THE SHADOW
OF
GRITSTONE

David Rousham

To my family, friends and the inspiration of the Peak District, England.

ACKNOWLEDGEMENTS

Dave Farbrother for his life-long friendship and counsel. Andy Southan for creating the graphics and sharing the vision. Jill Moat for providing the time and space to write.

Contents

Chapter 1 - *Harvest*

The reverend looked at the single rope hanging down from the church bell in the small steeple of the Methodist chapel. A gruesome image came to his mind as he pictured a limp body gently swinging, the end of a life beyond hope. He knew the history of the chapel.

The vivid colour of Harvest Festival gifts from the community and local farms was a stark contrast to the austere gloomy tones of the wood used for the pews and roof beams of the chapel. It presented a once-a-year scene in which nature and goodness were let into the normally somber mood of a building more used to serious worship and even more serious commitment to hard work, which the parishioners hoped would result in an after-life of rewards, unknown in today's tough world of recession, double-digit inflation, high unemployment and a stock market crash. This was 1950s England.

The chapel was located centrally in the village, across the lane from the village pub and local primary school. Langley was a picturesque rural village, overshadowed by a large looming hill called Teggs Nose. It bore the scars of decades of quarrying gritstone, an industry that had only become financially unviable a few years previous. The name Teggs Nose came from the fact that from certain angles the hill resembled a sheep's head. Teg being an old term for a two-year-old sheep. In other directions, Langley was at the end of a river valley whose source stretched up into the Cheshire/Derbyshire moorlands to the north and east. This landscape provided a large catchment area to provide sufficient water for four large reservoirs to be constantly replenished.

The Harvest display was plentiful this year, perhaps an effort by the villagers of Langley to offset the woes of the wider U.K. economy. Sheaves of wheat and barley acted as columns with baskets of apples from local orchards, supplemented by more exotic fruits gifted by market stall holders in the nearby town. The vegetables were amongst the best examples from the recently held village fete. Even the prized 120lb pumpkin was on show, celebrating the efforts of one particularly proud parishioner. The whole scene of nature's prosperity warmed the hearts of the congregation as the local scout and guide groups marched into the church.

Oliver Aspinall proudly held the green Scout flag, a reward for taking on the role of Patrol Leader in the troop the previous week. He was beaming with a smile as wide as a Cheshire cat. In her first-ever church parade, walked his young friend Sara, who had just become a Brownie Guide. She looked at Oliver with complete awe as he knelt down by the alter for the vicar to take the Scout colours from him and mounted them in an umbrella stand, cleverly repurposed as a flag holder for the day by the clergyman. Twice her age, Oliver and she had been friends forever, just as their parents had been. He was a child of the harvest, having been born on 4th October 1940, in Langley. Oliver had spent many hours playing in haystacks with his mates, but since Sara had arrived, he had adopted her as his little sister, and some of his more boisterous games had been tempered by his generosity of time in looking after and playing with her as she grew. Oliver was a gentle and kind-natured boy, always quick to help those who needed defending in the playground, but only if he sensed that fairness was under threat. He had never met his father, but everyone spoke very fondly of him, and he was told that he bore an amazing resemblance. With Oliver as a mentor, Sara gained confidence on top of already being a very bright child. Small in stature and with a highly developed intellect that sponged in all new facts and figures that the nursery teachers and parents threw in her direction. She was the only child of a hard-working couple, the mother was a legal secretary, and her father owned the northwest of England's most successful pipe-laying business in partnership with Oliver's uncle. Both had fought and been honoured in World War II.

After passing their flags across to the minister, Oliver walked back to the pew together with the other flag bearers. Sara was allowed to sit next to him, just in case she wasn't comfortable on her first outing with the uniformed organisation. She was oozing with pride to be able to sit with her best friend and other senior Scouts and Guides; showing off her brand-new Brownie uniform. Settling into their pews, Oliver nudged Sara and pointed out that her parents were wearing the same colours as the mountain of lemons and limes that were positioned next to the pew in the chapel where they had chosen to sit. Giggling softly, Sara pointed out

Oliver's mother and grandparents, dressed in their Sunday finest (which happened to also be their only finest), positioned next to the prized pumpkin and a barrel of turnips. Oliver's grandma - Gwen – was as tall as she was round and rather resembled the giant pumpkin, that was placed next to her pew. Oliver pointed out this observation, and Sara's giggles were now audible enough for her to receive a reproachful look from the eldest of the Girl Guides sitting next to them in the pew. The little girl blushed with embarrassment and moved closer to her best friend for protection.

As a new minister, Reverend Hinchcliffe was keen to see whether the bloated congregation, attracted by the Harvest festivities and the uniformed children, would still be quite so sizeable in the darker days of winter. The Reverend had just replaced a popular, life-long minister called Reverend Hamish Pottinger. Many of the congregation had not previously worshipped under the new minister and were keen to hear his sermon style. Reverend Hinchcliffe cleared his throat and called for the introductory harvest festival hymn – "We plough the fields and scatter..."

Amused by the mixed quality of the singers around them, Oliver and Sara were enjoying the freedom of being able to sit together, and away from the close behavioural controls of their families. Whilst joining in with the theatrical yodeling, Sara giggling at his strange noises, Oliver leant against the varnished shelf of the pew, where the bible and prayer books lived. Many layers of varnish had been used on these old dark pews, but his fingers rubbed over some uneven surface and on closer inspection, he realised that the scratches spelled out letters. As the hymn came to an end, Oliver sat down and tried to make out what the letters spelled out. In the dim glow of the church, there was insufficient light to even notice the letters. Having a better angle, he guided Sara's little hands towards the shelf and over the surface, he asked her to spell out the shapes of the carved letters. Closing her eyes and moving her fingertips, Sara mouthed the following letters – 'C.A. & B.L.' These were the initials of Oliver's parents. He pressed his fingers into the grooves of the carving and closed his eyes, searching for knowledge about the father who died before he was born.

CHAPTER 2 - *HARD LABOUR*

In 1928, the quarry on Teggs Nose was a hostile and noisy place for sixteen hours every day of the year. The peace emanating from the hilltop at midday was disquieting for the village below. Henry Aspinall was apoplectic. The quarrymen at Teggs – his quarrymen – had downed tools in protest. At other neighbouring quarries, the workers continued to mine the gritstone, much needed for the building of roads and buildings, as the industrial growth of northern towns exploded. Money was being made everywhere, except – it seemed upon Teggs Nose, at his quarry. In fact, two of Aspinall's major competing quarry owners – Thomas Whetton and Philip Broadhead – had been subtly boasting at the local Business Guild supper the previous week that their income had doubled thanks to the Teggs Nose debacle.

Quarrying gritstone was often hazardous and tiring, hours long and the wages low. A tough breed of people was needed to extract this material from the – often inaccessible locations along the western edge of the newly formed Peak District National Park. Explosives were used to weaken the veins of gritstone rock before men could use sledgehammers to loosen them completely and eventually winch the slabs clear of the quarry for cutting and final shipping. The explosives were essential yet were unpopular amongst the Langley villagers as rocks would often fall through farm buildings or damage power cables and plunge Langley into darkness.

The quarry owners formed a cartel to protect any wage inflation by agreeing not to poach employees from each other, thus suppressing wages. Hourly rates in 1928 were one shilling and three pence per hour, well below the pay of most other labour-intensive industries.

The chief foreman at Teggs Nose was a mountain of a man – Silas Ledger – known as "Sledge" by the workers and his close friends. He was respected not only for his powerful frame, having helped him to become a rather reluctant arm-wrestling champion in the local pub league, and the only person able to wield a huge sledgehammer that held a legendary status amongst the village kids – akin to Excalibur – King Arthur's sword in the stone. Sledge was also highly respected for his fair and equitable dealings with the teams of men working the stone face.

Sledge was now forty years old and the very epitome of the industry he represented. His features were craggy and his face scarred by many encounters with rock fragments from the shattering of stone. There was not a spare ounce of fat on his body, just sinew from working with rock since the age of 12, when he was used as an expendable powder monkey, the term used for the young boys who laid the explosive deep in the rock fissures.

Six months ago, Sledge had listened to his team of

quarrymen complaining about the fact that the gritstone that they were quarrying, over ten yards beneath the surface, was twice as dense as the seams closer to the surface and so took twice as long to cut and remove. There was truth in this observation as Aspinall was earning more money for the higher quality stone, yet none of this was being seen in the hourly rate that the men were earning. Having had several conversations with Aspinall, Sledge warned that he might have to side with his men and call a strike to make sure that their demands for fair wages (three pence increase per hour) were acted upon. Before striking, Silas had requested the support of the wider Union in the region, but it was not forthcoming due to cartel pressure and the omnipresent backhander to the Union leaders that seemed to be a pandemic within the industry of the time. Several times, Sledge had been offered personal bribes to back down, but his fair play ruled his value set and he always refused.

A meeting was held at the Setter Dog public house with the workers to discuss tactics. The publican was Dick Avery – a friend of Sledge's – and an enterprising man always looking for a ruse to supplement his publican's salary. Much of the pub's income was reliant upon the Teggs Nose quarrymen blowing their wages on drinking on a Friday night following a tough week of battling gritstone that firmly wanted to remain in the earth where nature had formed it.

The small communal bar at the Setter Dog was rammed with two dozen quarrymen, all intent on listening to the update that Sledge had for them. The atmosphere was thick with tobacco smoke and clinking glasses. Outside, the rain was cascading down the tiles, overflowing the gutters and creating waterfalls that crashed into the paving stones. The door creaked open and the space was filled by the shape of Sledge, who had just come from a meeting with Quarry owner Henry Aspinall and his management team. The room hushed and became expectant of news. None of the quarrymen could afford to miss another hour's pay, let alone stay out for the whole day.

Sledge made his way through the crowded bar and took up position by the fireplace. A lurcher dog, who had been curled up peacefully, benefitting from the warmth of the crackling flames, moved away hastily to make room for this human form with tree trunks for legs.

Sledge turned and addressed his team. He spoke slowly and deliberately, commanding respect with every word. "Men, today we made a stand against the unfair treatment that Aspinall and his shareholders have forced upon us. The stone we cut is the best in Cheshire and commands the highest prices, yet the wages we make are amongst the worst." A unanimous murmur of agreement arose through the smoke.

"Shame on Aspinall and his family – bloody shits." A small bespectacled quarryman uttered under his breath. This was Gustav Coccini, a refugee from Sicily, who was reputed to be hiding out in Cheshire, having escaped his homeland due to troubles with mafia gangs. He was the kind of man who courted trouble and trouble courted him. Coccini's role at the Teggs Nose quarry was the storage, handling, laying and detonation of dynamite. He was an expert in this area, and given the inherent danger, he was respected amongst the quarry workers and his less savoury characteristics were forgiven. "What about our pay rise?" Gustav demanded.

Sledge responded, "You all asked me to negotiate a 3p per hour pay rise with Aspinall. He rejected this and said that there would be no increase to the basic pay, but he did offer a bonus of 50 shillings a man – payable at the end of the year – if we could increase our output to meet the demands of the new reservoir dam wall."

A new reservoir, called Trentabank, was being built nearby at the head of the Langley valley, to satisfy the growing needs of the local town's fabric manufacturing industry. Aspinall had interests in the success of the reservoir as he was the landowner of the required flooded area and had received a large compensatory sum of money. Little thought had been spared for the livelihoods of the two tenant farmers and families that would lose their farms in the planning of the flooded valley.

The offer of a bumper pay-out at Christmas (a week's extra bonus) produced a ripple of excitement in the bar room and caused the lurcher to rouse from its new location under a table. The truth was that few of the men believed a basic pay increase was possible, because of the strict cartel that the local quarry owners had agreed. An increase at Teggs Nose – despite the less easy to extract and higher-quality millstone grit – would be unacceptable as it would lead to an inflationary pay increase amongst all of the local quarries – unacceptable to the capitalist profit-seeking Aspinall and his quarry-owning fraternity.

"Well done Sledge – that's bloody good going, fella." Fred

Needles shouted out. Fred was the second biggest man in the room after Sledge, but half his age. He was best known amongst the local community for his fearsome bowling and was a key member of Langley village's cricket club – the social and sporting hub of the area. His physical frame was that of an evolutionary freak, whose arms hung down to his knees, connected to coat hanger-like shoulders.

Sledge acknowledged Fred's support with a nod. The quarry worker's strike was over within a day, but there was something that was clearly still troubling him. Few of the men thought any more of it as there was a call at the bar from Dick – the publican – for *drinks on the house* and a cheer erupted. The Setter Dog's income was safe for a while yet and the quarrymen could head home later with news for their families that, despite the general hardship, Christmas 1928 would be a good one.

The disquiet in Sledge's look escaped all but one person in the room – Jack Moat. Jack was Sledge's best friend, although ten years his junior, and was the only person that Sledge could confide in. Jack was well educated and had previously been a bank clerk in Marple, but had lost his job due to a bank robbery in which a safe had been blown and a small amount of money stolen. The bank needed a fall guy, and as the junior clerk, Jack had been fired despite no evidence and his protestations of complete innocence. Jack had moved to Langley following an offer of employment by Henry Aspinall as a stock taker and financial controller at the Teggs Nose quarry.

Jack ushered Sledge to the only corner of the bar room where there was space sufficient for a private conversation.

"What did that skunk Aspinall really say Sledge?" asked Jack.

Sledge raised his furrowed brow, "The bonus payment for providing the gritstone for the dam means that the valley will be flooded earlier than expected, and the farms will be lost. Ned and Sid will be devastated."

The two farms involved were Nessit Farm – leased by Sid Bayley, and Trentabank farm leased by Ned Lovatt, Sledge's brother-in-law. Both were sheep farms, and the flooding would take place in February without any recognition of the lambing season and what this would mean to two families that were heavily involved in Langley village life. Martha Lovatt – wife of Ned and Sledge's sister – was the local village school teacher, and Sid Bayley was also a lay preacher at the local Methodist chapel, in addition to running his farm.

There was no compensation for the loss of the farm lease. Henry Aspinall had informed the farmers that they would lose their farms to the reservoir two years previous, yet at that stage, they were promised new farm tenancies local to Langley. The economic recession had caused Aspinall to rethink and revoke any previous promise, having already secured a legal defense as the original tenancy agreement had only ever been based on a handshake. Aspinall's values could easily be shifted if potential profit was at stake. The early completion of the dam and the creation of the Trentabank reservoir could bring him considerable wealth, dwarfing any loss in the provision of a paltry Christmas bonus to his quarrymen.

Jack knew that this situation would take a heavier toll on Sledge than anyone. Sledge believed in justice and felt strongly that every man had a right to employment and a fair reward for the efforts that they make in life. His whole value system was being uprooted by the Aspinall bonus offer, and he felt torn between doing his best for his fellow quarry workers, or trying to support his two farming friends. What he was in effect doing was to accelerate the pain that Sid Bayley and the Lovatt family would experience.

The two friends left the pub without any farewells and started their way down the path back to the village of Langley and their families. They walked in thought and an idea came to Jack that he felt unable to share quite yet. Once back in the village, Jack went to his house, where he rented a room, and Sledge continued along the main road to the terrace where his family lived.

Silas Ledger had always been a deeply moral man and had shied away from courting girls in his late teens. His physical size had often frightened any potential female admirer away, and this just fed his shy nature and he had tended to avoid social situations with girls. His early years were spent in and around the farming community of Langley, yet his father was a quarryman and soon he had followed his father up Teggs Nose to start his practical education on the stone face. His physique, even from an early age, had been to his advantage in this activity. At fourteen years old he was able to lift stones that many of the adult quarrymen struggled with. This gave him respect amongst his father's peers, which he enjoyed and allowed him to think that he could be more outgoing and take more initiative.

His first foray into courting was at a local village dance at the cricket club and was a disaster as he was simply too big and kept treading on the toes of his much smaller partners. It wasn't until he was seventeen that he attended a youth group organised by his elder sister – Martha – at the Chapel. It was a youth group that attracted a number of teenagers from outside of the Parish, and a friend of Martha's – Gwendoline (Gwen) – attended and immediately drew attention to herself because of her abundant confidence and bubbly conversation. Silas was mesmerised by Gwen; never had he met a girl who was so eloquent and keen to debate on all sorts of topics. The one debate that she led on "The right to trespass" was of particular interest. This was 1910, girls were supposed to be demure and secondary to their male counterparts. Not Gwen – this was the time that Emmeline Pankhurst was creating the Women's Social and Political Union (WSPU), dedicating their movement to "deeds, not words." Gwen had been to hear a young Emmeline Pankhurst speak in her birthplace – Moss Side, Manchester – and was struck by the power of her message. Gwen had become a disciple of the suffragette movement and had every intention to spread the gospel around the communities of East Cheshire.

At that first meeting, Gwen spoke with great authority about how landowners had made the U.K. a land of "no go zones", and she felt that people should have the right to roam across the countryside, and boundary fences were made to be crossed.

Silas was humbled by this small packaged maelstrom of feminism. On first meeting Gwen, he was uncertain as to how to interact. He simply bowed and mumbled his name and the fact that he was Martha's younger brother. Gwen grabbed his hand and shook it firmly. That was their first touch, and both quickly recognised kindred spirits of very different natures. Their values around justice were foundation beliefs that allowed them to understand each other and then grow to love each other.

Silas and Gwen got married in 1914, just as the Great War began – Silas was expected to stay at the quarry rather than fight, due to it being a critical service to help provide material to help the war effort with gritstone being used for military runway construction. Gwen was all for heading to the front, but she settled to retraining as a nurse in preparation to support the injured soldiers returning from war. They had two children: Elizabeth and William. By 1928, the Ledgers lived in a small terrace cottage in Langley, Beth was 13 and Will 11.

When Silas entered the cottage following the resolution of the strike, it was with a heavy heart. Gwen recognised his mood and without words, she beckoned him over to the fire and busied herself, making him a hot cocoa – one of the luxuries they could afford. The children were already in bed. Gwen had been in her garden all afternoon; it was her pride and joy. During breaks, she busied herself by sending vitriolic and effective letters – under a male pseudonym – to the local papers about how women needed to play a greater part in leading commerce and society through this barren economic period. A local newspaper editor thought that Gwen's writing presented a balance to offset the masculine rhetoric that was omnipresent in the political section, and so agreed to publish her writing in a regular column, whilst maintaining her male pen-name. Beth was very proud of her mum's writing, and became a young disciple, writing her own stories with female heroes that always placed men in the villainous role. The staff room at her school marveled over the young girl's courageous social stance and supported her pushing literary boundaries.

Gwen's garden had won this year's village "Best Kept Garden" competition. And she was justly proud of the rosette hanging above the fireplace, although she secretly wished it could have been a journalism award instead. The mass of purple wisteria had almost disappeared at the front of the cottage, but the climbing roses, honeysuckle and jasmine were still attracting bees to their blooms. The lavender was abundant this year and spread a cloud of scent when any passerby brushed the bushes. The cottage always had cut flowers in a vase at the front, and Gwen chose the colour of the display to reflect her own mood. Today were fiery red roses – accurately matching the passion in her most recent letter to the editor, who had kindly suggested that she toned down some of her anti-authoritarian rhetoric. The vase of red flowers was also noted by Sledge as he walked through the door. Despite his size, Sledge delicately approached the stooped shape of Gwen busily scribbling away at her writing desk. He put his giant hand on her shoulder:

"Darling, you put more energy into your writing than most of my quarrymen put into their stone saws on the hill," he gently whispered. Gwen jumped, having been totally fixated on a sentence to justify why a feminine approach to managing the local power company would have led to less wastage and greater prosperity to the region. "Hi you, how was the meeting with that shark – Aspinall? Did you manage to find a solution?"

Sledge sat down on the window seat; "Yes and no. There is no improvement on the basic pay, but he has offered us a significant bonus, if we are able to meet an increased delivery of stone to the dam builders."

Gwen looked up and stared at Sledge; "and what does that mean for Nat and Martha?"

"It means that my sister and her husband will be homeless earlier than expected and before the lambing season has been completed." he wasn't surprised that Gwen had quickly seen the dire consequence of a positive outcome on one side, would lead to challenges for others.

"How can Aspinall be so focused on corporate greed and money-making before the well-being of simple farming folk like your sister's family? It makes my blood boil!" Gwen exclaimed, and in-so-doing made her face turn the colour of the roses in the window.

Sledge replied through gritted teeth, "There are other people I will talk to, but I'm not sure if we can slow down the inevitable."

Jack Moat was in his own rented room on the village's main street, finishing off his weekly report of stock from the Teggs Nose quarry for the Aspinall's bookkeeper at head office. He noticed that there was an anomaly in the section reported as an electrical cable. On checking he found that this had been a repeated error for the past 9 months - meaning that the quarry had been ordering more explosives cable than it could ever use. Probably an innocent mistake made by someone who thought the denser gritstone would need a greater level of detonation to remove it. Given the hard conversation he had had with Sledge on the walk down from the Setter Dog meeting earlier, he decided to call it a day, closed the inventory book and headed to his bed.

CHAPTER 3 - *BEYOND THE BOUNDARY*

Beth Ledger was in a foul mood; she had been shouted at by a gamekeeper on the Estate that separated the school field from the cricket club. She and her best friend – Molly 'Moll' Brampton – had been at an after-school drama club and had been keen to get to the cricket club quickly so that Moll could ogle the elder teenage boys in the nets. At that age, Beth thought that the male of the species was generally the spawn of the earth and responsible for any woes that had befallen society – ever. The only male she respected was her father – Silas.

"Why does that man need to shout at us when we have every right to walk across that land? What gives the Aspinall family the ownership of land that has been common land for centuries?" Beth added indignantly. "He's already forcing my uncle and aunt off their land by flooding the valley. He's now employing thugs to enforce the law. It's not fair."

Moll nodded in response, recognising when Beth needed no further encouragement to vent her frustrations over an undemocratic, male-dominated world. Moll was more interested in the selection of boys that were stretching in front of them, preparing to bowl in the nets. Adam Bostock – Langley's first XI Captain - had just arrived at the nets to oversee the youngsters and try to spot any talent that he could nurture into a senior squad player.

Village cricket in East Cheshire was taken very seriously, and Langley punched well above their weight, thanks to Henry Aspinall investing money in the Club and attracting players from outside the area. This had been highly controversial amongst the Cheshire Cricket Committee until Aspinall agreed to sponsor their annual trip to the Oval to watch England play against Australia in the 1926 Ashes. The Committee was most satisfied with Aspinall's 'favour' as they saw two legends of the day - Herbert Sutcliffe scoring 151 and Wilfred Rhodes taking 4 wickets for 44 runs. These performances helped to secure the Ashes for England and send the Cheshire Administrators back north with a sense that Langley was a team that justified support.

Young Mark Shannigan was bowling impressively in the two active nets and seemed to be getting the better of the batsman – Charles Aspinall – the son of the Club's sponsor. Two successive balls had removed the off stump and middle stump, and Shannigan was revving up for a hat-trick ball. Adam Bostock, recognising the importance of maintaining Club politics and peace, suggested that the two batsmen switch nets to get a variety of bowling and primarily as a chance to protect Aspinall junior's dented pride and maintain the healthy purse strings that Aspinall senior provided.

Unfortunately, the switch of batting didn't help much as a new bowler was immediately claiming an LBW with a cry of "howzat." Bostock frowned; how could he be expected to promote his paymaster's son given Charles' inability to keep his wicket intact?

Charles Aspinall was a realist, he accepted that perhaps his talents did not lie on the cricketing field. He despised his father's domineering attitude towards life. Everyone was expected to bow down to him – including his only child. This strict paternal upbringing had led Charles to turn away from pursuits that his father forced upon him, and more towards activities that demonstrated intellectual ambition. Cricket was of great interest, but less around the playing of it, more around the myriad of statistics that lay within the folds of the cricket scorebook – a venerable treasure chest of carefully calculated arithmetic.

Having finished his enforced net session, Charles returned to the clubhouse to remove his batting equipment. He knew that the longer time he spent doing this, the less time he would have to spend returning to the nets and bowling at the other younger boys who would take it, in turn, to see how far into the cow field they could hit his bowling. As he was removing his pads, he noticed two girls near the sight screen, one of them was giggling and pointing at him, and the other one was looking embarrassed and seemed to be admonishing her friend. He had seen these girls a few times before but had never spoken with them. He completed the removal of his batting pads and decided to pluck up the courage to walk over to them and ask what they were doing. Anything to avoid heading back to the nets for further humiliation.

"Hi – what are you two up to?" asked Charles.

"Are you Charles Aspinall?" Moll Brampton asked with a smirk. "Is it true that your father owns the whole of this valley?"

"Yes, I am – unfortunately," he admitted. "And he does not own the whole valley, but most of it."

Moll added provocatively, "My friend here – Beth Ledger – reckons that nobody has the right to own that much land." Beth pinched Moll on the arm.

Beth jumped to her own defence; "No, I did not say that, but I do think that everyone should have the right to enjoy the common countryside. Your father's gamekeeper has just shouted at us both for crossing that field." She said, pointing to the field between the cricket club and the school. Beth was on a roll and she quickly added, "The public should not be denied access to open countryside fenced off by wealthy landowners and patrolled by fascist gamekeepers."

Charles waited for Beth to finish her statement and responded with a smirk; he liked the fire that this girl seemed to have in her argument. "Thank you for sharing your politics with me Beth Ledger, and can I just say that I totally agree with you. The next time you cross that field, I will request that my father's gamekeeper escorts you, showing common courtesy and assisting you in getting over the fences."

This response rather threw Beth and set Moll off into a fit of giggles. "You didn't expect that, did you, Beth?" she said.

Beth bit back, "No, I did not indeed, Mr. Aspinall. Are you being sarcastic, as if you are that would be most rude?"

"Not at all. I think my father is abusing his status as a major landowner in this valley and I'm totally against the forced eviction of the tenant farmers and his arrangement with the local Water Authorities to dam this beautiful area, there are already three reservoirs, why should a fourth be built? I hope that helps you to understand my views," Charles finished.

Both girls stood there, not really knowing what to say next. Thankfully, a stray cricket ball broke the silence as it rolled to a stop just next to Moll. She picked it up and tried to under-arm it back towards the net practice area. In doing this she managed to throw it over her head back into the 'no trespassing' field.

"Let me retrieve that for you," Charles offered. "I hope that Archie Talbot – the gamekeeper – won't shoot me!"

They all laughed and Charles retrieved the ball and threw it back to the cricketing activity. He looked at Beth and, with a level of unexpected sincerity, spoke directly to her, "Perhaps we can further the conversation about politics at a later date, Miss Ledger. It's been a pleasure to make your acquaintance."

Charles bowed his head to the girls and turned to walk back towards the cricket practice. Waiting until he was out of earshot, the two girls looked at each other open-mouthed – not quite knowing how to react to an encounter that they did not expect in any way.

Moll started, "Can you believe it? I think you have found the most unlikely follower in your mission against unjust and tyrannous land ownership. Plus, I think he fancies you!" Hiding a slight blush, Beth pushed off the comment, but something stirred inside of her for the first time. A man – other than her father – had struck her as being someone that she just might want to get to know further.

CHAPTER 4 - *VILLAGE MESSENGER*

There was only one phone in the village of Langley in 1928. It was located at the Post Office. Villagers used the number for incoming calls and paid Percy Ricketts a small fee for any call received and the associated delivery of the message. The Post Office owner had thought this idea to be a useful additional source of income, but as he was ageing, he found the chore of messenger to be somewhat arduous. This is where his neighbour, the fourteen-year-old Will Ledger, was able to put his head to money making. For a penny – payable from the caller's account – he would act as Percy's messenger and would run a note onwards to whoever in the village it was meant for.

As the Post Office was next to the Ledger's cottage, when the call was taken and the message fully understood, Mr. Ricketts would use his walking stick to knock on the wall, and Will would sprint around and pick up the message and set off at a pace to deliver it. On a good day, outside of school hours, this would bring Will six pence per day, three of which he would pass to his mother for the inconvenience of having her peace regularly disturbed. Will was semi-committed to study. Diligent but nowhere as quick to learn as his sister Beth. He knew that if he could achieve a certain level at school, he would not have to follow in his father's footsteps up the hill to the quarry. He secretly harbored thoughts about working full-time for Ricketts, who had no family that could inherit the Post Office. Will could see himself as the new Postmaster, taking over the store that he thought he could run much more profitably. In the meantime, he spent much of the day doing odd jobs in the shop and running the messages.

Tap, tap, tap – the familiar sound of the walking stick on the wall. Gwen looked disapprovingly at the wall as each time the tap was made, her prized painting of a spaniel skewed sideways.

"Dam, that telephone!" she said under her breath. "Will, the bank's opened," she shouted up the stairs. Will sprung up from his reading, having already heard the noise, and moved rapidly towards the door before the third tap had been struck. Within a minute, Will returned:

"Easy money," he cheerily hummed. "This message is for Father. John Croker wants to see him after his shift today." Gwen looked up from her crocheting and moved uneasily in her armchair. Croker only ever wanted to see Silas if there was some serious news coming. Usually, the quarry management left Silas to manage his team without too much interference as long as the stone was being milled and the quality was maintained.

She commented: "Will, as it's such easy money, it's important that your father gets this message urgently. Can you run up to the quarry and pass it directly to him so that he will be able to head down into Macclesfield after his shift before coming home. That will save him time."

Will looked incredulous. "You want me to run up Teggs Nose and deliver this note? That'll take me thirty minutes at least?" The whole of Langley was only a five-minute run from one end to the other, so Will's messenger job was usually very quick deliveries other than the outlying farms, which required a ten to fifteen-minute run. Begrudgingly, Will set off and started the long climb up the sheep track. After about a mile and a half of clambering, he rested on a large stone and looked back down towards the village. The lights were gradually lighting up as the October evenings were getting longer and sunset was not far away. He had just started up the final mile when his sight was distracted by a man, stooped low and scratching between a tree stump and a clump of bilberry bushes. Will stepped behind a thicket of gorse and kept watching the man. It was then that he recognised Gustav – one of his father's workmates. Gustav had been a relative newcomer to the team and stood out due to his thick foreign accent and his weaselly physique. Will had learned on the first meeting that this was not a person to fall on the wrong side of. He kept silent as Gustav finished his business and moved on. Will tied a hanky to the gorse bush and moved onwards along the path. He would return to that spot later and investigate what Gustav had been burying.

Will entered the quarry site at a jog and saw Fred Needles. Will liked Fred as they both shared a common love of cricket and Will particularly loved the crazed look on his face that Fred had just before he ripped a fastball passed the peaked cap of an opposition batsman. The village boys often imitated this look and it was known as 'The Needles.'

"Why so out of breath, young Will?" Fred chuckled.

"Hi Fred, do you know where Dad is?" asked Will.

"Sledge is wielding that weapon of his at a tough piece of rock down on the lower level. Give him ten minutes and he'll be up again," Fred replied. "How about a bit of target practice in the meantime?"

Will knew exactly what this meant and he eagerly agreed. Setting up a small pile of rocks on the edge of the site, Fred and Will moved twenty-two yards back – the length of a cricket wicket – and measured a run-up. They bowled small rocks at pace towards the target. The first to hit won a point. After three goes, Fred was ahead. Will took careful aim and put extra effort into his fourth attempt. It went high and wide of the target and over the edge of the cliff. A weird sound was heard from down below, and Will grimaced as he looked towards Fred. And Fred looked back, bemused with what or who had let out that yelp. Thinking it was a stray sheep, they didn't think any more of it until the bloodied head of Gustav Coccini appeared, swearing in Italian, "Merde, coglioni – which of you bastardos threw that stone?"

Mortified, Will stepped forward to take the wrath that was coming, but at that instant, Fred beat him to it and admitted that it was his errant throw that had caused the pain. Given Fred's fiery reputation and physical presence, Gustav decided that it was not in his best interest to further the confrontation and slinked off. Gustav had given Will a wicked look suggesting that he had a clear idea as to who the real perpetrator was. The commotion had drawn the attention of a few other quarrymen, and laughter broke out at the situation as Gustav was not the kind of person one could easily warm towards. Silas also arrived and greeted his son, although he showed surprise at seeing him on site at this time and without a prior invitation. Will passed the note across from Croker and Silas read it and screwed it up, putting it in his pocket.

Patting him on the back, he said, "Thanks, son, looks like it'll be a late one for me. Can you head back home and tell your mum to keep the meal on the stove? I'll be home as soon as I've found out what Croker wants." Will shook hands with Fred and exchanged knowing smiles, headed back down the hill, following the way he had come. When he got to the gorse bush with the tied hanky – he looked back towards the hillside where Gustav had been. He made his way across there and found concealed and buried beneath the root a small wooden box with a loose lid. Upon opening the lid, he found several pieces of electric cord that left him puzzled. Why would Gustav be hiding lengths of electric cord in a box beneath a tree? He mused to himself.

Will bounded back down to Langley across the hillside and down the sheep track. A thick broth was waiting for his tea, and Gwen was just ladling two bowls for herself and Will. Beth would be late, given that tonight was the boy's cricket nets and she would be with Moll watching practice and sizing up the boys, helping Moll control her teenage girl's fantasies about which one of them might want to take her to the next Village dance. Gwen knew that her own daughter had no such aspirations about men just yet.

"Did you get the message to Father, Will?" she uttered, without turning her head to see who had clumsily bumped their way through the front door.

"All good," replied Will. "Dad said he would be home late from Macc and please keep his meal warm."

With that already in mind, Gwen put the broth back on the stove and sat back to eat. She had some uneasiness about the sudden request from John Croker, having never known Silas to be summoned to appear via a phone message before.

Between spoonful's of the tasty broth, Gwen said, "Eat up quickly, Will. We have choir practice at the Chapel in thirty minutes." Choir practice was a lowlight of Will's week. When he was a young child, it provided the entertainment of an evening and a chance to avoid an hour of boring homework, but now that he was fourteen, it was the last thing he wanted to do, especially given how exhausted he was feeling from the run to and from the quarry. Plus, he wanted to have some free time to think further about the intriguing discovery of Gustav's box up on the hillside.

Percy Ricketts also acted as choirmaster and was clearly the keenest amongst any of the gathered villagers, many of whom felt that their attendance might look good when St. Peter checked them in or denied entry. Percy used his walking stick as a baton and conducted from the pulpit like some demented fiend, barking out instructions amidst regular admonishments of Will and his equally challenged adolescent friend – Mick Shannigan – who would have much preferred to be back at the Cricket Club. Mick had been a proud alto in his younger days, singing solo in a pitch so high that Ricketts thought that only the cherubs in the upper stained-glass windows could truly hear. Now that puberty had hit, Ricketts likened Mick's voice to that of the Gargoyles if only the

Methodist's architectural budget could have stretched that far.

Reverend Hamish Pottinger sat smirking in the back row of the choir amongst the male bassists. It was his one chance of the week to be led rather than lead an activity in the Chapel, and he rather enjoyed watching the whirling Ricketts vent his anger on young Mick's barking voice and generally try his hardest to make a very mediocre choir into something that wouldn't shame him or the village at the Macclesfield Christmas Choir Festival planned for mid-December. Sid Bayley was also amongst the bass male singers but was staring into the recesses of the Chapel, looking detached from the action in front of him.

Sid was single and had never managed to find a wife suitable to take on the tough responsibilities and often thankless tasks of a farmer's life. Having reached the age of forty, Sid had taken the tenancy of Nessit Farm and committed his time to raising sheep on the surrounding hills. In his solitude, he found comfort in devoting himself to the bible and had become a lay preacher helping the affable Reverend Pottinger to tend to the righteousness of Langley's human flock. However, today, Sid was feeling very low, having had the devastating news two years ago that he would lose his farm due to the creation of the Trentabank reservoir. He had just discovered that he would need to move out of his farm before this year's lambing season had started, only months away. The forced move of his farm and sheep business, ahead of lambing, would likely bankrupt him. Especially as the landowner – Henry Aspinall – had offered no alternative land to move his flock on to. He would have to sell all of his heavily pregnant ewes and pass on any profits to new owners.

With a final flourish of his walking stick and having almost toppled himself out of the pulpit, Mr. Ricketts brought an end to the evening's 'caterwauling' – the word he used to sum up Langley's choir performance that evening. Motivational speaking was not one of Rickett's strong points. He called out, "Double practice next week, please, everyone. And Shannigan, make sure you gargle with salt before coming back!"

The choir dispersed, although most of the adults headed towards the Dunstan Inn led by Reverend Pottinger. The Dunstan was the village pub located about two hundred yards down the single high street, and the good Reverend was the most loyal of customers. Many would suggest that most of his sermons were dreamt up by staring at the bottom of his large pewter tanker – kept behind the bar – and given to him by the previous landlord as gratitude for his service to the ale industry. Sid remained behind in order to prepare for the Sunday service the following day, which was due to be a celebration of the Harvest in 1928. Sid didn't feel much like celebrating. He knew that he would be homeless by the year's end, kicked out by bad fortune and the greed of one man – Henry Aspinall.

CHAPTER 5 - *SHOP STEWARD*

Silas had made his way down the far side of Teggs Nose and walked the two miles into Macclesfield to the large, gloomy, dark granite building that acted as the Head Office for Aspinall's growing commercial empire. He entered the building and a small female receptionist gasped at the sight of a giant in human form, still dirtied by the day's work in the quarry and looking like a mythical creature capable of death and destruction in equal measures. However, Silas took off his cap and wiped his brow with a clean handkerchief that he pulled from his pocket, grateful that Gwen had - reliably as ever, placed it there first thing that morning. He smiled graciously. "Beg your pardon, Madam, I'm here to see John Croker on Teggs Nose quarry business."

The woman relaxed and smiled at Silas, relieved that this wild Neanderthal had morphed into a gentle giant within the space of a few polite words. "Of course, sir, who may I say is here?" she obliged.

"Silas Ledger, Ma'am," the kind-looking giant responded.

The receptionist showed him to a waiting room, where he sat down on a sofa as none of the single chairs looked sturdy enough to take Silas' proportions.

Ten minutes later, Silas was aware of some shouting happening overhead, around three floors above him, and then the approaching sounds of steps hurriedly coming down a staircase. John Croker appeared in the waiting room. Greased back hair, a hooked nose and a slick suit, he looked in every way the slime-ball type that Aspinall would employ to carry out his dirty tactics. This was the thought that immediately entered Silas' head. Without offering a handshake as a greeting, John Croker started in his usual formal manner. "Ledger, thank you for coming to see us. Please follow me upstairs to the Board room."

John Croker had known Silas for several years but had never once looked him in the eye, preferring to issue instructions and assume all was fully understood. He visited the quarry monthly but much preferred to spend time with Jack Moat rather than Silas. Silas felt that perhaps his size intimidated Croker and trusted Jack to pass on any relevant information. It seemed to work.

Silas followed Croker up the stairs, noting the portrait paintings of various august local establishment figures, staring at him as he passed. It seemed like they had passed judgment on many people previously, and it had a discomforting effect on Silas as the door to the Boardroom was opened.

"Mr. Silas Ledger," Henry Aspinall greeted him. Silas had not expected Aspinall to be at this meeting in person, and in his mind, the whole meaning of the meeting took a direction that he had not been prepared for. "Sit down, please. We have got a few things to discuss, haven't we?"

Aspinall was at the head of the large rectangular boardroom table. Behind him was a grand portrait of himself with the shape of Tegg's Nose as background to the picture. It was a statement of ownership, man over nature. Silas felt slightly sick in his stomach. Henry Aspinall Esq. was a vulgar man, born with a silver spoon and an unhealthy disregard towards anyone of a lower social status than himself. Related to slave traders from the East India Company, he believed that only material wealth mattered in this world and Godliness comes from those with the deepest pockets. He was revered and feared in equal quantities by the business community of Macclesfield. He demanded respect from all, most of all from his family.

Before Silas could sit down and gather himself, Aspinall continued, "Thank you for coming over this evening. We have not met for some time, and there has been much happening at the quarry which gives me concern. Should I be concerned, Mr. Ledger?"

Silas breathed in and collected his thoughts. "No, Mr. Aspinall, everything seems in order. The team is working again following the slight disagreement around their terms and conditions. Despite the fact that cutting the lower gritstone seam is getting harder and..."

Before Silas was able to finish, Croker cut in, "Mr. Aspinall, what Ledger is saying is that they are back at work now for the same pay rather than shirking their responsibilities to us and their families!"

Aspinall hissed, "Shut up, Croker. I've heard enough from you today. I want to know the truth from the man who leads the quarrymen, not from the man who spends his time pushing paper and drinking my sherry." John Croker visibly whitened and sat back in his chair recognising that his role in this meeting was becoming quickly superfluous, and that his own employment status was rather more fragile than he had thought.

"Please continue, Silas," Aspinall stated. "Explain the situation at the quarry and the feelings amongst the men. Am I going to get more future agitation that I can ill afford?"

Silas leant forward and placed both of his hands on the table. "Sir, what you have at Teggs Nose is a committed workforce that is willing to forego a fair basic pay in favour of a bonus payment if we can supply sufficient millstone grit to complete the Trentabank dam wall this side of Christmas." Silas sat back in his chair but continued, "That's all I can say, and I trust the men following a meeting that we held two nights ago at the Setter Dog. Evidence of that is today, we mined and cut more slabs than we have ever done on that hillside. The Teggs Nose stone will be used to complete the dam wall according to the timescale that you demand."

Aspinall smiled. "That is very pleasing to hear, Silas. I commend your faith in your team." Aspinall continued fixing his eyes directly on him, "And how does that make you feel about your sister's situation at the farm? Are the Lovatt's prepared to leave earlier than they had thought?"

Silas felt a sharp pain inside as this was the unease that he'd been feeling all along. Supporting his work colleagues in their quest for a bonus payment at Christmas would also lead to his own sister's family becoming homeless sooner, and he knew his brother-in-law - Nat was suffering in silence, unable to cope with the reality of the situation. Silas took a deep breath to help quell any emotion in his voice: "I understand your desire to open the reservoir earlier as the Town's industry demands more water. However, the cost of doing this will pay a heavy toll on the two families whose farms and fields will be flooded. They have nowhere to go."

Croker was enjoying seeing Silas reach the begging point – this is the reason why some people were born to be white collar management, whilst others would forever be their working minions getting their hands dirty – he mused. Aspinall, sensing Croker's enjoyment, turned on him. "What would you do if you were Nat Lovatt then Mr. Croker?"

Croker rocked back, suddenly horrified to be the subject of his boss' attack. He blurted out, "Well, er, well, er... I would have known that this was happening years beforehand and I would have made arrangements to safeguard my future." Croker offered up without much conviction.

"Exactly," said Aspinall. Croker visibly eased. "That's exactly why I have no sympathy for your brother-in-law, Mr. Ledger. He had his chance and he didn't take it."

"What chance did he ever have, Mr. Aspinall? You are his landlord and you demanded rent from his land right up until the dam wall is completed. How could he move when you offered no alternative land for his sheep?"

Aspinall stared blackly at Silas, "I don't care about the Lovatts and their bloody sheep; I do care about the completion of this reservoir and the money I will then get for the flooded land." Aspinall did not like being challenged. "I employ over five hundred local people; it is this money that keeps the wheels of industry well-oiled. Make sure you remember that, Ledger!"

"And there is one more matter I need to inform you about." He added spitefully. "I will be halving the size of the Teggs Nose quarry team as I have purchased a new cutting engine that will replace the need for manual workers to cut the stone. I'd like you to decide which of the workers will be leaving my employment at Christmas."

Silas got up from his seat, swallowed the words he wanted to say, and simply muttered, "Thanks for your time, Mr. Aspinall," and retreated out of the boardroom with an even greater burden on his broad shoulders than that which he had arrived with.

CHAPTER 6 - *ROCK BOTTOM*

Sid Bayley sat back down in the choir stalls of the now empty chapel. He looked up at the stained-glass window and the memorial stones of old villagers who had once worshipped there. With the choir and the Reverend having vacated the chapel, everything was peacefully still. He glanced over through the vestry door and saw neatly stacked sheaves of wheat and baskets of vegetables that villagers had started to donate to bring the Harvest festival alive. No doubt the village mice would be eyeing up their own harvest feast later. As much as the Harvest felt like a celebration of the year, Sid had a heavy heart. Reverend Pottinger had asked him to lead the sermon on Sunday about the blessings of nature and the Autumn season's deliverance of food from the fields and orchards. He had searched his soul and he could not conjure up any words of hope and wonderment about God's plentiful creation. He could not see a future where the sun shone and the crops grew. And certainly, there would be no more fields full of joyfully bleating lamps prancing in the Springtime. He could see no future thanks to Henry Aspinall's greed.

He got up from his seat and strode purposefully towards the entrance where the single bell rope was tethered. With little hesitation, he looped the rope into a noose, clambered up the bookcase where bibles and prayer books were housed, placed the rope around his neck, and fell.

The jerk of the rope snapped Sid's neck immediately, and the bell tolled loudly and fitfully. The sound of the bell was heard in the nearby pub.

"What's that for?" enquired Ned Croucher – the publican, "It's not last orders, that's for sure", he added with a smile.

Reverend Pottinger put his tankard down on the bar and listened to see if there were any follow-up rings. There was a secondary faint peel and then silence. His heart missed a beat. As a devout Christian who had led the parish for the last decade, he was very aware of the challenges that the congregation of Langley had. He knew all about the struggles over unfair wages up at the quarry and the consequence of the dam being built in the valley. Martha Lovatt had shared the news with him about the incentive bonus that the quarrymen had been offered for increased productivity to meet an earlier deadline for the dam completion and subsequent requirement for the Lovatt's and Sid's farm to be vacated at Christmas.

The Reverend collected his thoughts and excused himself from the choral drinkers. He moved with increasing speed towards the Chapel and tried to push the main door open. Something was blocking the door and stopping it from fully opening. He moved to the open vestry door and stepped over the harvest offerings. Coming to an abrupt halt as he entered the main church, he gasped. In front of him was Sid's limp body swinging against the main door – lifeless, his face drained of colour.

A very troubled Silas walked the last half mile towards Langley. The latest revelation that Aspinall had shared was almost too much for him to contemplate. During an economic recession he was expected to decide on the fate of a dozen of his team. People he had spent all his working life with. And then there was his sister's family and their pending eviction from the farm ahead of the creation of the reservoir. Lost in his troubles, he entered the cottage and served himself the broth that Gwen had left warming on the stove. Both Will and Beth were upstairs in the attic room that they shared. Will was counting his pennies for the week collected from his post office chores, and Beth was finishing off reading a newspaper article from an unsold paper that Mr. Ricketts always passed on to Will at the end of the day otherwise, it would be abandoned and he knew how much Beth devoured national news in her interest in becoming a journalist.

A single bell rang out from the chapel.

Silas had just dozed off in the armchair when he was awoken by the familiar tap, tap, tap of Rickett's walking stick on the door. Will shot downstairs. "Why would Mr. Ricketts be needing me at this time of night? Who would be calling on the telephone?"

"Perhaps he just misses you!" mused a partially dozing Silas to his son. Will slammed the door as he exited the cottage.

Within a minute, he was back. Will blurted out – "Dad,

something awful has happened. Sid Bayley has been found hanging in the Chapel. He's dead."

Silas leapt to his feet. "Stay here, Will, and don't tell your sister." He ordered. "I'm going to the Chapel and I'll get your mother from the Dunstan on my way."

Silas passed the Post Office and overheard Ricketts using the phone to speak with the Macclesfield police station to report the incident and ask for help. He swiftly moved passed the Dunstan – which seemed unusually silent. Ahead of him, near the entrance of the graveyard, he saw the reason. All of the choir's merriment at the Inn had turned to a somber hush now. The shape of a body in the entrance to the church had been covered in a curtain. Reverend Pottinger was standing with the rest of the group, there were several sounds of sobbing. Silas placed his hand on Gwen's shoulder and felt it shake. Gwen's rhythmic sobs were silent, others in the group were letting their emotions out more loudly. The shock and immediate grief was palpable. How could a person who had sung with them all only an hour previous have reached a level of such utter despair that he had decided to finish it all in such an awful way?

It didn't take long for some of the group to move from grief to anger. "Poor Sid, he must have been desperately sad about losing his farm. That thieving bastard - Aspinall is to blame." Spat Ned Croucher.

Gwen turned her teary face up to Silas and sobbed, "What about Martha and Nat? We must do more to help them, they must be going through the same kind of trauma that Sid was feeling. We can't just watch this happen!"

Silas had no words. He had a high regard for Sid Bayley ever since he moved into Langley and diligently got on with his farming work. Sid had often lent his largest shire horse – Battalion - to Silas to help shift some of the heaviest of the quarrying equipment around the Teggs Nose site. The quarry company refused to invest in their own horses and expected the workers to manage the machinery moves themselves. Many times, men had been injured in trying to move machinery. Battalion had become a firm favorite up on the hillside, and his presence often pulled a crowd as Sid guided him in shifting huge machine parts of iron and timber into place. Sid was happy to be able to help Silas and the other Langley quarrymen. He was usually the lone man quietly sipping his ale in the Dunstan, or celebrating the glory of God in one of his sermons in the Chapel, but when he and Battalion were on show at the quarry, he knew that he'd be the talk of the village, and his tankard would never be empty that evening.

Silas realised how far things must have got for Sid to decide that ending his life was preferable to fighting for his livelihood despite losing his farm and his sheep flock. Silas looked across at Jack Moat – who was no chorister, but had heard the bell and was aware that odd things were afoot – he had been second on the scene and had helped Reverend Pottinger lower Sid's body to the floor, and ripped down a curtain to cover the body.

"Jack, let me get Gwen home, and then I'll meet you at yours, we need to talk about this," Silas said quietly.

Jack replied, "Okay Sledge, give me half an hour. The police will want to get my story first and then I'll see you at home."

Jack, being a single man in the village and a similar age as Sid, had formed a close relationship with him and also respected his dedication to God and the tending of his farm.

Silas guided Gwen back to the cottage, a Ford Model T police car passed them. Only in the most serious of incidents did Macclesfield order their one police car out on the roads, and it had never driven the road to Langley previously.

Once home, Silas called Beth and Will downstairs and asked them to comfort their mother and pray for the departed soul of their friend Sid Bayley. He then turned and walked back towards Jack's house and let himself in knowing that the key was kept in the flowerpot to the left of the porch. Sledge never usually drank, but right then, he needed something to calm himself down, sufficient so that he could make sense of the day that he had been through. He reached for a half-full bottle of brandy that was sitting on the desk next to Jack's paperwork for the quarry inventory. In the accounts file, he noticed one underlined section in red ink that was identified as 'electrical cable' with a question mark. He thought no more about it and took two large gulps of brandy. Whilst he waited for Jack to return home.

CHAPTER 7 - *THE SICILIAN*

Gustav Coccini sat back in his small apartment in Macclesfield, he preferred town life to rural village life. It was grittier and reminded him of his days on the streets of Palermo – Sicily, where he had grown up and learned the art of survival. Having come from a poor fishing family, his father had never come home from one ill-fated fishing trip on the Ionian Sea, and his mother had reacted by hitting the grappa bottle far too hard. At the age of 8, Gustav had been thrown out of home and expected to fend for himself. He had become streetwise by working for a gang that specialised in shop-lifting in the winter and picking pockets of tourists in the summer months. For this, the gang gave Gustav a place to stay and sufficient food to keep the wolves from the door. As he was slight of stature, Gustav was mainly used for some of the gang's more ambitious money-making ventures. He was often lifted up and pushed through small vents that had been left open in various houses to help with cooling during the hot summer nights. Gustav would then let the larger, older gang members through the front door to complete the robbery – with or without the use of additional force, depending if the occupants were still at home. By far, the most profitable of these break-ins were the money exchange shops that were located near all of the tourism hotspots along the main shopping street of Palermo, by the cathedral and along the waterfront, where most of the restaurants were located. The gang could only plan and carry out two of these heists per tourist season so that the local Authorities and banks would not add further security systems. Plus, several members of the gang's family were members of these banks who could be counted on to provide paid for information on when and where the largest opportunities lay.

Although Gustav was small enough to be used to fit through any unshuttered hole, often there was a need to find another way to blow the security door from the inside to let other members of the gang in to lift the safe and make off into the night. This is where Gustav was introduced to the power of explosives. As a more expendable member of the gang, it was considered right that Gustav should plant the unstable explosives, charge and detonate them whilst trying to shelter – as best he could – from any of the shrapnel. He practiced his techniques in the countryside and learned that the risks of personal injury were lessened if he could calculate the right length of electrical cord that carried the charge to detonate the dynamite. Through this crude trial and error, Gustav picked up several deep facial scars from rock fragments. This pockmarking stayed with him for life and defined his character. Gustav largely educated himself in the art of laying explosives and the science behind dynamite. This skill was one that he used effectively whilst working with the criminal fraternity in Italy and later in the more legitimate role of quarrying in the UK.

Gustav had been pondering for some time how to make

more money than the paltry amount he was collecting from the risky work he undertook up on Teggs Nose, and he'd been slowly acquiring the appropriate equipment to take his skill back to the dark side. Over the last six months, Gustav had been taking small amounts of dynamite – a block at a time – and rather than laying it in the quarry wall to blast some more gritstone, he'd been hiding it away in his jacket and storing it in a hiding place on Teggs Nose. Similarly, he'd been stealing small lengths of electric cord and concealing these in an air-tight container in another location on Teggs Nose. What he would do with this stash, he had not yet considered, but if an opportunity arose to make money, then Gustav would have the resources.

Jack returned to his small cottage to find Silas refilling his glass with brandy. "Can I pour you one brother?" Silas greeted Jack, "How were the police?"

"Thanks, Sledge, I need one of those so much!" replied Jack.

The police had questioned Jack alongside the Reverend and taken statements. Given the knowledge that Sid Bayley had been under a great deal of personal stress caused by his pending home eviction and loss of livelihood, they quickly concluded that this was a sad case of suicide. They concluded that no further investigative action was necessary.

"Bloody suicide, Sledge, it's all crap!" Jack muttered. "More like murdered by Henry Aspinall. He should be the one that the police are interviewing, and what's more, they should be locking him up and throwing away the key."

"You're right," said Silas. "But that's never going to happen."

The two men looked at each other and took another gulp of their drinks. Silas took a deep breath in and started to impart his own news. "Today, I went to Aspinall's Head Office, as John Croker had summoned me. We met at the reception and took me upstairs to the boardroom. Henry Aspinall was there, and he thanked me for getting the boys to agree to return to work for a single bonus to deliver more stone to help the dam wall get completed ahead of time."

More deliberately, he added, "Then I asked if Aspinall could do any more to help Sid Bayley and the Lovatts given their positions as good tenant farmers to him and generally good local people who deserved support. Aspinall dismissed any support outright and accused my sister's family and Sid of being lazy by not preparing for the inevitable – he placed all the blame on them. Tosser! And now look what's happened – Sid's killed himself, and I just don't know what kind of state Martha and Nat must be in. I need to help in some way."

Jack looked at Silas and recognised the burden he was carrying for his sister's family and the guilt that he was unable to see the pain and dire stress that had led to Sid's ultimate action. "You've done all you can do, Sledge," Jack sighed. "You have helped more people by supporting the quarrymen in their need for money by agreeing on the bonus payment. Furthering the strike action would have helped nobody."

Sledge looked Jack in the eye. "It's all shit from Aspinall, he has no intention of maintaining the workforce on Teggs Nose. He has asked me to identify a dozen men who will lose their jobs, as he feels that mechanisation is needed, and he plans to invest in machinery by Christmas."

Jack gasped, "No way – how can you be expected to do that – it's so unfair. We need to do something about this." Both men stared for minutes into the glowing embers of the coal fire. Jack broke the silence. "We need to give Sid a good send-off – he deserves that. We need to pull together as a village and make sure that we sort out any of his belongings and try and find any distant relatives he might have. I have an idea for Battalion – could we stable him up on Teggs Nose at the quarry. We could use him for many more activities than we do today, plus he could be used to cart larger slabs of stone down to the dam wall as we will need to increase the delivery volumes."

Lost in deeper thoughts, Silas replied, "That's a good idea, Jack. Perhaps you can get that approved by Croker in the morning. I need to go and talk with Martha and Nat." He picked up his coat and walked towards the door. "Good night, mate. We have a lot to do to put this world right."

Silas thought his day would never end. It was now just before midnight, but he felt he must make an effort to go and see his sister that evening. He had fleetingly seen her amongst the faces outside the Chapel mourning Sid's death, and he'd noticed that Nat was with her. He reckoned that by now, they would have headed home up the lane towards their farm higher in the valley. Silas crossed a field and climbed the steep bank of the dam before descending into the lush pastures of the upper end of the valley. Within the next six months, these pastures would all be flooded and the farming life would be sent to a watery grave. The sounds of the night were magnified as if they also knew that their days were numbered. The whinny of a horse in a distant field made Silas remember the conversation he had just had with Jack about Battalion. The quarry would care for that shire horse well, and each time it would appear to pull a cart, Sid and his diligent industry and commitment would be remembered and honoured. He was aware of sheep scattering ahead of him and a small shadow rapidly approaching, it was Jess – Nat's border collie dog – forever watching over the sheep. Jess was overjoyed to see the large shape of Silas approaching. She bounded up to him and jumped up to receive the customary embrace that Silas always offered. For Silas, it was nice to be with a warm body who was immune to the harsh reality and troubles that that day had brought, and he clung to the active shape of Jess for a good while. They continued together across the field for a further five minutes until the shape of the farmhouse appeared, the kitchen window being illuminated by an oil lamp, signifying that Nat and Martha were still up, no doubt in the kitchen mulling over the happenings of that evening.

Nat had been crossing the fields earlier, on his way to collect Martha and walk her home from choir practice, when he'd heard the single toll of the bell. Five minutes further on, he saw Jack Moat and Reverend Pottinger stopping people entering the Chapel and asking them to move back to the entrance gate. It was here that he saw the ghostlike look on his wife's face as she was there with Gwen, her sister-in-law. Both were gently sobbing on each other's shoulder. Just as he went to comfort Martha, Silas arrived to take hold of Gwen. Neither of the men spoke to each other, recognising that whatever had happened was serious enough to respect silence at this time.

Jess nuzzled up against the kitchen door and managed to push it open. Silas followed: "Nat, Martha," he called out. "It's me – Silas." The kitchen door opened fully, revealing the warm glow of a fire and a steaming kettle just coming to the boil.

"Come in," Nat beckoned, giving Silas a respectful handshake on the way past, "good to see that Jess rounded you up." His attempt at humour helped to lighten the sad atmosphere a little.

Silas kissed his sister and Martha poured him a cup of tea without even asking. They all sat down and Silas started. "None of us can truly understand the kind of pressure Sid was under to decide to take his own life. But there is no escaping that you two have similar pressures going on, and I want to make sure that you know that myself, Gwen and the rest of the village are there for you." On the walk down from the part-constructed dam wall, Silas had considered telling Nat and Martha about his failed attempt to seek clemency from Aspinall that evening. But given everything else that had happened, he felt that this was unnecessary and might only spark further upset.

Martha was the first to respond, "Brother, don't you worry about Nat and myself, we knew that we would lose the farm two years ago. Yes, the fact that we need to move quicker than anticipated is unfortunate, but we also have some better news that we cannot make public yet." Martha looked at Ned and received an affirmative nod. "Okay, you must not tell anyone of this yet, Silas – do you understand?"

Silas looked puzzled. "Of course, what's the secret?"

"Nat, do you want to tell him?" She directed the conversation across to her husband, Nat took over, "I was at a recent sheep auction, trying to see how much I could get for the flock, and a representative of the Whetton Estate approached me and suggested I should find time to meet with Mr. Thomas Whetton. At first, I was confused, but when he said that it might be to my benefit, I arranged a meeting the very next day." Nat took a sip of his tea and continued. "I called over to the Whetton Estate office and was met at the door by Thomas Whetton himself."

"Go on." Silas urged, sensing the excitement building in the room.

"Well, Mr. Whetton offered me a good price for the flock but, better still, offered me some land just over the county border in Staffordshire. It's good moorland, not as lush as the Langley valley, but it's more than half decent. And what's more – there is a tenancy on a farmhouse and barns where we can move to in the new year."

Silas looked open-mouthed at Nat and then turned to Martha and hugged her. "That's fantastic news! I am so made up for you both. Good news is what we need right now."

"Silas, it's important that you should not tell anyone, but oddly Mr. Whetton sent a note to me this morning asking if I may ask you to go and see him also."

Silas sat back down, he paused and looked up at the ceiling, wondering what Whetton might want with him. He knew that Thomas Whetton was a very able businessman. His corporation had investments in shipping, canals, textile manufacturing, quarrying and mining. The gritstone quarry that Whetton owned near Teggs Nose was considered a professional set up and Silas had heard from a number of sources that the quarrymen there were well treated and had other benefits provided to help make up for the low basic pay. Indeed, some of his own men had moaned to him about the fact that Whetton's quarry was like a summer camp compared to the harsh conditions at Teggs. These thoughts were put into the background. He was overjoyed that Martha and Nat had a future to look forward to, and although it would be away from Langley, it was only across the hills, about a two-hour brisk walk away.

Silas spoke, "It's not the time to celebrate yet, but when we can tell Gwen and the kids, we must have you round for dinner, when might that be possible?"

"Not until we can clear the tenancy agreement exit with Aspinall. I don't trust that snake," Nat said forcefully. "I know that he will not want to lose the flock to one of his rivals."

CHAPTER 8 - *SOCIAL INJUSTICE*

The gentlemen's only cigar room was full at the Macclesfield Chambers of Commerce October Business meeting. The agenda had been completed and the new Board had been voted in unanimously. Henry Aspinall was relaxing in a large leather chair, satisfied that his nomination for re-election as Chairman had been supported without any challenge. There was only one niggle that was causing him a mild frustration. One agenda point was about how the section of the canal from Gurnett to the Staffordshire border had been targeted twice by gypsy gangs. The reports back to the Chamber from the Police had concluded that there was little that they could do without setting up costly patrols along what was a remote section running through few villages or towns. Unfortunately for Aspinall, both attacks had been on narrow boats carrying his goods and now he was in debt to companies in Stoke that were starting to demand compensation.

There were three other men in the cigar room with Henry Aspinall. Two of them were also Quarry owners – Thomas Whetton and Phillip Broadhead – and a local civil servant/politician – Joshua Padgett, the Vice Chairman of the Chambers and a Director of the Cheshire East Water Authority. Padgett was the kind of person who dabbled in many commercial activities where personal gain was possible. However, over time, he also recognised that gaining political status allowed him to leverage those around him to do the work whilst he was able to skim the cream by providing them with political support that paid him handsomely.

"So, Henry," Joshua started in a loud voice, "are we going to get our new reservoir in time? The Water Authority is currently unable to provide the mills the volume of flow and water pressure that they demand from Langley."

Aspinall responded impatiently, knowing that Padgett was well aware of the timelines for the Trentabank reservoir. "Of course, you'll get it as planned. I only have to evict one farmer now, as the other one felt that it was a better option to kill himself – poor bugger." Aspinall chuckled. "Very convenient for us, really."

Padgett goaded further: "You should've evicted them earlier and we could have had the dam wall complete by now, and the water would have been flowing through to the town. The plan for piping is already in place across the Hollins, and the Water Authority is keen to be charging mill owners more money." Padgett continued, "Farmers and sheep pay a pittance compared with the produce of industry... not that you can get any of your produce to the factories anymore without gypsies getting in your way!" he added sarcastically.

Thomas Whetton gripped his port glass a little tighter. He was a non-smoker and had only entered the cigar room in order to speak with Phillip Broadhead about plans for investment in quarry machine equipment, and how he was planning to retrain his workers to maximise the value of the investment. The conversation he was listening to, suddenly brought a realisation to him about the water supply and the fact that these two selfish bastards controlled it.

Whetton disliked Aspinall intensely and thought that Padgett was the worst kind of industrialist – born to a wealthy family that had also made money from the slave trade. Even though the slave trade in the UK had been abolished in 1807, Padgett still felt that his family had a right to treat all of his workers as unworthy citizens who should still bow down to the owners. Padgett's Silk Mill in Macclesfield was highly successful, but it had been built on the sweat, blood and tears of the workers. Their work conditions were horrendous and the management had quickly quashed any attempts at unionisation. Now that Padgett had moved towards local politics gave Whetton no further peace of mind.

Unsurprisingly, Aspinall and Padgett competed for least liked person in Whetton's life. Phillip Broadhead, on the other hand, was a decent man with a modern, forward-thinking mentality and an engineering background, hence the need to discuss how mechanisation might be introduced to the quarrying industry, but at the same time consider the evolving role of the quarryman. Aspinall and Padgett were stuck in a period of profiteering off the pain of others, whilst Whetton felt that he and Broadhead understood that sustainable business success must incorporate recognition and reward for the workers. Whetton had heard about the sad story of Sid Bayley and had vowed to see what he could do. He also wanted to attend the funeral. He was forming an idea in his mind that could deal a blow against the unacceptable face of Macclesfield industry and support the march into a new age of greater fairness and modern values.

First off, Thomas Whetton had felt a need to talk with the farmers most impacted by Aspinall's actions that the Water Board and Padgett were demanding. Two weeks previous, he had asked a trusted worker to request an audience with Nat Lovatt and Sid Bayley, independently. Knowing that a direct approach with Aspinall's tenant farmers could further their trouble, Whetton needed to go via a third party. Fortuitously, that very day, his contact had met and spoken to Nat at a sheep auction, but no contact had been made with Sid. Perhaps if circumstances had been different, a conversation with Sid may have resulted in salvation of a sort, and certainly a different outcome. When Thomas eventually met Nat in person, he found him to be a gentle yet strong individual who loved his family and felt a deep connection with nature and his sheep. Nat also talked with fondness of the close connections he had with villagers in Langley, especially his brother-in-law Silas Ledger, who seemed to run the quarry at Teggs Nose. He opened up about the eviction order that had been placed on his farm and the need to sell his sheep ahead of the profitable lambing period. Thomas listened to all of this and felt compelled to make an offer to Nat there and then. Thomas had been fortunate to have completed a land deal in recent times that included a section of Bosley Cloud, a prominent local hill on the borders of Cheshire and Staffordshire and about seven miles from Langley. He had not known what to do with the moorland that was too rugged to be farmed but could sustain sheep. Thomas felt that this was an option too good to miss and made an offer there and then to Nat. Nat had pinched himself and shaken Thomas' hand immediately.

A further week passed, and that week proved the difference, as Sid's despair got the better of him. Thomas felt wretched that he was unable to act as saviour to another – no doubt – innocent person who had fatefully and fatally fallen under the Aspinall axe.

Thomas Whetton needed to be in London the week before Sid's funeral and shortened his visit to catch a train north, ensuring he was able to be back by Friday midday, allowing him time to walk from Macclesfield railway station over Teggs Nose to Langley. Despite being able to afford any number of chauffeur-driven cars, he preferred to walk so as to find time to clear his head from the bore of daily business matters and think about how he might be able to better himself and the world around him. On that early afternoon, he was also very much deep in thought about the main reason he was heading to Langley – to pay respects to a hard-working farmer who had taken his own life – driven to despair by the acts of greed by people who were in the same business circle as he was.

The path he walked that morning was purposefully chosen as it passed by the Teggs Nose quarry, enabling him to observe the site and see how Aspinall had structured his operation. Thomas was impressed at how the quarry seemed to be moving large amounts of rock from the face to the cutting area using a very muscular-looking shire horse. He had decided that a rail system of trollies would be more efficient at his own quarry, but given the size of the cart and contents that this horse was shifting in a seemingly effortless way, he did think that the majestic beast seemed suited to the role. He also noted that the cutting team was not wearing helmets or safety goggles, as they used their pick axes and hammers to break the larger rocks before putting them into the crushing machine. He continued passed the hut that acted as the equipment store and small office – surprised that nobody had even asked what he was doing - a friendly face appeared at the door.

"Afternoon, sir, can I help you?" Jack Moat called out over the sound of the crusher.

Thomas shouted back, conscious of the booming crashes of metal on rock, "Hello, I'm heading down to the village and the path took me this way."

"No worries, I'll show you the way. I'm heading there myself," Jack offered, grabbing his jacket and locking the door behind him. As the two men started to walk together, Jack noted the expensive yet practical nature of the man's boots and the quality tweed overcoat that he wore.

"I'm Jack Moat – the Stock keeper here at the quarry," he announced.

"Thomas Whetton, pleased to meet you," came the reply.

"Oh, Mr. Whetton, I do apologise. I didn't recognise you in your coat," Jack said, shocked to be in such company. The last time he'd seen Thomas Whetton's face was in a regional business magazine at the barber's – the picture portrayed an image of a man collecting an industry award, surrounded by besuited people applauding. Jack hesitated for a moment and then said, "And so what brings you out this way, Mr. Whetton?"

"Please call me Thomas, and sadly, I am on my way to a

funeral to pay respects to a man I did not know but one who I feel was greatly wronged in life – Sid Bayley."

"I'm also going to the funeral," Jack replied. "I'd be honoured to accompany you to the chapel and introduce you to a few of Sid's closest friends, not that he had many."

Thomas was impressed by the polite and amiable nature of his fellow walker, and the two men chatted easily over the final two miles down the sheep track to the village of Langley. Jack was only too pleased to be able to share a few facts about working in an Aspinall subsidiary, including the fact that it was Sid Bayley's fine shire horse – Battalion – that Thomas had seen near the quarry face. Plus, the fact that despite many requests, only two workers had been given permission to attend the funeral by John Croker – the Teggs Nose Quarry's Commercial Manager.

The Chapel was full of Langley villagers. Sid Bayley was a well-liked member of the community, even if he was a little shy and socially awkward. Everyone admired his work ethic and his ability to manage a busy sheep farm alone but always attended to his church responsibilities as a lay preacher. His regular sermons were always impressive, and he took pride in weaving in metaphors relating to farming life, which brought amusement to the adult congregation whilst making it easier to understand for the younger members. His charismatic shire horse – Battalion – often appeared in his stories, and always appeared physically at the Village fete and allowed four children at a time to ride on his massive back. He had a revered status at the primary school, often being the subject of the first animal painting that a young pupil produced. Sid was proud of this and annually brought Battalion to the school to help present the art prize. Jack and Thomas joined the throng of villagers in the chapel and took up a position towards the back. It had been agreed that the bell would not be used to summon the congregation – for obvious reasons – and the bell rope had been sensitively hidden out of view.

The organ player stopped his solemn playing and the silence signaled the entrance of the coffin. There were six coffin bearers paired in height to help stability. Nat Lovatt and Ned Croucher were at the front, two other farming friends of Sid's were in the middle, and then at the rear were Fred Needles and Silas Ledger. The coffin sloped quite precariously towards the front because of the height of the third pairing, but the funeral director expertly steered the six pallbearers to the front of the chapel and placed the coffin on its stand.

Jack nudged Thomas and pointed out Silas as some of the discussion on the way down the hill had been about Silas and how he was the only other quarryman to be given permission to attend the funeral, although Fred had slipped out in his lunch break and sprinted down the hill to be present. Thomas paid particular attention when Silas was pointed out and noted that he was not difficult to spot in a crowd, given his size. He also noted the solemn look on his face and thought that maybe today was not the opportunity to talk to him about the idea he had. Across the aisle from Jack and Thomas sat someone who looked the spitting image of Henry Aspinall but a much younger version. Thomas thought of the awful irony of the day if Henry Aspinall – the main architect of Sid's passing – was in attendance. Thomas checked with Jack, and it was confirmed that this young doppelganger was, in fact, the fourteen-year-old son, Charles Aspinall.

Charles was next to 'Adam Bostock, a face he recognised as one of the better village cricketers of the county. The organ music started again and boomed out the first cords of The Lord's My Shepherd. Reverend Hamish Pottinger moved towards the coffin and waited for the final words of the hymn to end.

"My dear friends from Langley and elsewhere – welcome to what is a very sad day upon which we say our farewells to a lovely man and dear friend of this Ministry and us all." The Reverend's voice tailed off and he took a moment to collect himself again.

Thomas could not help but be drawn to look across at the Aspinall boy. Although he had a very similar physical look to his father, he had a softer, gentler face, and the sincerity of his presence was palpable. As various people spoke such warm words about Sid, Charles seemed to acknowledge the words and nodded his head in agreement. Thomas felt a bitter distaste for Aspinall Senior and he thought that the cold-blooded nature of the father must also somehow flow through the veins of the son. But Charles was looking respectfully at the speakers and listening intently to the emotional accounts of Sid's life on earth and how his unnatural death would not alter his ascension into a positive afterlife.

It was only later that Thomas learned from Jack why Charles Aspinall needed to be present at Sid's funeral. Charles had been sent away to boarding school from a very early age, and for this reason, he had developed few friends back in the Langley area. During summer holidays, in a house that offered a child little love and enjoyment, from the age of ten, Charles had looked beyond the boundaries of home. He had ventured across his father's estate and had come across Sid Bayley's farm. Sid was toiling in the fields, cutting and tying off bundles of hay for storage in his barn for later use for bedding in the lambing sheds. Charles had watched from the side of the field and had recognised that achieving this task alone was a tough, laborious job. On the third day he watched, Sid had beckoned him over and had asked Charles to tie off the bundle whilst he scooped up the grass into a large tuft. With both of them working in partnership, the hay was collected in double quick time. Sid was delighted with the boy's company and his intelligent questions about farming and outdoor life. And Charles was happy to be outdoors with an adult who was happy to share his knowledge. They became firm friends, and both looked forward to school holidays and, particularly, the harvesting season when they could spend hours together catching up on school life and farming life.

The funeral service finished and the private burial took place with just a few close friends in attendance. Charles Aspinall was amongst them, alongside the Lovatts. The rest of the congregation had been invited to the Dunstan Inn for a wake. Thomas and Jack were first into the pub, Dick Avery – the publican at the Setter Dog – had agreed to come down the hill and help out at the Dunstan, knowing that it would be busy following the funeral. Dick poured two pints of bitter and passed them across to the two men. A throng of funeralgoers entered the pub and the somber mood of the chapel was quickly forgotten as memories of Sid and his sermons started to get recalled. After thirty minutes, the five pallbearers arrived and Nat called over for a round of brandies. Fred had excused himself and headed back to the quarry to finish his afternoon shift. Silas entered the pub last, having to stoop to avoid an encounter with the low beams. Jack caught Silas' eye and beckoned him across.

"Sledge, can I introduce you to Mr. Thomas Whetton? Thomas, this is Silas Ledger," Jack announced, pleased that he was able to link his new friend with one of his oldest. Handshakes were exchanged.

"Why do they call you Sledge?" Thomas asked.

Jack intervened proudly, "Because he can wield a sledgehammer harder than any other living man." Adding with a smile, "Plus, his name rather fits."

"I see," Thomas replied with a smile. "That seems to make sense." He added. "Now, Mr. Ledger, I would like a chance to talk with you in private about a little proposal."

Silas spoke for the first time, "Thanks, Jack, I'll take it from here. Mr. Whetton, I am very pleased to meet you, and on behalf of a good man – Sid Bayley – thanks for paying your respects today, it means a lot. Let's talk outside, I don't think we'll get much privacy in here." Thomas immediately warmed to this oversized human and felt that this was a man he wanted to get to know better. They walked down the main street towards a streetlight beneath which a bench was located. They sat down.

"Mr. Whetton", Silas started.

"Just call me Thomas."

"Mr. Whetton... Thomas, I want to thank you for your kind offer to help my sister and brother-in-law – the Lovatts. Nat told me confidentially what you've said to him, and it is the most generous of offers and will help a family out of a desperate situation. Nat and Martha will repay you, I promise, through hard work and good husbandry of your land."

"I have no doubt of that"', interjected Thomas,

"Nat also told me that you wanted to talk to me?" Silas suggested.

"Yes, Silas, may I call you by your first name?" Thomas asked.

"Of course," Silas responded.

Thomas spoke plainly, "I would like to address the imbalance that I feel has been dealt to the people of Langley by Henry Aspinall. He has grown rich from the natural resources that he has inherited and is now exploiting his position by punishing hard-working folk. Sid Bayley and your sister's family are just one example. It also seems as though Aspinall's dubious operating ethics at the Quarry are putting men at risk – in order to increase productivity and his profits." He continued, "Also, once the Trentabank reservoir comes into operation, he has already planned additional income from the installation and rent of pipes required to move the water across the Hollins and down into the town, producing the required pressure for his textiles mill, as the river Bollin will not be able to take the additional volume. This will mean the destruction of more arable land that the people of Langley farm." Thomas paused to gauge a reaction from Silas. The larger man sat there staring down at the ground. The new revelation about the reservoir was sinking in.

Silas raised his head. "But surely all of the mill owners in Macclesfield – including you – will benefit," he challenged.

Thomas quickly responded, "That is correct in the short

term, but there is no doubt that Aspinall has plans to work with the Water Authority and his friend Joshua Padgett to increase the tax of the new water supply over time and this will give them the power to drive out some mills who will need to spend more on their energy, thus filling the coffers of Padgett and Aspinall even more."

Silas contemplated this new information. He was being drawn into the kind of dark intrigue and tactics that he believed was rife in commercialism and that he had long ago wanted to distance himself from by simply staying with his quarrying job on the hill. A job that he had felt safe in until recently, when the pressure of suppressed low wages had forced him into a representative role for his workmates.

Thomas continued, "Now that the timescale to complete the dam has been accelerated, there is much more pressure on the laying of pipes across the Hollins. Is there any way that you can engage the help of the farmers to raise an objection about the loss of agricultural land, in the County Court? This could at least delay the start and give me time to petition higher Government to ensure a more sustainable level playing field for mill owners and workers."

There was a moment of silence whilst Silas soaked in the new revelation. He spoke. "I hear your words, depressing as they are, and I agree that we need to act. I will raise your concerns at the monthly village meeting next week and ask for support."

Both men stood up. Firmly shaking his hand, Thomas said, "Thank you, Silas, I promise you that this will just be the start. I also want to support the situation at the quarry, as I recognise you as the man in the middle, supporting your fellow workers whilst being unfairly pressured by upper management. I'll be in touch." And with that Thomas turned and walked away.

Silas returned to the Dunstan Inn and sat back down next to Jack. "Well, Sledge, what did Thomas want to talk to you about?" Jack asked eagerly.

Silas turned to him and simply said, "We've got work to do, my friend, but it's all good. I think we have found a useful ally."

CHAPTER 9 - *THE SCOREBOX*

From the chance meeting at the cricket nets, Charles Aspinall had been very keen to manufacture further opportunities to meet the intriguing Beth Ledger. To him, she seemed to offer a spark of energetic rebellion that was so alien to his privileged but shackled upbringing. Charles was the only child of Henry and Florence Aspinall. His father had little time for his family especially as he felt that his only son and heir was more of a mother's boy. The fact that his wife had failed to provide him with any further offspring was always a contentious issue in the family. Charles' mother had reacted to this by finding relief for her depression in the bottom of a bottle from an early stage of her married life. Charles had been brought up by a nanny until the age of five when he was sent away to boarding school. Charles endured a dozen years of hardship at his prep and then secondary school at Hoarwithy, just over the county border in Derbyshire. Suffering regularly from bullying due to his skinny frame and complete lack of ability on the sports field. However, he had excelled in all intellectual pursuits – particularly mathematics and sciences.

One day, when Charles was thirteen and the Hoarwithy School's first XI cricket team was playing – all boys were expected to line the boundary rope and support the team – the Cricket Master – Mr. McCrory, called him over. "Aspinall, can you go to the scorebox immediately please? Mr. Grainger needs some assistance."

Charles immediately jumped up and hurried across to the scorebox. Mr. Grainger, an old boy, now seventy-four years old, had religiously scored for every one of the school's 1st XI games since he had retired from his job in the Civil Service, opened the door. Charles was welcomed by a pleasant old gentleman with the words, "Hello, son, I've heard you love numbers; come on in."

This is where Charles' love of cricket scoring started. Mr. Grainger taught him everything about the scoring system and how to annotate the various scores into the enormous loose-leaf scorebook. Each batsman and bowler were identified by a different colour, and each ball needed to be recorded accurately. It was a focused task requiring a high level of concentration – Charles loved it. Soon enough, Mr. Grainger was able to lean back on his chair and simply oversee Charles creating his numerical and artistic masterpiece on the paper, and pull the appropriate strings to change the scoreboard. Mr. Grainger was happy that he had found a protégé, and Charles was happy to have found a passion and a person who would treat him with kindness and respect.

During the summer holidays, Charles returned to his family home on Ridge Hill, overlooking the village of Langley. Despite the cold and unloving welcome he received from his parents, he escaped to the village cricket club as often as he could to score for the Langley home teams. He gained respect from everyone down at the ground, not because his father was the major Club benefactor, but because of the beautiful scoring sheets he could provide for each match, together with precise bowling and batting figures for each Langley player. Many of the better games ended up having their scores recorded and framed on the walls of the clubhouse. Adam Bostock – the cricket captain – always looked out for Charles and respected him for what he was – an ace scorer. Henry Aspinall – on the other hand – had no respect for his own son. Whenever he visited the Club, Henry showed great disappointment that his son was not striving to get on the honours board as a player. Compiling statistics was not the job of an Aspinall. Adam and Fred Needles often made it known to Aspinall Senior that Charles was a much-admired member of the Club, and in fact any team in the league would be proud of the scorebooks at Langley. However, Henry refused to see it, and more often than not, left the Club muttering to himself about his son's failings in life.

Charles had just turned seventeen and was in his final year at Hoarwithy. His father had destined that Charles would enter the family firm and serve an apprenticeship under John Croker, possibly completing some accountancy qualifications. Henry did not believe that higher education was needed, and he wanted Charles closer at hand so that he could influence his character more. Charles dreamt of a university education and certainly had the intellectual capacity to handle it. But ahead of his final year, he had a summer to endure at home and enjoy down at the cricket club.

It was the first week of the holidays that Charles had first spotted Beth and her friend – Moll Brampton – crossing the field from their school to the cricket nets. However, it was not until the end of the holidays that he plucked up the courage to speak with Beth. As soon as the two started conversation, there was an electricity that neither had previously recognised – a warm and pleasant feeling entered their bodies.

There were two weeks left until Charles had to return to Hoarwithy. He needed to make the most of this new found relationship. Following their first encounter – when they'd verbally jousted but agreed over the rights to trespass – Charles had found out that Beth lived on the main road through Langley, next door to the Post Office. That night he'd slipped out of the mansion house on Ridge Hill, descended down into the valley and slipped a note under the Ledger's front door – addressed to Beth.

The note was neatly written using a different colour for each word. It said, "Meet you again tomorrow at 2 o'clock in the cricket scorebox, where I'll allow you to trespass again! CA."

Will was up first as he had a newspaper job at the Post Office, and Mr. Ricketts insisted on all papers being delivered before 6 am. Will noticed the slip of neatly folded paper on the floor. He picked it up and took it to the room he shared with Beth. "Sis," he gently whispered into her ear. "You have a note from an admirer!"

Half asleep still, Beth acknowledged his words but kept dozing. It wasn't for another hour that Silas knocked on the door and announced that it was time for breakfast. Beth needed to be up to help her mother at the chapel to dress it with all of the harvest festival gifts, a chance to create a warm and fresh feeling in the usually austere Methodist chapel – made even more so following Sid Bailey's recent funeral. The note fluttered to the floor, and she picked it up and read it.

How odd, and why the colours? She quickly guessed the initials meant Charles Aspinall, and she smiled with the thought that he might be interested in progressing the relationship further. She thought that she was, too, especially with someone who seemed to share the same values. Although, why did he, given his upbringing of privilege, surrounded by wealth, intrigued her even more so? She quickly got dressed, had breakfast and headed out to the chapel, where her mum was already creating large bouquets of meadow flowers.

Beth wondered whether she should tell Moll about the note, who was also at the Chapel with her mother. But she realised that any shared news with Moll meant that the whole village quickly knew, too, and Beth needed to understand more about Charles before any gossip got to work.

She completed all the tasks that Gwen needed help with and quietly slipped out of the vestry door without saying her goodbyes to Moll. She bumped into Reverend Pottinger coming up the graveyard path. The vivid hues of the flowers adorning Sid's grave provided a stark contrast to the grey stones surrounding it – paying their own respect to the latest inhabitant of the village cemetery. "Thanks for your help, Beth. I'm sure the inside looks wonderful," The cheery minister said. Beth smiled and continued passed him with increasing speed just in case his voice had alerted the inquisitive Moll.

It took only ten minutes to head up the lane to the cricket club, and Beth managed to navigate her way stealthily around the boundary rope using hedges, sight screens and ground rollers as camouflage before she arrived at the scorebox – which was basically a small shed with a door at the back and a scoreboard on the front from which the score was showing that the Langley 3rd XI were 75 for 1 wicket after 10 overs. It was the final game of their season, as Summer was very much turning to Autumn. She knocked at the door.

"Enter!" Charles' voice called out from within, in a falsely deep voice. He had seen Beth's appearance on the far side of the pitch and followed her attempts at discretion with increasing amusement. Beth entered the box. Charles was sitting at a desk with his work in front of him. Coloured pencils and an eraser were being picked up, used and put down – at a rapid speed. Without losing concentration in any way, he pulled up a second seat next to him and beckoned her to sit down. She did, liking the calm and cool way that Charles seemed to be rapidly multi-tasking.

"Thanks for coming, Miss. Ledger," he said with a mocking formality. "And here begins your education in the fine art of cricket scoring." Beth relaxed and put down the two apples that she'd pinched from the Harvest goodies.

Charles then spent the next half an hour entertaining Beth with a running commentary of the scoring and his actions in the scorebook. Her job was to change the scoreboard following his instructions. She laughed at what she thought was an illogical game with rules he seemed to be making up. Using alien words like *silly mid-on* and *deep fine leg,* he described the field in front of him and made-up fun names for the opposition fielders based on their physical forms. He was a witty entertainer – and seemed as confident about the sport he was scoring as about the fact that he was in a small, confined wooden hut with a new female companion.

The cricket teams broke for tea, and Charles put down his pencils and ceased his amusing commentary, having described the cream cakes and finely cut sandwiches that were likely being made and served by Hilda Bostock, the diminutive mother of Adam, the Club Captain. From below the table, Charles produced a small wrapped tablecloth that he laid out on the table in front of them. As it unfolded, Beth saw that Hilda's cakes and sandwiches were being reproduced in front of her. Hilda admired Charles and his unusual love of scoring, she knew about his harsh home conditions and so felt it was her duty to befriend the teenager. Hilda had been delighted to package up some of her much-admired tea items for him, as she knew that during tea, he'd likely be involved in more of his statistical summations. Charles also had purloined a small flask of scrumpy cider from the bar and two glasses.

"Mademoiselle Ledger – your food is served," he said in a mock French accent.

Beth was highly amused at the whole scene and loved the fact that Charles had chosen such a creative way to get to know her further. Very different from the boys who had tried and failed to woo her at the occasional village barn dance – where she had no interest. This was different. Charles was a charmer but also a much deeper thinker than the other village boys. They ate the food and Beth produced the apples, which made a crunchy addition to the cold cider that Charles poured out. "Now tell me more about your thinking around trespass," he said, changing the course of the conversation away from Hilda's clotted cream and jam Victoria sponge.

Beth looked at him, she was up for the debate! "Surely your ideology is not that of the free spirit? With all of the land that your family own and the team of gamekeepers that patrol it, do you not want to keep that countryside to yourselves and fence it off?"

Charles looked intently at her. His previously charming and fun demeanor changed, and he spoke with genuine gravity. "My father is the landowner; he employs gamekeepers and he has fenced off our estate. If you ask him, he believes that as he has legitimately inherited the land, then he has every right to do with it what he wants and only those with permission to enter are allowed to." He grabbed her hand and seemed to speak from the very depth of his soul, "I detest everything my father stands for!"

Beth looked up at him and shook her hand free. "Prove it then. Come with me next week on a trespass on the moors, just the two of us."

Charles looked at her, admiring the fire that burned inside. This charming idealist was everything that he wasn't – free to think for herself, free to act on her convictions. Could he dare rebel like her? "I will go with you, Beth, I promise."

The week passed slowly for Charles; his mother's health was worsening by the day, and the regular visits from the doctors suggested that she was unlikely to live for much longer. His Father was absent, as usual, preferring to spend time at his private Old Boy's Club or with his most elite friends talking about business and how to grow their share of wealth. Charles decided to pack his large trunk early for the upcoming winter term at school. He was determined to achieve a scholarship to university that he had discussed with his old friend – Mr. Grainger. It seemed like the Old Boys Alumni provided an annual scholarship to any boy who might need support in obtaining a university education if he does not have the requisite financial support to do this. Charles had discussed his father's desire to move directly into the Aspinall family business as an apprentice rather than support his ambition to go to university. Mr. Grainger admired Charles' growing independence and immensely enjoyed the company over the summer months whilst the two of them spent hours together scoring the school's cricket teams. He gave Charles the idea of applying for the scholarship once he turned eighteen, the age at which he was legally able to decide for himself which path in life he was to take.

The final items were being packed in the trunk when one of Aspinall's housemaids brought up an apple wrapped in a handkerchief. Charles looked at it quizzically for one moment and then realised the likely meaning. Attached to it was a folded note with the initials CA on the front. Charles unfolded it and smiled as he read it, "See you on Friday at 4 pm by the Saddlers Way signpost. BL."

Charles was heading to Hoarwithy on Saturday, so he'd have one last chance to see Beth before term started. He felt a thrill of energy race through his veins. He so wanted to share in Beth's rebellious streak and feel the joy and freedom in which she seemed to live her life.

Beth was already back at Macclesfield High school for girls. As usual, she had finished her Latin assignment well ahead of the rest of the class, and she was sat staring out of the window at the hills in the direction of Shuttlingsloe and the Derbyshire moors. She was thinking about Charles and what a fun time she'd had with him in the cricket club scorebox. She was surprised how quickly he'd agreed to meet up with her again and join her in her quest to challenge society's inequalities. Beth had decided that she wanted to go to university to read sociology and politics. Education came easily to her, and she was forever lost in her reading. Each evening, when the Post Office/Newsagent had closed, she would hungrily digest any of the newspapers or magazines that Will would bring back from Mr. Ricketts. Often, she would debate the hottest political topics of the day with her mother, who also had a passion for how society was developing and how the woman's role was gradually being better represented in all facets. Silas used to sit at the kitchen table bemused by how his wife and daughter could create such passion between the two of them debating any number of topics. He observed and was rarely asked to contribute as the maelstrom of feminist argument was too powerful to ever consider contradicting! Both he and Gwen were so proud of how Beth was developing her strong personality and sharp intellect. They had no doubt that she would attend university and it was their responsibility to help her afford the college fees. Every spare penny that Silas and Gwen earned went into the college fund, and even Will – who had his Post Office ownership dreams – added to the fund with the occasional penny from his messaging runs income stream.

On the way to school that morning, Beth had left early to

deliver the apple to the Aspinall house on Ridge Hill. She was stopped at the gate by Arthur Brice – the Aspinall Estate Manager and Head Gamekeeper. He recognised her as the girl who regularly took short cuts across the estate land near the cricket club. "Hey Missy – you need to start taking heed of the notice that says 'Private Land, Stay Out' – or you could get yourself shot!"

Beth smiled and decided that charm was the best approach this time to achieve her goal, "I'm so sorry, sir, I'm short-sighted and struggle to read notices without my glasses on. I'll pay more attention in future." Before allowing a response, she quickly added, "Please, can you deliver this to the house? It's for Master Charles."

Arthur Brice took the apple parcel smiling and quipped back, "I will as long as you didn't pinch this from our estate orchard!"

"Thank you, and I'll be sure to read the signs in future." Beth giggled and turned to walk away. As soon as she had turned her head, her face lost any sense of humour, and she vowed to go on another apple raid before too long!

The signpost at the start of Saddlers Way was a well-known marker point directing walkers either up Teggs Nose and onwards towards Macclesfield or up on to the Moors and towards Buxton. Charles was there well ahead of the four pm invitation. He was excited but apprehensive about what plans Beth had in store for them that afternoon. Four o'clock came and went, and Charles was getting anxious that Beth would stand him up. Thirty minutes passed and he was just about to give up when he heard a distant voice call out from below. It was Beth climbing the path as fast as she could. Breathless, she crossed the last few yards and sat down on the grass. Panting, she laughed, "I'm so, so sorry – what must you think of me?" She caught her breath, "I was asked to stay behind at school to help some of the younger girls with their reading."

Charles offered his hand to help her up. He was so happy to see Beth's unkempt hair hiding rosy cheeks and that intelligent yet mischievous face. He was already smitten. Beth grabbed his hand and started to move at a pace up the path towards the moors. The energy she had seemed to pass through her hand like electricity and he felt so alive. They must have walked about three miles and were now well above the sheep fields and entering the heather and peat bogs that marked the start of the moorland, plateauing for several miles before the Buxton valley came into view. Beth was a dynamo of conversation, finishing most monologues with a question, "So, what do you think?" But before Charles had any chance to answer, Beth cut in with her own answer. And so it carried on. Charles estimated that it was a quarter of an hour before he was able to stop her from talking and force her to listen to his own point of view. They laughed, and Beth apologised for being such a chatterbox.

National politics were the main discussion point – including the perilous state of the economy and how it was becoming increasingly tough on the working classes. Charles – despite being as far away from economic hardship as it was possible to be – agreed with all of the points that Beth made and presented a genuine sentiment towards the inequality that was rampant in society. Beth had decided to steer clear of the obvious example happening down in the valley beneath them – the building of the Trentabank reservoir – for the benefit of the wealthy, with no thought of the consequences that impacted the little people. The forced eviction of her aunt and uncle – and, of course, the tragedy that it had also caused in the death of Sid Bayley.

Beth said that she was keen to stand as a counsellor at the next local elections, although she also wanted to go to Durham University to study Politics. Charles found himself absorbing all of this information and responding in the affirmative when space allowed. He did question how she was going to break into the male bastion of the local County Council, but all this did was to raise the energy in Beth's voice even more as she listed out her political agenda and what she would stand for – which Charles roughly interpreted as Progressive Libertarian Modernist. Charles had never met a person who was so determined about the direction they were taking and a cause so worth fighting for. Beth felt very comfortable in Charles' company and appreciated his support and his ability to add new thinking whenever there was a pause for her to take a breath!

They reached a point in the north facing path where a fence meant that they had to take a left turn and follow in a westerly direction. The sun was just setting over the Cheshire plain and the distant Welsh mountains. Beth only took two strides and then halted. She stopped, turned and looked at Charles. "And this is what we are here for," she said with increasing ferocity. "This fence has been put here to stop us walking across the moors. The landowner is the Earl of Derby and he claims that the public should be kept off the moors as we disturb the nesting grouse that help fuel his and his friend's disgusting hunting hobby." Beth pulled a pair of pliers from her small pouch. "I would like to introduce you – Charlie Aspinall – to my little friend and the tool that I use to fight back against the pompous landed gentry." Beth took the pliers and easily snipped through the three lengths of barbed wire that made up the fence. She stepped to the other side of the now broken fence and beckoned Charles through. "And now, sir, I welcome you to the fightback and the world of trespassing!"

Charles looked shocked at the destruction of the fence, but in Beth, nothing was surprising now. He took her hand and walked through to the other side of the fence. They laughed and started skipping between the peat bogs, bilberry bushes and heather. No grouse rose up to shrill an objection, but a family of lapwings took to the air and circled the joyous couple as they enjoyed the freedom of their crime. After about ten minutes of playing hide and seek, Beth and Charles retraced their steps and headed back down the way they had come. Passing the fence, Beth handed the pliers to Charles and he defiantly cut several more gaps in the fence to make it as difficult as possible for the gamekeepers to mend. Once on the path back down Saddlers Way, the two friends brushed shoulders whenever they were close. At the signpost where they had met, Charles reached out his hand to express his gratitude for what had been one of the most exhilarating experiences of his life to date and certainly one of the most illegal. Beth brushed off his formality and threw her hands around him and gave him a hug. He was more than happy to reciprocate. Beth knew that term time for Charles would mean that she would not see him until Christmas, ten weeks away. She would miss getting to know her new friend further.

CHAPTER 10 - *SHAMEFUL PRACTICE*

The monthly Langley village meeting took place in the Dunstan Inn on the last Tuesday of the month. Ned Croucher rearranged the bar area so that seats were around the outside of the room, and whoever had a point on the agenda was expected to stand in the middle and present their item. All agenda points for the meeting needed to be registered through Percy Ricketts at the Post Office by Tuesday lunchtime. There were always plenty of matters arising across the spectrum of the village's needs, from the formation of a crochet group proposed by Hilda Bostock to the need for a working party to help with drainage on the village playing field. Most of the items were relatively trivial and dealt with in minutes. The larger and more controversial matters were dealt with at the end of the agenda, which meant that often, the Dunstan would still have its lights burning well beyond 11 pm.

The final agenda point was reached and Percy invited Silas to address the group. "Fellow villagers," Silas started, "firstly, I'd like to invite Nat up to say something given that he and

Martha and Sid – may he rest in peace - have always been closest in our thoughts due to the creation of the Trentabank reservoir and their forced eviction from their farms."

Nat – never a man to seek public speaking opportunities – gingerly got to his feet and took off his cap. "Thanks, Sledge," Nat mumbled, "I'd just like to ask everyone to pray silently for a moment and think about our dear friend and fellow farmer – Sid Bayley." The entire group rose to their feet in unison. The men removed their caps and stood with their heads bowed. Many of the dogs – mainly sheep dogs awoke from their slumber, expectant of a move home, but then also stood in silent thought. After a minute, Nat thanked everyone and they returned to their seats. "I'd just like to take this opportunity to tell everybody that the Lovatts have got a new place to live over near Bosley Cloud and will be moving our flock to a new farm on the Whetton estate, and what's more, we will be taking on Sid's flock, thanks to Thomas Whetton's vision to create a larger more sustainable sheep farm."

Many of the group gazed and looked across at Martha. Relieved at seeing a comforted look, they cheered and clapped Nat on the back, unanimously positive that the horrible situation that had befallen some of their friends and indeed caused the untimely departure of Sid, had been rescued by the good fortune that Thomas Whetton had provided to the Lovatts. "What about Battalion?" called out a voice from the group.

"Don't you worry yourself," reassured Nat. "Battalion will be looked after by Jack and the quarry team up on Teggs Nose and will be on call to help any villager with any heavy moving needs. I think that's what Sid would have wanted." A sound of respectful approval erupted from the room.

Nat sat down, and Silas returned to the floor. "It is good news that Nat and Martha have a new home and that the new reservoir can be built on schedule, but we now have a further challenge that we must face together." Silas registered a new level of attention paid to him by the group. "The river Bollin serves the needs of Macclesfield's industry to date and has been effectively used as the water supply from the three existing reservoirs. However, with the addition of the Trentabank reservoir, the volume of water increases by around sixty percent. The Bollin does not have the capacity in its current course to handle that additional volume of water at normal, let alone peak times. The village would be susceptible to flooding on regular occasions. The Water Authority has proposed to lay a series of large pipes from the reservoirs up over the Hollins to take the excess water to the town that way," Silas paused.

This news was completely new to the group, and it needed a few moments to be fully absorbed. "Sledge, what does that mean to those of us farmers who farm over the Hollins, and where exactly is the pipeline going?" challenged Donald Hough, a local farmer.

"A relevant and good question, Don," Silas replied. "I don't know of the exact route of the pipeline or how much disruption laying it will be, but because the Hollins is part of the Aspinall estate, I don't believe we have any legal right to stop it happening." He continued in his slow, controlled manner, "However..." Silas had the attention of the whole room waiting expectantly – "However, planning permission has been agreed between the Aspinall Estate and the Water

83

Authority, but not shared in public. It is my understanding that the contracts for the laying of the pipeline are also about to be issued."

"We must see those plans!" demanded Don Hough. "They may have grave consequences on our own futures, given how Aspinall's Estate has treated the Trentabank farms."

A very clear consensus of agreement arose from the bar room. Anxious faces and words were exchanged across the floor. Silas's voice rose above the rest. "Everyone, let's calm down. Please hush for one more minute," he continued. "We need to act singularly here. If I have your approval, I will petition Macclesfield Planning Authorities to make public the plans for the pipeline and insist that no work or contracts for work be started before we have a fuller understanding of the impact."

Jack Moat's voice was the first to be heard, "Sledge, I think you have everyone's support here. And I think we need an agreement to meet again as soon as any further information is forthcoming. Could we also ask the Planning Authority and the Water Board to come and meet with us as a matter of urgency?" A murmur of agreement arose from the room.

Percy Ricketts, who was busily taking minutes of the meeting, spoke, "Is that a note for the minutes then? That Silas will write to these Authorities urgently requesting a sight of the planning permission papers, and also inviting them to a meeting with this forum?"

Looking at the room and noting a nodding consensus, Silas added, "Thank you, Percy – yes, I will pursue those actions with haste".

The meeting closed, and the group spilt out into the main village street, clearly concerned by this worrying new news. When Gwen and Silas got home, Gwen was very animated. The news about the pipeline was new to her, too, as Silas had agreed with Thomas Whetton that he needed to tread with caution about who knew what. "I think you need to personally go to the Town Hall in Macc tomorrow, Silas. They will need to give you a response if you are there in person. Writing will take too long."

"I agree, dear. I will go via the quarry so that I can ensure the first work shift is running smoothly. Tomorrow is the first day that we need to deliver double the quantity of rock over to the dam wall at Trentabank."

Silas was up early and knocked on Jack's door on his way to the path up Teggs Nose. "Morning Sledge..." Jack announced from his bedroom window. "Give us two minutes." The pair walked and talked their way up the sheep-track to the quarry, with Silas rehearsing the way in which he should ask the various departments at the Town Hall to divulge and agree to Langley's demands for information. They also discussed how they would best achieve the required quota of gritstone to be carted across to Trentabank. On reaching the quarry, Jack headed to the store office, and Silas met up with Fred Needles to pass on instructions to ensure that everyone understood the importance of meeting the new demands for gritstone, as this was the basis upon which John Croker and Henry Aspinall had agreed to a potential bonus. It seemed as if Fred was confident that the team were positive about the task ahead. Silas set off for Macclesfield.

He arrived at the Town Hall just as the St. Michael's Church bell next door was ringing nine o'clock – the opening hour of the civil service. Silas entered the building and noted the dusty, stale smell of paper pushers. Very different from the fresh air at the quarry, despite the regular smell of nitroglycerin from the explosives, and the resultant cloud of rock dust. "Silas Ledger", he announced to the first paper pusher who raised their head, "I'm here to see the Water Authority and the Planning Officer."

The man scurried away, rather intimidated by the sheer size of Silas. He hadn't come across such a behemoth of a human before. After ten minutes, a well-presented young lady approached Silas and gestured to him to follow her into a nearby office. "Sir, I presume you do not have an appointment today. Is that correct?" she asked politely.

"No, madam, I don't, but I will not be leaving this building before I see those people who will give me answers," Silas spoke back in a cool and determined way.

The lady seemed impressed with Silas's direct approach. "Well, sir, I am the new Planning Officer for Macclesfield, and as luck would have it, I have no appointments as this is my first day in office. What can I do for you?" she said, clearly wanting to set a good example during her first day in post with her first customer.

Silas smiled, thinking that he had struck lucky to find such a welcoming newcomer, not yet affected by the burden of excessive paperwork and bureaucracy. "I am here on behalf of a group of Langley villagers who would like to see the planning permission application for a possible pipeline that crosses the Hollins from Langley into Macclesfield." The lady got up and headed off to the filing cabinet behind her in which all planning applications were filed.

As she ruffled through the files, she asked whether Silas knew who could have filed the application. "The Water Authority would own the pipeline," Silas informed. "And the land upon which it would be built is Henry Aspinall's, yet he rents it out to a number of farmers who use the land for arable and grazing purposes."

"Okay – so that should be the Water Authority applying to the Aspinall Estate." She replied and thumbed through the section that it should have been in but found nothing. "That's odd. Perhaps I need to check with the Office across the way who looks after all of the Water Authority administration?" As the planning officer left the room, Silas sighed at the thought of a job involving endless bureaucracy. But in this case, bureaucracy in the form of planning regulations might just achieve the means to an end.

After a few minutes, the door was pushed open forcefully by a mustachioed man with a slight limp. "Sir – I am Victor Knight, the manager for the local Water Board - for what reason are you requiring this information?" He spat out with an unjustifiably aggressive tone. Silas repeated the reason that he had previously explained to the planning officer, but added that Langley had suffered previously due to the rather slapdash approach to the way the Trentabank reservoir scheme had been forced through two years previous. Victor Knight sneered at Silas – "I can assure you that everything has been progressed with due diligence paid to the correct planning process."

"I'm sure it has" responded Silas. "So, can I see the

application as I am representing the interests of a number of farmers who might be impacted by any pipeline laying?"

"I'm sorry, sir, I am unable to show you the document right now." And with that, Victor Knight walked out of the office.

The fact that the planning permission could not be found aroused suspicions in Silas' mind. Could it be that the Water Authority, in the form of Joshua Padgett, had simply *done a deal* with Henry Aspinall directly without any consideration of the consequential impact – a pipe-laying operation that might have an impact on more farmers' livelihoods? In his head and heart – Silas knew that this was very likely to be the case.

The Planning Officer, whose name was Melissa Kirkham, had witnessed, on her very first day, the fact that local politics were alive and breeding in the Macclesfield Chambers of Commerce. She accompanied Silas to the front door. Mr. Ledger, she addressed Silas, "Let me do some more digging around and I will get back to you as I do think we owe you an explanation."

Silas responded courteously, noticing her name label on the lapel of her jacket, "Thank you, Miss Kirkham, that would be greatly appreciated." Silas needed to get back up to the quarry, as he felt there was no more he could do, right then, to follow up further on the Hollins pipeline situation. He headed up the lane towards the path that would take him back over to Teggs Nose.

Melissa Kirkham had had a tough induction on her first

morning, but it was about to get very much worse. Just after a tea break at 11 am, Victor Knight burst into her office, looking very flustered. "You need to go to 16 Duke Street immediately," he said. Melissa had no idea what this meant, but she realised that the urgency in his voice suggested that he had been instructed to make sure she went to this address in haste. Melissa grabbed her coat and was given instructions on how to get to Duke Street by the door steward, who also acted as a security guard for the Town Hall. It was only a five-minute walk if she hurried. She was apprehensive as she had no idea why she needed to go to this address other than it was important. Melissa arrived at the front door of the building and knocked using the large lion door knocker. On the third clang, the door swung open and revealed a uniformed man. She introduced herself, and without saying a word, he ushered her in and took her coat. He then beckoned her to follow him. The corridor was long and dark but covered in portraits of important-looking gentlemen. The usher knocked at the end door.

"Enter!" came a voice from within. The door opened on to a large office with heavy red velvet curtains and a large dark patterned Turkish rug on oak floorboards in front of a gigantic walnut desk. A cream chaise longue located at one side of the desk was the only light item in the room. A floor-to-ceiling bookcase on one wall housing leather-bound files of encyclopedias and business documents interspersed by antique-looking machine parts. More oil-painted portraits of serious-looking gentlemen and hunting scenes hung on the oak-paneled walls. The whole place wreaked of a male bastion of arrogant wealth and pomposity.

A slightly balding, silver-haired man sat at the desk with

his back to Melissa as she entered the office, and the door closed behind her. "Please take a seat," the man said, pointing with his right arm to the chaise longue. Already feeling uncomfortable, Melissa sat down at one end of the couch.

"Miss Melissa Kirkham," the man announced as he swung his chair around. "May I introduce myself? I'm Joshua Padgett – Managing Director of the Cheshire East Water Authority and Vice Chairman of the Macclesfield Chamber of Commerce." Melissa looked at his wrinkled, smiling face but recognised no hint of kindness behind his look. He reminded her of an old headmaster who had enjoyed dealing out corporal punishment with a cane, so much so that he was eventually fired by the school governors for abusing his power when one young pupil was hospitalised after one such beating. "How are you enjoying your first day in my planning department?" he said condescendingly. Without waiting for an answer, he continued, "Let me get this straight from the start, Miss Kirkham – you work for me – indirectly, I admit, but you work for me all the same, and anything I say, you need to do. Understood?"

Melissa was sitting rigidly on the couch. She had wanted this job badly, but she was beginning to regret what seemed to be some of the conditions that went with it. "Mr. Padgett," she started. "I have been selected to ensure that the Planning Application process is adhered to in the borough of Macclesfield, and that's what I intend to do. I hope that meets your needs?"

Joshua Padgett repeated his cold grin. Getting up from his desk, he moved across to the couch and sat down next to her. Uncomfortably close. To Melissa, he smelt of cigars and liquor, and she noted that his dark red tie closely matched the pattern on the rug. She found it hard to imagine a more repugnant human being. It was as if she was back in the Headmaster's office about to be brutalised. Padgett reached his hand over and touched her leg. Melissa froze, unsure whether to slap him hard across the jaw, or get up and run for the exit. She decided to stay stock-still for the moment.

"Mr. Padgett," Melissa said, edging her body as far along the couch away from him as she could and trying desperately to focus the attention on strict business matters. "There seems to be a missing application for a pipeline across the Hollins – could you shed some light on this matter, please?"

"Melissa, may I call you Melissa?" Padgett hissed. "I think we can come to some arrangement – you and I – don't you agree?"

She moved his hand away from her leg. "What do you mean?" she stuttered.

"I mean that you should approve the planning applications that I ask you to, without hesitation or question. If you do this, then we will get along just fine."

He lunged towards her with both his hands and grasped her body, groping for her breasts. Melissa felt she was in some kind of twilight zone. Surely, she was not being molested by this man? It could not be true! She pushed Padgett away and kicked out with her left knee – making contact with his groin – and sending him crumpling to the floor. She got up and fled towards the door. Opening the door, she turned around to see him staring at her, with that fixed cold smile still on his face, although now there was at least a trace of pain etched in it.

She ran down the corridor, leaping down the stairs, grabbed her coat and forced her way past the door man, who seemed not in the slightest bit surprised. She vowed that she would never return to Duke Street.

Collecting herself on her walk back to the Town Hall, she recalled the pleasant and genuine nature of Silas Ledger and remembered that not all men were like Padgett. As she got back to her office, Victor Knight appeared, he was highly agitated but contrite. "I'm very sorry, Miss. Kirkham, but your first day is also your last day working here. I have been told by a senior authority in the building that your work contract has been terminated as of now, and you will need to leave the building immediately. You will get paid for the single day you have worked."

In reality, Melissa was mightily relieved as it saved her from handing in her notice, which was exactly what she was about to do as soon as she could get to the Personnel Office to lodge a complaint. She took off her name badge, grabbed a piece of paper from her desk, and walked straight out of the building, relieved that despite being jobless, she was away from the beast that was Joshua Padgett and the corrupt and deplorable practices that he seemed to thrive in.

CHAPTER 11 - *ILL-GOTTEN GAINS*

The basement of the warehouse was thick with smoke. It was rare that illegal bare-knuckle boxing fights were arranged in Macclesfield, but occasionally, the stars aligned and one of the Manchester gangs championed one of their own – in this case, a street fighter called George Jonas – and pitted him against all comers in one of the surrounding working-class towns. The publicity for the fight had been broadcast across the pubs and working men's clubs of the region – but no location had been advertised due to the need to make this at the last minute for fear of the law stepping in and halting the event. It was only the lunchtime of the fight that the location was revealed, namely Harrison's Paper Mill in Bollington, a few miles to the north of Macclesfield. There was a special atmosphere brewing on this night because the traveller community had selected one of their big young fighters to take on Jonas, an unbeaten fighter who was very experienced in the murky underworld circuit.

It was nine o'clock and the preliminary boxing bouts had proven to be a great success, with a lot of money exchanging hands. It was often understood that one of the fighters or the other would throw in the towel in a certain round in order to share in some of the betting reward, which paid far better than the purse for the winner. Betting on the outcome of any fight was always a lottery. However, the sense was that the main bout carried with it more than just money – it was the pride of the traveller community in the region versus the might of the city of Manchester.

This was just the scene that Gustav Coccini thrived. It reminded him of his origins, where he needed to scrape a living together back in Palermo. Coccini had set himself up as an amateur bookmaker – taking in bets on the outcome of fights – and in which round a particular fighter might hit the ground for a partial or full count. Coccini was skilled at working out if and when there was an agreed fix and setting his book up to ensure profits for himself.

He had a good feeling about the main bout of the evening, he had made a small profit on the earlier bouts – none of which were fixed – or so his various informers had suggested. Therefore, he was able to lay a large bet on the George Jonas fight. He was scheduled to fight against a largely unknown Gypsy lad. Gustav had been given a strong indication that the raw Gypsy would fight strongly in the early rounds to add more backers in his favour, yet he would throw the fight in round four, and his Gypsy followers would – having bet on the opponent to win in that round – pick up a sizeable compensation for losing, as would the bookmaker.

Gustav Coccini closed his book after round 2, with the Gypsy winning convincingly, expending enthusiastic energy early on, rocking his opponent back on his heels in the early stages of round 2. Between rounds, Gustav felt a sharp tap on his shoulder – it was the walking stick of a gentleman in a top hat – unusual to see such headgear amongst the mass of flat caps – he turned round fully and was faced with Henry Aspinall alongside Joshua Padgett. They'd heard where the fight was happening and had decided to see what this bare-knuckle fighting was all about. Especially as Padgett had a senior contact in the Manchester gang, namely Edgar Fitch, who had given him a tip about the dead certain outcome in return for some pipe-laying contracts. Edgar Fitch had been in HMP Strangeways Manchester for half of his life and had built a reputation as a gang leader inside and outside the prison walls.

"Can we have £50 on the Gypsy kid?" Aspinall demanded of the bookmaker, urged on by Padgett.

Gustav could not believe his luck – suddenly, this looked like the easiest of easy money – and what's more, it was from the owner of the Teggs Nose quarry, who had refused to give any of his workers an improvement in their basic pay nor proper safety equipment. Gustav smiled wryly; "Are you sure sir? I had closed my books as it looks like a foregone conclusion, but why not, it would be a pleasure to help you secure a big win," said Gustav graciously. "£50 on the Gypsy – done."

Gustav took the money and put it in the leather bag that was tightly buckled across his chest and around his shoulder. He was delighted that he'd collected a large bonus – particularly as it was from the much-despised Henry Aspinall.

Round three started and thirty seconds into the round, out of the corner of his eye, Gustav saw Jonas' manager look over at his boxer and make a very subtle signal. Gustav blinked to check through the smokey haze of the room whether he'd seen what he thought. But as if to confirm it, George Jonas took an innocuous upper cut to the chin and was floored, looking totally unconscious. A mighty roar went up from the Manchester side of the ring. Gustav recognised that it was surprisingly not that of disappointment, whilst the Gypsy supporters were also roaring in a similar way. Confused chaos reigned. The referee was on his knees next to Jonas' prone body, counting him down.

"1,2,3..." the count continued. Gustav couldn't believe it, the Manchester mob had thrown the fight but won the jackpot on the basis that their man fell first.

"...4,5,6,7..." the referee continued. The Gypsy lad was begging George to get up and continue the contest, but George was not going anywhere, comfortable that he'd lost his unbeaten record but won a very healthy losing bonus from his sponsors.

".....8,9,10." the referee slapped the ground, and all hell broke loose. The big Gypsy punched George again, who miraculously recovered and pretended to crawl across the floor towards his camp. Chairs were getting thrown along with the dirtiest of insults. Gustav, despite feeling totally duped, sheltered behind a heavy wooden chest, seething that his informers hadn't advised him of the double-cross.

Gradually, the pandemonium died down and the Gypsies left Harrison's Paper Mill and went back up to the canal sidings, where many of them had their lodging on working barges. The Manchester gang quickly sought out the bookmakers, including Gustav, to claim their winnings.

Gustav had almost covered all his losses and was only ten pounds down, but that was a fortnight's work at the Quarry. He felt gutted.

Gustav begrudgingly handed all that he owed across to the Mancunians and watched as they carried a pride-bruised but financially happy George Jonas out of the building to one of a number of motorised vehicles, horse-drawn carriages and carts. The cavalcade set off although the Gypsies did manage a few final blows as they rained beer bottles and lumps of coal down on them from the aqueduct that ran through Bollington.

Henry Aspinall and Joshua Padgett, had had a most entertaining time, helped enormously by the fact that the reliable information that Padgett had been given by the Mancunians had guaranteed a doubling of their bet. Both men had loved the gritty reality of bare-knuckle boxing – much more fun than Queensberry rules, they both agreed.

"Thank you, Mr. Bookmaker, it's great doing business with you," sneered Aspinall, as Gustav counted one hundred pounds out in £20 and £10 notes. Each note felt like a cut to his wrist. Someday, somehow, he would get his own back on these two wealthy pigs, how dare they come down to his murky level of society and beat Gustav Coccini at a game that he usually always won.

Gustav was the last to leave the musty, makeshift boxing theatre and make his way back up to the Canal sidings where the gypsy patriarch – Ivan Boksic, lived. The fracas with the Manchester mob had passed. Boksic had invited Gustav up to crack open a special bottle of Cutty Sark whiskey – a recent acquisition from a theft – ironically – from one of Aspinall's barge consignments on their way to Stoke on Trent. At least, this was small compensation for Gustav that night, but he needed more than this to quench his thirst for revenge. It was Boksic's nephew who had won - and lost - the boxing bout that night, and he was also invited to join the group as they cracked open a second bottle and passed it around. As they did this, Gustav had a thought that just might be something that he could interest the Gypsies into supporting. He would wait for a suitable opportunity to discuss it with his trusted friends.

CHAPTER 12 - *WORK CONTRACT*

Melissa Kirkham spent a few days at home with her parents, privately reliving the nightmare at Duke Street and the whole madness of that one day's employment at Macclesfield Town Hall. Although she had told nobody about what happened with Padgett, the fact that upon returning to her office, she was asked to leave by Victor Knight from the Water Board suggested that Padgett demanded a fully compliant Planning Officer in more than a professional sense. And all the better if she was a 'pretty girl'. The thought of it made bile rise in her throat.

Melissa remembered back to earlier on that fateful day, and her interaction with Silas Ledger. She felt an irrational need to explain to him why she was no longer able to support his request – given her resignation from the role – to understand the planning application for the pipeline. However, she had no idea how to get back in contact with him. Her priority right then was to get another job, and she managed to secure a temporary job at a local solicitor – she felt that the legal profession might just be a useful location for her if Joshua Padgett ever resurfaced in her life!

Jack Moat, on top of his regular work at Teggs Nose, acted as a junior clerk for several small Macclesfield businesses. He completed their monthly accounts on top of the daily inventory and procurement work he did at the quarry. During a visit to one of the companies he supported, he noticed Melissa speaking to another girl. Jack had not seen Melissa previously but was very keen to be introduced. The reason for his visit was an ad hoc inspection of accounts and sign-off on the accuracy at this small law firm. The permanent finance manager was a very capable individual, and so the audit usually took only half an hour. A full hour later, the accountant returned and asked Jack whether he had found any errors, but Jack's meticulous and laboured study of the numbers was merely an excuse to remain in the office long enough to manufacture an introduction. Finally, Melissa walked past and Jack glanced at her and smiled. Given recent experiences, Melissa was in no mood to meet any new man. However, Jack struck her as a mild-mannered, intelligent, slightly shy individual who had a healthy complexion looking like he worked outside a lot. Plus, the fact that as a new member of the team, she needed to know who was who.

"Good afternoon, sir. I'm Melissa Kirkham, and I'm the new interim Office Supervisor here at Sperry & Burroughs Solicitors," she said as a way of a formal introduction.

"Please call me Jack, and I'm their part-time auditor. I just check the very good accounts that Winston here keeps."

Melissa enquired further, "Part-time, eh? What else do you do?"

Jack replied "My full-time occupation's up on Teggs Nose at Aspinall's Quarry Company – I look after inventory and orders up there."

As soon as Melissa heard about the quarry, her interests were pricked, "So, do you know Silas Ledger by any chance?"

Jack smiled, "Sledge? Of course, I do. He's a good friend – and one hell of a guy."

Melissa smiled at Jack's use of Silas' nickname. "Sledge – that's a very good description of the man. We met last week and I think I can now help him with something that previously I couldn't."

Jack looked puzzled. "Sure, how about later today? We could walk over to Langley together after work, and I could introduce you to Sledge. His shift at the quarry should be over by then. I can also show you the delights of the village of Langley."

Melissa felt that she could trust this bright, intelligent person, "That sounds great – let's do that."

The end of the day was almost upon them anyway, and so Jack quickly completed his work with Winston's accounts and then the two of them left the Solicitor's office together. It took about twenty minutes to walk along the canal and up Jarman Road to Langley. Jack talked easily about his background in banking before landing a job at the quarry and falling in love with the Peak District and the outdoors lifestyle. It was hard, but it made him feel alive. With every word, Melissa warmed to Jack's enthusiasm and genuine love of nature. At every opportunity, he pointed out spider's webs, sparkling with early evening dew, the heron standing stock still by the canal

– waiting to spear an unsuspecting fish – and the moorhens in the reeds.

The most impressive description was the way Jack delighted over the architectural build of the snail bridge in Gurnett, where the footpath moved from south to north with the bridge meaning that the barge-towing shire horse did not need to be decoupled from the rope pulling the barge. Jack was talking a lot, his general reaction to being nervous. He thought Melissa was a stunning looking girl and very different to other girls he had come across in recent times. She was an independent, educated woman and a few years younger than himself. She listened to him with genuine interest and laughed at his simple jokes. By the time they reached Langley, Jack had practically forgotten about the reason that they were heading that way.

He stopped in his tracks. "Ahh, now, Sledge – let's go and find him." They strolled past the Post Office, and Will waved to them through the window. Jack waved back and beckoned him outside.

"Hi Will, do you know where your dad will be about now?" Jack said.

"Hi Jack – yeah – he should be heading down from Teggs. He'll be home in ten minutes or so," Will replied, giving Jack a smile and a cheeky wink when Melissa turned away. Jack and Melissa carried on down the main road, passing the Ledger's cottage, the Methodist Chapel and the Dunstan Inn. Jack's commentary on everything 'Langley' continued without much time for a breath.

Eventually they reached the cottage where Jack had rented a room. They stopped outside as he'd spotted a figure just rounding the corner coming down from the small reservoir at the bottom of Teggs Nose.

"And there he is – Silas Ledger – Sledge." Announced Jack – gesturing up the path. "Come on in and you two can discuss whatever you need to in my humble abode." Melissa entered the cottage whilst Jack stayed outside to intercept Sledge. Silas came into hearing range – Jack beamed up at him and shouted out, "Sledge mate, do I have a surprise for you? I have a young lady who has something she wants to talk to you about."

Silas looked quizzically at him. "What are you talking about, you clown!" At that point, Melissa showed her face at the window, and Silas took a double take before nodding. "Arrr – now I understand..." he announced. "Jack, you come in on this too, as you may be able to help work out what we can do next."

The three of them sat down in the shared lounge. It had been two weeks since the village meeting and the request from the farmers for Silas to understand more about the plans that were in place for the laying of the pipeline over the Hollins. Melissa recognised a healthy friendship and respect between Silas and Jack immediately. They complemented each other perfectly. Jack was the energetic, creative dynamo, whilst Silas provided the worldly wisdom that could bring practicality and logic to any of Jack's wild ideas. She felt very comfortable.

"Mr. Ledger," she stated,

"Please just call me Silas or Sledge," Silas quickly interrupted.

"Sledge, I promised that I would try to help you understand the planning application for the Trentabank pipeline, but I didn't know how to make contact with you. Fortune would have it that I left the Planning Department that very day, the job was not for me," she paused just long enough for both men to think that there was more of a story here. She continued, "I am now working with a business that Jack freelances for, and it was great fortune that he knew you and brought me here today." She stopped, realising that the penny was now dropping with Jack, as to why Melissa wanted to speak with Sledge.

Jack asked, "So you were working in the Town Hall Planning Department two weeks ago when Sledge visited, and so why are you now working at Sperry & Burroughs Solicitors?"

The look on Melissa's face seemed pained, "Let's just say that the enquiry I made into the pipeline planning application led me to a confrontation with Mr. Padgett, a confrontation that led me to leave that job rather quickly. But not before I learned something." Melissa pulled the small piece of paper from her pocket that she'd grabbed from her desk just before vacating the Town Hall. She handed it to Silas. The note was handwritten in scratchy writing but was quite clearly legible.

November 1928

Mr. Edgar Fitch,

This note hereby commits all Trentabank-Hollins pipeline work near Macclesfield to be carried out by your work teams until the project reaches completion.

Costs to be agreed and paid by the East Cheshire Water Board

Yours,

Mr. Joshua Padgett

Sledge read it a second time and then passed it to Jack. He looked at Melissa.

She offered the answer to the question without it needing to be asked, "After we met, and I could not find the Planning Application filed for any Hollins pipeline, I then asked Victor Knight – the Water Board Manager – he also claimed no knowledge, but I was quickly summoned to Joshua Padgett's offices in Duke Street." Melissa took a breath and then continued. "Let's just say that I met with Mr. Padgett, and I am convinced that there was no application made for the right to build a pipeline across the Hollins. And despite it being Aspinall land, the fact that the farmers who farm on the Hollins have tenancy agreements filed means any change of land usage by the landowner needs their approval if it falls within the period of the tenancy."

Silas stopped her and reflected for a moment. "We know that Aspinall has no regard for planning permissions given that he blatantly and illegally evicted Sid, Martha and Nat from their farms at Trentabank in favour of the Water Board and their reservoir. This looks like another illegal gentleman's agreement between Padgett and Edgar Fitch, possibly without the knowledge of Henry Aspinall. "

Jack looked at Silas and excitedly started, "Sledge – this might just allow us to achieve several objectives at once.

Listen to this thought. Firstly, we know that the pipeline needs to be laid, as the Bollin Valley does not have the capacity to be the only way water can move from Langley to the town. If we ask the farmers to accept the disruption to their farmland on the Hollins on the condition that they are compensated by payment for their machinery to help lay the pipelines." He continued, "Secondly, we propose new work shifts at the quarry that will move half of the team on to pipe laying duty (which pays more per hour), thus enabling us to achieve no layoffs – at least for the year it will take them to lay the pipes over the Hollins. I cannot see how Aspinall will not support this idea as it provides him with control over the pipeline rather than the Water Authority, and an additional income stream.

Melissa was enjoying listening to the two men discuss solutions and felt that she had something more to offer to avenge some of the pain that Padgett had dealt her.

"And as for the work commitment note that I took from the file, Joshua Padgett has written a note to whoever this..." She looked at the paper again. "...Edgar Fitch is. Well, he'll just have to suffer as he will need to renege on this irregular arrangement."

Jack looked at Sledge and then looked back at Melissa. "Edgar Fitch is a gangster and one of the most vicious thugs in the North West – Padgett will indeed suffer consequences of any change to that agreement."

"Good. That arsehole deserves anything coming to him," Melissa hissed. Both men looked up, surprised by the venom with which these words were issued.

CHAPTER 13 - *POACHING*

The quarry on Teggs Nose was now regularly producing record amounts of crushed stone, and the full-time introduction of Sid Bayley's shire horse – Battalion - meant that the stone was getting across to the dam wall at Trentabank much more quickly than before the industrial action. This was happening at the onset of a really harsh start to winter with regular snow flurries across the hills. The quarrymen were involved in back-breaking labour but were still taking home a paltry basic wage. Only the promise of a Christmas bonus kept their grumbles in check. However, the talk at the Setter Dog Inn was all about what would happen in the new year when they had spent any bonus and they were back to basic wages only. There was also a rumour going around that once the Trentabank reservoir was completed, some of the machinery used there would be moved up to the quarry, and this would put pressure on jobs. Nobody in the workforce, other than Jack, knew that Silas had been asked by the management to nominate around a dozen of them who would not be needed moving forward.

Those quarry workers who were married needed their wives to be working in the textile mills in Macclesfield. Two incomes just about allowed a family to survive, with young children being looked after by relatives or friends and elder children being expected to help with chores and support their parent's income by running basic errands. Single quarrymen, other than trying to look for partners, often looked for ways of making money in shadier ways. Gustav Coccini had questionable links with illegal gambling and always seemed to have plenty of money himself. Two other quarrymen well known for secondary nefarious incomes were Andy Soutter and Robin Brampton – Moll's elder brother.

All of the workers at the quarry knew if there was a special occasion in the family where some special meat was needed, then a quiet word with Dick Avery – the publican at the Setter Dog – would see the appearance of a rabbit, pheasant, grouse or goose, at a very reasonable cost. For particularly special feasts, prize cuts of wild boar or even venison could be ordered. Salmon and trout were also available during Spring and Autumn. Dick Avery was the public face of the illegal meat and fish business, but the real workers were Andy and Robin. Langley boys from birth and close school friends. They were now both twenty years old and knew every piece of woodland and stream in the Langley area. They were able to set snares or lay lines in locations that they knew were optimal for the capture of specific game. Naturally, they were singularly the biggest nemeses of Arthur Brice – the Aspinall Estate Manager, and Archie Talbot – the Head Gamekeeper.

On regular occasions, the two village youngsters – using their own guile and wit, regularly toyed with the elder estate professionals. On one particularly daring occasion, Andy Soutter imitated the blood-curdling squeals of a snared wild boar thrashing around in the undergrowth near the woodland by the Estate Manager's cottage. As soon as Arthur Brice was seen moving as fast as he could across the field towards the coppice, brandishing a shot gun, Robin Brampton had broken into the game shed, behind the cottage and filled a wheelbarrow with a variety of meats that could have proudly adorned a window of a very upmarket butchers' shop in Macclesfield. Once clear of the game shed, Robin hooted like an owl, and the wild boar was suddenly silent. The boys were tired but jubilant with their haul as they pushed the wheelbarrow back up Saddlers Way to the Setter Dog and a happy publican. The meat raffle that Friday night at the pub was a good one, whilst the Aspinall dinner in the Banqueting Hall of the Manor House that same night had to be quickly provisioned, at great expense, from a specialist butcher in Buxton.

There was a code of silence around the village, recognising that the nature of this kind of poaching was purely redistributing wealth in the times where everyone unanimously believed that the Aspinall's could suffer a little loss in income to support what on occasions were quite literally families that were starving.

Both being members of Langley Cricket Club and active at the Methodist Chapel, Andy and Robin were keen to ensure that both establishments were beneficiaries of their adept skill. Hilda Bostock – who looked after all the Cricket Club's catering needs – turned any meats that magically appeared in the Club kitchen into "game pie". Ironically, and to the vast amusement of the cricketers, even on the occasions that the Club's benefactor – Henry Aspinall – was present! At the Chapel, in these austere times, Reverend Pottinger often celebrated the appearance of a large salmon on the morning of a communal supper by being inspired to remind the congregation of the miracle of the loaves and fishes, always delivered with a wry smile on his face.

The police were also keen to turn a blind eye to this kind of petty crime despite it being a regular subject that Arthur Brice and Henry Aspinall complained about bitterly and repeatedly. The police diligently made enquiries, but nobody seemed to know anything about any rural crime called poaching – especially as the master poachers were always scrupulous at clearing traps and snares away to leave no evidence. The local Sutton & Langley bobby – PC Keith Aikin – was rather partial to a goose at Christmas and a pheasant at Easter. Remarkably – those birds seemed to appear at precisely those times – on his doorstep, and this went a long way to making any poaching enquiry considered a low priority on the rural crime agenda.

In any case, the police needed to focus more on a growing concern that was appearing—the spread of gangland Manchester and its extortion activities, encroaching on the sleepy suburban towns of East Cheshire.

CHAPTER 14 - *FAMILY BREAKDOWN*

In the winter months of 1928, Beth Ledger and Charles Aspinall exchanged letters on a weekly basis. They loved the written word and were both discovering how the language of love could be magically weaved into everyday dialogue. Beth filled much of her writing with expansive thoughts around political activism and the rights of women to become a much more pivotal part of society. In turn, Charles responded with supportive comments contradicting the privileged upbringing he had experienced. Privilege in materialism but completely bereft of family warmth and love. Charles was experiencing – for the first time – the power and energy that feelings of true love were having upon him. His cold school dormitory was brightened and warmed exponentially when he read the letters from Beth.

Beth shared the fact that she was applying to attend Durham University to read Politics and Sociology, supported by her whole family, who recognised that Beth's ambitions were well beyond the cobbled streets of Macclesfield and its mills. Gwen and Silas were often embarrassed by their elder child's school reports, where the teachers often requested that they slow down Beth's insatiable desire for learning. She led debates on many subjects in class where she ended up presenting for and against the motion, as her classmates and most of her teachers were unable to keep up with her sharp brain and dynamic tongue!

Beth wrote as she debated – answering her own questions and presenting both sides of every argument. However, it was quite clear that social reform and gender equality were her pet subjects. Charles' letters entertained her immensely. He presented fun questions relating to the cricketing scorebook and teased her with facts from Wisden's latest almanac, which he used to read most nights in order to memorise the statistics of that year's top-performing teams. He also shared his own ambitions around attending university to read Law, as he felt that he had seen sufficient social injustice in his young life to want to provide a stronger balance in arguing right from wrong. The bigger challenge he shared with Beth was that, unlike her supportive family, his father was wholly against Charles' own thinking about his future.

Christmas holidays seemed to take an age to arrive for the young eighteen-year-olds. But arrive they did, and Beth was at the railway station in Macclesfield to meet the train that brought Charles back from Hoarwithy boarding school. As the train slowed down and the steam dissipated, Charles saw Beth running towards his carriage door with a massive smile on her face and she threw herself at him. What he failed to see was the shocked look of his father – Henry Aspinall – who was standing next to the Station Master, having just himself returned from London. It was coincidental that he was at the station when Charles arrived, as he had not even registered that his son was due home for the Christmas break. He was astonished to see a girl running towards his son and enveloping him in such a tight embrace that it seemed to take the wind out of him, but it was clear that he was also holding her just as closely.

As soon as Charles let go of Beth, who was already chattering away about how much they were going to do over the holidays, he saw his father looking dumbfounded. He had never seen his father looking quite so surprised, but that look soon changed to a dark stare of disapproval. Charles felt that this was as good a time as any to introduce his special friend.

He walked hand in hand with Beth towards Mr. Shankins, the Station Master and his father. "Good afternoon Mr. Shankins," said Charles politely. The Station Master doffed his cap and smiled at the courteous nature of the smart young man in front of him. "Good afternoon, Father." Charles continued, "I would like to introduce you to my very good friend, Miss Beth Ledger."

Henry Aspinall stared at his son, still shocked by the sight he saw. For the first time, he wasn't facing a cowering lonely child but a young man who had grown noticeably in terms of his physical form and clearly in confidence. Henry found himself speechless. He shook Beth's outstretched hand and the two youngsters walked onwards to the station exit. Beth looked over her shoulder and giggled sweetly. By the time he had collected himself and bid farewell to Shankins, Aspinall Senior moved towards the exit, but there was no sign of the teenagers, who had already headed towards the main road back out of town towards the Hollins and Langley.

Henry Aspinall needed a drink. He hurried towards his private Gentleman's Club, muttering to himself. Had he really just seen his son with a girl whose surname was Ledger? Could it really be Silas Ledger's daughter? No way could he allow his son to associate his family with the working class. Not only that, but with a family whose patriarch was a quarry worker and so clearly despised everything about Aspinall and all that he stood for.

His associate, Joshua Padgett was having his usual early evening aperitif – an orange and brandy. There were two other men over at the far end of the bar room, playing billiards. Aspinall recognised them as Thomas Whetton and Phillip Broadhead – fellow land and quarry owners. He needed to have a word with Broadhead as he had been requesting a review of the basic pay of quarry workers as there was pressure to increase, and Aspinall wanted to continue to suppress. He was refusing to even talk to Whetton as he had recently discovered that he had offered refuge to the Lovatt family, who he was evicting from Trentabank Farm, and he had hoped to take over the entirety of their sheep flock as he thought they would have no option but to give them to him at a knockdown price. As it was, Whetton's offer of land over at Bosley Cloud had allowed the Lovatt's the ability to take their flock with them.

"A double whiskey, straight," Aspinall demanded from the barman.

"Hello Henry, sounds like you've had a tough day?" Padgett mused.

"Yes, thank you," replied Aspinall as he took a position next to Padgett at the bar. "I have had better days." Aspinall was still finding it hard to acknowledge what he'd seen at the railway station, and he declined to describe the disgust that he had felt when introduced to the Ledger girl. Glancing at the billiard table, Aspinall spoke softly to Padgett, "Do you know what that bastard Whetton has done to me?" Padgett leaned towards him and shook his head. "Those two softies are wanting to redistribute my wealth." Padgett looked quizzically, and Aspinall explained the reasons why he had so much of an issue with the billiard players.

"Now I understand why you might be so upset, Henry. You should challenge them to a bare-knuckle fight. I'm sure my friend Edgar Fitch could set it up for you," Padgett jested.

Henry Aspinall took a large gulp of his whiskey – his thoughts turned to what he'd witnessed at the train station. He needed to act swiftly with his son. Charles needed to understand the implications of developing close friendships with a lower tier of society. He finished his glass and headed home to Ridge Hill to confront his son.

Charles delighted in walking home with Beth, feeling her soft hand clutching his, breathing in her sweet smell, and being bombarded by her constant excited chatter about life. It was no time until they were next to the Post Office in Langley, next door to the Ledger's cottage. Beth had described her family to Charles in her letters, and Charles knew who William was thanks to Will's occasional appearance as a twelfth man in the Langley Cricket 1st XI. He had also seen Silas at the funeral of his good friend – Sid Bayley – carrying the coffin. However, he had spoken to neither of them and had never met Gwen.

Will suddenly appeared on the pavement next to them. "Who's the posh-looking fellow?" He said cheekily. Beth playfully cuffed her brother round the head. "This, young William, is Charles Aspinall. We have become good friends over the last few months."

"I know you," said Will. "You're the ace cricket scorer at the Club, aren't you?"

Pleased to be known for this rather than the wealthy landowner's son or the inept cricketer, Charles replied, laughing. "Yes, Will. That's right I am Langley CC's statistician, and please just call me Charlie."

"Nice to meet you, Charlie, but please don't listen to everything my sister talks about. You'll risk having a permanent headache!" Will raced off as he was on a chore for Mr. Ricketts from the Post Office.

The young couple rounded the corner and entered the cottage. Gwen was in the kitchen making a hot pot and baking bread. "Hi Mum," Beth said.

"Hello Mrs. Ledger, what a beautiful garden you have. I'm Charlie Aspinall," added Charles.

Gwen spun around, surprised that she had an uninvited guest in the house and she hadn't had time to plumb the cushions or tidy away Will's dirty football boots. "Oh, hello, Charlie, very pleased to meet you." Gwen blushed. "What was your surname again?"

"Aspinall," Charlie repeated slowly. "But please don't hold that against me," he added, laughing.

Gwen took his coat, and sat Charles down on the small

couch, having quickly swept her hand across the cushion to remove any stray cat hairs. She asked Beth to put a kettle of water on the stove. Charles thought he'd never been in a cozier nor happier family environment, helped by the wonderful smell of freshly baked bread. The three of them discussed the school term, and quickly, Charles understood where Beth got her spark and vitality from. Gwen had a steady flow of questions to ask him about his boarding school and life in a big manor house, as well as his ambitions beyond school. Charles enjoyed this inquisition and he quickly relaxed, thinking how lucky Beth and Will were to have such a warm and bright mother. It further highlighted to him the challenges he faced with his own sick mother, but it also made him think that he should make his way back up to Ridge Hill and face whatever his father had for him, given the quick interaction they'd had at the station.

Just as he was putting on his coat, Silas returned home from Teggs Nose. He had a bloodied face as he'd been cut by a stone chip, and this made him look even scarier, given his enormous physical presence. Gwen and Beth both swiftly moved towards him and gave him a hug. He was easily able to hold on to both women and still look over them at Charles.

Silas' face – despite the trickle of blood and the cloud of dust appearing when he removed his cap – was a kind, gentle one with deep-set eyes that shone brightly. He greeted Charles with a giant hand.

"Excuse my appearance, young sir. The gritstone today was particularly difficult to extract."

Before Charles had a chance to speak, Beth and Gwen both spoke at once, but Beth hushed in order to give her mother the honour of introducing their guest. "Silas – this is Charles/Charlie Aspinall. Beth found him outside and seems to have befriended him."

They all laughed, and Silas spoke. "Well, Charles/Charlie, it's great to meet you and I hope the Ledger girls have made you welcome."

"Thank you, Mr. Ledger," Charlie said. "You have a very welcoming family, and I very much look forward to seeing you all again soon, as I need to head home now." Beth and Charlie made their way out of the house onto the pavement to share a more private farewell. Silas took off his jacket and sat down on the now vacated couch. He thought to himself that there might be a challenging time ahead based on his daughter's choice of boyfriend. He would be proved right in so many ways.

Up on Ridge Hill, Charles entered the Aspinall manor house at the same time as John Croker, the Teggs Nose Quarry's commercial manager. Words were not exchanged, but Croker gave Charles an odd sneering look as they passed. Little did Charles know, but his father had ordered John Croker to come to his house – a rare event – to receive one instruction. That instruction was clear – set up a meeting with Silas Ledger for tomorrow morning first thing.

Charles entered the drawing room, his school trunk was already there, delivered directly by Hoarwithy School. He sat down on it and thought how cold and inhuman this house was compared to the warmth of the Ledger cottage. Small and compact as it was, it held within it – life, love and energy. All he could think about in his own house was his ill mother drinking herself to death and his father, who seemed to despise the earth that his son walked on. His father had a need to control his son's life to the extent that Charles felt claustrophobia in this house, and all he wanted to do was break free from the burden of the Aspinall name and all that it stood for.

A housemaid broke the silence. "Good evening, Master Aspinall – welcome home – dinner will be served in ten minutes in the dining room."

Charles felt the controlling nature of his father descending on him like a dark cloud. All he wanted to do was disappear to his room, pick up his pen and write to Beth, or even better climb down the wisteria and run across the fields, through the wood to meet her and kiss by the light of the moon. That romantic image was shattered by the ring of the bell announcing that those eating should make their way to the dining room. Charles entered and he saw a large table with three places set. He sat across from his mother, and his father was sat – predictably at the head of the table – in the power position.

Florence Aspinall raised her head at his entrance. "Hello Charles, welcome home. I'm sorry I have not been able to visit Hoarwithy during the term. I've had a few health issues." She coughed to highlight the fact that those issues still continued. Charles had sympathy for his mother – living with his father for the past twenty-five years was sufficient to drive anyone to drink.

"Good evening, Charles. I trust you were able to find your own way back from the railway station?" Henry Aspinall said with a clear hint of sarcasm.

"Yes, thank you, Father," Charles replied. "Beth was lovely company and we enjoyed our walk home immensely."

Florence looked up. "Beth? And whose Beth?" she inquired. Before Charles could reply, Henry looked daggers at his wife, who visibly shriveled in her seat.

"Let's eat, and then we have a lot to discuss about what the expectations are to being an Aspinall."

Charles was seething, but he bit his lip for now. Soup was served in silence, and only some very vague conversation happened between Florence and Henry about his trip to London. Charles ate in silence. A cut of venison was served as the main course. Henry remarked that the meat had to be purchased due to the blasted poachers having made deer on the estate so rare that Archie Talbot – their gamekeeper – was unable to track any over the last two weeks.

"I must get rid of that old codger – he's past his use-by date," Henry said out loud. Florence tried to protest, reminding Henry that Archie had been a gamekeeper on the Estate since the age of fourteen, and he had served both Henry's father and grandfather. "All the more reason to put him out to pastures now!" was the cold response from Henry. Charles remained silent, waiting for the subject to change to the scene that Henry had witnessed on the Station platform.

After the main course, Florence excused herself and left the dining room. A chink of glass from the library was heard, informing that she was in need of another stiff drink before bedtime.

"Charles, I have some very serious words to impart to you

about the Aspinall tradition and how I expect you to uphold it," Henry started what sounded like a monologue of rules and conditions. Charles was prepared for most of the monologue, and he was fully loaded for a response. His father had never had his son challenge him. Tonight was going to be the night.

"Charles, you will finish your final two terms at Hoarwithy, and I suggest that you head back early after Christmas, and then you stay at school over the Easter break revising for your final exams. Once you have completed the term, you will return here and you will start your apprenticeship with the Aspinall Company. John Croker will act as your manager initially and you will work with him on improving the profitability at the quarry on Teggs Nose. Depending on how that goes, I will then move you into a new position, possibly at one of my London institutes, as I'd like you to build your business network in the city well away from the influences of East Cheshire. You can live at my London apartment."

Charles simply stared at his father, thinking how one man could believe that he had so much total control over another. His father was about to experience a fightback.

Henry continued. "This will allow you to access multiple debutante balls in the capital, and I would expect that you may be able to find a suitable future Mrs. Aspinall. A wife who will be able to support your needs as a successful businessman and raise your children, my grandchildren. How does that sound?"

Henry looked over at his son, expecting the nod of compliance he was used to. Charles paused for a moment; had he really just had his whole life planned out by his father? He took a deep breath. "Father, I understand that you have an expectation of how my life will unfold. I believe that I'd like to take an alternative path." Charles noted the brooding look on his father's face. He continued, "I feel that I would be well placed to enter higher education at a university and study law. I believe that I can make a good living away from the Aspinall Company and might even be able to support it but from an arm's length in an advisory capacity." His father shifted uncomfortably on his seat and fixated his stare towards the coat of arms that was carved into the wooden beam of the dining room.

Charles paused briefly, but as his father said nothing, he decided to continue on to what he knew was – if anything – an even more contentious subject. "I have been very good friends with Beth Ledger for the last three months, and neither of us knows where the relationship will go, but who I choose to see as a partner will be my choice entirely, and it will not be made based on social status or the wealth of an inherited estate. Wealth for me comes from within a human, not from the state of their bank account or the title that has been handed down to them."

"You silly idealistic child, you have no idea of the real world," hissed his father.

"And neither do you!" shot back Charles. "Do you know how people survive below minimum wage? Do you know how 98% of the country's wealth is held by 2% of the population? Do you know that landowners have obliterated the right for people to cross national parks by building fences?" He continued with a more personal assault on his father, "Do you know that I attended the funeral of Sid Bayley, a generous, lovely farmer who was a tenant of yours? Your forced eviction, with no option to move to an alternative farm, was the sole reason for Sid to take his own life." Charles stood up and jabbed a finger towards his father. "You have blood on your hands!"

At that point, Charles left the room and headed up to his bedroom. He left silence behind. Charles was surprised that he was able to have the last word in the dining room. Never before had his father not had a discussion where his view had the final say in any conversation. What was his father thinking? He was to find out quickly enough the next morning.

The following day, Charles descended the large sweep of stairs and was met by the housemaid, who passed him a formal-looking letter with his name on it. He sat on the bottom step and opened the letter – it was from his father:

Dear Charles,

It is beyond disappointment that I write to you today. I stated my plans for you quite clearly last night, and you countered with your own ludicrous and misguided thoughts.

If you do decide to follow your poorly considered dreams, you will do this unsupported by me or the Aspinall trust fund. I suspect that this warning is sufficient for you to come to your senses, but if not. The Aspinall family will disown you.

Your Father

In some ways, it was cathartic for Charles to read this stark message. There was no grey area. He existed at the polar opposite end of the spectrum to his father. Henry Aspinall was unwilling to compromise, and now neither was his son.

Charles sat on the stair and started to think about what he must do in order to fulfill his ambitions. He was comfortable that he had enough support from his school in order to complete his education and the promise of a potential university bursary fund from his Hoarwithy Old Boy and cricket scorebox friend – Alastair Grainger, supported by Mr. McRory, who had just been promoted to deputy Head Master.

Charles decided to head outside to clear his head. He walked across the field through the wood, up over the almost completed Trentabank dam, only weeks away from being completed. He walked across the meadows that he used to help Sid manage over the harvesting periods, and he got to Nessit farm – now empty apart from the scurry of field mice. He thought about what this farmhouse would look like in a few weeks' time with thirty feet of water above its roof – never to be seen again. Deep in his heart, he knew that Sid's passing was a turning point in his life. His father was the architect of Sid's death, and everything that his father had stood for was the antithesis of what Charles felt was ethical and fair. It was at that point that he knew that he must grow up and face the truth or live his life as a hypocrite, continuing to support the poison of the Aspinall way of life. He felt a brush across his shin and looked down – there was Mew – Sid's black and white cat. Charles knew that he must make sure that she was rehoused before he returned to school and the valley was flooded.

He returned to the Aspinall manor house on Ridge Hill for the last time. His mother had arisen, unaware of the previous night's conversation. However, she had read the letter that Charles had left on his still unopened school trunk. Without a word, she reached out and embraced him. It was a warm tender moment, and one that Charles only wished that he'd experienced before. Florence Aspinall had been so suppressed by her dominant partner that Charles thought that his mother had lost the power to love. Within that one embrace, he had felt more love than he had for the previous decade.

Florence knew that Charles had to leave if he was to become the man that she knew he needed to become. She wished she could have been that strong, but her fate was sealed. There was one thing that she could do for him, and that was to provide him access to her own small trust fund, which she had managed to squirrel away during the years when her wits were stronger and she felt more able to plan her own escape from Henry's cruel dominance. But as the years passed, the life was sucked out of her and the bottle became her constant companion, replacing any hope of marital liberty.

Florence passed a note with some bank account details on to her son, who accepted it gratefully. They hugged for one last time before arranging for his trunk to be returned to school. Charles took a hamper from the Cook, who realising the sad finality of the occasion, and shed a tear whilst she filled the basket with all of the types of food that she remembered he liked. Charles then set off back down to Nessit Farm, where he planned to stay for a few days as there was enough firewood in the store to keep it warm until he could return to school.

CHAPTER 15 - *THE PIPELINE*

Silas had not been too surprised that John Croker had appeared at his cottage on the previous evening to deliver a message. An urgent invitation for him to attend a meeting at the main Aspinall Company offices in Macclesfield first thing in the morning before the quarry opened.

At 5:30 am, Silas had set off to walk the three miles into town. It was a crisp winter morning, and the sun was yet to rise. He pulled his thick coat around his shoulders and puffed out large clouds of condensation into the air. As he walked, he mused over the coincidences that had led his own daughter and Henry Aspinall's son to become close. He knew that it could spell trouble for himself, but he was also aware that there was a brewing discontent amongst the quarry workers who had been slaving hard over the last few months, producing much more gritstone per hour than any other quarry in the region. They were doing this without any firm commitment about their Christmas bonus payment. It was only their total trust in Sledge that gave them the confidence that the bonus payment would appear. He also knew that

Croker and Aspinall would be expecting an update on the reduced manpower that mechanisation would drive in the new year. Given how hard all of his team were working, the thought of releasing any of them was causing Silas a real challenge. He was keen to present a new idea to the quarry management that he and Jack had conceived around how he could retain the team in spite of the new machinery arriving.

Silas entered the reception area of the Aspinall headquarters building. His last visit was two months ago. Nobody was manning the reception desk, so he sat down and took in the surrounds again. The large oil paintings of various Aspinall patriarchs stared coldly down at him from the dark oak-panelled room. A naked coat stand stood there, suggesting none of the administration workers were yet to arrive. Silas felt like a trapped bird inside this building, there was a feeling of foreboding, a feeling of loss of control. Aspinall held the key to so many things – a comfortable Christmas for his quarry working colleagues, a blessing on a growing relationship between Beth and Charlie, and a commitment to the villagers of Langley that they will be dealt with fairly in the building of the Hollins pipeline.

John Croker walked in just ahead of Henry Aspinall, who had his chauffeur drop him off in his Daimler car, one of only two in the county of Cheshire. The two acknowledged each other and took off their overcoats. Silas got up and nodded to both gentlemen.

"There's work to be done Mr. Ledger," Croker stated in a dark melancholic way.

"Indeed, there is," Aspinall added bluntly. He walked up the stairs to the Boardroom. "Mr. Croker, can you bring myself and Mr. Ledger two cups of tea, please? I'd like to see Mr. Ledger alone for the first part of this meeting." John Croker's shoulders slumped. Tea maker was not something that a Commercial Manager should be asked to become regardless of the situation – he silently muttered to himself.

Henry Aspinall sat at his usual seat at the Board table, with his own portrait positioned behind him on the wall. Confronted by two images of the same person, one illustrated in oils, Silas pondered as to whether his own resentment for Aspinall doubled also. The outcome of this meeting might allow him to further evaluate his resentment scores.

"Mr. Ledger, it seems like my son has made friends with your daughter, and I was certainly unaware of this fact until yesterday. Can I ask when you were informed? And whether you condone this relationship, as I do?" Aspinall announced as if he were starting a business meeting.

Silas took a deep breath. "Mr. Aspinall, I also only found out about Beth and Charlie's relationship yesterday, but I fully trust my daughter to decide for herself who she has as friends. Plus, Charlie seems to be a very polite and honorable young man. You should be very proud."

Upon hearing Silas refer to his son as "Charlie", Henry Aspinall visibly winced – not once had he ever referred to his son in any form other than his full name with which he was christened. In the societal circles that the Aspinall's should inhabit, colloquial nicknames were seen as a very common form of address.

"Mr. Ledger, that does not surprise me at all. Your daughter would be most fortunate to associate with persons of a higher social class, and I wish her luck in her climbing ambitions. However, that will not be with my son – *Charles*." Aspinall exaggerated the last word for effect. He continued, "As of this morning, I have forbidden *Charles* from associating himself with your daughter. And I wish that you also respect my views by insisting that your daughter breaks off any such friendship. If I do not see evidence of this, there may be further consequences for you."

This was almost amusing, thought Silas, if his livelihood did not depend upon the Aspinall Company. Not allowing nature to dictate the course of events in relationships seemed comical to him, and contrary to everything he believed. Indeed, Silas felt that nature would dictate the outcome with no need for his involvement, and if he knew his daughter as he did, he was fairly sure that she would have the strength of conviction to overcome any medieval societal norms or parental direction that might hold nature back. He decided not to respond to Aspinall and just sat there wondering how such a pleasant young man like Charlie could possibly have such an odorous father as Henry Aspinall. As for the veiled threat of consequences for him if he were not to appear to be condemning Beth's relationship with Charlie – well, he felt there were plenty of other larger consequences that were likely to hit ahead of these.

The awkward silence was interrupted by a knock on the door. John Croker triumphantly entered, having managed to pass servitude down the chain. A young female receptionist followed him in, carrying a tray with a large pot of tea and three cups. Croker positioned himself across from Silas and ushered the receptionist to pour the teas personally. As she reached over Silas, out of sight of the other two, she mouthed the words "Good luck with these arseholes!" and smiled.

Henry Aspinall started the official meeting, having felt that he had got his message over in very clear terms about Charles and Beth. "Mr. Ledger, we have brought you here today to discuss two business matters. Firstly, we would like to hear who you have decided to lay off at the quarry and secondly, we would like to discuss the bonus payments promised to your colleagues if they were to achieve sufficient additional mining of gritstone to complete the Trentabank dam construction." Silas nodded and listened as John Croker took over the first agenda point.

"So, Ledger – who are the unlucky dozen of your chums who will be released?" he sneered.

Silas took a deep breath and raised himself in his seat to his full height. This caused Croker to cower back in his chair. "Mr. Croker, Mr. Aspinall, may I just remind you that my team have worked tirelessly in filthy conditions to mine, cut and crush more gritstone per man than any other quarry in the area. We have achieved record daily amounts of stone and transported it across to the dam construction site, which was not part of the original work scope. Not one of my teammates has taken a day off since October. They have earned their bonuses, and they do not deserve to then be rewarded in the new year by losing their jobs."

John Croker interrupted. "Ledger, it will be up to myself and Mr. Aspinall to decide upon the bonus payment thank you. I repeat, who are the twelve workers you are letting go?"

Silas felt like he needed to land the new employment proposal quickly for fear of losing any attention on anything but Croker's demands for human suffering. "Gentlemen, I have a proposal for you that may serve all of us in the long run. We know that there is a pipeline to be laid from Trentabank up and over the Hollins. The skill sets to lay pipes and quarry stone, are not dissimilar. The Teggs Nose quarry would like to manage labour shifts to support the laying of the pipeline, thus providing jobs for all existing quarrymen whilst also allowing the new quarry machinery to be introduced in the new year."

John Croker was looking incredulous – how could a mere quarryman under his management be formulating a creative shift in the business and undermining his own authority? Croker looked across at his boss and was shocked to see Aspinall looking half interested in this hair-brain idea.

Silas added, "This approach will also allow the villagers of Langley to support the project as any of the deeper digging needed to lay pipes could be supported by local farmers and their digging machinery." He noted that Aspinall was looking interested, whilst the reddening complexion of Croker suggested total opposition. He continued, "There is a village meeting next week, and it would be an ideal opportunity for you – Mr. Aspinall – to attend and launch this initiative yourself."

Silas knew that this last bold suggestion might just play into the Aspinall ego. Of course, the game he was playing entirely relied on the fact that Aspinall knew nothing about the agreement between Joshua Padgett and the Manchester mob. He had no idea where this might go, but it was worth it rather than the alternative of simply giving in and laying off a dozen good men.

"Thank you, Mr. Ledger. Do you mind waiting outside so that Mr. Croker and I can discuss this proposal? I do accept that the bonus payment will be paid to the workforce, as the Water Board has agreed that they are ahead of schedule with the dam construction," Aspinall said whilst stroking his chin in thought. Like Croker, he felt no desire to agree with anything that Silas suggested, but where there might be personal commercial gain, he was always willing to revisit.

The positive news about the Christmas bonus was more than Silas had expected, and the fact that Aspinall did not reject the pipeline proposal immediately made Silas feel positive about the eventual outcome. Only time would tell, but he left the Boardroom with a feeling that Jack's idea and Melissa's information about Padgett's dirty tricks might just allow for a good Christmas after all. And at the very least, he had confirmed the bonus payment for the quarry workers with respect to their hard work over the Autumn and Winter periods. He had less certainty about Aspinall's threat around the relationship of Beth and Charles. Time would tell.

After Silas left the Company Boardroom, Aspinall asked Croker to remain in the room. Having been outshone by the initiatives of a mere quarry worker, John Croker was very much on the defensive. "So, what do you think of the quarry diversification idea?" asked Aspinall.

Knowing that he was in a tight spot, Croker thought quickly. Could he interpret the fact that his boss – always outspoken – had not immediately rejected it and belittled Ledger further, making him think that it just might be politic to agree with the proposal and support the idea of forming a pipe-laying subsidiary. "I think that Ledger has had a good thought Mr. Aspinall. I was thinking similarly, in fact." He blatantly lied but continued, "And I believe that we could manage shifts to allow sufficient labour to lay the pipeline project."

"Good" said Aspinall. "That's what I want you to put into place, and as soon as my son – Charles – has finished his final term at School, I want him to take over that project under your supervision."

John Croker breathed a sigh of relief. He'd chosen the right option. He despised the fact that Silas had come up with the idea, but at least Henry Aspinall seemed to be satisfied with the outcome. Although the result for Croker might have to be a need to deal with that wretched, spoiled boy – Charles Aspinall. However, there were six months until his schooling finished, and much could happen in the meantime.

CHAPTER 16 - *RED NOTES*

Henry Aspinall decided to retire to the Business Club for an early lunch and a chance to share this bright plan about the pipeline with the Water Authority Director – Joshua Padgett. He was sure that Padgett would be delighted given the fact that Aspinall could place more pressure on his own men to complete the task for minimum wages and ahead of time – just like he'd managed to achieve at the Trentabank dam wall. The Trentabank reservoir needed six months to settle following the official opening. Those six months would allow it to fill and the sediment to settle, and for the Water Authorities to ensure that there were no dam wall leaks. The pipe laying project should be completed by the end of next Summer, in time for the following Autumn and the additional demand for water that the growing textiles industry was creating.

Aspinall arrived at midday and was reading a copy of the Financial Times, happy to see that the price of land in the North West of England was going up. A chance for him to review the rents that he charged his tenants, which he had consciously only fixed on an annual basis, allowing him to maximise profits by raising rents even when it did not seem justified.

The doorman entered the library and passed Aspinall an unmarked envelope. "Sir, a young boy passed me this envelope and asked me to pass it to you."

He opened it to find an empty betting slip inside. On the back of the slip was written in red ink.

'Remember Titanic!'

He looked at it and was pondering further what the meaning could be of a sunken ship reference when Joshua Padgett walked into the room having just wandered down from his own office in Duke Street. "Hello, Henry, putting a bet on something," he quipped, seeing the betting slip. "Do let me in on any sure winners!"

Aspinall folded the note and shoved it in his wallet aggressively. "Afternoon Joshua – I do have a winning bet to share with you, but not of a sporting variety. Sit yourself down and listen to this idea that I've just committed to."

John Padgett ordered his normal lunch and sat down on the Chesterton armchair, "Come on then, Henry – share your new money-earning venture," he said quietly so that they could not be overheard by any of the waiting staff.

Aspinall leaned over to him and started, "I have my own low-cost pipe laying team ready to start in the new year, not only that, but I've managed to get around any issues we have with the Planning Department over where the pipe will lay and what impact it will have on my tenant farmers. The farmers will also benefit as I will pay them for some of the work that requires heavy digging machinery. In addition, I have Charles lined up to support the project management after he completes his schooling – I need to quickly get him involved in business before he is swayed by other distractions."

Aspinall moved on with increasing enthusiasm, "I can deliver the project for less money as I will be paying quarry workers' wages rather than the higher basic wages of pipe layers. I'll get paid by the Water Authorities an amount that we agree, and then skim off the profit before we pay the labourers. For you and me, it's a win-win." Joshua Padgett looked away; he was not looking as cock-sure of himself as he usually did. "What's not to like?" added Aspinall quickly.

Padgett stared at his friend and slowly said, "You cannot do that – I have already contracted that work to a third party." Aspinall's mouth opened wide, and his furrowed brow demanded more information. Padgett continued. "I have an agreement with one Edgar Fitch to have a team of his boys come down and lay the piping," he stared, looking blankly at the corner of the room.

Aspinall baulked, "What! Joshua – you need to break that agreement and tell Fitch that he is no longer needed."

Padgett closed his eyes. "Henry – it isn't that easy. I owe Edgar Fitch a favour, and this is how I was going to pay him back."

"But Fitch's mob isn't even registered to do such work as pipe laying," Aspinall protested.

"It'll be easy for him to obtain false licenses allowing his men to work, he has most of the Manchester Chamber of Commerce in his pocket." Padgett fired back.

"Well, Joshua – it's your problem. You need to sort it out.

The pipeline crosses my tenant's land, and I am not having any of Fitch's 'Sons of Strangeways', anywhere near the Hollins." Flustered, Aspinall stood up and headed out of the room, leaving Joshua Padgett still staring at the corner of the library. 'Sons of Strangeways' was the self-styled nickname that Fitch's gang went by, as most of the members had been recruited by Fitch himself during his regular spells inside at His Majesty's Pleasure.

Henry Aspinall decided to walk home – via Teggs Nose. He wanted to firm up directly with Ledger that the Teggs Nose Quarry team would split and take on the pipeline work in the New Year. He had realised that John Croker was a worthless individual who had managed to get to an elevated position in his Company by keeping his head down and not taking any risks or having any original thoughts. Aspinall couldn't wait for a time in which Charles could take over from Croker and move the quarrying and soon to be, pipe-line laying business forward.

Aspinall rarely went up to the quarry, but what he saw was a group of workers busying themselves just next to the quarry face. A small man beckoned to the other workers to take cover behind a corrugated iron shield leaning against a couple of large boulders. The man looked over at Aspinall and scowled without removing his eyes – he put his fingers to his ears and BOOM! An enormous explosion threw large fragments of rock tens of yards in the air, and a large cloud of rock dust enveloped the scene. As the air cleared, the group of men headed back into where the blast had come and sounds of pick axes and sledgehammers on the rock were quickly heard.

The small man headed over to where the largest of the men was swinging the biggest of hammers.

He shouted out in a foreign-sounding accent, "Bellissima – Sledge - that was a good one. I think I've blown the main seam wide open, that should be the last one needed today."

Aspinall saw the large man turn round. "Thanks, Gustav," he said. "Put any of the spare dynamite back in Jack's store. I agree. No more fireworks from you today."

Aspinall recognised where he had seen that small man before – he had been the bookmaker at the illegal Bollington boxing fight and had been particularly reluctant to pay him and Padgett their winnings – ill-gotten as they were. Noticing Aspinall's appearance through the dust cloud that was now quickly dissipating, Silas shouted out, "Hello, Mr. Aspinall – pleased to see you again so soon after this morning's meeting. How can we help you?"

"Hello Ledger – I wanted to immediately come up to the quarry myself to thank you for the proposal you shared with me this morning. I would like to take it up and I have asked John Croker to start planning the project immediately," Aspinall announced.

A flicker of a smile appeared on Silas's face, never one for extreme emotion – this was indeed – good news. "Thank you, sir. I will go and inform Jack Moat – he had the idea in the first place and will be able to help Mr. Croker to sort out a work schedule. Does that mean you can attend the village meeting next week and announce this to the Langley farmers and, particularly, those that farm across the Hollins tract of land?"

"Yes – I will be there, together with Mr. Croker," said Aspinall.

"Good news, thank you," said Silas. They shook hands, firming up the arrangement.

Aspinall walked on past the quarrying operation and looked over the Langley valley – most of which comprised his estate. He looked at the newly completed dam wall and the area that would soon be flooded to create the Trentabank reservoir. He traced with his eyes the route that the pipeline would take over the Hollins and down to Macclesfield. He felt good, he felt fully in control. If only his son could see the opportunity ahead of him to follow in his father's footsteps. Henry was sure that when he got home, his son would have seen the light.

Joshua Padgett was in a stew. Following his depressing lunch meeting with Henry Aspinall, he had returned to 16 Duke Street to find an envelope on the doormat. It had no name on the front, he tore it open. It was a betting slip. The words in red on the reverse read:

'*Water & Fire*'

He was in no fit state for silly games and he tossed the slip in the top drawer of his large desk – he had bigger issues to confront than a silly prank. It was critical that he spoke with Fitch before any news broke from Aspinall that the pipeline contract would officially be awarded to the Teggs Nose Quarry team. He had hoped to get Water Board approval for the Fitch contract as there would be no alternative. He had misplaced a duplicate note to Fitch offering him the contract, and this note was supposed to be made up into a formal contract and filed at the Town Hall planning office. However, quite clearly, Aspinall's deal to retain local jobs and appease any negativity from local farmers, would get the Water Board's full backing, especially as it also offered a better commercial term for everyone. Fitch's contract would have lined Padgett's pockets with gold, but would have been more costly to the Water Board. How could he reverse his position with Edgar Fitch and his gang of thugs? That was the challenging question facing him.

He decided that a phone call to Edgar Fitch might be the best option. A face-to-face meeting with Manchester's most notorious mobster seemed most undesirable. He settled himself behind his mahogany desk in his Duke Street office, picked up the phone and dialled. "Mr. Fitch's Office," a coarse Mancunian male voice barked out. If ever you wanted a less welcoming voice as a first impression of a business empire, this was it.

Joshua Padgett steeled himself, "Hello, it's Joshua Padgett here from Macclesfield. I'd like to speak to Mr. Edgar Fitch."

"Hold on, I'll see if Mr. Fitch is in." came the stark reply.

Two minutes passed; Padgett's pudgy face started to bead with sweat. "Hello Joshua," Fitch's gravelly voice sounded non-plussed to be speaking to him. "What more can I do for you today?" he enquired with a strong hint of sarcasm.

"Well, hello Edgar, I thought I'd just call to clarify a conversation we had just before the Bollington boxing event that you kindly sponsored." Padgett breathed rapidly, wiping the now-falling beads of sweat from his brow.

"Ah yes, I remember it well, Joshua, you and your friend Mr. Aspinall won a lot of money when my boy George took a fall," Fitch stated factually enough. "And in return, you agreed to give me a lucrative work contract for my boys."

Padgett was at least pleased that there was no more small talk, he might as well get the pain over quickly. "Yes, Mr. Fitch, and that's what I need to talk to you about. Rather, unfortunately, another highly reputable company has appeared and has been given the pipe laying contract, so I'm afraid I need to withdraw that offer of work."

There was a sizeable pause at the end of the phone. Padgett's sweat started to flow more rapidly. "I see," said Edgar Fitch, "Well, that's not how we do business around here Mr. Padgett. A promise is a promise and I have a copy of a note right here committing to that work. I demand that you honour your side of the bargain or there will be consequences." Fitch's threatening last word set Padgett's heart racing. Fitch continued, "Of course, it could all be forgotten if you pay me £10,000 by the end of January. I will leave it up to you. A confirmation of the work contract, or the cash."

With that, the phone line went dead. How was he going to be able to resolve this? Whilst everything in Henry Aspinall's world seemed to be working out, Joshua Padgett's world was falling down around him. He needed to find a solution and fast.

Aspinall had arrived home from Teggs Nose with high

hopes that he would meet a chaste Charles ready to conform to his father's desires. But it was Florence, his wife, who he first saw in the entrance hall. One look told him the answer he was dreading. Florence looked dishevelled. She had been tearful most of the day, coming to terms with the fact that her one remaining ray of sunshine – her son – had now decided to make his escape from the clutch of his father. An escape that she had wanted to do for many years herself but was too weak to achieve. Her escape was through the bottle, which she knew – confirmed by the doctors – would eventually kill her. The ultimatum note that Henry had left for his son was the final offer, and Charles had decided that the threat of severing family ties was the only option left to him.

Henry Aspinall had little to no love left for his wife, and now that Charles had left, it struck him that if Florence had been stronger, then she might have been able to support him better and keep their son on the correct path. "Go to bed, Florence. You look dreadful!" he snapped. The fleeting moment on Teggs Nose, when life seemed so good, had truly passed. He needed to quickly bury himself in where he was most comfortable. Managing his business affairs and making money. He asked the nearest maid to run down to the gatehouse and ask Arthur Brice – his Land Manager – to come up to the house. It was about time that he got rid of Archie Talbot for being too old and incapable of keeping those damned poachers out of his estate.

CHAPTER 17 - *VILLAGE MEETING*

The village meeting at the Dunstan Inn was more populated than ever before. Once more, Ned Croucher had to beg the services of his friend from the Setter Dog – Dick Avery – to help behind the bar. Given the identity of the special guest expected, Dick decided against bringing down any spare cuts of meat his two poaching friends had provided him in the last week. That would have to wait! There were seventy people inside the Inn and a further twenty outside listening through the windows. Reverend Pottinger was not present, but he had been asked to announce at the Sunday service that, as promised, Silas Ledger would have news about the pipeline, and a special guest – from the Aspinall Company – would be present to update any interested parties. This local village word-of-mouth, plus the obvious importance of the topic, had created quite sufficient excitement to draw a large crowd.

Once everyone had managed to get served at the bar – Ned's pre-requisite for loaning the village meeting his premises – he called for order by banging two large ale jugs together and asking the Chairman - Percy Ricketts to take to the floor to announce the agenda. There were no crocheting clubs or Langley Village fete committees to organise this month, the agenda was focused on one item from the last meeting: planning permission for the proposed pipeline from Trentabank over the Hollins to Macclesfield. Mr. Ricketts proudly announced the agenda point as if it were a royal proclamation and introduced the special guest, who had been kept hidden at the back door of the Inn by a very excited Mrs. Croucher. "It is with great pleasure that I introduce Mr. Henry Aspinall – our esteemed local squire and landowner – to respond to the agenda point itemised previously." With a flourish, Ricketts stood aside, allowing the crowd to see Henry Aspinall appear accompanied by John Croker and the large looming shape of Silas. There was a muted reaction to the sighting of Aspinall, as he rarely appeared in public in the village. Croker was unknown to everyone other than the quarry workers, but a cheer went up when Silas appeared – that caused some clear discomfort for the other two men.

Having had his enthusiasm for the idea severely dampened by the loss of his son as a future driving force behind the project, Aspinall had considered withdrawing from this village meeting as he felt he owed nobody his precious time – yet he did feel a need to understand more about the types of people who had so affected his son's sense of values that he had decided to abandon the guarantee of a lifetime of social wealth and material riches. He started his address slowly as it was clear to him that some of these numbskull farmers might not understand King's English quite so well. "Gentlemen... and Ladies present, my ancestors owned most of the land in this valley, and I feel that I have become a strong and fair guardian of that inheritance..."

"Not to Sid Bayley, you're not," an anonymous voice rang out.

"Hush, hush now," said Mr. Ricketts. "Let Mr. Aspinall have his say."

Having heard the random heckle and the clearly sensitive subject matter, Aspinall continued unperturbed. "I own this land, and by my generosity, many of you have livelihoods that you may not have done under other landlords. The quarry on Teggs Nose offers employment for many of you villagers. The farms in the valley are all effectively run by yourselves for very reasonable rents." Another murmur of dissent was heard – but Mr. Ricketts quickly tapped his trusty cane on the counter, demanding silence. Aspinall continued, "I know that many of you women work in textile and paper mills in the town that I own." He paused for a moment and looked around the room. Through the window, he recognised Beth's eyes staring back at him – never had he seen such a hateful look other than from the eyes of his own son on the night before he left the house. He temporarily halted and lost his place in the speech. Redirecting his gaze back onto the people in the room, he got on to the real reason for his presence that evening. "You all know that a new reservoir – Trentabank – will open in the new year. And please come to the opening ceremony where we believe that we will have royalty present." A few oohs and aahs arose from the room. "That reservoir will only mean the loss of two farms – Nessett and Trentabank, and the additional water it will be able to provide Macclesfield's industry will secure jobs for generations to come. The river Bollin catchment is too small to be used as the vehicle to get the water to the town, and so engineers from the Water Board have designed a pipe network that will be able to bring the much-needed water up and over the Hollins."

"Where exactly?" enquired Donald Hough, one of the Hollins farmers. Knowing that this was the crux of the matter and on cue, Aspinall made way for John Croker to appear from behind him, holding a large piece of paper. Between he and Mr. Ricketts they held it such that Aspinall could commentate and point to particular landmarks on the map, showing the route between the reservoir and the Hollins. Those from the front of the room, near the poster, helped to communicate details towards the back of the room where people could not see. There were, in fact, two routes, both skirted the village, one to the north and the other to the south. One crossed three different farmer's fields, and the other went across two but also went through a small woodland.

The map caused a great deal of discussion, but the fact that there were two routes allowed Aspinall to make the room think that they were involved in the discussion. In fact, he cared little about which route the pipeline took. The consensus from the room suggested the southerly route crossing two farms and through the woodland – would be preferable. In part because nobody other than Aspinall's privileged huntsman friends were ever allowed in that woodland. Only Robin Brampton and Andy Soutter looked disappointed by that decision, as they knew that woodland well and had caught several deer in its leafy shade.

"Thank you all," Mr. Ricketts brought the meeting back to order. "I feel we have a decision on the southerly route." A small cheer of support broke out, and the room took on a much more relaxed atmosphere. The two farmers that would be impacted, were told that they could earn good monies from the use of their tractors with the heavy digging requirements. This seemed to placate them.

Henry Aspinall took the floor again. "What's more, I have decided along with the Water Authorities that the Teggs Nose quarrymen, who so ably delivered the requisite gritstone to complete the dam wall, will be used to lay the pipeline. A job that will secure their employment for the duration of the project." A cheer went up from everyone in the room – although Jack Moat and Silas remained muted as they recognised that following the pipeline project, there remained a question as to what futures the quarry workers had, but at least this diversification allowed for more skills and hopefully more opportunities, if a good job was achieved.

Aspinall had successfully turned his fortunes around with the villagers, from pariah in some of their eyes due to the forced eviction of the Lovatts and the suicide of Sid Bayley – he had become a forward-thinking and amiable landlord willing to be flexible in dealings with the village.

"Let me buy you a pint," shouted out Fred Needles, knowing that the support of Aspinall as the Cricket Club sponsor was key to helping Langley punch above their weight in the local Cheshire league.

"Thank you, but I must be off now, I need to firm the agreed pipeline route up with the Water Board. But please buy Mr. Croker one instead," replied Aspinall, relieved that any thought of socialising with this riff-raff could be avoided by a simple excuse. Fred Needles looked disappointed but ordered at the bar all the same.

Aspinall exited the Dunstan Inn via the front door. He wanted to try to catch Beth without her father around. Nobody else was on the street outside as everyone had been intent on pushing into the bar room as soon as the map had appeared. He saw Beth on her own, heading back towards the Ledger's cottage and in the shadows between two street lamps. He quickly caught her up, spinning her around, he hissed, "You little bitch, what have you done to my son?" He grabbed her by the neck and pressed on her airway, "If you have anything more to do with Charles, your father will regret it, do you hear me?" Aspinall let her go and walked off into the night. Beth collected her breath and could already feel the bruising appear where Aspinall's grip had been tightest. She got to her front door, stepped inside and collected herself, she could not put her father at risk. She shuddered at the thought of that man's hand around her throat. Will was upstairs asleep, so she sat down on the sofa and thought of Charlie all alone at Sid's doomed farmhouse, was their relationship also doomed? Little did Henry Aspinall know that his physical attack had only re-strengthened Beth's resolve to save Charlie from the sufferance of his father forever.

Back at the Dunstan, an impromptu early Christmas party had started with the farmers and the quarry workers both believing that the good news was weighted in their favour. Dick Avery and his two young poachers, were doing a roaring trade in bookings for new year meats and fish. It would be a busy few nights in the coming week for Andy Soutter and Robin Brampton. Jack and Silas had found the only quiet corner and were sitting down, generally satisfied with how the evening had gone. John Croker was getting merrily drunk listening to Fred Needles talking about the fine art of hostile swing bowling and how he had drawn blood from three of the top four batsmen from Toft Cricket Club over in Knutsford.

"Jack, you should be proud of how your idea has taken wings and become a fully-fledged plan," Silas said, patting him on the back, "Regardless of not knowing the longer-term future for the quarry team, the fact that we will all have new skills gives us a good chance of future employment. Good men will always rise to the top." He added, "Let Aspinall and Croker take the credit for the idea, we all know where it came from."

Jack looked back at Silas. "It wasn't just me; a good deal of credit needs to go to Melissa for sharing the note from Padgett about the Manchester mob workers. That triggered the thought that we could do better than any of them."

Silas smiled to himself – he knew that Jack was lonely and that Melissa had sparked a new interest in him. It would be good to see his friend happy. He was less sure of how the ember of love he'd seen flicker between Beth and Charlie would cope with the differences in upbringing and societal norms. And the destructive force that was Henry Aspinall.

CHAPTER 18 - *ROUGH SLEEPING*

It was Christmas Eve 1928, the High Street in Langley was decorated with Christmas wreaths of holly and mistletoe on the doors of houses and the school had had their end-of-term nativity play, choreographed as always by Martha Lovatt. The stable scene had been transferred over to the Chapel to form the centre-piece for the Christmas service period. The first of which was a candle-lit service that evening. The choir was performing carol songs outside the Dunstan Inn, joined from inside by a less musical rendition of 'Hark the Herald Angels'. Those that were considered sufficiently sober were welcomed to join the choir and the general congregation inside the Chapel where Reverend Pottinger would conduct the service.

A shadow slipped unnoticed across the graveyard towards the procession of candles. Gwen joined her sister-in-law Martha in the front pew alongside the Brampton family, minus Robin, who was busy in the woods with Andy Soutter, fulfilling the late-game orders made on the evening of the pipeline route unveil. Beth loitered at the back of the church and sat in the back pew, away from the candle-illuminated section occupied by the proportion of the congregation. Charlie Aspinall slipped in through the main door after all the villagers had taken their pews. He sat next to Beth. Charlie had been staying for the last two days at the empty Nessit Farm, with only Mew – Sid's old cat – for company. He was desperate to see Beth again and had managed to get a message to her via old Archie Talbot, the Gamekeeper. Archie had been a loyal worker on the Aspinall Estate but had recognised the increasing distance that had been growing between young Charles and his father. He had winced with pain when he saw Henry take a horse whip to Charles on his thirteenth birthday when the young lad had refused to shoot a fine stag whilst hunting between the copse near Saddlers Way and the moorland. Henry had shot the creature anyway and commanded Archie to bring the carcass back to the Manor House. Henry was with Arthur Brice in the stable block when Archie returned, and Henry summoned Charles to join them next to the still-warm body of the stag that was still bleeding from the neck. Henry was quite clearly raging at his son's failure to attempt to shoot the stag. Without any warning, Henry had wiped his hand across the bloody neck of the stag and slapped his son with his hand, marking his face in blood. Henry then took his whip out and gave Charles three sharp lashes to his body. Both Archie and Albert were shocked by the brutal physicality of father to son, but Archie was equally shocked – and impressed – by the way that the teenager had taken the beating and had looked emotionless and steely-eyed back at his father. From that moment, Archie swore to himself to try to support Charles in any small way and look at an escape route out of the service of Henry Aspinall despite having been Gamekeeper to the Aspinall family for the last two generations.

It was Archie Talbot who had been spoken to by Florence Aspinall a few days ago and asked to try and find her son following his departure and make sure that he was ok. Archie may have lost his skills as a tracker of animals in his old age, but he knew enough about the Aspinall Estate to know where a young man might hide out. He also knew of Charles' fondness for Sid Bayley and had watched them bale hay together several times over the previous few years. He had found Charles at the abandoned Nessit Farm and had sworn to him that he would not tell his father where he was. Archie had also brought him extra provisions, helped by Florence. It was Archie who had passed a note to Beth to tell her to meet Charles at the back of the Chapel at the candle lit service on Christmas Eve.

As Reverend Pottinger called for prayers, Beth and Charlie knelt down on the prayer cushions and held hands. They hadn't spoken to each other for three days, and a lot had happened. Charlie told Beth about the ultimatum note that his father had written. He also told her that it was the last straw and that he had conceived the escape plan, helped enormously by his mother's blessing and financial support. He would need to go back to School on Boxing Day. Ironically, this was the day that the Aspinall's had traditionally given gifts to the poorer members of the Langley community. But in recent years, it had ceased to happen because Florence was no longer well enough to travel down to the village. Thankfully, she had given her son one final gift – the ability to escape his father.

As the hymns were being heartily sung at the front of the

chapel, Beth and Charles continued to catch up on what had happened. He told her about Nessit Farm and the fact that he had all he needed to survive a few more days before he could return to Hoarwithy School – thanks to Archie. He also told her about Mew the cat and asked her to look after him once the reservoir started to form and the farmhouse flooded. He reminded her about his ambitions still to go to university, helped by Mr. McCrory, the newly appointed Deputy Head; and Mr. Grainger, his old friend from the Hoarwithy cricket score hut. He spoke with a new positive energy and a fresh passion that she had not detected before; it was like he was starting life anew.

Given the burning glimmer of positive hope in his eye, Beth decided not to tell Charlie about the fact that his father had half-throttled her and threatened Silas if she did not cease to see his son. Having made the sacrifice he had done; Beth was not willing to hurt Charlie further. She loved him and wanted to prove that those neck bruises were insufficient to influence her life. She was worried about her father, but also knew that Silas was a force of nature himself, and would survive any blow.

As they were kneeling, Charlie pulled out a small knife from his pocket. He opened it and started to carve into the dark wooden shelf in front of them. He carved the initials CA & BL. He looked at Beth and, in the shadow of the chapel, gave her a soft, tender kiss. Her eyes filled with tears, and one drop fell on the newly carved initials.

"Don't cry, my love, we have so much living to do. I will write to you from Hoarwithy. I promise." And with that, Charlie slipped out of the Chapel door and darted back into the night across the fields to Mew and Nessit Farm.

Christmas Day passed uneventfully in the village of Langley. Jack had been invited to the Ledger's for Christmas dinner and was overjoyed by the best present possible that he had been thinking about a lot recently. Just as the Christmas pudding was brought in by Silas, smothered with cooking brandy and burning with a blue flame, a knock was heard at the door. Will sprung up to answer the door, and there was Jack's present - Melissa Kirkham – wrapped up in a thick red cape and jaunty bobble hat. Her red cheeks complemented her looks perfectly. Jack swiftly made room next to him.

Silas had shared with Gwen his thoughts about Jack and Melissa, but thought no more about it. However, his wife was a much more proactive type when it came to match making. Gwen had taken a detour home from work, and called into Sperry & Burroughs Solicitors on Christmas Eve morning, and introduced herself to Melissa. Gwen immediately warmed to Melissa's easy-going nature and the fact that Jack was mentioned several times without any prompting made Gwen's job easy. An invite to come for Christmas dinner was presented and accepted, although Melissa did say that she'd have to excuse herself from the food as she'd promised to cook Christmas dinner for her parents, but as soon as they were both asleep, she'd walk up and arrive mid-afternoon.

Gwen beamed brightly when she saw Jack's reaction to Melissa's appearance. Her match-making was coming together nicely. Silas placed the pudding on the table, and Gwen served everyone a plate. Only Beth was subdued. Her thoughts were with Charlie. He would be alone at Nessit

Farm, with only Mew as company. Regardless of his bravado from the Chapel, she knew that he would be lonely and she vowed to go and see him before he left for Derbyshire and his Boarding School.

Having had one final glass of port, Silas joined Gwen on the sofa. The result of over-feeding on a beautifully cooked goose – courtesy of the Setter Dog Inn's magical game store – was contented sleep. A brandy-enhanced plum pudding, all washed down with a fine bottle of port that Gustav Coccini had acquired somehow and had gifted to Jack in return for a couple of water-tight storage boxes from the store – meaning that loud snores could be heard from the Ledger parents. Will was upstairs practicing batting strokes, in a mirror, with his new Stuart Surridge cricket bat. Jack and Melissa took the opportunity to slip out of the door and head over to his cottage. Beth quickly put on her mum's coat, wrapped a scarf around her neck and headed out in the direction of the Trentabank dam.

The wind was chill and flakes of snow were in the air. The dam rose up from the Bollin valley like a colossal, ungodly black wall, countering the natural beauty of the surrounds. She was sad that industrialisation and the demands of man had desecrated her home so much. She thought of Sid Bayley and the Lovatts and the mental anguish that they had been made to suffer because of this wall. But above all, she thought of Charlie on the other side of the dam in the Farmhouse on his own. She quickened her step and rounded the side of the dam, dropping down into the meadow before reaching the Nessit Farmhouse that lay in a natural hollow. The Lovatts had already moved across to Bosley Cloud, and so Charlie was the sole human living in the soon-to-be flooded valley. The snow was getting thicker and had started to stick on the grass before her, she hurried herself further, keen to get out of the biting cold wind. A small plume of smoke was coming from the farmhouse chimney.

She called from the farmyard, "Charlie, are you there?"

The door opened, and a smiling Charlie was standing, silhouetted by the glow of the fire behind him. He had made a bed out of a stack of bales, and an upturned box was being used as a table. He had a pot of water on a hook over the fire. It wasn't quite the scene of cosy, domestic bliss that she'd left at her parent's cottage, but it was pleasant enough for a man on the run!

"Come in, you must be freezing," Charlie said, beaming. He enveloped her in his arms and wrapped a blanket around her. "You shouldn't have come. There's a winter storm brewing."

"Of course, I needed to be here. I couldn't stand the thought of you being alone, and I needed to see you before you left," she said, lifting her face to look into his eyes. "I can't stay long, but I needed to know that you're okay." Mew shifted from his cosy position by the fire, looking perplexed by the fact that the farmhouse door had been opened and let in a bolt of cold air.

"Honest Beth, I've been fine here, and I feel so alive now that I have finally been able to tell my father that I am in control of my own destiny, not him." Charlie was still holding her tight, and he closed the door behind him. Mew settled back into his bed, helped by a piece of goose that Beth had smuggled out of the house, alongside some plum pudding and a small flask of port. They had only been friends for three months, but they had shared so much. They had recognised each other as soulmates from two very different worlds, and their coming together had created a storm, but one that they would survive.

Outside, the winter storm started to howl ferociously. What was in store for Beth and Charlie outside of the sanctuary of Nessit Farm? Would their relationship survive or would it drown in the troubled waters stirred up by Henry Aspinall, in the same way that the low-lying Farmhouse they sat in right then was soon to be submerged under the waters of the reservoir?

CHAPTER 19 - *FLOODING*

The new term was two weeks in. Beth was worried as she had not received any letters from Charlie. She knew that he had returned to Hoarwithy because a chance meeting with Archie Talbot had confirmed that. He had taken a letter from Charlie up to Charlie's mother just last week, so why had Beth not received any, particularly given that she had written half a dozen letters to him already?

It was the official day that Trentabank reservoir would be opened, and the first waters would start to fill as the dam gates were blocked. Langley Primary School had been given the day off, and Martha Lovatt was leading the schoolchildren along the access lane to climb that side of the new dam. Nat had decided not to be present for sentimental reasons and as he was focused on the future and the new farmstead that Thomas Wharton had been kind enough to provide for them and their expanded flock of sheep, having combined Sid Bayley's remaining flock.

The children made their way slowly up the bank of the new dam, chattering away excitedly, expecting a sudden wave of water to fill the large expanse of the higher Bollin valley. Of course, this was a symbolic closing of the stop gates, it would take many months to fill the reservoir with over one hundred million gallons of water. It was planned that by the Autumn of 1929, Prince Henry would be present at the full opening of the Trentabank reservoir alongside the Duke of Gloucester, who was the current Minister for Waterways in the UK Government of the time. The pipelines over the Hollins would need to be complete by then and able to shift a volume of water over to power the mill industries.

There was a large platform at the top of the dam wall where a reception was being held. As the landowner of the valley, and the person who the Water Authority had purchased the land from, Henry Aspinall had been given the privilege of waving the flag to close the stop gates far below at the base of the dam wall. Many of the villagers had made their way up to the platform and mingled with a number of business men from the town, many of whom would benefit from this new and improved supply of water. Amongst them were Thomas Whetton and Phillip Broadhead. Victor Knight, the Water Board Manager, had the honour of acting as the master of ceremonies. Joshua Padgett was also present in his capacity as Director of the Water Authority and Vice Chairman of the Macclesfield Chamber of Commerce.

Padgett looked over at Aspinall and seethed at the fact that he was looking so full of his own self-importance. Their relationship had taken a turn for the worse since the Hollins pipeline project had been granted to the Teggs Nose Quarry (and now) Pipeline Company.

"That arrogant shit, I hope he falls on his own sword." He thought to himself. Aspinall looked over at him and smiled, wondering how Padgett had dealt with the Manchester mob. The truth was that Padgett had not dealt with the Manchester mob, and he had only two weeks before the deadline for the £10,000 compensation payment was to be made – and no idea how he was going to muster this money together.

Victor Knight signalled for quiet and passed the starting flag across to Henry Aspinall to wave. Aspinall enjoyed the public spotlight, especially when a number of his peers were present. He started, "Gentlemen and Ladies, Boys and Girls – it is with great pleasure that I bequeathed this land for the betterment of the United Kingdom and her many industries – I herewith declare Trentabank Reservoir open." Flourishing his flag, the workmen down below turned the cog to close the lock gate. A grating sound could be heard, and then nothing. The children were all disappointed that the reservoir had not suddenly appeared, and let out a collective sigh. The adults, recognising that there now followed a good six-month period of filling, started a ripple of applause, loud enough for Silas up at the Teggs Nose quarry to hear and look down towards the dam – happy that he was not close enough to be party to the pompous Henry Aspinall lauding it over all those around him. It was Aspinall who had convinced the Water Authority to pay an inflated price to acquire the land in the upper Bollin valley, and allowed him to make a fortune by allowing the building of the reservoir.

Joshua Padgett was suddenly aware of a burly man with a scar on his face approaching him and thrusting a note into his hand. "Regards from Mr. Fitch," he mumbled menacingly before moving on.

Padgett opened the note. The message could not have been clearer:

£10,000 two weeks today!

CHAPTER 20 - *DIRTY DEALINGS*

A further week had passed since the opening of the reservoir. Beth woke up in a cold sweat. She had been sleeping poorly because of the lack of correspondence from Charlie, she was worried something had happened. But it was for another reason that she had suddenly awoken. "Mew!" she gasped. Sid Bayley's cat had been left in the farmhouse, and the valley behind the dam was starting to fill up with water. She shouted over to Will, "Will, get up! We've got to go and rescue Mew."

"What!?" replied Will, upset that he had been so rudely awoken by his sister.

"Mew – Sid's cat – he's still in the Nessit Farmhouse," said Beth urgently.

Will slowly computed the facts – the Farmhouse was in a very low part of the valley and would likely be amongst the first parts to fill up with water. He had also liked Sid Bayley a lot and, as a fourteen-year-old, had been badly affected by the way Sid felt that life was no longer worth living. Will had never been so close to the brutal facts of life before. "Okay sis, we'd best get a move on. There's a cat to be rescued." He sprung out of bed and put on his jumper as the house was freezing; the morning fire had not yet been stoked back into life. Will had not realised that his sister had such strong feelings towards the feline world, but he didn't know that this cat represented a life force that his sister associated closely with the first person she had ever felt love for – Charlie Aspinall.

The two of them slipped out of the slumbering cottage, managing to leave Gwen and Silas asleep in their room. They moved hastily up the lane, passed the Chapel and took no time in clambering up the dam wall, ignoring the multiple flood warning signs that had been placed all around the catchment area. The blanket of snow on the meadow had largely melted, and tufts of grass were visible. Beyond the meadow, they could see the roof of Nessit Farm, but as it was in a dip in the land, they could not see if the flooded valley beyond the dam had reached it yet. Certainly, other lower parts of the valley were already under flood water. They squelched over the sodden meadow, now saturated with snow melt as well as a rising water table. As they neared the brow, they could see the farmyard completely under water, and the buildings were now islands within a small, dirty lake. Will estimated that the water was already a yard deep inside the farmhouse. Pieces of debris were floating in the steadily growing lake. Old wooden cartons, pieces of timber, an old teapot and a milk urn meandered unnaturally around the farmyard.

Beth spotted an old water trough floating near the still visible top of an old gritstone wall that used to be a sheep pen. She saw a movement from on top of the trough.

"Mew!" she exclaimed excitedly, seeing the drenched and scared cat shivering at one end of this makeshift life raft. "Will, there's Mew." Ignoring the freezing cold water, Beth waded into the lake, breaking the thin layer of ice that had formed in parts. She grabbed the trough and pulled it back to where Will was shin-deep in mud. Will picked up the scared cat, who was protesting loudly, yet also recognising that he had better accept human intervention at this point as he had little better option. Will wrapped Mew up inside his still-dry jumper and Beth and he helped each other out of the muddy field and back towards the safety of the dam wall.

"What now?" asked Will.

"We'll take Mew back to the village; someone will want to look after him," Beth replied through chattering teeth. Her body was shivering still, although she could feel some blood circulation coming back to her frozen limbs.

"I know!" exclaimed Will. "The Post Office is suffering from an infestation of mice right now. Mr. Ricketts is constantly complaining that his baked goods have been nibbled. I reckon I could convince him to take Mew as a mouser."

"Great idea Will, but let's take him back to ours first so that we can warm him up and give him some milk – he must be cold and starving," said Beth.

"Not as cold and starving as me!" Will winked back at his sister. Beth smiled; she was also frozen, but at least she had saved Mew for Charlie despite not having heard anything from him for weeks.

Hoarwithy Boarding School was situated on the Derbyshire, Staffordshire border, not far from Chatsworth House. It was a wealthy school with large grounds and its closest town was Bakewell, about two miles away along the river. There was a twice-weekly mail delivery from the main sorting office in Bakewell, up to the school and vice versa. One of the school caretakers – Angus Jordan – used to deliver and collect the post on Tuesdays and Fridays. He regularly complained about all the care packages arriving from wealthy parents, guilty of sending their children away for months at a time. The care packages were heavy and meant that he was regularly hauling three or four sacks of parcels up two flights of stairs to the School Office for distribution. Occasionally, a particularly sweet-smelling parcel of goodies used to accidentally find its way to his small office in the basement rather than some spoilt, expectant student. Their small loss was his tasty gain.

At the start of the January term, before the pupils had returned to their dormitories, along with some early care packages, he received a letter unusually addressed to him with a Macclesfield postmark on it. Angus knew nobody in Macclesfield and so was surprised that it was addressed to him personally. Inside were two crisp ten-pound notes and a letter:

Dear Mr. Angus Jordan,

Sources tell me that you are in charge of all post arriving and departing Hoarwithy School.

I would very much appreciate it if you would help me in my endeavour to keep my son focused entirely on his final two terms at School.

Please put to one side any incoming letters arriving for Master Charles/Charlie Aspinall. Open them, and if they are from a Beth Ledger – under no circumstances – pass them on to my son. Similarly, if there are any outgoing letters to Miss Beth Ledger from my son, simply destroy them.

If you do this, I will ensure that the money I enclose in this envelope is doubled at the end of term.

Yours in expectation,

Mr. Henry Aspinall Esq.

Angus was used to odd requests from parents, but this was one that he could support with relish, particularly as it generated such useful additional income. Forty pounds was a fortnight's pay for a lowly caretaker. He sat back and popped another delicious chocolate bonbon from Harrods into his mouth.

It was four weeks since he had returned early to Hoarwithy School, and Charlie was beside himself. He could not believe that Beth had not responded to any of his letters. He felt that their relationship was so strong, particularly after he had made the decisive move away from his father's control. His mother had secured funds from her private account to complete the terms he had left at School, and he was confident that the bursary funding from his friend Mr. Grainger and his alumni group of Old Boys would see him able to at least start University after which he would need to get a part-time job to support ongoing funding. Charlie was willing to sacrifice so much to take control of his own destiny, but losing Beth so early in his quest was unforeseen and unfathomable.

Charlie had few friends at school who had close relationships with girls and certainly no friends that he knew of who had severed ties with the parental silver spoon that fed them. He was lonely and sought console in his books. More firmly than ever, he felt that the study of Law would be the direction in which he wanted to throw his passions. The logical argument and meticulous study of legal precedents that the profession demanded reminded him of the joy he got from his cricket scoring and study of Wisden almanacs. Having been one of the few boys who had returned to Hoarwithy so early, he had been invited to lunch with the Deputy Head – Mr. McCrory – and his young family. Upon hearing about Charlie's preference to study Law at University, Mrs. McCrory shared some of her own insights into the hard intellectual challenge that the many years of Law School would entail and the fact that many lawyers drop out due to the sheer amount of study required. This only fuelled Charlie's desires further. Perhaps because of his difficult upbringing, he felt a need to fight for the rights of all people – rich or poor. He could well recall Beth's comments about how the wealthier classes simply grew richer at the expense of the masses. He had witnessed this first-hand in his own home. Charlie felt his destiny had to be doing his bit to redress the balance.

It was approaching the end of January, and the deadline day for the payment of £10,000 to Edgar Fitch. John Padgett had few options ahead of him, he would have to remortgage his house and ask the bank for a crippling loan. Why was life treating him so badly? Then a thought came to his mind could he interest Edgar Fitch in an investment idea that an old friend of his, who was now a Director of the Liverpool-based Cunard Line Shipping Company, had suggested to him during a game of bridge at a North West England Chambers of Commerce event. It was after several large brandies, but the investment – although with great risk – sounded like it could be feasible.

Prohibition in the USA throughout the 1920s meant that there was a high demand for foreign alcohol – particularly spirits. The illegal manufacture of liquor in the USA had been ubiquitous despite an ongoing crackdown by law enforcers. Prohibition of alcohol was almost considered a lost game, and reform was just around the corner. The idea was that as the Reformation Bill was still in its early stages in Washington D.C. There would be a relaxing of policing governing the import of alcohol from overseas. Padgett's contact in Cunard could, for a small anonymous fee, guarantee access to one large container onboard the Cunard ships out of Liverpool for each crossing to Boston and New York. On the surface, it would be for the movement of textiles manufactured in the mills of Macclesfield. That's what the export papers would read. In truth, the fabric material would be used as mere padding around crates of English gin, Russian vodka, Scottish whiskey and French brandy. Backhanders to the underpaid stevedores in Liverpool and the US ports could soon be made to ease the cargo through any of the port checks and onwards to the US distributors. Padgett had liked this idea at the start but had no understanding of the murky underworld in the

America to be able to manage the distribution. Mob rules was an area that he knew Edgar Fitch and the Sons of Strangeways knew all about, but would they be interested?

It was 30th January 1929, John Padgett was in a public house called the Railway Tavern in Stockport, he had a cheque for £10,000 in his pocket, but he had no intention of passing that to Edgar Fitch, as firstly, it would nearly bankrupt him, and secondly his export idea had great potential and it could make both Fitch and himself, by his rough calculations, about £1000 clear profit per Transatlantic crossing. With five Cunard crossings per month, the debt from the loss of the pipeline contract, would be cleared in two months. After that, he was going to suggest an even split of profits with Fitch.

The landlord ushered Padgett through a side door away from the public bar into a private area. Padgett nervously followed the landlord through the door. He immediately recognised the burly man with the facial scar who had handed him the reminder note at the Trentabank dam wall two weeks earlier. He was standing to the side of Edgar Fitch. The sight of this hardened criminal puffing on a Cuban cigar made Padgett twitchy, perhaps he should just hand him the cheque and exit quickly.

"Hello, Mr. Padgett. I hope you have some good news for me?" Fitch said as a way of introduction. "It's been too long already and my boys were very, very disappointed about the pipeline contract."

"Me too," blustered Padgett, taking a seat facing Fitch. "I

have your money, but I also have an alternative proposition I would like to share with you, as it's an opportunity to make much more money than the paltry value of the pipeline contract."

Fitch took a long draw on his cigar and blew the smoke directly into Padgett's face. "Go on, I'm listening, you have two minutes to convince me."

Padgett outlined the idea at pace. Using the network of midlands and north west canal waterways to collect together and transport the liquor and textiles. Packing the crate in Manchester's docks before using the new Ship Canal to take it to Liverpool's docks and transferring it to the Cunard ship. Padgett's time was almost up – the tell-tale beads of sweat on his forehead indicated the stress was building. He finished with a summary of how much money this venture could make and finally made his offer, "May I suggest that we look at a 50/50 split on the profits for such a business – I think that this would be more than fair." Padgett took a breath.

Fitch smiled, enjoying quite how uncomfortable Padgett was looking. He paused before sighing: "Mr. Padgett, thank you for your offer, you have clearly been thinking hard about how you need to make up for the disappointing start to our relationship. He paused and took another long drag. "I suggest that we look at a 60/40 split in my favour, but only after you've proven this can work by giving me my £10,000 first within those first two months of operation, and then we continue, in partnership. I will help by providing you with US distribution through my network from the start and support in packing the product."

Padgett winced – but accepted that he was not in a strong

bargaining position right now. He was feeling increasingly optimistic that this could actually work, such that even the loss that he'd take in the early stages due to Fitch's demands would be palatable in the medium and long term.

CHAPTER 21 - *PUBLIC SCHOOL*

It was early on a Saturday afternoon in mid-March, the earliest spring lambs were just appearing in the fields. Beth had just stepped off the second bus of the day at Bakewell's central bus station. She had become so concerned about the lack of correspondence from Charlie that she had decided to entrust her story to her friend – Moll Brampton. Moll had responded with incredulity as she could not believe that Beth had kept this intriguing love story from her for so long. "You simply must go to Charlie's school and find out what's happened," was Moll's clear directive. Beth had been stewing over why Charlie had been so unresponsive to her letters when she should not have left it two months before finding an opportunity to see him face-to-face. The following Saturday, she had walked to Macclesfield early in the morning, caught a bus to Buxton, and then onwards to Bakewell.

"Excuse me, where would I find Hoarwithy school?" she asked a couple of middle-aged women who were just entering a butcher's shop.

One of the women answered, "Just follow the river path along for about two miles and you'll come upon the school's boathouse. The main school building is up on the hill behind it. Just a warning, though, they don't like single girls up there." She winked at Beth and laughed with her friend.

Beth set off along the river path toward the direction that the two shoppers had pointed. It was a lovely spring day and the crocuses and snowdrops were appearing in the woods. Mallards and moorhens were busying themselves in the river reeds, collecting material in preparation for the nesting season. The rolling hills around Bakewell seemed very tame in comparison to the wilder moors above Langley, Beth thought. She felt more at home in the wild.

Forty minutes later, she saw a large, part-stone, part-wooden building right on the edge of the river, and some young boys were outside painting two rowing boats in the maroon colours of Hoarwithy, supervised by an older boy who was busily trying to ensure the youngsters got more paint on the boat rather than themselves. The elder boy noticed Beth and tipped his cap politely. Beth nodded her head in acknowledgement and walked on past the only footpath available to her. She entered a grove of overhanging beech and horse chestnut trees, at the end of which a large number of playing fields stretched out before her. The school's Saturday sports day was happening and the maroon of Hoarwithy was playing against a team in royal blue colours. It was the rugby season, and each age group seemed to be playing at the same time, meaning that there were hundreds of boys scattered across the grounds. Most spectators appeared around the first team pitch with the eldest boys playing nearest the school buildings. With this number of people, it was easy for Beth to blend in as she walked around the younger boys' pitches towards the first team pitch. She knew that Charlie would not be playing rugby, that was not his calling, but she did know where he just might be.

For the rugby season the cricket scorebox conveniently converted itself to show updates of the first team rugby score. And there was Charlie standing adjacent to the wooden structure with a box of tin numbers ready to hook on next to the 'Visitors' or the 'Hoarwithy' nameplate. He was chatting away to a friend of his, both had their prefect blazers and school caps on. Beth was relieved to see him, having not known where he'd been for the last month, but she was also incredibly angry to see him looking so nonchalant performing such a menial task and joking with his schoolmate – looking like he didn't really have a care in the world.

She was only about ten yards away when Charlie spotted her. His expression changed instantly, he pushed his friend to one side and rushed towards her. His embrace crushed Beth, but the passionate strength of it was also reassuring in its tenderness. Charlie guided her to the back of the scorebox and, in passing, his bewildered friend said, "Monty, can you take charge of the scoring? I need a few minutes."

Now out of sight, Charlie kissed Beth with such ferocity Beth lost her breath and pushed him away: "Charlie – hold on!" she said, laughing and wiping away her tears of joy that had appeared the instant that she felt Charlie's arms enveloping her so firmly. "Why haven't you been writing to me?"

Charlie, still holding her close, replied, "Why haven't you?" And then realised what had been happening. He held her closely again, "Bloody hell, I know what's happened. Our letters have been intercepted somehow by my father. What a bastard he is! He's still wanting to control me, control us."

Beth recalled the way that Henry Aspinall had nearly throttled her on that dark December day following the Langley village meeting. She shivered, "He is a bastard. Why is he so horrible?" Charlie had no answer as a large cheer went up on the playing field – Hoarwithy had scored a try.

Monty appeared around the corner and coughed politely, "Excuse me, Aspinall, how many points is it for a try?" All three of them laughed at Monty's inability to have taken on the finer points of scoring despite having been Charlie's reserve scorer for several seasons.

"Don't worry, I'll do it!" Charlie said. As they waited for the attempted conversion, Charlie introduced Beth to Monty referring to her as his girlfriend. Monty looked highly impressed, if not a little disappointed.

The rugby games finished and the spectating parents and players retired to changing rooms and the dining hall for tea and cakes. Charlie excused himself from his normal prefect duties – ensuring all of the younger boys had showered and changed back into full school uniforms.

He and Beth walked across the now empty playing fields towards the tree grove and the boathouse beyond. They passed the painting party on the way back up, with the young boys having what looked like maroon war paint all over their hands and faces. The supervising prefect gave Charlie a look of exasperation as they passed by and added a sly wink when he saw Charlie's female companion.

The two of them sat down on the boathouse dock, looking out across the river. Alone, other than the brooding waterfowl and the occasional trout rising to the surface to snare a fly. Beth again thought how totally different this schooling landscape was to that that she had back in Macclesfield. Could they overcome the differences of their upbringing? Could they survive the aggressive and evil acts of Charlie's father? To what extent would he go in his effort to halt their relationship? These were all questions she kept to herself. Just then she was content just being in Charlie's arms and able to be held by him. Charlie was thinking in a more practical way – how could the two of them maintain a relationship without his father knowing and possibly making it even worse for the two of them?

"Beth, given the circumstances at home, I can't make it to Cheshire for Easter. How about every two weeks we meet here?" He continued his stream of thought, "Without my parent's permission, I am not allowed to leave the school grounds, but on Saturdays, I'm sure we can do what we've just done and you may even be able to come up to the cricket scorebox again, and this time I'll introduce you to my very good friend – Alistair Grainger – the old man who thinks he can help me with a university bursary."

Beth looked at a ring of concentric circles that had just appeared in the river. "Of course, I can come to you, that's easy to manage. I've told Moll Brampton about us, and I'm sure she can help make sure there is a cover story for my absence. I trust her."

They talked easily for half an hour about what had been happening in Langley and how Will and she had rescued Mew from a flooded Nessit Farm. "And where's Mew now?" he inquired.

"He's at the Post Office, and Will proudly comes home every evening with my newspaper, magazines and a new tally of how many mice Mew has caught. Mr. Ricketts has even suggested renting Mew out to anyone else in the village who has a mouse infestation." They laughed, realising how good it made them both feel and, in part, making up for the many days and weeks not knowing why their written communication links had been severed.

Over the coming months, Beth and Charlie met many times, often at the boathouse but also on occasions at the cricket scorebox. Alistair Grainger was delighted to meet Beth and recognise such a bright and ambitious girl and a wonderful partner for Charlie – who he had grown very close to – and would miss once the cricketing term was over. In fact, on the odd occasion when Beth had been questioned by several patrolling teachers as to why she was in the Hoarwithy School grounds on a Saturday, the agreement was that she was Mr. Grainger's grand-niece and simply paying him a visit.

The fact that no more letters were being written had prompted Angus Jordan – the caretaker whose job was to intercept any correspondence – into thinking that his job was done, and so he wrote to Henry Aspinall to ask for his additional money. On receiving this news, Aspinall was delighted and had quickly reached the assumption that the relationship was over and that there might be a chance of Charles returning to the family fold once the final School term was over. Little did Aspinall Senior realise that university applications had already been submitted and both Beth and Charlie had applied to attend Durham University – Beth to study Politics and Sociology, and Charlie to study Law. Charlie had received confirmation of funding from the Hoarwithy Alumni bursary fund and a strongly supporting reference from his Deputy Headmaster – Mr. McCrory.

CHAPTER 22 - *DYNAMITE*

Gustav Coccini had opted out of the slightly higher-paid work on the pipeline to stay at the quarry, he realised that there were fewer eyes on him on Teggs Nose and that provided more opportunities for him to increase the size of his explosives stash. Gustav had only used the dynamite once for personal gain since he'd started to divert some away from the Quarry store to build his own private store, hidden in weatherproof boxes around the hillside. A few years ago, a fellow Sicilian immigrant living in Hazel Grove had identified a bank over in Marple that was undergoing a refurbishment. Some of Gustav's other Italian contacts had suggested that it would be an easy target, and so he had partnered with one of them.

Following some reconnaissance by his friend, they had gone to the bank on a Thursday night, ahead of the normal Friday pay day in town. His friend had sworn that the bank would be easy to access and the safe would be easy to blow with Gustav's skill with dynamite. Indeed, both these facts were true, but the safe contained only £35 in cash. The error made was that the Italians had forgotten that there was a Wakes Week holiday and payday was not until the week after.

The debacle caused a split in the friendship, and Gustav swore to work alone in any future money-making scheme. The irony of the whole affair was that Jack Moat had been the bank clerk in Marple, and he was fired as the bank considered he was the least experienced amongst the staff and would take the fall for the bank's lack of security systems. For the first two months of Jack's employment at Teggs Nose, Gustav was convinced that Jack had been sent there to monitor him as a suspect in the robbery. As time passed, it became clear there was no link, and Gustav felt some sympathy for Jack, given that he had been directly responsible for Jack getting fired and having to restart his career outside of banking.

After the heavy financial loss Gustav had taken at the Bollington bare-knuckle boxing event, he had grown closer to the local Gypsy community, recognising that these nomads were a little like his Sicilian roots where he was on the periphery of society needing to work in shadow industries to make any kind of a living. He particularly liked the leader of the Gypsy group – Ivan Boksic. Every few weeks, he would head down to the canal basin near Macclesfield and meet up with Boksic at their encampment. The caravans and horses were allowed in a field adjoining the canal, where the Gypsies had a legitimate business moving coal by barge up from the surface cold fields down in North Staffordshire. Boksic knew how to maintain a low enough profile with local Macclesfield businesses not to provoke, yet he also knew when and where to take opportunities. Boksic recognised Gustav Coccini as a man he could work with, and they had both been burnt badly by the Manchester mob that had rigged the result in Bollington, plus they were threatening to move in on some of their East Cheshire protection business.

Ivan Boksic and Gustav were gathered around a campfire at the Macclesfield basin, chatting and sharing a bottle of port. It might have been the way that the rum had loosened Gustav's thinking, but he felt it the right time to share with Boksic that he had in his possession a large amount of dynamite and if there were any opportunities to use it on any money-making scheme – especially if it was at the cost of Henry Aspinall and Joshua Padgett, then he would be happy to oblige for a share in the profit. Boksic looked at the port bottle – recognising it to be one of the last ones from the consignment that his gang had stolen – at knifepoint – from an Aspinall Company barge just before the Bollington event. An idea struck him, why should they not take it a step further and blow up one of Aspinall's barges and then employ an elaborate blackmail to guarantee that no more harm would come to the Aspinall Company if they paid a protection fee? He kept it to himself for now, but the seed was planted, and Boksic was the kind of man who would store up those ideas and revisit when the time was deemed right.

CHAPTER 23 - *FAREWELL PICNIC*

It was now early Summer, and the lambing season was over. The Lovatts had settled into their new farm over on Bosley Cloud, despite the move of their heavily pregnant flock from Langley, they had had a very good number of lambs with an unusually high number of twins and triplets being born. Plus, the additional flock that the Lovatts had inherited from Sid Bayley meant that their flock was now over 1000, this provided Thomas Whetton with some additional rent for the tenancy, which Nat was happy to pay, but Whetton had refused the additional rent for the first year. His benevolence had not been for the sake of money but more for the opportunity to rebalance social justice and irritate Henry Aspinall.

Silas, from his look-out location on Teggs Nose, was able to see the gradual rising waters of the reservoir, the highest point of Nessit farm – the chimney stack – was now underwater, and he estimated that it would be around five more weeks until Trentabank Farm – which stood on higher ground - was totally submerged. Appropriately, the track between the two farms was called Dark Lane, and Silas watched daily as Dark Lane slowly vanished beneath the rising waters. Gwen suggested to Silas that they mark the day that the Lovatt's old Farmhouse disappears forever by inviting them over to watch from the platform on the dam where Aspinall had so pompously announced the opening five months previous. Silas thought that this would be a good idea, and he also thought of Thomas Whetton and what support he had given Martha and Nat. He decided that he should also send an invitation to Whetton, not really expecting him to respond.

It was a hot Sunday and the Ledgers and Lovatts met after the Langley Chapel service and walked up to the dam. There were three people already there – Jack and Melissa were there as was Thomas Whetton. They all smiled to see the group forming – greetings were exchanged. Silas, aided by Will and Beth, had been carrying a large picnic basket and the Lovatts had a couple of flagons of cider and ginger ale to toast the final farewell. "Thank you for coming, Mr. Whetton," Silas said as he shook Whetton's hand.

"It's a pleasure, Silas. I could not possibly miss an opportunity to join the Ledgers now that they are my best tenants. Their sheep seem to be multiplying by the day!" Wharton quipped. "And what's more, Jack here has just agreed to give my freight barge business some more work by bringing in all of the new pipework for the Hollins pipeline."

Jack looked proudly over at Silas, "That's right Sledge. Mr.

Whetton's barges have much greater capacity as they're proper freight carriers."

Thomas added, "That's good news, especially as Aspinall doesn't have these barges. I'll feel like I'm earning good money from him for his pipeline project!" The three men chuckled.

"Look everyone!" Beth exclaimed pointing towards the reservoir, just the very top of the hay barn at Trentabank farm was still visible. It was a poignant moment, and the men of the group took off their caps. Everyone stared towards the dark waters and stood silently for a moment. It was apt that Nat broke the silence.

"Now, who wants some scrumpy cider?" he announced. The somber moment was broken, and Melissa and Martha helped pour drinks to toast the ever-rising water.

The pipeline work had begun three months earlier, and Jack had been manically involved in the new project. He and Silas had agreed with John Croker on how the quarry workforce would be divided, and Jack took the lead in project managing the pipeline laying team. He'd also taken Battalion, the powerful shire horse, down from Teggs Nose and he was now stabled in Gurnett, where Whettons' barges brought the heavy ten-foot-long clay pipes. A small pulley system had been erected on the aqueduct and the pipes were offloaded and lowered on to a cart that Battalion then hauled up the hill to where the labourers were laying the groundwork. This was helped by Don Hough's brand-new tractor with an excavation tool, which John Croker had rented as part of the Hollins farmer's compensation agreement.

The operation seemed to be going according to plan, and the pipeline was on target to be complete by the time the full opening ceremony was due to happen up at Trentabank when the Duke of Gloucester and his royal guest would appear in the early Autumn.

Jack was weary, but very happy, as his work was always brightened by the appearance of Melissa at the end of the day. He supervised the final pipework unloading and the two of them would bring Battalion back to the stables in Gurnett before regularly retiring to the local Inn for whatever pie was on offer that day or simply walking together to Melissa's home and her parents, where Jack had become a firm favourite with her mother.

Very occasionally, Henry Aspinall would accompany John Croker to the site of the pipeline. Croker was careful to get a full briefing ahead of time from Jack. This was obvious to Aspinall as whenever he asked a question on detail, Croker deferred to Jack rather than answer it himself. Aspinall recognised in Jack a highly able individual, and one that his son Charles could have learned a lot from.

The fact that Charles was intent on severing his ties completely from his father was hurting Aspinall badly. Rather than enter the family business and move through an apprenticeship as he had done with his father, Charles had applied to university supported by means that Aspinall did not know about. He had begun to believe that his son was a lost cause. But may be, in time, Charles may return to the family fold, and a legal qualification might help the family business. Right now, it was crucial that the Hollins pipeline was completed by the date of the Royal opening. Failure to do this would be a severe embarrassment to the Water Board, the Cheshire Chamber of Commerce, but, in particular, Henry Aspinall. This could not happen.

CHAPTER 24 - *VENDETTA*

Will Ledger was fifteen years of age and, unlike his sister Beth, had lost interest in academics. His real passion was being an entrepreneur. He'd made some good pocket money from the chores that he had been doing for Percy Ricketts at the Post Office, but Silas was keen that he should pick up new skills, and what better place than where he could keep an eye on him – the Teggs Nose quarry. If Jack wasn't so manic with the pipeline, and spending every other waking hour courting Melissa, it would have been good to get Will mentored by him.

It was agreed with Mr. Ricketts that after his paper round, Will would spend the mornings at the quarry and the afternoons at the Post Office. Will enjoyed being outside, he had his father's sturdy build and could already strike a sledgehammer as hard as most men other than his dad. He particularly loved the occasions that he was allowed to join his father at the Setter Dog Inn with some of the other quarrymen. He loved listening to Fred Needles and his endless cricketing stories. At the quarry, he was paired up with Robin Brampton and Andy Soutter – two quarrymen who were also involved in a poaching sideline – but were utterly trustworthy in Silas' eyes. Silas had split his team into four units of three men, and he trusted Andy and Robin to show Will all of the skills needed to operate safely in a quarry.

During a rock-crushing session, and despite wearing all the right headgear, a splinter of rock shot up and caught Brampton in the side of the head. It was a minor injury, but required an overnight stay in Macclesfield Infirmary. Will noticed that Soutter was looking particularly distressed at his good friend's injury.

"Don't worry, Andy," Will said. "I'm sure Robin appreciates a night's rest in the hospital!"

Andy replied, "It's not Robin I'm worried about, it's the large order we have for mid-summer celebrations."

"What!" Will looked puzzled.

"We must go out and trap some rabbits tonight as we have an order for seven, and we've promised Dick Avery that we'd have them for him by the morning," Andy said, sharing his thought aloud with Will.

Will knew that the two of them were involved in poaching, everyone in the village knew, he took the opportunity of learning a new skill.

"I can help tonight, Andy, go on. Give me a chance!"

Andy looked at him and smiled. "No – your dad would kill me," he replied.

"Honest," Will said, "he won't know a thing, and it will just be a one-off before Robin is back. And I won't take any pay."

This final offer was too much for Andy to resist, and they agreed to meet at Saddlers Way at midnight.

Will was excited that evening. He had completed his chores for Mr. Ricketts, picked up Mew from a house down the road that needed the cat's expert mousing skills, and returned to the cottage with Beth's reading material for the night – yesterday's copy of the Financial Times. He went to bed at 9 pm but was nervous about falling asleep and missing the rendezvous. He got out of bed at 11 pm, tiptoed past his sleeping sister, still clutching the FT, and quietly went down the stairs, picked up a coat and went out of the house. He was down the street and halfway up to Saddlers Way when he realised that he was wearing the rather oversized coat of his father. No worries, he'd return it before dawn, he thought.

It was almost a full moon and as it was close to mid-summer, the night was not too dark. Andy was already at the agreed meeting point, as he'd started early and laid a number of snares across a stretch of grassland and bilberry bushes. "Hi Will, it looks like a good night for rabbiting. I need you to skirt around the hill and then come down the hill when you hear my owl sound." Andy pursed his lips and made a very authentic-sounding owl noise. "The rabbits will be out grazing on the grass, when they see and hear you approaching, they'll bolt for holes. I have set traps, so it should be a big haul, we may even get all we need in one go."

Will nodded with enthusiasm, that sounded easy enough, and he took off up the hill. En route, he passed near the tree that, many months previous he had seen Gustav Coccini hide a box with detonation cords inside. He detoured to see if the root still hid the box. It did, he opened the box and there was more cord inside. He took three cords and put them deep in his coat pocket. For what reason, he was unsure but thought that he'd take them anyway. He continued up the hill and crouched, waiting for the owl hoot.

Twit-twoo, came the rather human bird sound.

Will started moving down the hill, and from all directions, he saw rabbits scattering to find their sanctuaries. He heard enough unnatural sounds to suggest that there had been quite some carnage. He got back to where Andy was standing. "How many do you think we've got? There were hundreds out there!" Will exclaimed.

"I think we've probably got half a dozen, there were a dozen traps laid." Andy started off back up the hill, followed by Will, Andy knew exactly where he'd laid the traps and checked each one. The first two were empty, but the next three had rabbits in them. They were either already dead or with a quick snap of the neck, Andy dispatched them. Will put the dead rabbits in a sack Andy had brought with him. They counted eight – it was a good night for the amateur poacher.

"Well done, Will – we've done well – Robin will be happy. Especially as he's had all night to chat up the nurses, too!" Will smiled, happy with his contribution. "Here you go," Andy said, reaching into the bag and extracting a medium-sized rabbit. "Take that home to your mum, but don't you dare tell her where you got it from." Will took the still-warm body and put it into a deep pocket in his overcoat. The two-headed in separate directions. Andy towards the Setter Dog Inn and a grinning Dick Avery and Will back to Langley village and his bed.

Joshua Padgett's liquor export business had started

remarkably smoothly. He had negotiated a good deal with some premium spirit distributors in the Midlands and shipped the cases via canal to Macclesfield. Boxes of freshly manufactured textiles were added to the cargo and the barges then started to arrive in Manchester, where Fitch's team took over. They repackaged everything into Cunard shipping containers, with the textiles positioned all around the liquor to give the impression of it simply being a textile consignment. They sealed it with a fake customs stamp that they had procured by way of a hefty bribe at Liverpool docks. Many of the stevedores employed to load the containers on ships at Manchester Ship Canal's main depot and Liverpool docks had previous connections with criminal gangs and so were used to turning a blind eye. It seemed as if Fitch had been true to his word and had developed agreements with New York and Boston-based crime syndicates who paid Padgett's asking price.

The first two months passed without a hitch, and this meant that the £10,000 profit that Padgett owed Fitch was fully cleared. So, it was with this happy fact in mind that he entered the Old Boy's Club in Macclesfield, flush with the knowledge that all he needed to do was maintain this momentum, and he'd start to see his own bank balance rise rapidly. He spotted Henry Aspinall at the bar discussing something with the doorman. "Hello Henry, I haven't seen you in here for a while. How's that lovely family of yours?" he said with a disingenuous smile on his face, knowing quite well that Florence Aspinall was an alcohol-fuelled depressive, and Charles Aspinall had decided to forge his own destiny away from his father, who had disinherited him.

Ignoring Padgett's snide remark, Aspinall shot back a

brusque retort – "Very well, thank you, Joshua." And immediately changed the subject, "And my barges seem to be keeping your new business afloat very well. Am I charging you enough?"

Padgett looked at him hard with a furrowed brow. *What did Aspinall know about the liquor export business he has with Fitch?*

He decided to play the game a bit harder. He replied: "They seem to be keeping up to my expectations in terms of delivery, but of course, I could use Thomas Whetton's barges, he seems to be able to deliver the Hollins pipeline project to you. Can you not do that yourself?"

Aspinall decided to ignore the goading from Padgett, he was quite happy with the fact that the larger freight barges that Whetton owned were the only sensible means of getting the pipes up the canal from the manufacturers.

Suddenly, Phillip Broadhead burst through the door. "Have you heard?" he said loudly enough for the whole room to stand still. Before anyone could reply, he continued without drawing breath, "There's been an explosion in a canal lock near Kidsgrove; one person's died, and several are injured."

Both Aspinall and Padgett looked at each other, "Do you have any more details?" pleaded Aspinall, thinking immediately about the fact that it could be one of his boats.

"I don't know any more details. I overheard a policeman tell the Station master at Macclesfield a number of them are heading down to Kidsgrove now." Broadhead finished his news update and demanded a drink, happy in the knowledge that, for once, he'd commanded the full attention of the Club. Too often, he was in the shadow of the more successful members of the Club, who generally commanded quicker information links than himself.

"Let's get down there now," Aspinall suggested to an ashen-faced Padgett. Whatever the situation, a closed canal system was bad for trade. "My chauffeur is outside; he can drive us down in the Daimler in an hour."

The chauffeur drove quickly, and Aspinall's estimation of an hour was correct. There was little conversation in the car as both men tried to calculate their own possible damage scenarios and the impact that it could have on their businesses. They could see a plume of smoke rising from about five miles away, and as they got closer, the distinct sound of fire engines was to be heard blasting water as sirens blared. The police cordon had been set at 100 yards, but a large crowd had gathered. It was difficult to make out, but it looked like a barge was still on fire in the lock itself and was listing heavily to one side.

Padgett and Aspinall ignored the safety cordon and moved quickly toward the nearest senior-looking policeman.

"Sir, that could well be my boat!" yelled Aspinall above the sound of the sirens.

"And that could be my bloody cargo!" added Padgett.

The Aspinall Company logo could quite clearly be seen on the burning hull of the barge. An inferno was raging on board fuelled by the crates of spirits that seemed to be regularly exploding and spraying more liquid flame around the whole of the scene. Thick, acrid smoke billowed from the engine room of the barge as it started to list further. On the quayside, there were firemen being attended to by ambulance staff. A little further back there was a single police officer standing by the form of a body lying on the floor, covered by a sheet.

A senior police officer approached them. "Gentlemen, can you come this way, please? I am Chief Inspector Milner of the Congleton and Kidsgrove Constabulary. I need to ask you some questions."

Shell-shocked, Padgett and Aspinall walked with the policeman across to a car park where a tent had been erected to act as a make-shift incident centre.

Gustav Coccini and Ivan Boksic were in a nearby inn, toasting their success. A large explosive had been placed above the waterline by one of the young gypsy boys. It was unfortunate that the lockkeeper had spotted it just as the lock gate had closed and was investigating it closely. The explosion had killed him instantly, but also shattered the stern of the barge. The inflammatory component of the alcohol was sufficient for fire to quickly spread across the deck, badly burning the two-armed security guards and three barge men from the Aspinall Company, they'd thrown themselves into the water and were lucky to be dragged out by some brave passers-by.

Coccini and Boksic had stationed themselves on the hill overlooking the lock system and could not see the detail, but celebrated in the likely scenes of devastation that the size of the fireball had produced.

"I warned them that fire and sinking would haunt them,"

said Coccini gleefully, referring to the anonymous notes that he had sent both Padgett and Aspinall on the same day following their pompous treachery at the boxing match in Bollington.

Boksic sniggered, "And it looks like they'll be more trouble for Padgett from Edgar Fitch, too, if that alcohol doesn't arrive in Manchester." Boksic knew that there were two consignments of alcohol on two consecutive barges, this was the method Aspinall had employed to make any piracy in the isolated Staffordshire stretch less easy. One was now a wreck, and the other one was a sitting duck queued up behind the damaged lock. His gang was in place, ready to strike this second barge later and steal a few crates of premium liquor.

"There is an additional bonus that we had not considered," said a delighted Coccini. "The freight barge carrying the pipe lengths to the Hollins will now also be delayed, setting back the completion date of the pipeline considerably," he laughed. Coccini couldn't care less about the pipeline or the fact that half the quarry workers depended on it for their livelihoods. He was making enough money now from his extracurricular activities, and his quarry job was purely a means for accumulating his weapon of trade – dynamite. He smiled with the thought of the public humiliation that both Padgett – on behalf of the Water Authority, and Aspinall – as the main land owner and the man responsible for laying the pipes in time for the royal visit would suffer in the press. How vilified would they be in the local community? He looked over at Boksic smugly and toasted the successful outcome once more. Boksic was content, but the humanity in him did wonder about the impact the death of the lock master would have on the young boy who'd laid the explosives. The Gypsy family bond was strong, and he vowed to ensure the lad was looked after well. Boksic also thought that the death would mean that further blackmail might be too risky in the near future. Although, ironically, more companies might be willing to pay him for greater protection.

CHAPTER 25 - *SUSPECTS*

Aspinall and Padgett completed their interview in Kidsgrove. A large question mark remained over the fact that Aspinall had no license to carry such large quantities of alcohol on board his barges, and Padgett had no license to supply alcohol at all. But this was the least of their problems, and they knew that a few words with their close friends within the Cheshire constabulary would see them clear. There were a number of more pressing matters to attend to. Padgett had the worry about the repercussions of not being able to fulfill the delivery of the alcohol consignment to Fitch. Aspinall had lost an uninsured barge plus all the associated revenue through the loss in transportation for a considerable time until the lock gate was fixed, and the partially sunken barge wreck removed. The major issue being that there would be a serious delay on the pipeline laying project.

Who was behind the explosion? Both men wanted retribution. Now was not the time to exact any sort of blame against each other. Who else could it be?

On returning to Macclesfield, Detective Inspector Cooper of the town's force was summoned to Joshua Padgett's office on Duke Street. Henry Aspinall was also present. "Cooper, we need your help in this mess over at Kidsgrove," Padgett opened the meeting directly.

"To be specific," added Aspinall. "We need you to stay very close to the Kidsgrove investigation and make sure that the licenses for the carriage and export of premium liquor are not a factor."

D.I. Cooper was a seasoned professional in the Police force and had for many years recognised that there were certain people that he needed to ensure were 'looked after' in the community. Padgett and Aspinall were two such people who could make his last year before retirement very uncomfortable if he failed their request. They had sponsored his membership of the Old Boy's Club in Macclesfield and paid for several golfing trips to exclusive resorts. This was payback time. "Of course, Gentlemen, I trained with the Chief Inspector in Kidsgrove, and I am sure he will come to me to check details through. I will confirm that all business matters are compliant and issue back-dated licenses, if necessary." One of Cooper's regular paid informants was also a master forger, and falsifying documents was very straightforward. He added, "The Kidsgrove investigation will be into the explosives themselves, as it was this that caused the death of one of their canal workers." Cooper looked over his shoulder during the last sentence to see if any of Padgett's staff were within earshot. They were not. "One question I have for you both." Cooper continued, "Who would have a motive to attack both of your businesses at the same time, or was that coincidence?"

Aspinall was sitting on the velvet couch. He stood

suddenly, arousing the attention of the other two men. He pulled from his pocket a small folded piece of paper from his wallet. It had been there for a while. It was the betting slip with the words *'Remember Titanic'* in red ink. He laid it out on the desk. Cooper and Aspinall stared at it. Pointing at the note, Aspinall asked, "I received this note back in the springtime. I didn't think anything more of it at the time, but could it have been a threat?"

Aspinall and Cooper were suddenly aware of Padgett's reaction. He was gasping and frantically opened his desk drawer and rummaged around inside it. Eventually, he found what he was looking for. He pulled out a similar betting slip and laid it next to the first. It read *'Water & Fire'*. The three men stared at the red lettering. Why would Padgett and Aspinall receive such anonymous forewarnings of what had just happened in Kidsgrove – a sinking of a boat and a destructive fire in the canal? Why were both notes written on betting slips and in red ink?

D.I. Cooper stated the obvious words that Aspinall and Padgett had already deduced. "Whoever sent these notes must have been responsible for the incident". Cooper carefully pocketed the two notes as evidence. "Quite clearly, you are both being targeted, and I'd like both of you to give me a list of people who might have a motive, and I will discuss how I can get my team here in Macclesfield to start the interview process. We need to control this carefully as it is a murder investigation."

Henry Aspinall walked home that evening, he needed to clear his head and he needed time to think clearly about who might he have upset sufficiently to commit this act against his property and reputation. He had already asked John Croker to estimate how much time would be lost to the pipeline project – his main concern. The good news was that Jack Moat had already come up with a plan whereby the lifting equipment at Gurnett could be deployed onto one of Whetton's freight barges and used to collect the pipe lengths at a point near Kidsgrove where a service tributary of the main canal ran. This could enable pipes to continue to be delivered to Gurnett, although in smaller numbers. The estimate for the entire repair of the lock and removal of his wrecked barge would be about a month and around £30,000 – a cost shared between the Water Authorities and businesses that used the canal at Kidsgrove. The cost of the barge replacement would be a further £30,000, and that's before the loss of income from other canal trade that he supplied. If Padgett was desperate, it might be that he would need to employ Whetton's barges to shift his alcohol through to the Manchester warehouses. Or Padgett might need to use the Gypsies who also had access to freight barges. The Gypsies – he thought – could they be responsible for all of this? No, surely not, they were involved in simple piracy and looting. Terrorism involving explosives was too much for them. He had also ruled out Edgar Fitch and his Sons of Strangeways – they were benefitting nicely from Padgett's business idea coming to fruition, so they would not want anything to halt the money flow. So, who else, and what was the relevance of the weird messages of forewarning?

He entered the Aspinall manor house on Ridge Hill, still twisting the whole sorry affair around in his mind. Florence was in the hallway and seemed to be humming happily to herself. "What's wrong with you?" Aspinall said sharply.

Assuming her joyful countenance had been supplied by her favourite Beefeater gin.

"I've heard from Charles and you'll not be happy with this!" She sang back to him, seemingly goading him.

"What have you heard?" Henry spat back. Since forbidding any communication with his son from her, he knew that someone in the household had been providing her with an open channel to pass messages. He had suspected that it was Archie Talbot, who, despite being sacked from his gamekeeping job, was still living as a lodger at the Gatehouse where Arthur Brice lived.

"What have you heard?" he repeated in a more forceful manner.

The next information sent a chill through him. "Charles is going to Durham; Charles is going to Durham." She smiled at him and added, "He's been accepted at University to start this year." Florence was genuinely delighted for her son, as this was what he wanted. However, she knew that this was the last thing her husband wanted.

Henry Aspinall could take no more. Upon hearing the news, he picked up a Chinese antique vase and flung it at her. It missed, but Florence lost her balance in evading the projectile and slipped over. He bounded over to her and kicked her squarely in the ribs. The furore caused a maid to come into the hall, and she immediately screamed when she saw the master of the house stooping over his wife with hands around her neck. Florence was struggling to breathe, but she was able to hammer one more piece of information home that stopped Henry immediately and possibly saved her from being strangled.

"Beth Ledger is going to Durham University, too," she stammered between breaths.

Henry Aspinall dropped his wife. This final piece of information was simply too much. He rushed towards his office and slammed the door, but not before shrieking at the maid. "Pick up my damned, drunken wife, and put her to bed." Once in the office, he headed over to his spirits cabinet and, filled a grand tumbler with whiskey from a decanter and took a solid swig. He went over to the window and looked out. He could see across the valley to Teggs Nose. The tragic incident down in Kidsgrove was serious, but the loss of his son, was ten times more painful to Henry. Charles had had his head turned against his natural destiny by a young girl from the village. This betrayal will never be forgiven. He mouthed the words: *Silas Ledger – you will suffer for this!*

Joshua Padgett had also been calculating the size of the loss that the Kidsgrove incident would have on his business. He was also nervous about the delay in the pipeline project and possible repercussions, yet his more immediate concern was the flow of premium spirits to the Manchester depot and maintaining the relationship with Edgar Fitch, now that it had started so well and proven highly profitable. He knew that the news of the explosion would have reached Manchester by now, and he wanted to be proactive with Fitch. His calculations were that he had completely lost half of one full consignment in the explosion. He would struggle to claim for the loss of this from Aspinall, and the cargo was not exactly an insurable item given the nature of the export business. If the canal network was blocked for a month, then he would need to move his cargo by road up to the Manchester depots and to Fitch's responsibility. He estimated that this would set him back about two weeks and lose three consignments. He knew that he'd have to pay compensation and was gutted that just at the point he was earning a tidy profit out of the business, this had happened.

He picked up the telephone. "Good afternoon, is Edgar Fitch there, please," he spoke humbly, rehearsing the tone that he felt he would need to exhibit.

"This is he," came the unmistakable voice of the mob leader.

"Oh, hello Edgar, this is Joshua," Padgett said confidently, thinking that first names might help the personalised nature of the conversation.

"Joshua, who?" questioned Fitch in his deep monotone voice.

"Joshua Padgett," Padgett replied, becoming more flustered by the second.

"Hello, Mr. Padgett. I was expecting your call. I hear you've been having some fun down in Staffordshire." Fitch enquired.

"Yes, sir, but nothing we cannot sort out quickly. I will transport the textiles and liquor via road instead of canal – starting tomorrow. The canal will be closed for four weeks, and we will resume once the lock has been fully repaired and the sunken vessel removed." Padgett paused to hear if Fitch had anything to say. There was silence. Padgett continued nervously, "And we estimate there will be about three Cunard sailings missed." This was the key fact that he knew would cause Fitch to react, and react he did.

"Well, that's not acceptable, Mr. Padgett. My US distributors will need to be compensated, and that means I will need compensation, too."

Padgett sighed in despair. He realised protesting was no good, and he did not want any more visits from scar-faced gangsters. "Yes, Mr. . Fitch – I will compensate you fully for your losses. Will £5,000 suffice?"

"Did you say £15,000?" Fitch said playfully, "that's the amount that my US connections will want. Wall Street seems to be crashing, and everything is becoming inflated."

Padgett had heard that the US stock market was in crisis but felt that Fitch was mocking him with this figure. He sighed and resigned himself to the fact that it would be several months until he made any profit from what was his idea in the first place. He agreed that payment would happen in the next week. Padgett would have to take out a loan to cover this and lose even more money through interest payments. He almost shed a tear as he put the receiver down. In front of him on the desk, he imagined the two betting slip notes and the conversation he had had with Aspinall and D.I. Cooper earlier - 'Remember Titanic. Water & Fire.' Who was it that was responsible for this sick and very painful joke? When had he seen that type of betting slip before? He wracked his brains.

CHAPTER 26 - *EVIDENCE*

In confidence, Aspinall and Padgett had independently put down all of the people who merited looking into it because of the fact that they disliked either of them. D.I. Cooper was amazed about how many names there were in front of him. Many of the names were known to him and quite a few were fellow esteemed members of the Macclesfield Old Boy's Club and the North West Chamber of Commerce. There was even a name of a cricketing umpire that had alleged unfair play due to Aspinall having paid a groundsman to doctor a wicket in favour of Langley – the team he sponsored. Of course, the umpire was found to be in the wrong, and had his officiating certificate removed.

Some of the names included people who worked for the two men. D.I. Cooper gathered his team of junior detectives together and then divided them into pairs to take on the interviews and house searches where necessary. Two of the detectives headed towards Langley and started by interviewing members of the Aspinall household. They contacted the local Policeman in Sutton and Langley – P.C. Keith Aikin. Aikin knew everybody who lived in the valley and could very quickly provide a profile on all of the names.

Following quick interviews with Arthur Brice and Archie Talbot, the detectives started to get a picture of Henry Aspinall as a much-despised local figure.

P.C. Aikin had called together an impromptu meeting at the Old Kings Head in Gurnett of all of the Aspinall Quarry workers who had been re-deployed to lay the pipeline. The lack of new pipe deliveries meant they had plenty of free time. They were generally non-plussed by both Joshua Padgett and Henry Aspinall as there was still a mistrust of anyone to do with the Water Board and the whole sorry Sid Bayley affair was blamed upon the Trentabank project. Their bonus for pipeline work completion was also now looking in jeopardy because of the lack of pipes being delivered. This fact alone convinced the detectives that they needed to look elsewhere.

Another couple of detectives had headed down to the Macclesfield canal basin to talk to the gypsies. Generally, the law steered clear of gypsy encampments for fear of uncovering all sorts of petty crime that would end up providing them with too much workload and endless paperwork, after which the gypsy accused would likely get off on a technicality. The detectives approached the camp and were aware of a couple of hastily covered-up crates. Not wanting to antagonise anyone, they asked to see the gypsy leader. Ivan Boksic was in his caravan and came out holding the leather leash of a salivating beast of a dog. "Don't worry, boys, he's had his lunch," Boksic quipped. "What can I do you for?"

The police asked a couple of basic questions on whereabouts, and felt that this was sufficient to then beat a rapid retreat away from the glare of the werewolf. A young child who was sitting on top of a pile of crates gave them the finger as they left, completing the usual sense of appreciation that lawmakers had when visiting the canal basin.

Another pair of detectives conducted interviews around the Town Hall, where again there was a general sense of revulsion coming from anyone asked about Padgett in particular – as his role on the Water Board and other committees – made him a regular attender of public meetings and events.

D.I. Cooper went up to the Teggs Nose quarry with one of his junior constables to meet up with the team from the Aspinall Company, who were keeping the quarry orders fulfilled. On arriving at the quarry, he noted that there were three quarrymen working the rockface and three others working the cutting and crushing machinery. A further team was employed to shift rock fragments around the site. Two more men were in the store shed, checking some paperwork. "Who's in charge?" Cooper bellowed above the sound of the machinery.

Silas and Gustav were the two workers addressed. Upon seeing the uniform, Gustav froze for a moment. "Sledge, I've got to go and set these charges off now." The Sicilian said urgently and scurried off.

Silas turned to the policemen and said in his slow drawl, "I'm in charge of today's operation, how can I be of assistance?"

D.I. Cooper and the other officer walked over to the store shed and sheltered from the incessant drizzle inside. They introduced themselves. "Are you aware that there was a criminal incident down in Staffordshire yesterday, connected to the Aspinall Company, in which one man died?" asked the senior officer. "We are here making inquiries across all Henry Aspinall's interests to see if we can gather the information that will allow a greater understanding of the crime."

"I am aware that a barge blew up in Kidsgrove but know little else about the details. I don't get newspapers delivered at the time I need to be up here", Silas said in a matter-of-fact fashion. "But happy to help in any way I can."

"Just take us through a normal working day then, please," piped up the junior officer, taking out his notebook.

Silas turned to the shed door and started to point out the different sections of the quarry site where operations were in full display. He explained about the way that the shift work was managed and that half of the team, since March, had been re-deployed over to the Hollins pipeline work, where a colleague of his – Jack Moat – was leading the project. A bell sounded, and then an ear-splitting explosion happened, rocking the wooden structure of the shed.

"And that is a planned explosion to loosen further gritstone slabs on the rockface," Silas chuckled at the way the younger officer had jumped with fright and dropped his notebook.

Whilst retrieving his notebook from the stone floor, the junior officer asked, "Can you account for all of the quarrymen and their whereabouts yesterday, please?"

Silas looked at the work roster for the week and identified that he had a full complement of the workforce in attendance yesterday, other than Fred Needles, who had been asked to represent the Cheshire Quarrymen in a cricket match in Chester. He did not consider it worthy information to share that Gustav Coccini was absent but on standby, as his specialist skill was only needed whenever the gritstone seam became too hard to deal with using pick axes and sledge hammers. D.I. Cooper noticed that the rosters were written in red ink. Indeed, Silas was holding a red pen whilst he had been checking the attendance record. He kept that thought to himself for the moment but asked if he could take a copy of an old roster for their records.

That evening, all of the detectives regrouped at the station next to the town hall in Macclesfield. The debrief took place with D.I. Cooper, and he then telephoned Chief Inspector Milner down in Kidsgrove. He reported no significant findings on day one of the investigation, but he also learned from Milner that there had been several smaller robberies happening from barges now stationary, queuing up behind the closed lock gate. Both officers just felt that these were merely opporrtunistic and unrelated to the act of terrorism on the Aspinall barge. Probably just kids being kids. Resources were too stretched to follow up on these given the fact that the explosion had caused death and so had been escalated to a murder case.

Once the call had ended, D.I. Cooper was keen to follow up on one piece of possible evidence. He took out the quarry roster and placed it next to the two scribbled notes that had been received by Padgett and Aspinall a couple of months previous. Although the handwriting was different, the colour tone of the ink was a perfect match. He had agreed to debrief both Padgett and Aspinall at the Old Boy's Club, where they were all members. This way, any conversation could be off the record. The three men went into the cigar room and chose cigars from the Club humidor. Both of the businessmen were looking irritated, they had just heard that they had lost several more cases of premium spirits from the second Aspinall barge, as the cargo was being transferred to horse-drawn wagons. Their bargeman had employed local labourers to do the heavy lifting, and three of the crates had miraculously disappeared.

"Any news on the investigation, Cooper? Have you found anything of interest yet?" Padgett asked.

"Nothing really, gentlemen," the officer replied. He debriefed them both on the interviews that had happened so far, and Aspinall laughed hearing about the fact that Archie Talbot, his gamekeeper, had been interviewed.

Aspinall exclaimed, "That old goat! Archie Talbot is a worthless individual. I wish he'd been at the lock yesterday. Nobody would miss him."

D.I. Cooper was tempted to reply with the caustic remarks that Archie Talbot had made about Henry Aspinall. Having happily served two previous generations of the family, in his statement to the police, Archie Talbot believed that Henry was the devil incarnate.

"There is one small matter that I will follow up on, though," Cooper added finally. "When I was up at your quarry on Teggs Nose, I was speaking to Silas Ledger. He was using a red pen that seemed to match the ink colour of the two notes that you both received." He continued, "Is it common that red ink is used in quarrying for any reason? And who at the quarry would be using it?"

Aspinall responded, "That's interesting. I know that red ink is used in all quarry operations because of the amount of rock dust. The red ink stands out more, so most paperwork just happens to be in red. Let me telephone John Croker to check on who at Teggs would be most likely to use red ink."

Aspinall left the cigar room and headed over to the Club Administration office. He barged in and asked the receptionist to leave as he had a private call to make. John Croker picked up the receiver immediately, he was over at the Aspinall Company head office on the other side of Macclesfield. Knowing that his voice would be recognised, Aspinall launched straight in. "Mr. Croker, can you tell me who in the Company's employment at Teggs Nose Quarry is most likely to be producing any sort of paperwork," he asked.

Croker was on edge, there had been several occasions recently that he felt under immense pressure and felt that Aspinall was looking at any excuse to fire him. "Mr. Aspinall," Croker replied, delighted at least that he was able to prove that he was working well after hours that evening. "There are three people who are more likely to be involved in Teggs Nose paperwork. Jack Moat will be the main individual as he will be completing orders for gritstone and also managing the stock reports, and producing monthly accounts for me to check. However, Moat will not have been there for several months now as he is full-time on the Hollins pipeline project." He took a breath, happy that he could impress his boss with immediate and accurate knowledge. "The next person would be Silas Ledger, he has been managing the planning rosters of men now that they are divided between the pipeline and the quarry, plus the men all trust him to apportion workload fairly. And finally, there is myself. I visit weekly just to cross-check all of the information and ensure that all orders are being properly fulfilled," he finished and felt positive that Aspinall would be impressed.

Aspinall was sitting on the desk, and whilst listening to Croker rattle on, as soon as the name Silas Ledger was mentioned, a smile broke out on his face. "Thank you, Mr. Croker, that's been very informative." His words were suddenly calm and assuring. "Now, you've been a very loyal member of the Aspinall Company for a while, and I'd like to recognise that with a bonus payment that will make Mrs. Croker very happy indeed. I have one task that I'd like you to carry out for me, but it is very much a secret task. Are you up for that, John?"

"Of course, I am, sir," Croker said, delighted that his boss was on the charm offensive. "What can I do for you?"

"It's a delicate matter, but I need you to take a half case of premium spirits, labelled *Export Only,* from my office and discreetly hide them in the back garden of Silas Ledger's house in Langley. It must be done tonight, and it is vital that nobody, nobody knows about this. If you get caught, I will deny any conversation." Aspinall finished the conversation with a final threat "If you do get caught, you will lose your bonus and lose your job."

The phone went dead, Croker put the receiver down. What was all this about? But he had no time to question Aspinall's motives, he simply needed to carry out his instructions to the letter and all would be fine.

Aspinall left the Club's administration office and returned to the cigar room. This was it, here was his chance to destroy

Silas Ledger and release the fury inside him that the loss of his son to that young witch – Beth Ledger – had created. The cigar room had started to fill up with other members, so Padgett and D.I. Cooper left the room and found a quiet corner of the main lounge. They sat down and Aspinall reported that there were three individuals who could have access to red ink and writing material. Jack Moat, Silas Ledger and John Croker. Aspinall immediately negated John Croker from the investigation as he knew that he had been with him at the time of the explosion.

D.I. Cooper suggested precisely the actions that Aspinall wanted him to do when he next spoke. "Tomorrow morning, we will conduct searches at both Moat's and Ledger's properties in Langley – simply as follow-ups to the fact that there might be a link with the red ink used on the suspect notes you both received a few months ago."

CHAPTER 27 - *STITCHED UP*

P.C. Keith Aikin was very proud that he'd been asked to coordinate the house search operation by D.I. Cooper, as he knew the village and individuals concerned well. P.C. Aikin had only been briefed very early that morning and had been given eight officers to manage the search. The decision had been taken to start at 7 am before Silas and Jack would be due to leave for their respective work locations, and the searches could be done with the suspects present. Warrants for the searches had been sped through the Cheshire County Court system overnight. Keith Aikin knew Silas and Jack well and was certain that there would be nothing untoward found, but the formalities of policing needed to be followed, and he was a letter-of-the-law type of policeman. Given the profile of the case, D.C. Cooper felt he also had to be present.

A group of policemen was positioned outside both houses, which were at either end of Langley High Street. As the village awoke, more and more people came out into the street to see why there were so many uniformed officers and vehicles. P.C. Aikin knocked at Jack's door and his landlady answered, looking rather embarrassed as she was still in her sleeping attire.

"Morning, Mrs. Rose," said P.C. Aikin apologetically. "I do beg your pardon, but we are here to see Jack and search his room and belongings."

Behind her, Jack appeared in his work attire. "Hello Keith, what's going on?" he said, totally surprised at having a house invasion. P.C. Aikin explained that it was just a procedure relating to the incident in Kidsgrove.

"I have nothing to hide, come on in," Jack said.

"Take your boots off first!" shouted Mrs. Rose from the bedroom that she'd retreated to, still shocked that not only had she been caught in her bedclothes, but also, she hadn't had a chance to put the kettle on and make all those handsome young policemen a nice cup of tea.

The search was conducted briskly and P.C. Aikin nodded to D.I. Cooper that all was in order. Jack was free to go, but further questions might arise and it would be useful if he kept any travel to minimal for the foreseeable future. Jack had no plans but thought the whole business was very odd. He did ask P.C. Aikin for more details, but he seemed not to know either and suggested that Jack direct his questions to D.I. Cooper, who had now made his way toward Silas's terraced cottage. Gwen had already left to walk to her work at the mill in Macclesfield. Will was next door at the Post Office sorting newspapers for delivery whilst Mr. Ricketts was out on the street trying to understand what was going on.

P.C. Aiken knocked on the Ledger's door and Silas answered. Beth was behind him, both looked like they were ready to leave for their day's duties. The policeman grandly announced himself on the doorstep, aware of the growing crowd of onlookers.

"Good morning, Mr. Ledger," he then whispered only to Silas. "Sledge, I have to be formal, but don't worry, it's just a routine check." Again, P.C. Aikin adopted his louder public voice. "The Macclesfield police force has been instructed to conduct a search of your property."

Silas filled the doorframe and there was no getting past him until he stepped out of the house with a bemused look, allowing four policemen to enter. "I would like to know the reasons for this search, please, Keith?" P.C. Aikin once more referred to his senior officer and pointed D.I. Cooper out who had located himself near the Chapel gate in order to observe from afar.

Silas called back inside the cottage, "Beth, can you just make sure none of these policemen knock over any of your mother's flowers? They'll be hell to pay when she gets back from work if anything is out of place."

The policemen started upstairs and then came down to the back porch. At the back porch stood a coat rack. One of the policemen took a large overcoat down and checked the pockets. He caught his breath as he pulled his hand covered in blood out of one of them. He called P.C. Aikin over.

"There's something odd in there, can you hold it whilst I get a cloth."

Silas was still around the front of the house standing next to one policeman with many neighbours peering around him to see what was going on. A flustered P.C. Aikin came out of the house. Without looking at Silas, he called over to D.I. Cooper. "Sir, can you come in here for a moment? I'd like to show you something."

D.I. Cooper moved towards the cottage and once again failed to make eye contact with Silas. The two policemen went through to the back garden. The large coat had been laid out in the garden, and a dead rabbit with a ligature around its bloody neck was laid on the jacket together with several pieces of detonating cord. As they were inspecting the odd contents of the overcoat on the ground, one of the other police officers shouted. "Oi – over here!" under an old tarpaulin was a half crate of premium liquor bottles labelled *Export Only*. P.C. Aikin stared at D.I. Cooper – all of these items seemed odd and just did not add up.

Beth came out onto the back porch. "What are you doing with my dad's coat?" she said before gasping at the sight of the rabbit and cord as the policeman carried the half crate of bottles over to place next to the overcoat. She screamed, "That's not my father's – where did that come from?"

D.I. Cooper asked one of his officers to take Beth back into the house. "We will need to take Mr. Ledger into custody in order to interrogate him further, he has a lot of questions to answer."

Two of the officers gathered up the items that needed to be explained, and put them in a police vehicle. D.I. Cooper and P.C. Aikin moved back through the house to the front entrance. Looking up at Silas, D.I. Cooper spoke quietly to him so that few of the people close at hand could hear. "Mr. Silas Ledger, I am arresting you on the charge of suspected gross criminal damage, theft and potential murder." A gasp went up from the nearby onlookers, and a ripple of conversation was passed to the more distant ones. Some people cried out in protest, but most were simply too shocked to comment.

Jack Moat was the first to speak, "Don't worry, Sledge – it's all a mistake – we'll sort it out."

Silas just looked upwards towards Ridge Hill; he felt the eyes of Henry Aspinall piercing him. This was his revenge, and Silas was going to be made to suffer for Aspinall's evil ways and the fact that Aspinall had failed as a parent. Beth flew out of the front door and hugged her father seconds before Will ran out of the Post Office and hugged him from the other side. In that very brief moment, as he held his children, he knew that it was the love of his family that he would always have over the lonely, loveless existence of his nemesis on the ridge.

Both Will and Beth raised their eyes to meet his. He held them close and spoke, "Don't worry, things will work out. Make sure your mother is ok. And we'll see each other again soon."

They struggled to adjust the handcuffs to fit around Silas' huge wrists before being led off to the police vehicle to be taken to the holding cells beneath Macclesfield Magistrates Court. His life had turned and although having lived his life as an honest man, right then, he felt that righteousness would not be his salvation.

Back in Langley, there was uproar. One of their most respected and loved villagers had been accused of something that nobody could understand. There were no facts currently being shared by the police, and people simply could not understand how this could have happened. Gwen, Will and Beth had a large blanket of community spirit wrapped around them. The gentle, caring, powerful, loving man who was their husband and father had been accused of the most heinous crimes that they knew could not be true. Mr. Ricketts and Reverend Pottinger called for a village meeting that evening. They invited P.C. Keith Aikin along in order to better explain the earlier actions. Both the Hollins pipeline workers and the Teggs Nose quarrymen considered downing tools in protest, but they decided to work until they knew more about the reasons behind the arrest.

Nat Lovatt made contact with Thomas Whetton, as he knew that Whetton had been a great supporter of Silas and had shown himself willing to help the Lovatt's following the loss of Trentabank farm. Whetton had been away on business, so had not known of any of the events that had happened. Once he found out, he kept to himself some of the mixed views he had of the incident and of the subsequent arrest. His basic thought being – if Henry Aspinall was involved, then there were dirty tricks just beneath the surface. He put a call into the law company in Macclesfield that he had on a retainer – Sperry & Burroughs Solicitors – and set up a meeting for the following morning.

D.I. Cooper checked the paperwork personally to ensure there were no technical errors relating to the arrest of Silas. This was likely to be a very high-profile case, and he was very conscious that his last few months of policing before retirement needed to be spotless (unlike decades of his policing previously) so that he could retire to his second home in Anglesey, Wales - on a full pension. He had promised an update on the house searches in Langley to Joshua Padgett, and particularly Henry Aspinall, who seemed to be the more enthusiastic about the result. The three men met back at Padgett's offices in Duke Street, where the policeman reported that nothing of interest was found at Jack Moat's rented room, and so he had been given a warning that he might be needed for further questioning later but otherwise released. He then moved on to Silas.

"At the Ledger household, we proceeded to make a thorough search of the property and it revealed sufficient evidence for us to make an arrest." Padgett gasped with surprise. Aspinall smiled, thinking that Croker had delivered his promise and that he must fulfill the bonus offer to help buy his ongoing loyalty and silence. D.I. Cooper continued, "The items of suspicion that we found were in an overcoat owned by Mr. Ledger. We found the remains of a rabbit with a ligature around its neck – suggesting that he caught this rabbit illegally. But beyond a clear illegal act of poaching, we also found several pieces of detonating cord, which, on further inspection, is the type used alongside explosives. The final piece of evidence that seemed incontrovertible was the discovery and seizure of a half crate of premium spirits labelled for Export only, hidden under a tarpaulin in the garden."

This time it was Aspinall who was gasping – theatrically – "What!" he erupted, "Ledger is the one who's been poaching on my land and blowing up my boats, as well as corrupting my son."

He shut up quickly, realising that the last point about

Charles – exposed due to his anger – was irrelevant to the police investigation. It only served to raise a question over the personal motives of Aspinall's desire to see Silas found guilty.

Aspinall was astonished, though, to think that Silas Ledger, a man so loved by his workmates and village community, could get involved in petty poaching. Joshua Padgett was simply pleased that, within two days, the police had someone in custody. It would not help with the unfulfilled alcohol export, but at least he could report the guilty party back to Edgar Fitch, and indeed, it confirmed that it was not the Sons of Strangeways trying to blackmail him by destroying the supply chain and extorting cash directly.

CHAPTER 28 - *POLICE CELL*

Gustav Coccini was confused. Why had two of the few people he had any respect for been identified as possible suspects in the Kidsgrove explosion? Jack Moat was totally engaged in the pipeline work, and he would have no reason nor motivation whatsoever to commit such a crime. As for Silas Ledger, he was the least likely person that Gustav knew who would risk all by a meaningless act. Silas was as honest as the day was long. He'd known that the police had interviewed Ivan Boksic at the gypsy camp, but that seemed to be standard procedure for any crime committed in the area. He had no worries that Ivan would successfully hide behind the fact that society owes life to gypsies, and to date, that translated into petty crime perhaps – but not murder and explosions. So why were two work colleagues at the quarry picked out for a particular investigation, and why had Sledge been arrested?

Gustav was at work that day, but he decided to head home early and asked Fred Needles, who had taken over the supervisory role from Silas, if he was allowed as he had a migraine caused by the gritstone dust. He was given permission and headed home quickly in order to pack a bag in order to ready himself for a rapid departure, if the police came calling at his door.

Silas had slept badly. He was not overly worried about the reasons for his arrest – he had seen that there had clearly been a setup. He just needed time to think it all through and sort out a plan of action. He was keen to be able to talk with his family and Jack Moat. His hearing had been arranged for the following day, where he would hear the charges against him. He would be allowed legal counsel, but as he was a man of limited resources, the State needed to select a lawyer. He sat in his holding cell, worrying about Gwen and the toll it would take on her. He knew that Beth would be strong enough but worried also for Will, who had more of his mother's constitution.

Thomas Whetton met with the law firm – Sperry & Burroughs. For such an important client as Mr. Whetton, both of the founding partners, Harold Sperry and Jonathan Burroughs, had made themselves available. Thomas recognised Melissa Kirkham – from the picnic on the Trentabank dam wall. "Good morning, Melissa, I didn't know that you worked here," he said, surprised at seeing her at the door,

"Hello, Mr. Whetton," she replied. "I'd heard you were coming, and I wanted to catch you before your meeting with the partners." Melissa was looking anxious and upset.

"Is your concern about Silas?" Thomas correctly guessed.

She looked up at him, "Yes, none of us know why he has been arrested and why he is a murder suspect. This is Silas. He wouldn't hurt a fly," she added. "Despite his size."

"No, Melissa, I am certain he would not, and we are going to make sure that whatever fabrications have been made up about him are torn to shreds before they even reach court," Thomas said reassuringly.

At that point, Mr. Sperry entered the reception room. "Arr, good morning, Mr. Whetton. I see you've met our new office manager, Miss. Kirkham – we are very lucky to have found such an efficient support."

"Indeed, hello Harold, I do know Melissa quite well" he said and turned back to her. "May I ask how Jack is doing?"

"Excuse me Mr. Sperry, I didn't mean to take up yours and Mr. Whetton's time," Melissa replied.

"That's alright, dear," said Mr. Sperry. "As long as you can bring in a fresh pot of tea and three cups, I know Jonathan doesn't function well without at least one strong brew inside him." He retired to the meeting room, leaving Melissa and Thomas together.

"Jack is in a bad state. Thank you for asking," she said quietly. "He could not quite understand why the police were searching his room in Langley, but when they searched the Ledger's house and found suspicious items, leading to Silas' arrest. He thought he was going mad."

Thomas looked at her, "I'd like to meet up with Jack as soon as I can. Do you know where he is now?"

She replied, looking much brighter, knowing that Jack

would be pleased to meet with Thomas. "Yes, I will meet him tomorrow at the Old King's Head in Gurnett at 5 pm, when his work day is done. You can meet him there too if you are free."

"Good, that's a date," he said. "Now, I must not keep Harold and Jonathan waiting any longer, and I think they need their tea!".

Thomas's meeting with the Solicitors was short. He asked them to take on the representation of Silas; all payments would be made by himself, and he wanted to be kept informed every step of the way. He highlighted the fact that he was certain there was a miscarriage of justice happening but did not share his deeper thoughts that there were senior members of the business community in Macclesfield who might be complicit in wanting Silas Ledger to suffer.

The following morning, the public balcony of the courthouse in Macclesfield was full. Gwen Ledger was there, together with Martha Lovatt. The solicitors had been quick to advise Gwen that it was wise to keep Will and Beth away at this point, as it could cause extra stress to their father. Harold Sperry would be the main legal counsel for the defense on this case and had already seen Silas and briefed him on what to expect at this first hearing when charges were to be read for the first time. Other than his wife and sister, the two rows in the public balcony were packed with Silas' supporters from Langley. None of his colleagues had been given permission by John Croker to be there, even Jack Moat was warned that if he had attended, he would be dismissed immediately. Percy Ricketts – who never normally left Langley – was present, as was Reverend Hamish Pottinger. Several members of the cricket club were there – including 'Adam Bostock – the first-team cricket captain. The two publicans at the Setter Dog Inn – Dick Avery, and the Dunstan Inn – Ned Croucher. Both were also keen to show support for their friend. Melissa had been given permission to be present as note-taking support to Harold Sperry. She sat downstairs where the legal counsel was positioned.

Downstairs at the back of the courtroom, Henry Aspinall and John Padgett had sought and been granted special permission to be in attendance. Their seats were located such that the balcony was unaware of their presence. Silas was brought into the courtroom. They had just about found handcuffs to fit him, and he was escorted by two of the biggest court security officers they could find. Even so, Silas towered over the two of them. He looked up to Gwen and the balcony, and tried hard to give a reassuring smile. Gwen and Martha gripped each other's hands for strength as they had never seen Silas looking so vulnerable.

The judge entered and the clerk for the court asked everyone to rise. He announced, "Please be upstanding for the Right Honorable Judge Lincoln Westbury presiding." Judge Westbury took his seat and waved the papers he had in his hand for everyone else to sit.

In the assured accent of a person who had never struggled financially in life, Judge Westbury formally announced the date and the fact that the court was in session. "The first case to be heard are the charges against Mr. Silas Ledger of the High Street in Langley. May I ask Detective Inspector Cooper to list the charges against Mr. Ledger, please?" The judge sat back and D.I. Cooper stood up.

"Your Honour, I would like to seek the Court's permission to keep Mr. Silas Ledger in custody for two further weeks so we can prepare the full case against him." D.I. Cooper took a breath and then continued. "Mr. Ledger is accused of involvement in an explosion in Kidsgrove, North Staffordshire, in which a man lost his life and several were injured. Also, in that incident, a barge belonging to the Aspinall Company and a consignment of goods – belonging to John Padgett – were destroyed. The total value of the barge and goods is estimated to be around £50,000. There will also be considerable costs involved in the repairs to the lock and a large loss of revenue as the canal system will be suspended through Kidsgrove for about one month."

An audible gasp came from the balcony. "Sledge couldn't have done that!" shouted Dick Avery standing up. "Bloody lies, it's all rubbish!"

D.I. Cooper looked up at the balcony and just thought of the peace and quiet that he'd enjoy in his retirement by the sea. He just had to get through the next few months. He ignored the heckle.

"Order, order," snapped the Judge. "Any more shouting from you, sir," pointing at Dick Avery. "Will lead to your immediate expulsion from the courtroom." The Judge directed his comments back to the police officer. "Detective Inspector Cooper, will you continue, please."

"Thank you, your Honour. In addition, I would like for the court to also hear a lesser charge, that of poaching, against Mr. Ledger." At this, Dick Avery shrunk back into his seat and looked rather coy.

"Thank you, Detective Inspector," said the Judge. "And can you provide any initial detail on the evidence that you have on why these charges are being brought today?"

D.I. Cooper continued, very keen for this to be over. "Our suspicions were first aroused when we saw two threatening notes written to Mr. Henry Aspinall and Mr. Joshua Padgett, making reference to a boat sinking and fire. This was written in an unusual and rarely coloured ink matching the ink that Mr. Ledger uses at his workplace. Upon a search of Mr. Ledger's property in Langley, his overcoat was searched, and small lengths of detonating cord used for explosive charges were found in one pocket. In the other were the remains of a dead rabbit with a ligature around its neck. Further investigation of the garden, unearthed a half crate of premium spirits matching some of the spirits that make up Mr. Padgett's regular consignment."

In the back row of the main courthouse, Joshua Padgett winced, nervous about all this public exposure of his unlicensed liquor. He hoped that in parallel to the court appearance, Cooper was obtaining his false back-dated license quickly, and equally, he hoped that no further attention would be turned on where the liquor moved beyond Macclesfield. He was working on an alibi for that at pace, for if anyone found out that he was in business with Edgar Fitch, then the tables would turn very quickly.

"That's all I have for now, Your Honour. I would like two more weeks to further investigate this case and hand all evidence to the prosecution and defense counsel for the case to be heard." D.I. Cooper concluded and sat down relieved that his part was over for now. He turned to look at the back of the courthouse. Henry Aspinall was sitting there; he could not hide the fact that he was smiling. Melissa had followed the policeman's stare and had also seen Aspinall's expression. She froze when she saw Joshua Padgett staring back at her. It was the first time she had seen him in the flesh since he'd molested her. She felt sick.

The Langley village meeting that evening at the Dunstan Inn was packed out, hoping to hear all of the details from the courthouse. Martha was staying with Gwen to help her come to terms with the stack of evidence facing Silas and just try to help make sense of why her husband had been framed in such a horrible way. Who would hate this wonderful person that much?

Will and Beth attended the meeting, and were given two seats near the bar in respect of their father being the main subject of the meeting. The whole of the quarry team was present, including Gustav Coccini, which was a rarity, as he preferred to drink alone or with his friends at the Macclesfield canal side inns. Jack Moat had met with Thomas Whetton earlier in the evening at the Old King's Head Inn in Gurnett and had been reassured that he would help in any way he could, already evidenced by covering the hefty cost of employing Melissa's Company as defense lawyers. Jack and Melissa had then walked up to Langley and after checking in on Gwen and Martha, had joined the village meeting.

Earlier in the day at the courthouse, Percy Ricketts had been taking copious notes. He signalled to Ned Croucher, behind the bar, to ring the bell and call the meeting to order.

"Ladies and Gentlemen of Langley, your attendance is appreciated in support of one of our own." Percy continued with added solemnity, "Today, Silas Ledger was accused of a heinous crime, one we are certain he was not involved in." The crowded bar had fallen silent at the ring of the bell but, at this point, bellowed their support for Silas in no uncertain way. Once the shouting had died down, Percy continued, "This morning, in Macclesfield, Judge Westbury read out the charges against Silas. One – causing an explosion in which a man lost his life, and several were injured. Two – causing the destruction of property valued in excess of £50,000. Three – causing the closure of a key waterway for at least a month, leading to a significant loss in earnings and additional costs to any number of industries. And finally, Four – poaching." Ricketts concluded by revealing the evidence shared by Detective Inspector Cooper: the half crate of premium liquor, the detonating cords, the incriminating red ink notes and the rabbit carcass and ligature.

The sea of faces in front of the bar was more and more open-mouthed as the charges were read out. Many looked over at Andy Soutter and Robin Brampton when the poaching charge was announced, as their extra-curricular occupation was well known and indeed accepted by the village as a way of getting affordable meat from the plentiful supply across the nearby Aspinall Estate. Robin and Andy looked at each other quizzically, not understanding why Silas was involved in their shady business. An eruption of conversation followed with everybody having their own opinion as to what might have happened to poor Silas.

Jack and Melissa were with Beth and Will, providing them both with support and encouragement. "Don't worry, you two, we'll get this sorted. Your dad is innocent of all of these accusations," Jack said confidently. Melissa looked at him, having been in court earlier and her face told a different story.

Will suddenly gasped. "Oh, my God! I know what happened." Jack ushered him out of the Dunstan, closely followed by Beth and Melissa. They sat down at a bench by the chapel.

Jack, keen to learn what Will knew but concerned that information needed to be controlled in the close confines of the village, said in a quiet voice. "Will, what do you know?"

Will spoke slowly and deliberately, "I borrowed Dad's overcoat a few days ago – I went out at night up to Saddlers Way. I picked up the snared rabbit as a gift for helping out Andy, as Robin was injured at the quarry and had to stay overnight at the hospital. I completely forgot that I'd left the rabbit in his coat."

Beth looked at him angrily, "You stupid idiot, why did you get involved in that." As a vegetarian, Beth was very anti the lust that people had for meats, let alone ill-gotten gains. "Look what you have caused," she scalded and lunged towards him. Will looked crest-fallen and deserving of a beating from his elder sister, at the very least. Melissa calmed the situation down and held Beth back from a likely sibling assault. Jack asked about the detonating cord, and Will revealed that he had also put this in the overcoat that night as he had found it in a hidden storage box on Tegg's Nose. He had known about it as he had once watched Gustav Coccini conceal it. Jack bit his lip, a realisation came to him, but it was too soon to share.

"Will, Beth – I do not want you to tell anyone about this

yet. We need to make sure that this information is more fully understood before we can use it to help your dad." Jack added, "And it still does not explain why there was a half case of stolen liquor found hidden in the garden." The four of them went back to the cottage to comfort Gwen and Martha.

The Dunstan was gradually emptying its doors. Once again, Ned Croucher – the publican – was happy with a good night's takings that these village meetings raked in. A drinker who was little known to Ned but was welcome as one of the quarrymen hung behind at the bar, having moved on to brandy some while back. He was a wizened-looking man for his age and notable for his foreign accent. Ned was about to ask him to leave, as the last orders had been called an hour previous, but the drinker seemed to want to engage in conversation.

"Thank you, Mister Barman," Gustav slurred. "Poor old Silas, eh? He's a good man, but something must have turned him to make him do all that," he added. "Looks like the evidence against him is cut and dried. What do you think?"

Keen to appeal to new drinkers, Ned responded with his own views. "You work with him up on Teggs Nose, sir? You must know him to be a fair and honest worker. It looks like a setup to me."

"I do work with him, and Silas Ledger does seem like a decent man, but something's sure been troubling him recently," Gustav replied, needing to lay as many seeds of doubt as possible to hide his own guilty tracks. "I reckon he was fed up with Aspinall making so much profit out of the quarry and pipeline work. This was his way of wreaking some havoc for Aspinall, but it sure has back-fired." Ned didn't want to hear any more of this nonsense and reminded Gustav of the fact that it was over an hour since the last orders, and he would need to ask him to leave – as quietly as possible, given the location of the pub in the middle of the village.

Gustav made his way out through the door unsteadily, collecting his coat on the way out. On his way home to Macclesfield, he pondered his good fortune and thought of how a piece of detonating cord from the quarry could have found its way into Silas' possession. All he knew now was that he was going to have to be very careful about all of the excess dynamite he had hidden in secret locations around the hillside. Perhaps he should relocate it all to the gypsy camp as they seemed to be immune from police searches of their property. He resolved to ask Ivan Boksic the next time he was with him.

CHAPTER 29 - *FOOTPRINT*

Silas had now spent a week in prison. He had a further two weeks to go before his trial would start. He had only been allowed visits from the legal representative that he had accepted, thanks to Thomas Whetton's kind support. Harold Sperry had spent some time with him ahead of the case being heard and had subsequently been busying himself with the building of a defense. The time they had each day was limited to one hour by a court ruling, and so Sperry arrived each day with a fixed set of questions that he needed to get answers for. The first few meetings had been all about the four items of evidence that the prosecution seemed to be betting their success on: the red ink of the notes, the half case of stolen liquor, and the short length of detonation cord found in his overcoat pocket. The ill-gotten rabbit seemed to be a distraction, yet was illegal, and therefore coloured Silas' character in a way that might influence any jury into believing that this was a man who could perform outside of the law.

Silas was unable to supply any rational explanation for any item of the evidence other than the red ink, which was used for all admin matters at the quarry. His belief was that only he and Jack Moat regularly used it, and as Jack was working on the Hollins pipeline, then he had very little opportunity to use the red ink that was only ever used by Silas in recent times. An additional issue arose during the discussion that bothered Harold Sperry. On the night before and the morning of the explosion, Silas had offered to help finish off some dry-stone walling over on Nat's land to the south of Bosley Cloud. Sheep had been escaping through a long length of wall that had been broken by the winter storms. At the same time, Nat was at a Farmer's market in Chelford, trying to get the best price possible for his eighteen-month-old lambs from the previous year. Chelford was sufficiently distant for him to have to take a horse and cart over with a sample selection of lambs, and it was a full day's round trip.

After the quarry shift, Silas had loaded up a cart with some of the cast-off stones from the quarry and headed over to where the wall needed repair. He claimed that he'd worked there alone for almost four hours that evening fixing the wall and until it was too dark to work on. As it was summer, Gwen had packed some food for him, and he had taken a tarpaulin, blanket and pillow and slept for five hours in the back of the cart. He awoke at dawn to complete the job. He had returned to Langley at seven am and had a quick wash before heading back to the quarry. Nobody could testify that he had spent all of that time fixing holes in the dry-stone wall. The problem was exacerbated by the fact that he was only five miles away from the canal lock in Kidsgrove, where the explosion occurred. Realistically, Silas could have gone to Kidsgrove late at night or early the following morning and laid the explosives at the lock, or more probably on the Aspinall barge itself, as it had overnighted at the lock awaiting the opening of the lock the next morning. It was also possible that Silas had used this time to steal some liquor.

Harold Sperry shared his concerns with his partner, Jonathan Burroughs. They realised that this was an area that the prosecution might target, and their defense was limited.

On the night of the Langley village meeting, when Will had revealed the answers to why Silas' overcoat had a detonation cord and a rabbit with a snare around its neck. Jack Moat had asked those present to remain silent until he had worked out how best to deal with this matter. If he had been honest straight out, then Will Ledger and two of the quarry workers – Robin Brampton and Andy Soutter – would have been arrested for poaching. At that time, poaching carried a minimum prison sentence of six months. Robin and Andy would have also lost their jobs. Plus, it would likely lead to the fact that Dick Avery – the Setter Dog Inn's publican and mastermind of the poaching racket – would also likely be arrested and charged too. He needed to think carefully about this delicate subject.

The other matter preying on his mind was the origin of the detonation cord found in Silas' overcoat pocket. If this was found in a container on Teggs Nose and had been hidden there by Gustav Coccini, Jack needed to find out what other skullduggery was going on with the Italian. He decided to ask Will to show him where the cord was found. After that, he would confront Gustav and get him to confess what had been going on.

Will had not been sleeping at all with the worry of everything and the fact that he was blaming himself, so it was with great relief that after a few days, Jack asked Will to take him up Teggs Nose and show him the hidden container where the cord had been stored. Will knew precisely where it was as he had been playing over in his mind every step that he'd made on that fateful night. Jack and he approached the sheep track up the side of the hill, and he looked across the scrubland towards the tree where the box was buried under the roots. Will got to within five yards of the site when he noticed that there had been a lot of fresh earth dug up and scattered about. Where the box had been hidden, was now just a dark hole and resembled a freshly dug badger sett. There was no sign of any box. Will was mortified, his story no longer made sense.

"I'm sorry, Jack," wailed Will, "I swear it was here, and I swear that I saw Gustav Coccini hiding it."

"Don't worry, Will, I believe you." Jack put a consoling arm around Will's shaking shoulders. "We'll get Silas out; we both know that he's innocent."

Jack sent Will back down the hill to the village. He was in no fit state to help any further that day, but Jack had a job to do. Once Will was out of sight, he turned his attention back to the tree roots and the soil. It took a little while, but he finally found a footprint in the soil and measured it against his own boot. It was a similar size, about an eight, and looked like the kind of solid boot that the quarry workers wore. Jack headed on up Teggs Nose towards the quarry.

"Hi Jack," called out Fred Needles, who was now supervising the quarry work. "Any update on Sledge? Has Gwen been able to see him yet?" he asked.

"Not yet," replied Jack, "the lawyer is seeking permission for a visit next week, hopefully."

"Poor guy, he was always such a decent person. None of the boys can believe what's happened." Fred looked down at the ground.

"Is Gustav around?" Jack asked casually. "I'd like to chat to him about something."

Just at that point, a large explosion took place on the quarry face. "There he is, the dynamite kid is at play," Fred said, looking up with a grin.

"Thanks, Fred. Take care." Jack walked off towards the dust cloud that had erupted from the quarry.

"Hi, Jack," Gustav spoke first as he appeared out of the cloud. "What a tragedy about Sledge. I didn't realise that he was like that." Jack found it hard to hide his disgust as he looked down at Gustav's feet and noted that his boots were a similar size to his own.

"Gustav." Jack stared directly at him. "When I was looking after the store shed, you alone had access to the explosives. Have you ever taken any explosives out of the shed without noting them in the log book and reporting them to me or Sledge?"

Gustav looked directly back at Jack. "Moat, what are you suggesting? I hope you're not thinking that I'm a thief. Or that I'm involved in anything that Sledge has done. How very dare you!"

They were now just inches apart, "I don't have any proof yet, Coccini, but I do think you know something about this whole affair, and I'm going to find out what!"

At that moment, Fred Needles appeared and noting that the two men were squaring up on the edge of a fifty-yard drop, pulled Gustav away, suggesting he needed to take a break. He then walked Jack away in the opposite direction. Gustav retreated, thanking his good fortune that he had removed the evidence of the box of dynamite and the separate box of detonation cords the previous day and taken them across to the Gypsy encampment, where they would be safe from the eyes of do-gooders like Jack 'bloody' Moat.

Jack accepted Fred's kindly persuasion not to cause an issue with Gustav just then. He needed to bide his time and collect more evidence before finger-pointing could happen. Justice would be served.

Jack continued along the path down into Macclesfield, he had taken the day off and was going to see Melissa at Sperry & Burroughs and take her out to lunch as it was almost her birthday. He also needed to tell Harold Sperry all about Sledge's overcoat and the reason why it contained the incriminating items. He hesitated about informing the lawyers about his suspicions about Gustav Coccini. Without any hard evidence, it would be impossible to convince anyone about his involvement. It seemed as if the police had slowed down any further investigations until after Sledge's trial, which was now only a fortnight away.

Later that week, some good news appeared from the Law firm. Harold Sperry had requested visitors' rights for Silas and had been granted one visitor for ten minutes. He called

Melissa into Harold Sperry's office and shared the news, suggesting that she be the one to arrange the visit with Gwen. He also asked her to collect as many character references for Silas as she could from people who were themselves reputable members of the community. She found no problem finding people who were queueing up to testify in his favour. Melissa brought the list back to Harold Sperry to decide upon the two who would attend the crown court in Chester and stand as character witnesses. The two he chose were Percy Ricketts, someone who had known Silas as a man and boy and also Reverend Hamish Pottinger. Any jury tended to be positive about a testimony from a man of the cloth.

Melissa told Jack about the opportunity for someone to visit Silas, and it was obvious that Gwen must be given the choice. It might have been that she could have found it all too upsetting, but Gwen was a strong woman and leapt at the chance to see Silas ahead of the trial. Melissa arranged all the necessary paperwork, and it was agreed that Gwen would see him for ten minutes only on the following Tuesday morning. Her work manager had been to school with Silas and so was supportive of releasing Gwen for as long as she needed.

Gwen arrived at the police station in Macclesfield an hour before the meeting. She sat patiently in the waiting room. After fifteen minutes, she saw John Padgett and Henry Aspinall leaving a room along a corridor to her right. They were sharing a joke with Detective Inspector Cooper and a very learned-looking gentleman who was wearing the gown and wig of the legal system. Padgett passed her without a glance, but Aspinall saw her and muttered in a hushed manner – "Send my regards to your husband, Mrs. Ledger." He stared mockingly and moved on. Gwen felt a cold shiver down her neck – she dreaded what that might mean.

Harold Sperry had just come out from the meeting cell where Silas was sitting. He spoke briefly with Gwen, just asking her to stay positive and upbeat, that's the way that would help her husband. She was then escorted into the cell by two burly policemen, who remained at the door throughout.

Having been told that she was unable to touch Silas, she sat down across the small desk. Silas was looking tired but still maintained a sparkle in those deep, dark eyes. Gwen thought that he was looking gaunt and had lost some weight. She remembered Sperry's instructions to stay positive and upbeat. She smiled and said how much Beth and Will were looking forward to him coming home. She started to talk about different members of the village who had passed on their best wishes to Silas.

Silas looked at her intently. Gwen was always the talker in their relationship. "Gwen, just be quiet for one minute," Silas said sharply. "I have a very important message that you must respect. Will never borrowed my overcoat that night. I took it with me to Bosley Cloud when I was dry stone-walling."

Gwen looked at him quizzically, "But Will said..."

"Quiet, Gwen," Silas ordered, "you must believe me when I said that I was wearing the coat." Gwen realised that with this factual statement, Silas was taking any blame away from his son and heaping it upon himself. Her eyes welled up, and she was looking at the only man she had ever loved and would ever love, potentially sacrificing his life for his family. If Will had been implicated in the poaching, that would have been serious, but if his handling of the detonation cord had pulled him in for being an accomplice for his father, then Gwen would have lost a husband and a son.

"Time's up, you two," said the senior of the two policemen at the door. Gwen couldn't control her emotions; she threw herself across the desk and hugged Silas.

"Sledge, I love you!" she cried.

"Now, Mrs. Ledger, out you come." The policemen firmly but gently loosened her grip. Silas was not able to move as he was handcuffed to the desk at his ankles and wrists.

"I am being moved to Chester prison to await trial tomorrow," Silas said as she was removed from the cell, and the door was closed behind her.

Harold Sperry was waiting for Gwen's return and took her out of the police station and walked her past the town hall and towards her place of work down Mill Street. "Mrs. Ledger – did Mr. Ledger tell you about his overcoat?" asked Sperry.

"Yes," said Gwen.

Sperry continued, "It is really important that we maintain the position that he used his overcoat that night. Otherwise, your son will be in trouble. As a lawyer, I can only advise on the likely direction a court might take. Whatever the truth is about the overcoat, I consider one truth to carry a higher risk than the other truth. And that is what I have advised Mr. Ledger as my client."

"I understand," Gwen stuttered. "Whichever truth we opt for, Sledge could be guilty, but with one, it means that Will is not accused of anything."

"Correct," The lawyer confirmed.

Harold Sperry and Jonathan Burroughs had, as promised, been keeping Thomas Whetton informed of how the defense counsel was developing its case. Much seemed to rest on the information that the prosecution could find out about Silas' whereabouts on the day of the explosion. The fact was that his whereabouts were only known to himself as there were no witnesses to say that he was at Bosley fixing dry stone walls. They had discussed Will's story, claiming that he was wearing his dad's coat that night, but they all agreed that this was only deepening the problem by involving another, slightly less innocent – given the poaching – member of the Ledger family. The key evidence was the hidden liquor in the garden. Nobody had any information as to why that was there. The prosecution could, no doubt, point to the fact that Silas was 'working' as he claimed, in the direction of Kidsgrove, with a cart – or a means of carriage for the box of liquor. A saving grace was that character witnesses could be found in their dozens to testify as to the true and honest nature of Silas Ledger.

CHAPTER 30 - *CROWN COURT*

On Wednesday, Silas was being prepared for the transfer over to Chester prison in readiness for his Crown Court hearing. He had been moved to the cell next to the police stables. He would be taken to Chester in the first Black Maria police vehicle that the Macclesfield force had received. The press was out in full to capture any opportunity for a photo of Silas Ledger, as it was such a high-profile case, but also of the Black Maria that would be used to carry dangerous criminals moving forward.

Silas was surprised to receive another visitor. This time, it was a less welcome one. Henry Aspinall was keen to get some one-on-one time with Silas ahead of the final court hearing. He wanted Silas to understand the pain he was going through in losing Charles, and he hoped that the pain that Silas and his family were having to endure came somewhere near his own.

"Hello, Ledger," Aspinall said in a low voice through the bars of the cell. "I hope that you recognise that this might be the last time you ever smell the air of your beloved Macclesfield!" He paused for a response, but none was forthcoming. "Surely you know by now that the odds are stacked against you. You'll be going down for a life sentence at least, but as a public servant was killed in your misadventure, there's a big chance of hanging," he smiled. "Just like your friend Sid Bayley."

Silas looked at Aspinall, knowing that he was being baited. He responded, choosing his words deliberately. "Sir, I know that you may have money and power, and you may well have bought the result of this trial. But at least Charlie recognises that all the money and power in the world cannot buy happiness."

Aspinall scowled and walked away, who gave this simple quarry worker the right to call into question the Aspinall reputation?

The Black Maria drove out of the Macclesfield police stable block at the start of its journey to Chester prison. The driver proudly waved to the press photographers from the local Express newspaper and several national titles. There were two policemen travelling with Silas, who was chained in the back of the vehicle. Nobody noticed at the time, but in the photography taken that day, behind the group of police cheering the Black Maria was one face who was looking deeply satisfied – one Henry Aspinall.

Thomas Whetton noticed the photo in the following day's Macclesfield Express, as it was front page news. He cut it out and stuck it on his noticeboard.

Gwen and Beth accompanied Percy Ricketts and Reverend Pottinger to Chester in Thomas Whetton's chauffeur-driven Bentley. Whetton had no need for it as he had travelled by train to Edinburgh for a business meeting. It would have been a most enjoyable journey for the group from Langley, other than for the reason of having to travel to Cheshire's crown court. Melissa accompanied Jonathan Burroughs and Harold Sperry in a rather less extravagant Austin Seven.

On the three-hour journey to Chester, Beth looked out of the window and allowed herself to daydream. She thought of Charlie and the wonderful times they would have at university in Durham – learning about love and life.

Charlie was spending the Summer up in Durham, ahead of starting his law degree, working at a solicitor's office that was owned by a Hoarwithy School alumni associate of his old friend, Mr. Alastair Grainger. He also had no real home in Langley that he could have returned to anyway, given that his father had banished him from the manor house, and his mother had further descended into a new depth of ill health and was bed-bound. Beth and Charlie corresponded each week via an arrangement with Mr. Grainger to stop any blockage in the postal service caused by his father. There was positivity in their hopes and aspirations for the future. However, the dominant shadow that clung on to everything was the outcome of Silas' trial.

It had been decided that Will would spend the day with Jack, continuing to bring pipe lengths up from Gurnett to the Hollins. There had been excellent work on the reparations to the Kidsgrove lock, and by the time of the trial, it was fully functioning again, with the canal having been cleared of the wreck of the barge within the first five days. Given the story that Will had shared about the overcoat, it was quite clear that he needed to be distanced from the trial proceedings – for his own sake and for Silas' sake, too.

The travellers arrived at Chester Crown Court, which was used for all of the county's most serious cases. Even though the crime had happened in Kidsgrove, North Staffordshire – as the initial case hearing had occurred in Macclesfield, it was felt acceptable for the final trial to take place in Cheshire too.

Chief Inspector Milner from the Congleton and Kidsgrove police force was present as a witness. He and Detective Inspector Cooper shook hands upon seeing each other, having not seen each other since the day of the incident. Milner also shook hands with Henry Aspinall and Joshua Padgett, who, as the main targets of the crime – were also in attendance as potential witnesses if called.

All of the court officials were introduced by the clerk of the court. Gwen recognised the prosecuting lawyer. He was the learned-looking gentleman who had been at Macclesfield police station with Aspinall and Padgett the day she had last seen her husband.

Silas had been asked to wear a suit for the trial, but he didn't own one himself. Therefore, Melissa had been instructed by her bosses to find the largest one available in a suit shop in Macclesfield. Unsurprisingly, the dimensions available were not sufficient for Silas' bulk, but for the jury, it made his appearance look smart, if not a little uncomfortable. Silas sat there looking solemn but was able to look up at Gwen and Beth – and gave them a reassuring look. In his ill-fitting suit, surrounded by the paraphernalia of the Crown Court, Beth never thought that her father had looked more vulnerable.

The presiding judge entered the courtroom, and everyone stood up. The jury was sworn in, and the opening statements began.

Harold Sperry performed very well, but for each challenge he had to the efficacy of the evidence presented by the prosecution, there seemed to be a strong counter-argument produced through the key witnesses.

The impact statement made by the widow of the Kidsgrove lock keeper was delivered with emotion and spite, directed towards Silas, suggesting that the accused was already considered guilty.

The red ink messages printed on betting slips were shown to the jury by the prosecution, followed by the red ink work plan roster written by Silas. It was quite clear that the handwriting was vastly different, but the prosecution laboured on the fact that several letters of the words *Titanic* and *Water*, from the notes, were similar to a couple of letters of the surnames of two of the quarrymen from the work plan that Silas had written. The prosecution counsel had called a handwriting expert in from Manchester who supported the idea that the two notes and the work plan could have been written by the same person. Not definitive evidence, but it was still compelling.

The key item of evidence presented, and the one that received the most conjecture, was the half crate of illegal liquor found under a tarpaulin in Silas' cottage garden.

Harold Sperry tried to convince the court that several crates of liquor had gone missing from canal boats in the North Staffordshire area in the last six weeks, it could be that someone else in the area was just using Silas' garden as a convenient hiding place. Had the police considered this? To distract the proceedings, Sperry added a pointed comment about whether the liquor was being transported legally in the first place.

The Judge immediately cut in, recognising that this was irrelevant given the case that was being heard. Even so, the prosecution counsel picked up on this immediately – and waved two licenses – one for Padgett's export business and one for Aspinall's canal transport business. The back-dating of these licenses made both valid documents. Padgett and Aspinall both looked at a smug-looking D.I. Cooper.

The prosecution lawyer also dammed Sperry's suggestion about numerous occasions where liquor had been stolen by linking the batch from the Aspinall Company barge that had sunken to the batch found in the garden. This evidence had also been contrived as it had been tampered with whilst being handled by John Croker before planting it in the Ledger garden.

Sperry asked for the character witnesses to appear just ahead of raising the idea of motive. Both Percy Ricketts and Reverend Pottinger did a spectacular job highlighting how the community of Langley truly respected the neighbour and friend who was Silas Ledger.

The court adjourned ahead of the summing up.

Gwen and Beth went outside for some fresh air, where

they met Melissa and Jonathan Burroughs. The lawyer felt it appropriate to share some truths with them: "The prosecution counsel is one, Benjamin Quincy KC, he is a renowned London barrister and rarely loses a case. He is almost never seen up north, as he is one of the most expensive lawyers on the network. Harold is doing well, but the prosecution has had a strong day. I need to warn you that there is a chance of us losing the case."

Beth and her mother hugged. Melissa looked crestfallen, although very confident of Silas' innocence, even she had felt that Quincy had argued the room into believing that he was guilty.

The five-minute bell sounded, and the court retook their seats. Benjamin Quincy KC summed up the case, playing heavily upon the emotional impact of the widow's statement and the fact that three young children will grow up without knowing their father.

He continued, "Four months ago, Mr. Ledger wrote two threatening notes to Mr. Joshua Padgett and Mr. Henry Aspinall, spelling out quite clearly what his intentions were."

He went on to remind the jury about the evidence of the hidden liquor and the detonation cords found in his clothing. He accepted that the poached rabbit simply highlighted that we were dealing with someone who flouted respect for the law.

Without any hint of humanity, he then looked at the Judge whilst pointing to Silas, and demanded the highest sanction of the death penalty. Gwen's shoulders began to shake, but she remained silent. Beth just sat there in total shock.

"Don't worry", Melissa leaned over, "It's Harold's turn now." She knew that she did not sound convincing.

Harold Sperry stood up, looking at Quincy. "Sir, you are so totally wrong. The Accused sits here before you all as an upstanding member of society who has befallen a series of vendettas brought against him. Mr. Ledger is a strong family and community man." Sperry looked up at the gallery to where Silas' family and friends sat. "Indeed, on the very night of the incident in Kidsgrove, he finished his day's work at the quarry and then went to his sister's and brother-in-law's farm to help keep their sheep flock safe. He had no idea what was happening in Kidsgrove. As for the detonation cords, well it is in everyday use in the quarry, and he may have just inadvertently picked some up and kept it in his pocket. The liquor in the garden was stashed there by some other criminal, and so was a mere – and very unfortunate – coincidence. The fact that there was a snared rabbit in another pocket – we have no answer to that, I accept, and if there is a lesser penalty of poaching that you wish to accuse us of, we will accept that." He concluded: "Ladies and Gentlemen of the jury – I implore you – look into the eyes of an innocent man and make your decision to release him today."

Sperry sat down and took a deep breath. Had he done enough? He was not confident, and when he looked at Silas, it was hard for him to hide that feeling.

The court went into recess whilst the jury met to decide the verdict. It was now down to twelve people to decide Silas' fate. Silas knew that Henry Aspinall had contrived to pervert the course of justice so that he could exact revenge for the relationship between Beth and Charlie that he blamed for the choice his son had taken.

What he could not understand, however, was why Aspinall seemed disinterested in finding out the real truth behind the Kidsgrove incident. Surely his hatred of Silas wasn't sufficient for him not to discover who his true enemy was?

Joshua Padgett and Henry Aspinall had not been called up as witnesses in the case. This fact pleased both of them, given that they would have had to perjure themselves based on having influenced the procurement of false documents for their business dealings, amongst other things. Benjamin Quincy had recognised that this was a delicate matter and had successfully steered the Judge and Harold Sperry away from this area of questioning.

Padgett was particularly pleased with the way the trial was moving, as any public questioning would have potentially opened up his dealings with Edgar Fitch, and that association would have immediately challenged all sorts of facts in the case. "Let me buy you a drink, Henry," Padgett said as they entered The Wig & Pen Inn next door to the courthouse. They sat down in a private booth away from other drinkers. "Well, it looks like we have caught our man," Padgett said triumphantly as he passed a pint of ale across to Aspinall. "I think Quincy did a fantastic job; I'm not surprised, given the money we're paying him."

Henry Aspinall took a long gulp and then looked at Padgett. "Joshua" he said, "I think we have a noose around Ledger's neck for sure. But he didn't do it."

Padgett looked back at him. "What? How can you say such a thing?"

"Let's just say that I know Ledger didn't do it. Aren't you interested to know who did it?" Aspinall said.

"It's a bit late now to be asking such a thing, don't you think?" Padgett said incredulously. His mouth remained open in disbelief at Aspinall's revelation.

"I'm not saying that Ledger is not guilty as hell and deserves everything he's going to get," Aspinall answered, "but he did not set the explosives off, nor did he steal any of your liquor. And we know that the threatening notes were not written in his handwriting, despite the evidence to the contrary that Quincy extracted from the handwriting expert."

Padgett just sat there looking at Aspinall and then spoke, "Why do you say this now? Why didn't you question this before?"

"I need Silas Ledger to suffer for the pain he's caused my family. This was the opportunity to do it. Once the jury has cast their verdict and the Judge has condemned Ledger to the gallows, then we can consider who really attacked us." Aspinall finished and took another long gulp of ale.

Padgett did not believe what he was hearing. "So, if not Ledger, who do you think could have been behind this whole sorry affair?" he said, desperately hoping that Edgar Fitch was not going to be raised as a suspect.

Aspinall put his tankard down, "Have you ever wondered why Thomas Whetton sponsored Ledger's defense by employing Sperry & Burroughs? Why did he loan his car to Ledger's family to drive them to Chester for the trial? Did he feel guilty about something?" He continued, "Also, which canal transport company would benefit most from the loss of my barge capacity and your demand for regular freight service through to Manchester docks? Whetton's - of course. He has never liked either of us, so my bet would be on him having paid someone to lay the explosive."

Padgett listened intently. All this new information needed another ale to help fully absorb, and he signalled to the barman for two refills.

"Whetton is one of us though." Padgett countered, "He is a member of the Old Boy's Club. He would not risk his reputation getting involved in dirty tricks like that."

Aspinall nodded his head. "I agree, but it's a theory. I have asked Detective Inspector Cooper to start investigating as soon as Ledger swings. We cannot open any line of inquiry before he dies."

The barman rang the bell by the bar and shouted that the court next door had rung the five-minute bell. The jury was about to announce their verdict.

Once everyone had settled back into their seats, and Silas had been brought back into the courtroom and remained standing. The Judge asked the question, "Do you find the defendant, Silas Ledger of Langley – guilty or not guilty of the charges outlined earlier."

The verdict was delivered by the foreman of the Jury, and it was unanimous. The courtroom was abuzz with tension. The jury foreman felt unable to look up from his notes as he uttered the word "Guilty."

Silas remained standing, showing little emotion. He

peered up to the balcony where Beth and Gwen were wrapped in each other's arms, consoling one another. Inside, he was hurting at the injustice of it all, but he would not give Henry Aspinall the pleasure of seeing him break down. Silas, by sacrificing himself, had also taken on the punishment that could have been dealt out on his own son. As a father, he had done everything for his son, something that Henry Aspinall would never understand.

The Judge repeated the *Guilty* statement and, given that a person had died in the explosion, had no option other than to deliver the most severe of sentences. "Silas Ledger, you are hereby sentenced to hang by your neck until you are dead. May God have mercy upon your soul."

Gwen and Beth both let out a cry from the balcony. How could their dear, sweet husband/father be taken from them in this most harsh way? This was an innocent man. Melissa and Reverend Pottinger tried to comfort them, but they themselves were finding it very hard to keep it all together.

It was through tear-stained eyes that Gwen saw Silas lead away. Would she ever see him alive again?

CHAPTER 31 - *A DAUGHTER'S TALE*

The whole community of Langley went into mourning when the news from Chester arrived. They could not believe the guilty verdict nor the ultimate sentencing. The shock was most felt up at the quarry on Teggs Nose and on the Hollins. Jack Moat, regardless of the busy work schedule, told all of the workers to down tools and they immediately did, regardless of being docked a day's pay. They all adjourned to the Setter Dog Inn. John Croker tried to reason with Jack as he knew that a day's loss in work on the Hollins pipeline could not be afforded. But he realised the severity of the feeling that the quarrymen had at knowing their friend was to hang for a crime that none of them believed he had committed.

John Croker also felt in no position to argue, as deep down inside, he knew that he was one of the main reasons why Silas Ledger would swing. He had hidden the export liquor under the tarpaulin in the Ledger's garden on the night before the house search was conducted by the police. His guilt was felt sharply but insufficient to offset the positive feeling he got from his wife when he had been able to announce the bonus that he was getting from Henry Aspinall. His wife had seemed to be growing bored with him in recent months, and this payment might help paper over the cracks in his relationship.

The quarrymen were all especially caring towards Will Ledger. They realised that this fifteen-year-old boy, who looked so much like Sledge, was about to lose his father. Jack decided to take Will up to the Setter Dog with the team. Fred Needles and Andy Soutter tried their best to keep the spirits up, but what can you say to a boy who is about to experience this kind of loss? Jack wasn't surprised that he could not see Gustav Coccini in the sea of faces in the crowded bar room.

Down in the village, the return of the Bentley car, carrying Gwen, Beth, Percy Ricketts and Reverend Pottinger – was greeted like a hearse carrying a coffin. In the car, Beth had already sworn to her mother that she would not go to University in Durham and would spend time helping Gwen and Will simply get by. She was also desperate to get back to her activism with a new direction – the abolition of the death penalty. She felt a spirit rising inside her that she often got whenever she saw an injustice. She always felt compelled to attack it with passion. The spirit she had felt when the sentence was served against her father – was the most intense feeling she had yet experienced. She had to do something, perhaps not in time to save her father, but it might be able to serve to save others who have had a miscarriage of justice served against them.

Upon arriving back in Langley, Gwen went with the Reverend to the chapel, where a number of people had met to pray for Silas and the Ledger family. Beth headed straight inside the cottage; her anger was such that she needed to express it through the power of the pen. She was well-known by the local press reporters for being a free spirit. She had contributed many articles on political reforms, particularly relating to women's rights. Some of her articles were published locally. This time, she needed to reach a larger and more influential audience, and she needed somebody with higher political power to help. If Charlie had been there, he would have had ideas, but she was alone and time was finite.

Melissa had been dropped off in Langley by Jonathan Burroughs. She did not want to be alone tonight and was hoping to find Jack around. She discovered that he was up at the Setter Dog with Will and his workmates. She decided to leave them to it and went over to the Ledger's cottage to see how Gwen and Beth were doing. She knocked on the door.

"Come in!" she heard Beth's voice from inside. She entered and saw Beth leaning over a writing desk, starting to write words and then crossing them out and starting again. She leaned over Beth and read the words across the top. *Hanging – a Daughter's Tale.*

"What are you writing about, Beth?" she enquired gently.

Without stopping, Beth replied, "Some people may be grieving and giving up. I'm fighting back, and when I fight, I write." She looked up at Melissa, "But I do need help. I need someone who may know London journalists and people in Government. Do you know who might have those connections?"

Melissa replied, "I'm sure Thomas Whetton may know some, or at least knows people who might know some."

"Good," she said, returning to her writing. "Can you ask

Mr. Whetton's chauffeur to wait for about an hour? He's currently in The Dunstan Inn, having just delivered us back from Chester. Make sure he does not leave before I can give him an envelope."

Melissa left the cottage to leave the whirlwind that was Beth at her desk writing furiously. She delivered the message to the chauffeur, who was more than happy to continue his conversation about new American car models with Ned Croucher, the publican. She then headed up to the chapel to join Gwen and other villagers seeking spiritual support.

Thomas Whetton's chauffeur stayed for several hours talking with Ned at the Dunstan Inn. It was a blessed relief compared with the emotion coming from the back seat of the car on the journey back from Chester Crown Court. Plus, he was impressed with the knowledge that Ned had of Chryslers, Cadillacs and Chevrolet cars – all gleaned from old car magazines that Percy Ricketts had given to him, having failed to sell them in the newsagents. Percy used to swap a magazine for a fresh tankard of ale every so often, and Ned kept the copies on the bar for customers to flick through if they so desired.

It was five tankards of ale and almost ten o'clock when the chauffeur rather clumsily knocked at the Ledger's cottage. Will was still yet to return from the Setter Dog, and Gwen had gone to bed. Beth answered the door,

"Thank you, Mr. Johnson, thank you," she said as she thrust a thick envelope into his hand. "Please make sure you get this to Mr. Whetton as soon as possible."

"Of course, that will be my pleasure," Johnson replied. "I

am due to collect him from Macclesfield train station tomorrow morning, first thing. I'll be sure to pass it to him."

"Please say it's from Beth Ledger, and tell him that it's very, very urgent," Beth said.

"Sure, I will, Madam," said Johnson and headed back to the car with the letter, walking rather unsteadily.

As Thomas Whetton's train was approaching Macclesfield, he looked up and saw Teggs Nose from a distance. He had heard about Silas Ledger's fate and wondered how his family were faring. He had been kept up to speed with how the investigation and trial had gone from Jonathan Burroughs, who had phoned regularly. From the descriptions given, it seemed like the evidence was stacking heavily against Silas, and when it was discovered that Benjamin Quincy K.C. had been appointed as the prosecution counsel, Whetton had seen the writing on the wall.

He was on the platform with the Macclesfield railway station manager when his chauffeur appeared looking a little hungover – puffing and red-faced. "Hello, Johnson. Have you been having fun when I've been away?" he said jovially and the station manager laughed.

Johnson blushed and passed the letter to Thomas. "This is from Beth Ledger, Mr. Whetton, Sir. She said that it was important you read it immediately."

"Thank you, Johnson. Wait for me in the car and I will use the station master's office to read whatever this is." Thomas looked at the station master for approval, of which he immediately got it. Thomas moved briskly into the office, which was located on the platform and sat at the desk. He opened the envelope and started to read.

Dear Mr. Whetton,

Today, I experienced the most awful miscarriage of justice. My father was wrongly accused and then found guilty of a crime in which a man died. The Judge then sentenced him to hang in the next two weeks. I beseech you to help us as I know that you are a good man and have helped my family before. I also believe that you also know the truth that my father is innocent.

Read the below and if you have it in your heart, please use all of your powers to get it published in any national newspaper. We need to bring this to the attention of the wider public and politicians so that this cannot happen again.

It may be too late for my father, but we can help others.

Yours in desperation.

Beth Ledger.

Thomas then opened another sheet of writing paper and read the title – *Hanging – a Daughter's Tale*. He read the next two pages, which were full of tenderness and passion about a daughter's love for a father, with an eloquently set out rationale as to why the carriage of justice needs to be more carefully examined before anyone can cruelly cut short the closest of family relationships. It was a clear-cut debate about modernising the justice system and the need to abolish capital punishment.

Thomas Whetton had read much about the reformation lobby and the need to consign capital punishment to the dark ages, but that had been written by academics and liberal politicians. Never had he read such a touching, personal and potentially tragic piece of writing as the one Beth had produced, and he was holding it in his hand. It called out to him to act and act immediately.

He left the station master's office. "When's the next train to London?" he demanded.

"Thirty minutes," came the reply from a porter who was moving someone's luggage along the platform on a trolley.

"Johnson," Thomas announced. "I'm off to London. I'll telephone you later to tell you when I'll be home next."

Thomas Whetton did not arrive in London until three o'clock in the afternoon, but he immediately hailed a black Hackney cab and asked for the Times Newspaper building on Fleet Street. He had read Beth's article a number of times on the train, and each time, a different aspect of the tragedy caused a tear to form in his eye. Beth had a magic way with words. It had implored him to act, and he hoped that it would do likewise with hard-nosed editors on Fleet Street.

It seemed like three o'clock was the bewitching hour for the newspaper industry; most stories had been put to bed for the following day, and the presses were now busily whirring away, producing printed copies for the following morning. Most editors had taken the opportunity for early doors at various local establishments. The doorman at the Times head office on Fleet Street pointed out a public house where most of the editors and top journalists tended to frequent at that time in the afternoon.

Aptly named *Ye Old Cheshire Cheese*, 145 Fleet Street, was alive with conversation when Thomas Whetton walked through the door. He moved through the crowd and asked a barman to point out any newspaper editor. The barman looked at him strangely and suggested he just target the man with the largest group of people around him vying for his attention. Thomas decided to chance his luck and pushed in upon the nearest group.

"Sirs, I have a story that will change history." He had decided that a bold statement might be needed. The group fell silent for a moment and then laughed loudly.

"Nice try, mate, but that's one of the least original lines I've heard today!" said the closest journalist to him, "best try a different tack."

Realising the important and urgent nature of the message, he needed to cause a distraction so that he could get close to one of the editors. On impulse, he kicked out his foot and tripped a waiter who was carrying a tray containing two bottles of claret and four glasses. In slow motion, the bottles and glasses floated up into the air and then slowly descended, only to rise again when the poor waiter hopelessly flailed at them to try and achieve the impossible – and catch them all. The result was chaos. About five people were doused with red wine, glasses and bottles smashed to the floor. The waiter was spread-eagled in a growing puddle of claret, and the rest of the pub was cheering.

Thomas moved in quickly and caught the eye of one well-dressed editor who seemed to be enjoying the comedic moment but not too excessively to suggest an overly sadistic nature. "Sir, a quick word in your ear if you don't mind." Thomas expertly maneuvered the editor to a corner where nobody else could get to him. "I have a story for you that is likely to appear in Parliament in the next two days, and I can let you have the scoop early."

The editor's attention was captured. "Go on, tell me more, but make it snappy," he stated.

Thomas gave him the title – *Hanging – a Daughter's Tale*, which immediately perked up the editor's ears. He was intrigued and Thomas gave a two-minute verbal summary of Beth's account. Knowing that he could never do justice to the power of Beth's own written work. But it seemed sufficient. The editor asked to see a copy of the manuscript, and within the first three lines, the prose clearly had an impact.

"What's your name?" He turned to Thomas, "Thomas Whetton, sir, and I am representing the daughter – Beth Ledger."

"Okay, Mr. Whetton, I'm Blake Theobold, and my paper is The Guardian. We have a strong readership in the North of England. I'll pay you £50 now if you let me run with that story, as I still have one space that I can fit in for the second edition overnight print. Is that good enough?"

"Mr. Theobold – thank you so much – my client will be delighted that her plight has been recognised," Thomas said, accepting the £50 note. He was utterly delighted that he had managed to land the first part of his plan, with only one unfortunate occurrence.

Outside *Ye old Cheddar Cheese Inn*, sitting on the pavement, was the waiter, nursing a cut lip and a very bruised ego. Thomas pushed the £50 note into his hand and thanked him for his help. The man looked at Thomas, confused but thankful that empathy was so profitable that day. Perhaps the occasional bar-room dive for a week's salary was worth it!

Thomas walked down Fleet Street and posted copies of Beth's letter in two other national newspaper mail boxes. He had spent much of the train journey from Macclesfield writing out copies of the letter so that he could target as many possible outlets as possible. He hailed another cab and asked them to drop him outside the RAC Club in Pall Mall.

Having purchased a Bentley just three months previously, Thomas had been given gratis membership to this most exclusive of Gentlemen's Clubs. He had felt that it was rather pretentious given that the staff certainly seemed not to understand his northern accent, but he recognised that it could provide a very useful networking contact list for the purposes he needed right then.

On the only previous occasion that he had entered its hallowed Pall Mall premises, he had quite literally bumped into an old Army Officer with whom he had trained at Sandhurst, with the name of Elliot Chapman. Thomas and Elliot had become good friends and partnered with each other in several British Army-sponsored motor races. Following decommissioning, the friends went their separate ways, with Thomas following his business interests back in the North West, whilst Elliot moved into politics and championed a more liberal and global approach to the extremist politics that had plunged the world into so much trouble in the Great War.

It was ironic then that Elliot and Thomas were both members of a most conservative of Conservative Clubs at the RAC, but both had a healthy disregard for the extreme formality of the Club rules. On their first meeting at the Establishment, Elliot adopted Thomas' thick northern accent, which caused great consternation amongst the established members. The fact that Elliot Chapman was voted in as MP to Winchester rather helped any small hiccup in his character get forgotten by the RAC, who appreciated having movers and shakers to call upon.

It was unapologetically for this reason that Thomas called ahead and arranged for a meeting with Elliot to happen that evening at the RAC Club. "Eh, up, my lad!" was the echo across the conservatory as Elliot welcomed Thomas to the RAC with the greatest level of northern charm he could muster. Thankfully, no other members were present, as it might have risked them swallowing their dentures in surprise.

"My dear Elliot Chapman M.P., how dam glad to see you again, old boy!" Thomas mocked back in the most pompous of southern English accents. They greeted each other and found a couple of armchairs. The butler arrived with canapes.

"So, Tommy, to what pleasure have you dragged me away from Westminster on this fine October day?" Enquired Elliot.

Thomas started to recount the Silas Ledger story and how his daughter had written the most remarkable piece of literature to present a case for reforming the law on capital punishment.

Thomas passed a copy of the letter to Elliot. "And what's more, Elliot, tomorrow morning, you will see this letter in print in the Guardian newspaper and possibly other Fleet Street papers who have the bottle to print."

Thomas continued to speak whilst Elliot absorbed the contents of the letter. Then Thomas stopped, and both men were silent for a while.

"Wow!" Elliot looked up from the letter. "I need to meet this lady – Beth Ledger – she writes so incredibly well." He thought for a moment. "I realise that any reformation of such a sensitive matter is a long-term play, and perhaps it is too late to save her father from hanging, but she makes a very strong and heartfelt plea for future cases to be considered more carefully in the instance that miscarriages of justice have occurred." Elliot continued with added momentum, "Perhaps, just perhaps, I can register this as a topic to raise in the House and call for a temporary cessation of any hangings until there has been sufficient time for a debate."

"Hallelujah!" Thomas exclaimed, jumping out of his chair. "That is exactly the conclusion I hoped you would reach, and I know for sure that a miscarriage of justice has occurred in the case of Silas Ledger, so it just may be that you can achieve that in time for his life to be spared."

"Sir," Thomas addressed the butler. "May you forego this fancy crystal decanter and sherry glasses and replace them with two tankards of the best ale from the Chiswick brewery!" The two friends laughed and enjoyed the rather shocked look on the butler's face as he headed off to discuss these strange drinks orders with the Maître d. Elliot often stayed in the lodgings provided by the RAC Club. Having had such a long day, Thomas was grateful to share his room.

CHAPTER 32 - *REPRIEVE*

The very next day, Elliot Chapman MP was true to his word, he lodged a paper with the House of Commons asking for an opportunity to debate the law on capital punishment. Within the day, this action and the Guardian newspaper article, which had received rave reviews, meant that any outstanding capital punishment cases would have to wait until after the paper was heard before they could be enforced. Instructions were issued to all UK County jurisdictions, and all prisoners facing a death sentence were immediately placed on a provisional three-week period – known as "three Sundays" – to await the Hangman's noose. Cheshire had only one such case. Silas Ledger was moved from his holding cell in Chester to the high-security wing of Manchester's Strangeways Prison.

The judge presiding in the case informed Harold Sperry, the defense counsel representing Silas, and he was quick to inform Melissa, knowing that she would be desperate to tell Gwen, Beth, Will and Jack about the development. It was late in the morning that Melissa had heard, and she phoned the Post Office in Langley where Mr. Ricketts answered.

"Hello, Percy, I've got some positive news for once. Can you ask Will to fetch his sister and his mother," she said excitedly.

Mr. Ricketts knocked on the wall of the store with his walking stick. Will appeared within the minute. "Will, please get Gwen and Beth to the phone as quickly as you can. Melissa has some good news from Mr. Sperry."

Once the three Ledger family members had gathered around the phone, Gwen took the receiver, and her children lent closer to the phone.

"Silas has been moved to Strangeways prison this morning. Something has happened that means his sentence is on hold for now." Melissa struggled as her voice was shaking with emotion. "Mr. Sperry is trying to find out what it is, but I'm sure Thomas Whetton has had something to do with it as he was in London yesterday, and he took Beth's article."

Melissa was calling from Harold Sperry's office, and as she was talking, a Guardian newspaper was thrust in front of her, open on page five. Sperry pointed towards an article entitled – *Hanging – a Daughter's Tale.*

"Gwen – quickly ask Percy if he has a copy of today's Guardian newspaper," said Melissa. Mr. Ricketts had one copy left. "Turn to page five," she demanded. The newspaper was opened, and Beth's article – less than forty-eight hours after she had written it – appeared in print in a national paper! "I'll leave you to it and see you later in Langley. And can Will go and tell Jack, please? He'll be as amazed as I am." Melissa put the phone down.

Gwen, Will and Mr. Ricketts absorbed the article in front of them. Beth just sat down on a stool, wide-eyed and stunned that her raw emotion and powerful energy had been turned into words that appealed so much to have been published so quickly. All three of the readers had their hearts twisted by the passion in Beth's words about her father and the fact that society could end his life so quickly without any opportunity to consider whether justice had been fairly dealt with.

Once Gwen had recovered her composure, she turned to Beth and hugged her. "That is the most beautiful thing I've ever read – I am so proud of you." She whispered in her daughter's ear. "But the journey has only just started, your father remains convicted of murder, but at least for now, he is still alive. It gives us a chance to clear his name completely."

Will was clearly moved, having read the article, and hugged his sister, too. He couldn't manage any words, but the tears rolling down his cheeks showed just how much he cared. "I'll run down to Gurnett and make sure Jack knows." He said, wanting an excuse to grab some fresh air and wipe away his tears.

Later that day, the London–Macclesfield train arrived, and a very weary Thomas Whetton disembarked. He went to the Sperry & Burroughs office and met with the Partners. He explained more fully how he had been totally captivated by Beth's article and had felt compelled to act. He told them that he had gone directly to Fleet Street and convinced the editor of the Guardian to publish the letter. He then told them that he had leveraged the good nature of a political friend to take up the cause, and that's the reason for the temporary pause to any execution across the country – including Silas.

The Judge in Chester also made contact with Benjamin Quincy KC at his Chambers down in London, updating him on the decision to defer the hanging of Silas Ledger. Quincy had a less pleasant duty to call Henry Aspinall and Joshua Padgett to inform them about the stay of execution.

"No, no, no. My God, how can that be?" Aspinall exclaimed. "That bastard deserves to die." Quincy was surprised at the venomous reaction of Henry Aspinall, whilst Joshua Padgett was more circumspect.

"I imagine it will be around one month until the debate in Parliament can be scheduled," added Quincy to both men. "During that time, Ledger will be kept at HMP Strangeways."

Joshua Padgett was disappointed but felt that execution was inevitable. It might simply take a little longer to complete. He met with an extremely agitated Henry Aspinall at the Macclesfield Old Boy's Club later that day.

Aspinall checked to see if anyone was within earshot before he spoke to Padgett. "Joshua, do you think you could get your friend Edgar Fitch to make sure Ledger regrets moving to Strangeways? In fact, make him wish that he had been hung instead."

"Henry! Calm down. Ledger will hang, he'll just have even longer to think about his crime," Padgett responded in a hushed voice. "But I will suggest that to Fitch as he has himself been inconvenienced by Ledger's actions."

Padgett remembered that Aspinall had made some suggestion that someone other than Ledger was responsible for the criminal damage but had put that to the back of his mind as all he cared about was getting his export business back up and running, and right now, the barges were moving freely along the canal and the Cunard ships were sailing again from Liverpool across the Atlantic. Silas Ledger was guilty of something, and he was the guilty party that had been sentenced and was the person that he could claim was responsible in order to calm down the psychotic tendencies associated with working with a business partner such as Edgar Fitch.

The message had gotten around Langley that Beth had written an article that had been published in the national newspaper and had influenced the Parliament of the United Kingdom to pause and reflect on a practice that had been enshrined in law for all time. One of Langley's own children had done this. Quite a few of the villagers were unable to read, and so it was agreed that Reverend Pottinger would recite Beth's article from the chapel's pulpit later in the day.

Following the Reverend's recital, there was not a dry eye in the house. Beth Ledger had poured out a daughter's feelings about her father. Yet, it was also the collective feelings of the village about one of their own sons. Silas Ledger was simply too good a man to end his life this way.

Reverend Pottinger and Percy Ricketts had spoken with Gwen and agreed that there would be a collection at the end of the reading to support Beth's dream to go to the University of Durham. Following her father's sentence, she had sworn that her place was at home supporting her brother and mother, but her writing was simply too good to accept this, and Gwen knew that Silas would want his daughter to fulfill her potential. Following the reading, everybody was only too willing to invest in helping Beth's ambition.

Edgar Fitch was pleased to meet up with Joshua Padgett back in the Stockport pub where the idea of the liquor export trade with Cunard was originally shared. He was becoming agitated that the Irish immigrant bootleggers in Boston were putting pressure on his margins, and the business was starting to lose momentum. Thankfully, New York was still operating well, and he wanted to talk to Padgett about redirecting more cargo containers through New York. That conversation passed easily enough, and Padgett agreed to discuss that with his Cunard contact.

"Mr. Fitch, I have a favour to ask of you that I believe you will be happy to consider. You know that Silas Ledger – the man who was found guilty of disrupting our business – has been transferred to HMP Strangeways, potentially delaying his hanging", Padgett said, "it would send a good message to anyone else who might want to challenge us if Ledger was made to suffer a bit."

"Are you asking me to kill him?" Fitch asked, looking at Padgett with a smirk. "What kind of man do you think I am?"

Spluttering a little, embarrassed by his descent into the murkier world of criminality, Padgett continued, "It's just a thought that you may yourself want to consider." He concluded, having intentionally moved any responsibility onto Fitch.

Fitch recognised this immediately. "Tut, tut, tut Mr. Padgett. However, if you can get me my New York containers,

I will have a word with one or two of my colleagues on the inside, and let's just see what happens."

Thomas Whetton had received a note of gratitude from Martha Lovatt, thanking him for taking up her brother's cause, deferring his sentence, and inviting him over to the farm in Bosley for Sunday lunch at which Gwen, Will and Beth would be joining her and Nat. Thomas was delighted to accept the invitation as it would give him a chance to get to know the author of that incredible article better.

He arrived at the farmhouse early and was met at the gate by Jess, Nat's lively sheepdog, he looked around the farmyard and thought how neat and orderly the whole place looked. He realised what a wise decision he had made to offer the farm tenancy to Nat and Martha following the atrocious treatment that they had received from Aspinall over at Trentabank Farm.

The Ledgers had already arrived and they were all sitting down around the main kitchen table. There was a large bouquet of fresh flowers from Gwen's garden that Martha was arranging into a milk jug. "Oh, I am sorry," Thomas said. "I have failed to bring any gift."

Martha scalded, "Don't be silly, Mr. Whetton. We're just honoured to have you visit us, and we cannot thank you enough for doing what you have for our Silas."

"Call me Thomas, please," he replied. "All I have done is act as a messenger. It is Beth that we all have to thank for her writing." He looked over at Beth and smiled. It was the first time that he had really looked at Beth, and he noted the strong, determined look of her father, combined with the warmth and passion of her mother.

"Please sit here – Thomas," Nat said. "We have a special joint of lamb that's been slow roasting all morning, and the smell has been killing Will and myself – our saliva has been overflowing!"

They all sat down and paid respect through Nat's grace.

"Mr. Whetton, I really am so very, very grateful. Please tell us how you managed to get my letter into the newspaper so quickly," Beth asked.

Thomas told the Fleet Street story together with the spilt tray of drinks at the Old Cheshire Cheese Tavern. They all laughed. He then talked about his wartime friend and current Member of Parliament – Elliot Chapman – and how he had managed to get a paper onto the Parliamentary agenda, leading to an immediate halt to any executions. Thomas reminded everyone that this was just the first phase, and they needed to keep on the pressure.

"It would be really helpful to Elliot if you," he said, looking at Beth. "Can come down to London with me next week and speak with him and others about your father and the need to spend time considering the role of capital punishment in society."

Beth looked at Gwen, who nodded her approval in positive encouragement. "Yes, of course, I will do anything to try to change this medieval act for Dad – and for anyone else who has been falsely accused."

"Enough for now," announced Will as he took the joint of lamb from the agar and placed it on the table. Nat had been sharpening the carving knife and plunged it into the meat, releasing a very satisfactory aroma. "Let's strengthen our resolve through the joy of lamb and mint sauce!"

CHAPTER 33 -
STRANGEWAYS

Silas Ledger was not angry. From a very early stage of the trial, and particularly after Henry Aspinall had got to him in Macclesfield just before the journey to Chester in the Black Maria, he realised the inevitability of the outcome. He had listened intently to Benjamin Quincy K.C. expertly presenting the case for the prosecution. Quincy had twisted the story so that the false evidence was weighted heavily against him. Silas had no issue with the way that Harold Sperry had tried to defend him. Henry Aspinall used his influence and power to buy the authorities and decide his fate. He had even more respect for Charlie and how he had put love and positive values above the tyranny and corruption of his father. Silas hoped that the power of love would continue to prosper for him and Beth.

The only area inside Silas' control, as the accused, was to keep Will out of any trouble. He still did not know why his son had been tempted to get involved in poaching. He thought that Will had stronger morals than that. But for Silas to take the blame for the poaching was of minimal consequence given the larger crimes that he had been accused of doing.

The surprise for Silas was that there was a sudden delay called to his execution. He had wrongly assumed that his transportation to Strangeways was to the hangman's noose. Instead, he was told that his execution would be delayed by several weeks due to some technicalities happening in London. He was told no more about this, but the rumour he picked up from overhearing a conversation between two prison guards was that some 'liberal do-gooders' had complained to Westminster and that had to be cleared before hanging could continue.

Silas was placed in a single cell on the high-security wing. He was still not allowed any visits other than from Harold Sperry, who seemed to have been paid to continue as his representative. Mr. Sperry was due to visit him in four days' time.

"Don't get too used to this comfort. You'll be swinging from the noose soon enough," came a gravelly voice from the next-door cell. "I've been here for a year now and only wish they'd finish me off."

Silas didn't fear death, but he did not want the hurt that it would cause his family. Gwen, Will and Beth were everything to him. And he hated to think what pain they were going through back home in Langley. He missed his friend – Jack Moat – and the camaraderie of the quarry workers; and the community of his village. In the courtroom, he had heard what Percy Ricketts and Reverend Hamish Pottinger thought about him in their character statements. He felt very humbled.

On the third day of his incarceration in the high-security wing of Strangeways, Silas was allowed to leave his cell for the first time and take a walk outside in a communal area. The internal courtyard was looked down on by many barred windows. The walls on all sides were so tall that natural sunlight never reached the floor where the inmates walked. Each prisoner was allowed to walk clockwise around the outside of the courtyard for ten minutes, observing total silence. They wore shackles on their wrists and ankles and needed to stay three yards behind and in front of their nearest fellow prisoner. Guards with thick truncheons stood in the middle watching and occasionally barking orders. Armed guards were stationed on a perimeter platform.

Silas stood out from the rest of the prisoners due to his massive size, and it was the first time that other inmates and the guards had seen him, so he was given extra attention. Silas just closed his eyes, breathed in the relatively fresh air, and simply walked around the circuit. He recalled the spring air and the smell of heather on Teggs Nose. He thought of sitting on the bench in his cottage garden, watching Gwen trim her beloved roses. He remembered the picnic on the dam at Trentabank, surrounded by his friends and family. They were all special memories.

"Ave it, you big fucker," he heard the words before he felt the sharp pain through his side. He looked down and saw blood soaking through his prison fatigues. A large shard of glass was embedded in his side. The only visible part had been wrapped in material, which was quickly turning red. Silas fell to his knees. Everything went black.

"Mr. Ledger, Silas, are you with us?" Harold Sperry spoke softly as he leaned over and bent towards his ear. Silas opened his eyes and blinked. Around him, he could see the stark inside of a prison hospital room. It was a crowded room. Three guards, one nurse, and Mr. Sperry.

"What happened?" were Silas' first words.

Harold Sperry responded. "Welcome back, Silas. We thought we'd lost you. You've been unconscious for twenty-four hours, and you lost a lot of blood," he continued. "You were attacked in the prison yard by a fellow prisoner. He stabbed you repeatedly."

"Why?" was all Silas could say.

"In these places, vendettas happen. Scores are settled. Your attacker is serving life anyway and is saying nothing." Sperry added, "We will likely never know who requested this hit."

Silas closed his eyes again. Are there no lengths that Aspinall will go to seek his revenge? He resolved to himself, 'I've no intention of dying right now. If the end is nigh, so be it. But I'm not going this way.'

Harold Sperry returned to Macclesfield and updated his partner, Jonathan Burroughs and Thomas Whetton, as to what had happened at Strangeways. Silas was stable, but clearly, there were moves afoot within the criminal fraternity to finish him off. Perhaps some of the inmates were upset that Silas received a reprieve, if for only a couple of weeks potentially.

Thomas had just returned from London once more. This time, he and Beth had been to do a follow-up interview with the Guardian's political editor together with Elliot Chapman MP. Beth had spoken to a group of fellow MPs that Elliot had gathered, who were all sympathetic to the abolition of capital punishment. They were all left spellbound by the power of this teenager to communicate her feelings as the loving daughter of a condemned man. "This is bad news," Jonathan Burroughs stated. "Even if we are successful in delaying the date of execution, or even getting the sentence reduced to life imprisonment, then this action means that there are evil criminal minds at work wanting to silence Silas forever."

Melissa had remained in the office as she also wanted to hear about Silas' state of health. Upon hearing these words from Mr. Burroughs, she felt that she needed to inform Gwen immediately – perhaps this development might mean that she will be allowed to visit. Melissa also needed to inform Jack and be with him. She was worried that he was suffering from depression, as he seemed to be spending a lot of time on his own, and she felt that more bad news might be a tipping point.

Melissa walked up to Langley and called into the Ledger's cottage. It was a difficult conversation with Beth and Gwen, and they were naturally upset and worried. Thankfully, Martha was at the cottage and could help them come to terms with the horrible environment in which Silas was just about surviving. Melissa walked onwards to Jack's cottage. He opened the door, looking like he had not slept in days, yet his eyes were sparkling. On the small desk in his room were many of the books that he used up at the quarry. All were written with the red ink that had previously helped to incriminate Silas.

"Jack, I need to tell you about Silas, he's been badly stabbed inside Strangeways," she paused for a reaction, but none came. "And he's now under observation in the hospital wing." Melissa was expecting at least a reaction from Jack, but it was surprisingly absent.

"Sledge is strong enough to take that – we just need him to survive another few weeks." Jack looked over at her and grabbed both her shoulders, staring her in the face with an excited look.

"Mel, I think I'm on to something that will help Sledge, but I need a bit more time. We just need him to keep going for a little longer." He looked back at the paperwork. "I might need you to arrange a meeting for me and Mr. Sperry in a few days."

Melissa reacted positively, but with caution, given that she thought this could be fatigue talking. What had Jack uncovered that was making him so excited? "Can I help in any way?" she asked.

Jack shook his head, "Not right now, but can you ask Will to come over as soon as you can please?"

CHAPTER 34 - *DETECTIVE WORK*

Will had been desperate to do something to atone for having been so absent-minded as to use his father's coat and leave what had become key evidence in its pockets. He felt guilty that his father was taking the rap for his error. He arrived at Jack's cottage and ascended the stairs to Jack's room. He went in and saw Jack still staring at the papers from the quarry.

"I cannot believe I've been so stupid," Jack said, not even looking up to see that Will had entered.

"What have you found, Jack?" asked Will.

"Look at this, Will." Jack insisted that the teenager study a large set of numbers in neat lines. None of it looked remarkable to Will, who had never enjoyed mathematics at school.

"What am I supposed to be seeing?" Will said.

Jack slowly talked him through what each of the columns and rows stood for. "The first column is for the inventory of items delivered to the store, the second column is the date it was delivered, and then my initials or your father's initials as the person receiving the goods. Then the volume amount." Jack continued, "Now look at these columns. This one is the date that they were taken out of the store and by whom. Then the amount." Will still failed to see anything odd about any of the information in front of him. "Now look at this." Jack pointed to a question mark in the margin and his initials. "This is my mark, and I used it to represent an anomaly that I noticed in the amount of detonation cords that we had. More were leaving the store than we needed for any explosive work in the quarry."

Will still looked puzzled until Jack pointed to the initials next to the row where the question mark had been written. "G.C." Will read out aloud, "Gustav Coccini! I knew it," Will exclaimed. "He was taking the detonating cord out to hide in his secret store. There's the proof!"

Jack sat Will down and explained that when explosives were used in the quarry, the same length of detonating cord was needed per explosion, but the amount of dynamite used was totally the responsibility of one man – Gustav Coccini – the explosives expert on the quarry. Consequently, it could be that Gustav had been able to hide dynamite, too. Jack also shared with Will that he had always thought that Will's story about Gustav and the hidden stash of the cord was right, and he had seen a size eight boot print in the soil on the day that they had found a presumed badger sett where Will had sworn Gustav had hidden the box. He also confirmed that Gustav wore size eight boots.

"Before going any further, we must collect more evidence. That's where I need your help, Will. Coccini had access to explosives. We need to find out where he was at the time of the Kidsgrove incident, and I need your help for that."

Will was excited. Perhaps what he was about to do to help Jack could directly lead to his father's release.

"Will, it's critical that you say nothing to anyone before we collect enough to approach the police. Otherwise, we could spook Coccini and he might make a break for it." Jack started to collect the papers together. "Tomorrow, I need you to go up to the quarry and ask Fred Needles to share the work roster from the days around the incident with you. We need to see if Coccini was at work that day or not, and if not, could he have been in Kidsgrove?"

Will headed out of Jack's cottage, feeling lighter than he had done for weeks.

The following day, Will was up earlier than usual. He completed his normal newspaper delivery round for Mr. Ricketts and then headed up to the quarry.

Fred Needles was overseeing the delivery of a new piece of cutting equipment. "Hi Will, I wish we still had Battalion up here, he would have shifted this saw blade easily," Fred said upon seeing Will. "Battalion is still shifting pipes down at Gurnett, but he could be done in a couple of weeks," Will said jauntily. "Any chance of having a chat about my dad?"

"Sledge? Of course, is he okay? I've heard he's been in trouble in Manchester," said Fred.

"Yes, but he's ok. It's a different matter. Jack just asked me to check something with you and I need to see the work roster from a month ago or so."

"Of course, come up to the store shed, and I'll get you out the papers," Fred replied.

Fred unlocked the store shed and allowed Will to take a look at the rosters. "Just lock the door again as you leave, and bring me the key. I need to get back to the delivery."

Will easily found the right dates as the work roster had been well ordered, initially by Silas, and Fred had maintained the neat order well. Gustav Coccini was not registered as having been at work the day before or the day after the Kidsgrove explosion.

Will left the quarry and headed over towards the Hollins to report the positive news to Jack. Just as he was approaching the path, he saw Gustav Coccini alongside Andy Soutter and Robin Brampton. He ignored Coccini's stare and looked at Andy.

"How's Sledge?" Andy enquired. He had felt guilt and relief that Silas had taken the blame for the snared rabbit that he'd given Will and had been found in the overcoat. He, Robin and Dick Avery had all reviewed their little illegal business and tightened up the security.

"He's okay," said Will, "and my sister is trying hard to gather support in London."

Gustav sniffed and dismissively said, "The written word of an eighteen-year-old girl will never make a difference. Unfortunately, I think your father is a goner."

They all looked shocked at the Sicilian. Robin replied, pushing him away with his hand, "Gustav, you can't say that about Sledge. He's one of us!"

"He may be one of you, but he's not one of me. I'm off for lunch down at the canal."

Jack was on the Hollins with one of the farmers who had been helping with the pipeline digging. The pipeline was nearing completion and only had another ten lengths to lay before water could effectively start to flow from Trentabank through to Macclesfield. The delay that had been caused by the canal blockage had been caught up by overtime from Jack's team of quarrymen.

Will found Jack and passed on the news about the work roster and Coccini's absence at the time of the explosion.

"I also met Gustav at the quarry, he was heading down to the canal for a lunch break," Will said.

Jack looked at Will. "Excellent, that might give me time. I need to get into his lodgings in Macclesfield. I need to check something out. Will you come with me and just keep an eye on the towpath and warn me if you see him heading home rather than back to work? I don't trust that rat."

Jack and Will headed down from the Hollins towards Macclesfield. They split up as they got near to the canal. Will perched himself in a position where he could see the canal basin, close to the gypsy camp. This is where Gustav would often go for some lunchtime sustenance. In the other direction, he could look towards town and see the building where Gustav lived. He saw Jack disappearing behind a wall next to Gustav's home, about half a mile away. If Gustav did head home from the gypsy camp, Will would have plenty of time to run down and warn Jack to get out.

Plenty of laughter and clinking of glass was coming from the gypsy camp, suggesting that lunchtime was being enjoyed with a glass or two of liquor alongside the stew that was always on the open fire in a large cauldron. The over-powering smell suggested that a lot of onions had been acquired to help flavour the meat that day.

The clink of glass gave Will an idea. He waited until he saw Jack give him a signal to say that he was clear of Gustav's building, and rather than go back over to the Old King's Head Inn at Gurnett, he headed down to the canal towpath. He walked towards the canal basin, making sure that he could not be seen from the gypsy camp. The canal was full of debris as it was a heavily industrialised area. Will fished a couple of recently discarded glass bottles out of the canal. He looked at the labels, smiled and hid them in his jacket. He headed back to the Inn at Gurnett.

Jack had used his charm with the gatekeeper to gain access to Gustav Coccini's building, yet he had had to use force to open the door to the room. He was surprised to see very little in the room. What looked like a hold-all containing Gustav's possessions was by the basin. Jack went to the small desk where there was a religious Madonna figurine standing – a reminder that he was in the room of a devout Italian Catholic – despite his alleged mischief. Two prayer candles stood on either side of the small shrine. Jack opened the drawer on one side of the desk. A book of betting slips was the only content. He carefully tore one of the slips and put it in his pocket. He then opened the other drawer – nothing. He tried to push the drawer closed, but something was wedging it open. Something was causing the drawer to stick. He put his hand under the desk and felt the object preventing him from closing the drawer. He felt himself go rigid – this was what he needed above all else – it was a small package of dynamite with a detonating cord attached. The same explosive that they had up at the quarry. This was proof that Coccini had been stealing explosives, and together with other evidence gathered. This was at least sufficient to get him arrested and questioned in relation to the incident that had led to Sledge being on the verge of execution – either by hanging or by the hands of some prison vigilante. He carefully detached the dynamite from the cord and wrapped it in a cloth. He exited the building swiftly, heading back past the gatekeeper, asking him not to mention anything to Mr. Coccini as it was all meant to be a bit of a surprise. The gatekeeper was a jovial type who seemed quite happy to be on the inside of a practical joke amongst the quarrying fraternity.

Jack raced back to Gurnett, taking great care with the wrapped bundle he carried before him. He met Will outside the Inn and just mouthed the words so that only Will could hear, "I think we've got him!"

Will and Jack walked at pace into Macclesfield and straight to the Sperry & Burroughs office. Thankfully, both of the partners were in, and Melissa opened the door for them both.

"Mel, we must see Mr. Sperry now," Jack insisted.

Melissa replied, "Okay, okay, I had suggested to him that you had something you wanted to talk about, but I thought you'd give me more of a warning!"

"Hello, Jack," Harold Sperry said, coming out of his office

door. "And you must be Will Ledger. You have your father's features."

Mr. Sperry shook hands with Will. "Come into the meeting room. Jonathan..." he shouted, "I think you might want to join us, please. Mr. Moat and Mr. Ledger Jnr. Seem to have something they wish to tell us."

The two lawyers stood on one side of the large table. Melissa stood by the window, with Will and Jack standing on the other side of the table. Jack carefully laid the wrapped cloth package on the table.

"We believe we have evidence sufficient to have a person arrested on the charges that were levelled against Silas." Jack said in a precise way, although his shaky voice was a giveaway as to how nervous he was feeling. Placing the betting slip on the table, he continued his show and tell. "I have here a blank betting slip, which is the same kind of slip on which the threatening messages were written in red ink." He then pulled out of his inside pocket a number of sheets of paper from the quarry. "Here I have proof that someone – that someone being a quarry worker - was taking an excess of detonating cord out of the store room at the quarry. This person has the initials GC." Jack pointed this out to the lawyers. He then explained that Will had found where this was being hidden many months ago, and it was from this location that he had picked up one of the pieces of cord and had, inadvertently, placed it inside his borrowed father's coat.

Jack continued, "This suspicion made me confident that more could be found about the individual, so I asked Will to check out GC's whereabouts using the roster book up at the quarry. Will can confirm that the rosters showed that GC was not at work on the day before and on the day of the explosion." Will nodded vigorously.

Jack was getting momentum and confidence up now. "We also did not ask ourselves the question of how easy it is to lay the explosives that caused the devastation in Kidsgrove. Well, I can tell you that it is a highly risky and skilled job, and quarries employ explosive specialists to lay dynamite. We only have one person at Teggs Nose who is licensed in this skill. He just happens to have the initials GC. Sledge has never been trained in laying explosives, so the likelihood that he could have ever caused the explosion at Kidsgrove must be challenged further."

Both lawyers were looking increasingly interested in every statement. Jack recognised the growing sense of anticipation and continued. "Explosives can only be handled by one person at the quarry, yet the amount that they use is dictated by that person depending on the requirements at the rock face. Gritstone seams are thick and dense, and so often, they will need a large amount of explosive to shift them. But sometimes, there are fissures in the rock, meaning that just a small explosion will be sufficient to break it. Only one person determines the amount and could easily have hidden additional dynamite for use personally."

With this final statement, Jack's eyes moved towards the cloth on the table. He carefully unwrapped it to reveal the dynamite and detonating cord. "This, gentlemen, was found in Gustav Coccini's lodging room in Macclesfield less than an hour ago."

The final reveal was a shock to the lawyers and they took several steps back. "Is it safe?" Harold Sperry asked.

Jack confirmed that if handled carefully, it would remain stable, and with no detonating cord, the explosives would be inert.

At that moment, Will stepped forward, thinking that his own discovery was minor compared to Jack's revelations.

"Excuse me, sirs, but I also have something to share." Will took the empty bottles out of his coat. "I found these floating in the canal, just down from the canal basin and the gypsy camp. I found them as Gustav Coccini was lunching with them, also about an hour ago."

The lawyers looked at the labels of the spirit bottles. Each of them had an Export Only sticker on them, quite clearly marking them as illegal for consumption in the UK. It also meant that they could be traced back to the supplier, who could very likely be part of Joshua Padgett's consignment that had been taken down at Kidsgrove. It proved that there were highly likely to be other stashes of liquor around the area, similar to that found in the Ledger's back garden.

Jack looked at Will and gave him a thumbs-up smile. "Well done, kiddo! Great detective work."

"Indeed, this all looks very compelling." Harold Sperry stroked his chin in thought.

"Melissa, can you call D.I. Cooper straight away, please and ask him to come to our offices." Jonathan Burroughs added, looking at the table, "I don't think it would be wise to move that dynamite too much more."

Detective Inspector Cooper and two other officers had responded to the phone call from Melissa, keen to understand what developments could possibly have happened over at the lawyer's office. Having heard the story of the evidence staring them in the face, the very least they urgently needed to do was to bring Gustav Coccini in for questioning. Police reinforcements were requested from the town station, and they surrounded the building that Coccini lived in.

From the canal towpath, Gustav Coccini peered across to the front gate of his home. He had been happy there for the last four years, but he knew that he needed to be more cautious than ever, given the strange looks he was getting from Jack Moat whenever they crossed paths. Thankfully, he had returned home before the police had arrived, and so he was now well away from the house, up on the hillside, looking back. He watched the police as they entered the building. Thank goodness for the fact that Jack Moat had had to break the lock on his door. The first thing that Gustav checked for was the explosive taped underneath the desk. Finding that it was missing, he realised that he needed to move fast. His bag was already largely packed in preparation, and it only took him a minute to pack the small statue of the Madonna in his bag and flee the building, careful not to be spotted by the Gatekeeper.

He needed to lay low for a while, and the Gypsy encampment would be too obvious a place, but perhaps Boksic had a barge heading out of the canal basin today, and he could hide aboard and get out of Cheshire. Coccini knew that he had been lucky to find such a scapegoat as Sledge quite so quickly. He was thankful that Henry Aspinall was so intent on framing Ledger, and he couldn't quite fully understand why he had not been questioned at all in the investigation. That fact had made him very relaxed about how easily he had escaped with such a major crime. He had not intended to murder anyone, only cause embarrassment and commercial loss to both Padgett and Aspinall. However, now the heat had been turned up, he had to vanish.

CHAPTER 35 - *APPEAL*

The very fact that the police found that Coccini's room had been vacated so quickly – confirmed by the security guard – and that there was no sight nor sound of him at the quarry or at the Gypsy encampment, immediately raised the likelihood that this new evidence had substance. A warrant for Gustav's arrest was issued and circulated across all local police forces.

Harold Sperry quickly lodged an Appeal with Chester Crown Court, backed by a statement from D.I. Cooper about the nature of the new evidence, bringing doubt on the conviction of Silas. The Detective Inspector had also spoken with Joshua Padgett and Henry Aspinall about the likely appeal, but it was a difficult conversation, and Aspinall insisted on meeting later that evening. Jonathan Burroughs strictly briefed Will, Jack, and Melissa not to treat this in any way as a done deal. It was important that justice was seen to follow due diligence. Gwen and Beth were informed but told not to expect anything to move quickly. Even so, Harold Sperry was confident that the Judge in the original case would support an Appeal hearing within the week.

D.I. Cooper had prepared himself for a caustic

conversation with Henry Aspinall, and so it was pleasing that Joshua Padgett welcomed him into his office in Duke Street with such a big smile. "Well done, Detective Inspector. It looks like we've got the real criminal behind this now." Padgett had been concerned with his ongoing business on the basis that Henry Aspinall had admitted to him that Silas Ledger was not responsible for the attack on the barge. There was nothing out there suggesting that another attack might not be in the offing.

"So it was that little Italian bookkeeper," Padgett said. "Bloody hell! I remember now that it was he who handed over the same betting slip at an event in Bollington that I attended. I should have remembered and linked the threatening notes and the betting slip, but it was months ago."

There was a knock on the front door. Padgett welcomed in Henry Aspinall. "Henry – good news – you recall the betting slips that we were given in Bollington, and that Italian bookkeeper. He was only an expert with explosives and worked for your quarry operation on Teggs Nose. It was all too obvious, really." Padgett quietened down as he saw the scowl on Aspinall's face grow.

"This new evidence might be strong, but what about the stolen liquor that was found hidden at Ledger's house? Surely, that still stands against him." Aspinall demanded.

D.I. Cooper realised that Henry Aspinall cared less for justice and more for seeing Silas Ledger behind bars or, preferably, worse. "Mr. Aspinall, so much liquor has been stolen from barges in recent months that it is turning up in several places – including earlier today by the canal basin. There might be a number of hiding places being used by gangs, but this does not necessarily implicate the owner of the location in which it is found. That will be the new line of defense used by Ledger's legal team."

In a weak attempt to console Aspinall, the detective added, "At least the snared rabbit carcass still provides undeniable evidence that Silas Ledger is a poacher."

"Have a whiskey, Henry," Padgett said, "trying to calm the obvious anger arising in his colleague."

Aspinall snatched the whiskey from him and downed it in one, thrusting the glass back for a refill. "Dam, that bloody lucky bastard, why didn't you get him killed at Strangeways?" Aspinall spat out the words

Joshua Padgett looked at D.I. Cooper with raised eyebrows and felt a need to move the conversation on quickly. "Ha, ha, Henry, good joke. Let's face it, the best news is that we have the right man now, and you have one less poacher to deal with on your country estate. D.I. Cooper – I'm sure you're needed back at the Police Station to complete paperwork. Thanks for calling over."

Padgett opened the door and ushered the confused policeman out of the door. Aspinall was already pouring himself a third large whiskey.

"Joshua, why could Edgar Fitch not sort out the killing of Ledger?" Aspinall demanded, "I thought he owned the corridors of Strangeways."

"He does," replied Padgett. "But I don't think they've come up against someone as big or as tough as Ledger before. Not many people would survive a multiple stabbing attack, yet he did."

"Well, he still owes me, make sure Fitch knows that."
Aspinall responded. Padgett looked at him and thought that
Aspinall really didn't know the kind of man Fitch was at all.

The Crown Court Judge at Chester allowed an Appeal to
take place within the week. The case was presented, and given
that the evidence against Coccini was that much more
compelling than the evidence facing Silas and that Coccini
had escaped custody, it looked more likely than ever that the
wrong man had been brought to justice.

Gustav Coccini became the number one suspect in
causing the explosion at Kidsgrove and the consequential
death of a lock-keeper. He had fled and was unable to face
trial, but all involved assumed his guilt. Silas Ledger's
sentence was reduced to six months for poaching illegal
game. Following his stay in the prison hospital, Silas was
moved out of the high-security wing of HMP Strangeways and
was moved into a shared cell in the main section of the prison.
An area that the Sons of Strangeways gang operated in with
total authority.

Although this move of location would bring Silas into
closer contact with the gang, at least he would be allowed
fortnightly visits from his family, and most importantly – any
threat of a legal death sentence had disappeared.

Thomas Whetton joined the gathering at the Dunstan
Inn. The news about the result of the appeal was sent to the
only phone in the village at the Post Office, directly from
Chester. Harold Sperry had made the call, and Percy Ricketts

had taken it. Although the village was holding its collective breath, there was confidence that the result would go the way of the Ledgers. The only shame was that the poaching element of the case still needed to be recognised, and Silas still remained in prison on this minor charge.

Thomas spoke to a small group, including the Ledger family. "Beth, do you realise what your father's case has done for justice? It has become a total endorsement and example of why the death penalty needs to be reviewed and handled with caution. An innocent man could have died if the sentence had been carried out. It would have been a total miscarriage of justice." He added, "This will hugely help our friend, Elliot Chapman, in his campaign at Westminster. I am sure that Parliament will at least agree to limit the death penalty further and it may possibly be the start of the end of this ultimate sentence once and for all. Only time will tell."

Thomas raised a glass and toasted Beth. Everyone in the bar cheered and raised their own glasses. Conscious that the true celebration would only ever be when Silas could be there with them. He tempered down his next toast.

"And we should also recognise Jack and Will for the magnificent work they did to help identify the true culprit. But let's also think of Silas and raise a glass to his innocence and his return to Langley in the not-too-distant future. God be willing."

At this point, Reverend Pottinger piped up, never one to miss an opportunity to remind the village about the need for spiritual enrichment. "Thank you, Mr. Whetton. That's a good opportunity to remind everyone that in God we trust, and I invite all of you to join me at the chapel tomorrow at the

Memorial service for Sid Bayley, as it's been one year since his very sad passing. We will also be saying a prayer for Silas and to ask God to speed him home to us."

CHAPTER 36 - *ROYAL OPENING*

It was a time of triumph for the Chamber of Commerce in Macclesfield. On the 2nd of October 1929, the water from the new Trentabank reservoir started to flow through the Hollins pipeline.

The Teggs Nose quarrymen had successfully diversified their trade, and, under the supervision of Jack Moat, completed the successful laying of the pipeline on time. The official opening of the Water Board operation was to happen in the presence of Prince Henry and hosted by the Duke of Gloucester. All of Cheshire's most important business leaders had taken the journey from Macclesfield, through Langley, and up to the dam wall.

Henry Aspinall, on whose land the reservoir was built and the pipeline had been laid, felt the need to be centre stage. Aspinall had suffered a rare defeat, losing his chance to use the law to destroy his nemesis, Silas Ledger. The hope was still there that a contract kill – inside prison – might be instigated via the shady network in which he was increasingly becoming involved. Joshua Padgett had introduced him to this through the illegal boxing bout ten months ago. The irony was that this illegal event had also brought him into contact with Gustav Coccini. And having been double-crossed and lost a lot of money, Coccini had exacted revenge by blowing up one of the Aspinall Company barges. Aspinall was learning fast that it was a dangerous game to play in the circles of organised crime.

But today was his day, on his land, and he demanded the highest of profiles. Henry Aspinall was also determined that Joshua Padgett – a man that he had worked with for the sake of monetary benefit – would be limited to the background of the event.

Some of the Langley villagers had boycotted the opening ceremony as they still viewed the reservoir with disgust, having involved the forced flooding of several farms and changing their beloved landscape forever. However, most had moved on and recognised that the town's industries needed the water supply in order to thrive.

As the chief sponsor of Langley Cricket Club, Henry Aspinall had asked them to put up a large marquee and stage a celebrity cricket game despite the lateness of the season. The festive atmosphere was helped by the attendance of a local brass band who had set up in the marquee and were already booming out many favorite patriotic tunes of the age.

The plan was to start the ceremonial event on the dam wall where Prince Henry was due to turn the valve to start the flow of water.

The weather had been kind, and the vast spread of the

reservoir stretched out like a mirror. At the far end was a small copse of deciduous trees, beyond which rose the moorland over towards Buxton. As this was all the catchment area for the reservoir, Aspinall had already done a further land deal with the Water Board to plant a large conifer forest for the purpose of building new longer term commercial opportunities in game hunting as well as logging. He had decided not to make public these plans just yet, as he knew that, again, the local villagers would resent him even more than they already did. Aspinall did not really care as long as there was money in it for him.

The VIP party was in place on the dam wall, and the over-sized valve tap was gaudily decorated with a red ribbon. The brass band from down below struck up the National Anthem, and everyone stood and sang. It was made more tuneful by the Langley Methodist chapel choir, who had been given a pound each to attend and add some volume. A flock of Canadian geese were startled into flight by the sudden loud and semi-coordinated sound.

The Duke of Gloucester nodded to Prince Henry, and the valve tap was turned. A round of applause followed, which had been stage-managed to be initiated by the directors and friends of the Water Board. The band struck up a version of Handel's Water Music, which amused the Prince immensely. The VIP party headed back to the road and was transported by a fleet of cars that had entirely blocked the access road. Others who had made the climb up to the top of the dam carefully descended and headed towards the Cricket Club for refreshments.

Henry Aspinall ushered the VIP party into a reserved

section of the marquee in order to avoid mixing with the masses and have the best view of the cricket match that was due to start on cue as soon as the brass band had finished their set.

Out of the corner of his eye, Henry spotted his wife, Florence. He was surprised to see her there as he thought she had been bed-bound for weeks. They had been living largely separate lives in the manor house for the last two months. Florence was looking unsteady on her feet and was making a scene while trying to get another drink from the waitress. Arthur Brice – Aspinall's estate manager – was trying to dissuade her from taking the drink, but it ended up spilling down his front.

Aspinall stared lovelessly at his wife and mouthed to his Estate Manager, "Get my wife out of here. Now!"

The last thing he needed was an embarrassing scene on his special day in front of his VIP guests. He turned his back on his wife and the struggling Arthur Brice, who was wrestling with Florence, to assist a quick exit. Florence was now loudly demanding to be introduced to the Prince. Aspinall looked round for help, and all he could see was Joshua Padgett, who he summoned over and introduced to the Duke and the Prince. Padgett was only too delighted to be the distraction. Aspinall excused himself and disappeared to confirm that Brice had been successful in taking back control of his wife.

"Why the bloody hell did you bring that woman here?" Aspinall asked.

"Mrs. Aspinall forced me to sir. I'm sorry." He replied.

"Just get rid of her now. Take her home immediately."

Florence turned round angrily. "Fuck you, Henry – you've lost Charles, you've lost me, but you don't seem to care."

"Florence – I have a drunk as a wife. I have a loser as a son. All I care about now is keeping the Aspinall Company afloat, and none of this is helping. Go home." He turned and walked away.

Thankfully, Joshua Padgett had done his job and distracted Aspinall's VIP guests, but a small yawn from the Duke suggested that Padgett's details of the Waterworks of East Cheshire had gone on too long.

"Excuse me, gentlemen, the time has come to ask Your Majesty to meet the cricket captains and umpires and toss the coin to decide the start of the game." Aspinall formally announced.

Just as the Prince was shaking hands with the umpires, Aspinall looked around the cricket ground. The weather looked to be set fair for the afternoon. Everything – other than the unfortunate appearance of Florence – was going to plan. Off in the distance, he could see Teggs Nose, where his quarry had been a consistent form of income for him over the years, and then the Hollins, where his pipeline had secured him more ongoing rental monies from the Water Board, on top of the sale of the land now occupied by the reservoir. His new conifer forest would provide a long-lasting legacy well beyond his time on earth. If only he had an heir to leave it all to.

In that instant, he refocused his gaze back on the cricket pitch. On the far side, he saw two young people, hand-in-hand, standing next to the scorebox. One was Beth Ledger; the other was a tall youth with a long coat and wide-brimmed hat. The closer he stared, the more he recognised the features. It was Charles, his son.

How dare he show up to his father's glorious day. The blatant audacity of the two of them! Henry Aspinall had banished his son from ever returning to Langley and to the riches of life that so easily could have been his inheritance. He had almost killed Beth's father and possibly still might do. Perhaps now, Charles was regretting the choice that he had made. Perhaps now, he would have preferred to be on Henry's side of the cricket pitch, inside the marquee, hobnobbing with royalty. However, this hope seemed forlorn, as the two young lovers were laughing and certainly enjoying each other's company as if nothing else in the world mattered. And Henry despised them all the more for it.

Beth and Charlie were just starting out on their studies at Durham University. Charlie had been there all summer working to supplement the bursary fund supplied by his school's Old Boy network, plus whatever allowance his mother was able to pass to him outside of the watchful eyes of his father. Beth had accepted the generous funding that had been given to her by the villagers at Langley, and a large one-off payment had been gifted to her by an anonymous benefactor in London, closely associated with the social reform work that Elliot Chapman MP was working on in Westminster. Her suspicions were that it was Elliot and Thomas Whetton together, although they denied any association when playfully challenged by Beth!

Charlie and Beth had decided to return to Cheshire for a weekend with the intention of seeing Gwen, Will and their various friends. There was no desire whatsoever to run into

Henry Aspinall. In fact, as soon as they saw him across the cricket field, they decided it was time to say their goodbyes to Moll Brampton, Beth's best friend, and a couple of the older cricketers who Charlie knew from his many days as a scorer at the Club. They took one last look over at the pomp and ceremony going on at the marquee and knew that the more enjoyable place for them was on the less populated side of the field with the hills and moorland stretching out behind them. They had promised each other that they would retrace their steps of a year ago and go back up to the moorland where they had trespassed and cut the wire fence high above Saddlers Way. The farmer or landowner had fixed the fence, but it didn't take them long to break the fence down once more... laughing as they did it.

One of the early subjects that Beth had been reading at university was around land ownership and the rights to roam on common land. She had joined an underground socialist youth organisation that was promoting the idea of trespass. This single act of vandalism made her feel like she was doing her bit to support the fight. Charlie just watched as Beth took out her plyers and went about cutting the wire. He felt like he had done a year ago – liberated and so much in love – but even more so.

CHAPTER 37 - *A WELSH MINER*

Gwen had been given special dispensation by the Macclesfield textile mill in which she worked. One day each month, she was allowed to take the train up to Manchester to visit HMP Strangeways and see her husband. On the third visit, she noticed that as she and Silas were talking, a number of the other inmates who were surrounding them were looking at Silas and speaking about him in hushed tones to their own visitors. Something odd was going on, she thought.

Silas seemed fine, but then he always did. She asked about the conditions he had now been living in, having been transferred out of the high-security wing. He shrugged and said everything was fine, and with good behaviour, he could be out of prison within the next four months.

"Best not count our chickens, Silas," Gwen would say, "the good news is that you will be back in Langley at some future date. That's so much better than what it had been at one stage."

She had updated him about how well Will was now doing,

working alongside Jack on a new pipe-laying job over near Congleton. She passed on regards from Fred Needles and, the quarry team, and the rest of the Langley community. She told him how the Christmas and New Year period had gone and how she had been mobbed by well-wishers wanting to pass on their season's greetings to him.

She listed out all of the updates like a newsreader on fast-forward! A smaller turkey dinner was had with Martha, Nat, and Will. Beth and Charlie had stayed in Durham as they had got holiday jobs together at a large Country Hotel, and the festivities of Christmas and New Year had demanded their presence. However, they would be back in Langley at some stage before Easter, as there was some big event near Kinder Scout that Beth had been twittering about in one of her many letters home. Gwen's crochet and knitting group was now twenty-strong, and there was even a first male member. Reverend Pottinger had promised that he would produce a cover for his own prayer cushion, and he was a quarter of the way through a very elaborate design of a dove holding an olive branch. The Reverend had wanted to produce two fishes to represent the occasional gift that appeared on his doorstep, but he considered that too risqué!

Silas looked at Gwen in wonderment. He had always admired her ability to paint the world in such positive ways. He could listen to her chatter forever. However, soon, time was up and the prisoners needed to return to their cells before the visitors were allowed to leave. Once more, Gwen was aware of people looking at Silas' large frame as he ambled towards the exit back to the main prison building. She also noticed that he was limping slightly. It was too late to ask him about that now, but she made a mental note to ask him the next time she visited.

For the three months that Silas had lived in the main section of the prison, he had been sharing a cell with an inmate called Owain Jones – a Welshman – who had been found guilty of arson. He was an ex-miner from near Aberystwyth and had found the gradual takeover of properties in the Snowdonia region of Wales by 'rich' Englishmen an atrocity against the Welsh nation. Owain's crime was to burn down a holiday cottage near Betws-y-Coed that was owned by a magistrate from Shrewsbury. He had been drunk on one winter's evening and had had an argument with a friend in a pub on his way home from a football match. His friend had said that Owain was all words and no action about his dislike of the 'English invasion,' so this time, Owain decided to act.

He had taken a can of heater oil from the back of a pub and walked through the snow into a nearby village. He saw a cottage that looked vacant but was clearly a holiday cottage. Doused its thatch in oil and set it alight. He then trudged back through the snow drifts to the pub to claim a last drink before heading off to catch the night bus home. The next thing he knew was the arrival of two police officers who had tracked his footprints back to the pub. The smell of paraffin on his clothes was sufficient for the arrest, and the matching footprint with his boots confirmed his guilt. He was sent to Strangeways for three years and had served two.

Owain immediately liked Silas and vice versa – a miner and a quarryman – kindred spirits who understood that their business was what kept the nation running. "Sledge, you're the first Englishman I've met who I like." Owain admitted, "and the fact that you're in here for poaching from a wealthy English landowner makes your crime all the more worthy!"

Sledge enjoyed Owain's endless description of coal seams underground and the joy he used to get from seeing what he would describe as black gold appearing following a few lusty strikes of his pick axe.

Owain was very aware that Sledge had travelled an unusual path since his sentencing at Chester Crown Court. Not many people sentenced to execution live to tell the tale, but here was a man who had courted death and survived. He was a bit of a celebrity in the main prison but hid from that new found status. Sledge just wanted to serve his time and return to his beloved family and countryside. Owain respected that and found it strange that some of the attention Sledge was getting started to become threatening. He soon learned that a large and influential gang within Strangeways wanted to cause Sledge harm beyond that which he'd already experienced in the stabbing incident within the high-security wing. Owain learned that he needed to have eyes in the back of his head in order to watch out for his cell mate. It's not that Sledge needed any physical help, really. Early on, three inmates had attacked Sledge in an unsupervised area of the canteen. The attack was over in less than thirty seconds. Two of the attackers were unconscious and bloodied, the third was squealing like a pig, with a broken arm and three broken ribs. The law of Strangeways meant that nobody ever ratted on another inmate, and so the three injured inmates all claimed to the prison guards that they had slipped or fallen over badly!

Sledge's mild manner and gentle countenance did not

mean that he would not defend himself if the need arose. Owain recognised that Sledge and he could be good for each other and was quite comfortable becoming another set of ears and eyes, scrutinising any interaction that prison life might throw up.

The hobble that Gwen had noticed was another incident which could have been so much more severe. Owain and Sledge were working in the greenhouse where Strangeways grew its own vegetables. Six of the gang, who called themselves 'Sons of Strangeways', had managed to get a corrupt guard to allocate them time in the greenhouse with Sledge and Owain. The guard then conveniently took a tea break with his partner, leaving the greenhouse without any supervision.

The largest member of the gang approached Sledge and hissed, "Mr. Fitch sends his regards." He swung a garden fork into Sledge's upper thigh. Stunned, Sledge looked at the fork in his leg, with the blood-forming around where the spikes had pierced his flesh. Most men would have been knocked over by the ferocity of the blow and the obvious pain that this would have inflicted. But like a mosquito being swatted, Sledge brushed the fork off his body, making the blood spurt out of the wounds. At this point, the other men started to attack Sledge with their own weapons – two spades, a hoe and rakes and another fork. Like annoying insects, Sledge repelled each attack with his massive arms and with the fork that he had removed from his own leg. Not that he was really needed, but Owain felt that he should wade in at this point, possibly to stop Sledge from killing these ill-advised gang members. Once Sledge had grounded the attackers and removed their weaponry, Owain felt it was his duty to deliver a few final blows to further incapacitate them.

The garden was a mess, with trellises and bamboo stakes ripped from their original positions and vegetation looking more like an unkempt jungle than a cared-for prison garden.

The two guards returned after five minutes to a scene they were not expecting. Six of the hardest prisoners in their custody, nursing their injuries whilst moaning in pain, were being looked down on by Silas Ledger, standing but using a hoe as a crutch. His left leg was streaming with blood. Next to Silas was Owain Jones, who was smiling whilst rubbing his knuckles, as if he were looking forward to a bell being rung and the announcement of 'round two'!

It took a month for the external damage on Sledge's leg to sort itself out, but thankfully, the fork had not pierced any major artery or bone. The muscle would mend in time, and the limp would only prove temporary. The Sons of Strangeways had again tried and failed to intimidate and hurt Silas Ledger. His legendary status within Strangeways just grew. The gentle giant was not to be messed with, and Owain enjoyed spreading this word further – the tales of the canteen and greenhouse attacks were significantly distorted in his favour – but always championed Sledge as an indestructible force of nature.

CHAPTER 38 - *TRESPASS*

Both Charlie and Beth were excelling at their university studies but in very different ways. Charlie used his naturally logical mind to apply structure to any legal debate. He was helped by having a photographic memory that allowed him to recall historical case studies in detail to better shape his argument. His professors were amazed at how advanced a first-year student could be. A local law firm in Durham had heard about this prodigy at a Law School dinner and had invited him to shadow a number of their Corporate Law Partners in order to get a better idea of how Law practice happened in real business life. Charlie loved every minute of this experience, and he craved time with the solicitors afterward to discuss how they had worked on a particular case. His thirst fuelled their work appetite further, and so he was a much-demanded resource to tag along on cases being heard at Durham Crown Court.

Beth was also causing a stir in her academic circle. Her passion for social justice had already been widely known due to the fact about her letter to the Guardian beseeching the Government to repeal or abolish capital punishment as a form of sentence. Beth continued to champion social reform regardless of how controversial it might have been. If the 'little man' was being trodden on by the 'big man,' then Beth wanted to challenge the status quo. She attended many lectures inside the university and increasingly outside, where radical groups – often with feminism at heart – had started to form wherever there were large student populations. One that she was particularly close to was a Marxist political group supporting public access to the countryside. Increasingly, wealthy landowners had been denying public access. Frustrated by the lack of progress achieved by lobbying Parliament, some groups had started to illegally trespass on privately owned land as a form of protest against wealthy landowners.

Beth had always been interested in this subject, and she had actively trespassed on a number of occasions, including several times with Charlie. However, she had never been on an organised trespass.

Kinder Scout was a large moorland plateau in Derbyshire that was a popular area for hikers to visit and enjoy the natural beauty. However, wealthy landowners had begun to fence the land and employ more gamekeepers to evict hikers, as it was felt that these trespassers were disturbing nesting grouse, which the landowners sought to profit from during the hunting seasons. Various different groups, including a group from Durham, had agreed to meet at Bowden Bridge quarry near Hayfield and walk in different groups across the moors.

Beth encouraged Charlie to come with her, and, as he was never able to deny Beth anything, Charlie agreed to join the peaceful protest. Around four hundred hikers met up at the top of Kinder Scout. There were a number of gamekeepers on the moor who had been asked to deny access 'by any means'. The gamekeepers were carrying shotguns and looked threatening.

"Fuck off, you scum!" one of the gamekeepers shouted at the group of hikers who were just sitting amongst the heather, making their point about their right to be there. A couple of protest songs had been rehearsed, including 'we shall not be moved,' an early African – American gospel slave hymn.

The verbal abuse was ignored by the hikers, but one of the Durham contingent did shout back. "I hope you enjoy your job mate." Not disguising the heavy hint of sarcasm.

This was a trigger for three of the gamekeepers to move into the group and start to physically push people away from the moor towards a path leading down into the valley. One of the hikers tripped and fell.

"Stop it now," yelled Beth, "you bastards need to understand what you're doing!"

One of the three gamekeepers shouted back, "We know what we're doing, luv, we're getting rid of rubbish from the moors. Go home, you're not wanted round here."

Charlie stopped Beth from confronting the obnoxious man. The sight of a hunting stick and a shotgun were enough for both to back down. They helped the lady up who had been knocked over, and continued to descend the clough. Occasional verbal insults were thrown backwards and forwards, but no other physical intimidation happened. As the hikers got closer to the valley floor, they noticed three police vans and around ten policemen.

The senior officer present addressed the hundred or so hikers. "We've had reports that there was a scuffle on top of the moor. And that you have all crossed into private land causing a nuisance to the rightful owners."

The crowd was incensed, and more jostling took place with the gamekeepers who had surrounded and corralled the group into a section between them and the police vehicles.

"Bloody shame on you all." Shouted a middle-aged man just next to Charlie.

"Get him," the senior officer pointed to Charlie. Two police officers with riot shields pushed through the crowd and marched Charlie off to the van. The man who had shouted was absorbed back into the crowd.

Beth did not believe what she was witnessing. Policing gone mad, society gone mad, and her innocent boyfriend being arrested for, she knew not what! She followed Charlie and the two officers to the van, protesting throughout, and once Charlie was in the van, she banged on the outside and demanded his release and that of the four other people who had been considered ringleaders. Her desperate pleas were ignored, and the police vans disappeared. The Authorities had some scapegoats – guilty or not – they'd done a job.

Beth was now on her knees, crippled by the weight of injustice. "This cannot be happening – where are they taking them?" she pleaded with one of the only remaining policemen.

Ignoring the excess of emotional outpouring, the officer stated very matter-of-factly - "They'll be heading back to

Manchester's central police station, Miss. They'll be charged or released on bail. May spend a night or more at Her Majesty's Pleasure."

Beth turned round, tears in her eyes. What more could she do? She and the group got back on their buses and all headed back to where they'd come from. As soon as she got to Durham, Beth went to see her Professor at Trevalyn College, who also tutored Charlie in one of their shared Sociology lectures.

"Hi Professor, I'm sorry it's so late, but I have a problem, and so does Charlie Aspinall," Beth said with a tired, broken voice. "We were involved in a protest action, trespassing on Kinder Scout Moor, to raise awareness of our rights to walk freely. Charlie has been taken off in a police van to Manchester. He didn't do anything wrong. The gamekeepers started a skirmish, and Charlie got blamed."

The professor looked concerned, "Oh dear, that's not good news. However, trespassing is not a criminal offense, so Charlie should be okay unless he did something else."

Silas and Owain were at breakfast, minding their own business, when Charlie was marched through the canteen holding a fresh pile of standard prison items that a newcomer is issued. Silas, never one to show much emotion, stared at the sight with his jaw open.

"Sledge? Are you alright?" said Owain, who had his back to the rest of the canteen.

"Charlie – Charlie Aspinall? Is that you?" Silas remarked, still with a look of disbelief on his face. "What are you doing here?"

By now, Owain had turned around and seen the procession of the five new inmates making the routine march through the canteen. He knew the lead prison officer, a fellow Welshman. "Hey, Jonesy, can you send that new lad over here, we'll show him the ropes. Saves you a job."

"Thanks, Owain Boyo," the lead prison officer replied. He pointed the seat next to Owain out to Charlie and directed him to sit.

"What? Why? How?" exclaimed Silas. "You are the last person I'd expect to be here!" He sat there incredulously, looking over Charlie, checking that it really was him. Charlie was dressed in his prison fatigues but still seemed so out of place in the soulless canteen of Strangeways. The Charlie that Silas recalled was so innocent and fresh-faced – loving nature and wholly invested in academia and love for his daughter! How could he have taken a wrong turn and ended up in prison?

Owain intervened in Silas' thinking. "Sledge, give the lad a chance to breathe, and I'm sure he'll tell us his story." He put a gentle hand on Charlie's shoulder and whispered. "Now lad, it seems like you know Sledge here, that's good as that makes you alright in my eye. Stick with us, and we'll see you right."

Charlie turned to Owain and thanked him with a nod of his head. "I appreciate that Mr. ...."

"Just call me Owain," the Welshman jumped in, "I'm Sledge's only mate here in the 'Ways, and we need as many people as possible on our side right now, so you are very welcome."

Charlie looked at Silas and spoke quietly. "Silas, firstly, let me say that Beth is fine and so looks forward to being able to see you again upon your release. We were both so delighted to know that your original sentence was repealed."

Charlie then went on to explain the reason that he had been imprisoned, but that he was hopeful that it would only be a short period due to the fact that he had been wrongly identified. His main concern was that his ambition to practice law professionally might be hampered if he had any kind of conviction.

Silas smiled with wonderment and pride that his daughter's activism had moved from paper and pen – albeit that which saved his life – and now moved on to protests to protect human rights. Having saved her father, she had now lost her boyfriend. He had to pay her back by helping to sort this out.

"Charlie, you must know how the legal system works, and I know that Beth will be working from her side to make sure you're out of here quickly. But do you have any legal representation?" asked Silas.

"Not yet," replied Charlie. "The arresting officer who escorted me here from the Police Station said that I would be contacted shortly."

"Okay, if you have not heard today, I will have a word with Mr. Sperry – my solicitor - later this afternoon, as I am due to see him anyway. We need to get you out of here quickly."

In Silas' mind, there were a number of reasons for this speed requirement. He did not want Charlie's innocence lost by being amongst some of the most notorious thugs in England. Silas remained a target close to the Sons of Strangeways gang, and any associate of his, especially a young one like Charlie, would be considered 'easy pickings.' Most critically, Charlie was innocent and somehow, they needed justice to be heard this time and he needed to get Charlie released so that he could return to Beth. Silas did not know whether Henry Aspinall would know about his son's wrongful arrest, but he felt that Henry would quite enjoy the idea of having his son's freedom taken away from him for a while and might see it as a fitting punishment for rejecting the life that Henry had planned out for him.

Harold Sperry was waiting for Silas in the meeting zone of the prison's visitor area. As was procedure, all of the visitors had been invited inside to take up seats on one side of small tables before the prisoners were brought in, handcuffed and led in by prison officers and individually seated facing their visitors. Rather than arranging private meetings for the two of them, Melissa – who was in charge of these meetings back at the Sperry & Burroughs law firm – had worked out that using this more public format would allow a greater number of meetings for the lawyer to meet with the client, and also allowed private messages to be exchanged too. Harold Sperry recognised that with Silas Ledger and his whole family, he was working with a good family who had been unfairly treated, and anything he could do to help, he was very willing to oblige. Melissa always made sure that Gwen knew when Harold would be visiting and as Gwen was there herself every three weeks, she generally used the Solicitor meetings to send letters or small home-cooked goodies for Silas to enjoy.

Having had these checked by the prison guards, Harold Sperry sat down at the table to await Silas' arrival. He looked around and realised that almost every other table had relatives at it. This was his only professional visit, yet he felt that given how close he had got to the Ledger family, it was appropriate that he felt able to act on a personal as well as a professional basis.

Silas' large frame appeared at the entrance door, emphasised even more so by the very small prison guard that had been assigned to escort Silas that day. "Let me guess?" said Silas, eyeing up the small wrapped bundle in front of Harold Sperry. "The unmistakable shape and smell of Gwen's scotch eggs!". Both men smiled.

"You may well be right, Silas. That smell has been torturing me all the way up on the train from Macclesfield." Harold smiled as he replied. "She's promised me my own batch next time. Now we have some business to do," Harold continued, "I am very aware that the longer you stay inside Strangeways, you will continue to be vulnerable to attacks from the dark side. So, we need to make this Appeal Hearing stick, and we need to get a release date agreed upon with the Judge. You have served sufficient time now to have your poaching sentence moved to parole, and given the mental pain that your death sentence must have had on you. We have a great chance."

"Hold it there, Mr. Sperry. Before worrying about me, I need to ask a favour." Silas halted the lawyer in full flow. "I have a new inmate that I need your help to support – one Charlie Aspinall."

Harold Sperry looked at Silas, astonished that his client

was able to move attention away from his own legal aid towards someone else – particularly the son of Henry Aspinall – a man who allegedly had a vendetta that led to Silas' imprisonment and, quite possibly, the ongoing threats from inside Strangeways. However, having heard Charlie's story as recited in detail by Silas, the lawyer agreed to head over to Manchester police station and seek a better understanding and, if possible, start an action to have the charges quashed and Charlie released from custody before any further action was needed.

Harold concluded the meeting, "Silas, I will help Charlie, but only on the condition that you will help yourself by reading this and agreeing to allow me to represent you at the Appeals Hearing next week. If we get a half-decent Judge, it may be that we can get both you and Charlie out of this hell hole in the next two weeks."

The lawyer stood and smiled at his selfless client – marvelling at a man who was able to survive in a hostile environment and put others before himself at all times. Harold Sperry kept one thought to himself. Knowing the breakdown in the relationship between father and son and also knowing the unsubstantiated suspicions that Henry Aspinall was behind some of the attacks on Silas within Strangeways, the lawyer did wonder whether having Charlie Aspinall under the protection of Silas in prison might avert future plans to finish off his client before release was possible.

Even without his father's influence, it seemed as if Charlie had some high-powered guardian angels out there. As Harold approached the front desk of Manchester's main police station, introducing himself and mentioning the Aspinall name, the on-duty sergeant exchanged a knowing look with him. "Ahh yes, Mr. Sperry, I have had several inquiries about this case. In fact, I have had one brazen young lady called Beth Ledger who refuses to leave the switchboard alone. She has made dozens of pleading calls today from Durham and, quite frankly, I'll be glad to get rid of Charlie Aspinall in order to reclaim some peace and quiet!" The sergeant continued, "The facts about the Kinder Scout trespass seem to be confused and it seems that some random arrests were made. In order to placate the landowners and estate managers, we needed to have some trespassers arrested and convicted. However, a learned University professor from Durham has already been interviewed on the radio stating that UK law does not consider 'trespass' alone to be a criminal offense unless damage to person or property occurs."

Harold Sperry urged the talkative policeman to continue, "So is Charlie Aspinall being held in prison illegally as the charge of trespass is in fact, not a crime at all?"

The sergeant looked at the lawyer and both understood what was going on without the need of words. Putting Charlie into custody would allow time to pass and a crime to magically 'emerge,' most likely involving the alleged assault of a gamekeeper. This might be sufficient to appease any of the landowners and put off any future protests by students and activists.

Harold shook his head in disbelief at the twisted world of law and wondered whether he should join his partner – Jonathan Burroughs – in early retirement. He knew that he needed to complete the Silas Ledger case, and if that meant also making sure that Charlie Aspinall was freed, then that's where his efforts should be directed.

It was pure coincidence, but the date of the appeal hearing for Silas was timed to be on the same morning as the case against the Kinder Scout activists. Both would be heard in the same courtroom at the City of Manchester Crown Court in front of a panel of senior magistrates.

The Appeal hearing was scheduled to be the first case heard in the morning, and Harold Sperry was confident that if Silas had taken on all of the advice that he had shared, then the parole release should be straightforward. It was a shame that there had been no developments on the manhunt for Gustav Coccini. For almost a half a year, Coccini seemed to have disappeared from the face of the earth, further sealing his suspected guilt in the tragic barge explosion. If he had been found and convicted, the court would have viewed Silas' case with even greater sympathy and moved to dismiss the poaching element completely.

However, the lawyer's heart sank when he saw Henry Aspinall's car draw up in front of the courthouse steps. As the landowner of the estate upon which the 'snared rabbit' had supposedly been caught by Silas, it seemed appropriate for Aspinall's appearance, but for such a trivial matter, really?

If Aspinall's presence was disarming for Harold Sperry, it was more than offset by the appearance of Silas' many supporters. It seemed as if the village of Langley had emptied and regathered in Manchester. Gwen, Beth and Will Ledger were in the front row of the gallery, together with Jack Moat and Melissa. Nat and Martha Lovatt were on the second row, together with Reverend Hamish Pottinger and Percy Ricketts – both of whom had been character witnesses at Silas' original trial. Thomas Whetton sat in the third row together with Jonathan Burroughs. Fred Needles, who had taken a day off from the quarry, sat next to Dick Avery, the publican from the Setter Dog Inn, and Ned Croucher from the Dunstan Inn. Both publicans looked like they'd justified their day out by additionally sampling some early morning competitive ales from a local Manchester brewery. Being only a mile from Piccadilly railway station, the commute from Macclesfield Station was easy enough for the group. Only Henry Aspinall had been driven by his chauffeur. He was sitting on the far side of the gallery with Arthur Brice – his Estate Manager – and presumably the one person who might be justified in seeing that the crime of rabbit poaching was being properly upheld.

Silas maintained his composure in the dock and confirmed his name with the presiding chairman. Harold Sperry then requested that the chairman and his two sitting magistrates consider a parole release given the good behaviour of the accused, and the fact that he had now served sufficient time for the crime that he had been found guilty of, and given the mental anguish that he had suffered due to the incorrect conviction for property destruction and murder, leading to a brief period facing a death sentence.

The chairman and magistrates retired to confer.

Henry Aspinall left the gallery, recognising that he had likely lost this particular battle, and did not want to witness the release of someone who he had spent the last eighteen months trying to finish. Aspinall was not used to losing, and as he left the gallery, he swore under his breath that this battle was lost, but the war was still there to be won.

It took all of five minutes for the chairman and sitting magistrates to return. The clerk of the court called proceedings to order and the chairman asked the defendant to stand. "Silas Ledger, you have served your time for the crime that you were committed. I now release you into a period of six months parole. You are free to go."

A great whoop of joy arose from the gallery and any number of people exchanged hugs and handshakes. Harold approached Silas and shook his hand. "We've done it, Silas. You are a free man."

Silas' response was as Harold expected, "I am, and now it's time to get Charlie off."

It was now late morning and the Court officials had stopped any more people from entering the courthouse. Students and protesters with placards had camped on the steps, and as soon as the door had reopened, they flooded into the court where the 'Kinder Scout Five' would have their charges read out. The courthouse was overflowing, so it was just as well that most of the Langley group had followed Dick and Ned across to a small brewery near the railway station to toast Silas' freedom and test the ales to see if they were potential for new barrel deliveries down to Langley.

Silas himself, together with Beth and Gwen, had managed to squeeze back into the Courtroom gallery to support Charlie. Silas was aware of the fact that Henry Aspinall had taken up a new position downstairs at the back of the main section of the courtroom floor.

The arresting police officer read out the charges, which highlighted the excessive use of force by the five protesters against the gamekeepers who were purely acting upon their rights to defend their land from these trespassers. The State allocated lawyer then took over and played down the importance of trespass and, in doing so, underlined that the case against the five protesters was purely around the physical attack that they made upon the gamekeepers, causing actual bodily harm.

At this, the courthouse erupted into a cascade of hysteria directed fully at the police. Placards were waved and paper was shredded and thrown like confetti. "Shame of you, shame on you" was the chant that was shouted in unison and directed at the court officials. Beth joined in with gusto, but Silas and Gwen considered it best to show their support in dignified silence. Harold Sperry, who was representing Charlie, stood downstairs with confetti floating around him, wondering once more about that early retirement option.

"Order, order," the Court Clerk shouted back, but to no use.

The Chair stood up, commanded a twenty-minute adjournment, and asked for the gallery to be cleared. The protesters stood on the steps of the court, still chanting, whilst the court resumed with a closed session.

After a further hour, Beth suddenly let out a scream. "Charlie!" and rushed towards a figure that was coming out of a side door together with Harold Sperry. Beth's scream attracted the attention of the wider crowd, and they all massed around Charlie and his lawyer, demanding to know what had happened.

"Can everyone hush, please and I will tell you about what has just happened inside the courthouse." Harold Sperry said in the direction of what was a group of about thirty people. Everyone started to quieten down.

"Okay, I am only representing one client – Charles Aspinall – and I can tell you all that the charges against Charlie have been dropped." Beth hugged Charlie tightly. Harold continued. "However, the other four people held have been charged with assault and will face trial. I am sorry."

At this, the crowd again erupted with a great deal of emotion, and the anti-establishment chanting began again. A small cordon of police had gathered at the bottom of the steps – prepared for some assertive crowd control. Harold beckoned to Silas and Gwen to follow himself, Charlie and Beth towards a side street.

Finally, away from the noise of the crowd, the five were able to huddle together. Gwen looked at Harold and asked, "Mr. Sperry, I don't understand what's just happened."

Harold looked back at her with his eyebrows still slightly knitted. "Mrs. Ledger, I don't really understand either. I was expecting all five accused to be treated in the same way, as none of the evidence pointed towards any individual. So, it would be common that the group all would face the same charges regardless of guilt. But suddenly, Charlie was identified as an innocent bystander who had been caught up in the violence in error. The chairman of the magistrates' panel dismissed the case against Charlie but enforced it against the other four."

Charlie shook his head, "That's just not fair though. None of those accused started the fight. It was the gamekeepers who initiated the aggression."

Harold added, "I simply cannot explain why Charlie was let off, but let's be grateful that he has been."

Gwen gave Charlie a big hug. "Let's get you back to Macclesfield."

As they were leaving for the short walk across to Piccadilly Station, Silas looked back towards the courthouse's main entrance, he saw Henry Aspinall's chauffeur passing a small package to the chairman of the magistrates.

Silas slowed down, allowing a joyous Gwen to walk ahead arm in arm with Beth and Charlie. "Money talks then, does it?" he shot a furtive glance at Harold Sperry. "Indeed, it does, Silas, indeed it does." The lawyer replied, confirming the thought that retirement couldn't come soon enough.

Henry Aspinall despised Silas Ledger for having escaped the death penalty issued by the courts and also that which had been promised by the Sons of Strangeways. And now Ledger and his daughter had welcomed his son into their family unit. However, he was not willing to see his son rot in jail and bring down the Aspinall family name further. Using his Chamber of Commerce connections, he had learned that the chairman of the magistrates appearing that day in Manchester Crown Court had some money problems and was susceptible to an offer. It seemed as if one thousand pounds was the sum required, and an agreement was reached. Charles Aspinall walked free.

CHAPTER 39 - *FREE AT LAST*

Ned Croucher walked back into the Dunstan Inn late that afternoon, together with the rest of Silas' supporters. Percy Ricketts had phoned the good news about Silas' release back to Langley and many of the villagers had already gathered in the pub to celebrate. Old Archie Talbot – who had been sacked from his job as gamekeeper by Henry Aspinall – had been taken on as a barman at the Dunstan.

"A round on the house," Ned shouted across to Archie, and a collective cheer went up from the bar room. "Silas will be home in the hour, so let's make sure that everyone has a full glass ready to welcome him home," Ned added, never one to avoid a marketing opportunity to sell a few more pints.

An hour passed quickly, then another one, but nobody seemed to mind as Dick Avery and Archie were entertaining everyone with their intertwining stories of poaching and game-keeping. They both laughed at the popular saying 'poacher turned gamekeeper,' as Archie recognised very clearly that he had now moved across from one profession into the heart of the other. By happy coincidence, a large tray of food was being passed around the pub – it contained wild boar sausages amidst chunks of venison covered in a rich berry gravy. Large chunks of homemade bread had been produced from the kitchen.

A crescendo of noise exploded from the bar room when Silas finally appeared at the Inn. He accepted the beer that was thrust into his hand and the numerous pats on the back from the crowd by the front door. "Thank you, thank you," Silas mouthed, looking humble and slightly embarrassed. Dick started off a round of 'For he's a jolly good fellow,' and the raucous villagers joined in. Silas caught Jack Moat's eye and followed it to the side entrance. He nodded to Jack and held up his hand to suggest five minutes.

Ten minutes later, Silas managed to move only about ten yards through the jubilant crowd to the side door where Jack was waiting for him. "Welcome home, big fella," Jack said, giving Silas a hug. "We've missed you. How do you feel now?"

"I'm just relieved to be home," Silas responded, "and so thankful that you and Will worked out that Gustav had something to do with this."

Jack stopped Silas. "Hold it, Sledge, without your amazing daughter, it would have been too late. Without her writing and Thomas Whetton's support, you would have been swinging from the rope half a year ago. She is the one you should be thanking."

"Regardless, you and Will proved my innocence by finding the guilty party. Do you have any idea where Gustav could be hiding out?"

Jack took another gulp of ale, "No idea. Fred and some of the quarry boys believe that he's gone back to Italy, but there is no record from the ports, so maybe he's hiding out somewhere in the UK. But the good news is that you are free. Are you going to go back to the quarry?"

Silas looked at Jack. "Are you serious? I need to distance myself from any business relating to Henry Aspinall. I have no proof, but I am certain he was behind framing me for the Kidsgrove incident and also for some of the troubles that I had at Strangeways."

"So, what are you going to do?" Jack asked

"Nat has offered me some work on his farm. He has miles of dry-stone walls that need fixing, and I cannot wait to get my hands on gritstone again." They both laughed as Silas pretended to shape a large stone in his giant hands.

Gwen had her whole family around her. She had had six months of hell without her husband, yet she had kept a positive countenance. She was immensely proud of how Beth was developing at Durham as an independent, confident woman, deeply in love with a wonderful, intelligent, caring man in Charlie. And as for Will, his mum was delighted with how he was working hard as an apprentice to Jack Moat and the pipeline business, which was prospering. Will was also maintaining his work, as spare time would allow, with Percy Ricketts, who was getting older and older and at some stage would need to hand over the Post Office to a successor – which Gwen knew Will wanted. She felt smug in a corner seat of the Dunstan bar room – she could see Silas in the far doorway with Jack. Will was laughing at the bar with Dick and Archie as Fred Needles tried to balance a beer mat on his nose. Next to her was Beth, who was chattering away to her old school friend – Moll Brampton. And by the window was Charlie – who had almost become an adopted son. Adored by her daughter and anyone who came into contact with him. Charlie was so intelligent, yet he made anyone he spoke to feel important. He had a sharp wit and a kind heart. Gwen, knowing how his own family had rejected him, was hopeful that Charlie would become a permanent part of their family.

Charlie was sitting on the other side of the bar room, engrossed in conversation with Harold Sperry. Harold was impressed at how advanced Charlie was in his law studies and was keen to help. With his partner – Jonathan Burroughs – seeking to retire later in the year, Harold was keen to strengthen the law firm by bringing on an intern so that he could move sedately towards partial retirement, and maybe Charlie was just what he needed.

Gustav Coccini had been very grateful for the ease in which Ivan Boksic was able to facilitate his departure from the heat that was growing in Cheshire immediately following the discovery of incontrovertible evidence linking him with the Kidsgrove explosion. Through Boksic's network of gypsy contacts on the canal system, Gustav had gradually been smuggled south. It was under the threat of death that Boksic had helped Gustav, getting the Sicilian to swear an oath around the gypsy's anonymity if he had been caught.

He had spent many nights on board narrowboats, curled up under canvas covers, with hard decking as his bed. His sleep was fitful at best. Often, he awoke to the magnified sound of rain hitting the canvas above his head or the feel of some vermin sniffing at his legs or arms. It was a horrible existence, but in some ways, he recognised that this was a small penance to pay for the troubles he had stirred up within the community he had left behind.

Whilst the narrowboats were moving, Gustav scavenged food and water from the crew in exchange for a few hours of work opening and closing many of the 158 lock gates of the Grand Union Canal, stretching between Birmingham and London. It was at one of these locks near Worcester that Gustav spotted a lock-keeper discarding a newspaper on a bench. He picked up the paper and returned to the narrowboat. Opening the paper up, he was aghast to see an artist's impression of his own face, with the headline:

Wanted for canal murder – Gustav Coccini – £100 for information leading to his arrest.

Quickly, Gustav returned to his make-shift quarters at the bow of the boat, he needed to double his caution now that his profile had been raised by the media. That night, he remained awake for hours, trying to conjure up a plan to hasten his escape from the country. Although he was frightened by the prospect of being recognised, however poor the artist's impression was, there was a comfort that at least a path towards justice was being trodden. Gustav had never been comfortable that a righteous and honest man like Silas Ledger could die because of a malicious act that he had committed. Sledge had recruited him at the Teggs Nose quarry and had always treated him fairly. Whilst others at the quarry had made fun of his poor English language and his foreign looks, Sledge had always trusted him. It was accidental fate that had led Sledge to be Gustav's scapegoat.

Gustav looked up at the cloudless night and traced the plough constellation with his eyes. The north star shone brightly, and he closed his eyes and prayed for Sledge and promised God that if the Almighty could preserve his freedom, then whenever there was a chance of paying back his debts to the Ledger family, he would do so without hesitation.

Gustav must have dozed off soon after a grating sound awoke him as the narrowboat drew along the side of a pontoon in order to moor up to await its turn in the queue for the next set of lock gates. Gustav pulled the cover firmly over his whole body, disappearing from any suspicious eyes that might be out there. What he had decided overnight was that he would use the canal network for another month and then make his way to one of the less well-known English Channel ports to escape to Europe and eventually return to Sicily and whatever his next adventure might be.

Chapter 40 - *Britain at War*

A number of years passed by and life in Cheshire ebbed and flowed with the changing seasons. Trentabank reservoir settled into the landscape, surrounded by a growing forest of conifers, planted by the Aspinall Estate to help preserve the water catchment area below the moors. The new forest would also make Henry Aspinall wealthier through the sale of timber and the sale of hunting licenses. Lush grass grew on the banks of the dam, and only during low rainfall seasons could you see any evidence of the two farms beneath the surface of the water when the top of a chimney stack appeared to excite the younger school children who believed the myth of a monster living in the dark watery depths.

The village cricket club, still sponsored by the Aspinall Company, was thriving in the Cheshire County leagues and was still punching way above the position they should have been as a small village team. Mainly thanks to the employment of several professional players, including an overseas player from Barbados, the first black-skinned man that many of the locals had ever seen. The very presence of him in the team, drew a crowd for the first few weeks he played. But in time, his lightening quick pace bowling became an even greater spectacle than his skin colour. Adam Bostock remained as the first team captain. Charlie had passed on his cricket-scoring skills to a youngster in the village who, like Charlie, was better with numbers than he was with the bat and ball.

Jack Moat and Melissa Kirkham had got married in a grand affair in Macclesfield and had purchased the Langley cottage in which Jack had previously rented a room. Jack was now fully in charge of the pipe laying business – owned by the Aspinall Company and was employing a team of fifty full-time staff. Will Ledger was now a team supervisor, under Jack's watchful eye. Melissa continued to work at Sperry & Burroughs Law firm, although Jonathan Burroughs was there solely in name, as he was now fully retired whilst maintaining an equity share and a place on the Board.

Charlie was completing his law articles, and was working full-time as an apprentice lawyer alongside Harold Sperry. Most of their work was local, although the Manchester courts were regularly visited, which always gave Charlie a strange sensation, given his one visit to the wrong side of the dock.

Beth had become a lead journalist with the Macclesfield Express but regularly had articles accepted by the Manchester Guardian. She also had become a member of a new feminist movement in London, that demanded monthly trips down to the capital. Each time she went, Thomas Whetton and Elliot Chapman were keen to take her out to dinner, and she often stayed over at their shared apartment.

Much to Silas and Gwen's delight, Beth and Charlie

became engaged and had moved in together in a small house in Gurnett by the canal, about two miles from Langley. Charlie had proposed to Beth on the moors above Langley, just the wrong side of a barbed wire fence.

Silas had been working at his brother-in-law's farm over on Bosley Cloud. The miles of derelict dry-stone walls that Nat had inherited had been transformed into weather proof and sheep-proof barriers of solid gritstone. It had taken a long time, but no farm in the region had such masterfully built dry stone walls. Just in time, really, as Silas had a new challenge ahead of him.

Henry Aspinall had been busy developing his business empire, so much so that the death of his wife came and went without any significant distraction. Florence eventually passed away from pneumonia and a loveless marriage. A small service was held at the Methodist chapel in Langley, presided over by Reverend Pottinger. Henry Aspinall did not attend. Charlie spoke eloquently and lovingly at the service. He mourned her lost soul whilst recognising that his mother's illness was one from which she deserved to find peace and – pointedly – an eternal escape from any tormentor.

The Aspinall Company had invested fully into the growth of the pipeline laying business, as the profit yielded more strongly than the quarrying business. Henry Aspinall decided to sell the Teggs Nose quarry to Phillip Broadhead, a fellow quarry owner. Aspinall's decision to sell would have been different if he had known that almost immediately, Broadhead had sold Teggs Nose onwards to Thomas Whetton. Despite Aspinall's protestations at the Chamber of Commerce, the quick transference of ownership from

Broadhead to Whetton, had been considered legitimate, and so he was forced to accept the decision.

The quarry at Teggs Nose at the time of sale was only employing fifteen workers, and had not been delivering positive profits ever since the completion of the Trentabank dam wall. The general malaise in the economy and the fact that the gritstone seam at Teggs was becoming even tougher to extract, paired with a new union agreement providing higher basic wages, meant that the operation was commercially unviable. The quarry was still being overseen by John Croker. The sale included the fifteen workers (and Battalion the shire horse), but Croker's role was considered redundant. Henry Aspinall had no more need for John Croker, who he had always thought was useless. Croker departed with minimal compensation. He was angry at his dismissal, and recognised that Aspinall had forgotten about the very large favour that Croker had done for him in the past.

As soon as the Teggs Nose quarry ownership rights had been signed in favour of Thomas Whetton, Silas was approached to take on the role of Quarry Manager for the new business, and not only the one quarry but also the second quarry under Whetton's company, over in Bollington. Silas was delighted, not only could he return to his beloved quarrying on the hill above his home, but he could also do this with an owner who he knew had integrity and the welfare of his staff as a core value. Silas immediately accepted on the condition that he could offer a job to Owain Jones, who had just been released from Strangeways and was looking for work in England rather than returning to the mines in Wales. Fred

Needles had been struggling to develop the commercial side of the quarry with little direction or support from John Croker, and so he was delighted to have Silas return, as were the rest of the quarry workers.

Henry Aspinall was upset when he heard about the quarry moving to Whetton ownership, but when he found out that Silas Ledger was returning to manage the business, he was apoplectic. He resolved to do something about it. From his manor house over on Ridge Hill, any view to the north happened to be dominated by Teggs Nose, and this made Aspinall wince with pain, thinking that he was being taunted and humiliated by Silas Ledger. With no other family member in the large stately home, he decided to temporarily move out and live in the apartment at his Head Office in Macclesfield until – in his mind – these wrongs were righted.

Aspinall had maintained a strong link with the premium liquor export business that Joshua Padgett and Edgar Fitch had set up. That link being the lower-risk canal transportation of the liquor from the Midlands distilleries through to the repackaging warehouses where Fitch's gang took over before being moved further to the docks in Liverpool and the Cunard transatlantic ships. He had needed to invest in much more private security on the canal barges to ensure that petty thievery and looting did not happen. This added cost, cut into the margins, and he was keen to make up for this elsewhere.

Aspinall bypassed Joshua Padgett and went straight to Edgar Fitch and offered to take over the full transportation element from the Midlands all the way through to the docks in Liverpool. Using Fitch's muscle to manage the security of the boats. He sourced new packing material from the pottery industry in Stoke, meaning that the repackaging of the liquor, camouflaged by Padgett's textiles, was not needed. This new agreement caused a major rift between Aspinall and Padgett, as Padgett's involvement had been reduced to the arrangement with the corrupt Cunard official. Both Aspinall and Fitch felt that, in time, they could cut Padgett out of the arrangement completely and take a greater share in the profits that were still growing strongly through New York. Both men viewed Joshua Padgett as a weak-willed man and someone who could bring the whole empire down with loose lips if the Authorities were to ever put pressure on him.

Aspinall had been disappointed with Edgar Fitch's efforts in finishing off Silas Ledger inside Strangeways, but this failure did not stop him from wanting to develop a deeper link with the undisputed leader of the North West's criminal families. He recognised a closer tie would ultimately protect his business, believing that Fitch was now elevated to a position of such influence that no Authority would be able to interfere.

No news about Gustav Coccini had been forthcoming.

On 1st September 1939, Germany invaded Poland. Two days later, Britain declared war on Germany. In Langley, the talk was not of the imminent war happening in distant lands but rather the forthcoming nuptials of Elizabeth Ledger and Charles Aspinall. Nobody could have known, but it would be the last truly celebratory event in the village for six years.

The First World War Memorial stood in the grounds of the Methodist Chapel and had been respectfully dressed with bunting by Gwen and Martha. The whole village lined the street, throwing confetti over the happy couple as they travelled in a smart carriage – loaned by Thomas Whetton – pulled by Battalion, who had been adopted and cared for by Jack Moat over the previous seven years and since Sid Bayley had passed away.

Some non-villagers were present, and Charlie had chosen his Hoarwithy school friend – Wyatt Montgomery 'Monty' – as his best man. He and Monty had stayed in contact throughout university, and become firm friends, both having decided that law would be their chosen career. Both were also delighted that another, much older Hoarwithy alumni – Alistair Grainger, had made it across from Bakewell. He could recall the first time that he had been introduced to Beth in the score hut at school and was delighted that two such charming youngsters were committing their lives to each other.

Gwen was in her element, fussing around the bride and bridesmaids from early dawn, helped by the very organised Melissa Moat, herself still glowing from her own recent wedding to Jack.

Hilda Bostock immaculately produced the wedding breakfast at the cricket club, and her crochet club colleagues produced some wonderful flower arrangements. Monty gave the most hilarious of speeches, making light of the fact that any sporting genes had passed both he and Charlie by whilst being replaced by the genes of justice and fair play – hence their employment of choice.

Beth could not help herself and demanded a chance to speak at her own wedding. Her articulation in words of her love and devotion to the causes she stood for around fundamental humanity were, for once, eclipsed by the way she spoke about love for her family and its newest member – Charlie. All Charlie could do was to hold her hand and stare at his new bride, besotted at her beauty and thinking how his life had twisted in the direction of light rather than the darkness he had been brought up with.

Silas walked his daughter down the aisle but asked Will to speak on his behalf to describe the tight-knit nature of the family. Silas' private words had been reserved for a more intimate moment with Beth and Charlie that left all three in tears, sharing the emotion of the day and the happiness that Silas felt in seeing these two together.

Although invited, Henry Aspinall could not find it in himself to attend or in any way bless the coming together of these two families. His bank balance could not have been healthier, but the sacrifice he had made was total. He felt empty and was too pigheaded to ever consider the offered hand of kindness intended in the wedding invitation. Instead, he had watched from afar, standing in the garden of his Ridge Hill mansion, gazing down on the village of Langley, hearing the church bell ring out in celebration. His heart remained just like the manor house behind him – cold and isolated. In a world warmed by the August sun, he recognised a frosty chill that was descending fast.

In the week following the wedding, the National Service Act was approved, stating that all UK males aged between eighteen and forty-one needed to make themselves available for military training. Agricultural workers and those that were in industries critical to the war effort were exempted.

Despite the dominant industry of farming, Langley had a dis-proportionate number of men who put themselves forward for the Cheshire Regiment – this included Will Ledger, Charlie Aspinall, Adam Bostock and Jack Moat. Several of the Teggs Nose quarry workers were also permitted to take on active service following a discussion between Silas and Thomas Whetton, and so Fred Needles, Andy Soutter and Robin Brampton were also accepted into military training.

It was a month after the Aspinall wedding in the Methodist chapel that these seven young men and their families, plus a large number of the Langley community, met again. This time Reverend Pottinger led a service devoted to prayers and well-wishes for those that were soon to depart to fight for Britain's freedom from the Nazis. The Cheshire Regiment recruitment officer from Macclesfield was present in his uniform. Following prayers, the seven young men stood at the front of the Church and the community queued on one side to shake their hands and wish them well.

Jack Moat was the eldest of the recruits and given his role in managing and leading a successful pipe-laying team, he had been automatically identified as Officer material. The other six had been given the lowest soldier rank of Private. Jack had made an early request to the Recruiting Officer that he wanted to stay with the other six as they already had a good degree of positive teamwork that should prove to be of great value out in the field. The Recruiting Officer had confirmed that this was often the approach when people from the same community joined together.

Jack was excited about the prospect of action, yet he knew of the challenges facing all of them in Europe. He knew that Melissa would be devastated, especially as she had lost two uncles in the Great War. Jack promised her that he would return as soon as he'd helped Britain give Hitler a bloody nose. This type of bravado upset Melissa, but she knew that Jack had a very high moral compass, and he considered that to fight for his country in a righteous war was something he must do as his duty to God and as a proud Englishman.

Similarly, Charlie felt that the atrocities being reported to be happening in Europe needed to be halted before Germany crossed the Channel and forced a Nazi dictatorship on Britain's democracy. He recognised that leaving Beth after just one month of marriage would be painful, but it would only be a brief interruption to what was going to be a wonderful life together. He was pleased that her brother – Will – would be with him as a constant reminder of his wife's upbeat character. He also felt stronger for being amongst a group of local quarrymen – surely with one of the hardest and toughest apprenticeships for being strong in combat. With this band of brothers, he felt that his less physical upbringing could be compensated for, whilst he might be able to offer something with his quick mind and more tactical thinking.

Following the service, Gwen and Silas signalled to Charlie that they needed a word. Charlie had become a son to them over the previous eight years, ever since their daughter had fallen in love with him, and he had been thrown out of his family home by his domineering father. He had become a perfect foil for their activist daughter – someone to calm her down when she kicked up a storm due to one social injustice or another. His considered and intelligent logic, combined with her fire and passion, made their partnership balanced and productive. The fact that their own son, Will, was leaving too just made it doubly difficult for Gwen, but she was also proud that he would be joining forces with Charlie, Jack and a group of his village friends.

"Charlie, we are very proud of you," Gwen started. "And we know that your mother would have been too." Conversations about Henry Aspinall were avoided nowadays due to the general opinion that he had disowned his son and wanted nothing more to do with him. Charlie had not spoken to his father for almost a decade, only occasionally seeing him at a distance, and both avoided any form of contact.

"We will pray for you, Will, and the other boys every day, and you'll all return to us – fit and healthy," Gwen stated forcefully. "Silas and I will look after Beth until your return, so no need to worry about that." She gave him an enormous hug, squeezing him so hard that he looked over at Silas with eyes that pleaded for him to interrupt!

Silas took the cue. "Charlie, I want you to use your brains to help keep the Langley boys safe. Brains have always won over brawn, and I'm afraid the others were blessed with one but not the other!" They both smiled as they looked over at Fred Needles – Silas' deputy at the quarry, who had desperately wanted to join up and prove himself in uniform. That's if they could find a uniform to fit his sizeable stature. He'd been spending less time on the cricket field and too much time at the Setter Dog Inn. Fred had developed a middle-aged spread prematurely. Perhaps life on army rations would help reverse this trend.

Silas continued, "Make sure you write to us via Beth and keep us informed about how you are all doing. I wouldn't have thought that any of the other boys even know what a pen and paper is for!" Silas then wrapped his arms around him, too and whispered in his ear, "Don't you dare leave me alone with these women for too long!"

The Army Recruitment officer had parked a small army truck next to the chapel and shouted out that he needed all recruits to get into the back of the vehicle. Final embraces, well wishes and kisses were exchanged from family and friends.

Beth had stolen Charlie away and they were behind the chapel, holding each other close. "Promise me you'll come home to me just as fast as you can, Charlie Aspinall," Beth said between sobs. "I cannot live without you."

Charlie's eyes were also full of tears. "I promise I will, my darling. I love you." Charlie wrapped her in his arms one last time and then turned and walked away. There were tears in his eyes as he realised that there was danger ahead, but the type that he had to confront as part of his duty as a citizen and as a husband.

The seven Langley recruits got into the mini-bus with a mixed sense of destiny. Excitement about the unknown was evident alongside the fear of what they were getting into. They all took great encouragement by looking around the small bus and recognising good friends who they knew they could rely upon in the best and worst of times.

Jack Moat was recognised as a smart, practical leader and was correctly fast-tracked in his officer training. He returned to Chester, where the rest of the regiment was based. The original recruitment officer, true to his word, had signalled that Jack had requested to lead a small troop of soldiers from the same village. This was generally a policy within the British Army and particularly supported by the Cheshire's as it tended to lead to greater cohesion when the pressure was on.

The Second Regiment of the Cheshire's departed in mid-1940 to support the evacuation of the British Expeditionary Force at Dunkirk. The Langley boys were in no doubt that war was far from glorious in those early days, as low-flying German aircraft strafed and bombed the beaches while soldiers with blank, lifeless eyes queued for transport back across the Channel. Jack realised that this was only just beginning and that this first experience of war was far from the romantic notion of valour and patriotic glory. He recognised how fortunate he was to have led his small troop of twenty men – six of whom were the Langley brotherhood – and he was returning to England with all twenty. A rare feat, as sixty-two thousand soldiers died over the week of the Dunkirk evacuation. Three hundred and forty thousand British troops successfully returned to British shores, transported on all sorts of boats, big and small.

The positive humour and camaraderie were evident on the small fishing boat that had picked Jack's unit up, cramming them on every spare foot of deck before eventually entering Ramsgate harbour. Fred Needles was proudly wearing a makeshift sling around one shoulder as he had suffered from a minor shrapnel wound on the beach. His mates, from quarrying times, ribbed him. "Needles, if you were a normal size, that shrapnel would have missed you completely," said Andy Soutter.

"Leave him be, Andy," said Robin Brampton. "I'd prefer to have Fred as a distraction to the Jerry guns than take one myself." He grinned as he poked Fred in the ribs. "Only joking, mate. All the girls will love you for having a war wound to show off."

"At least it wasn't in my bowling shoulder," Fred replied, "Did I ever tell you that I only need ten more wickets to be the most prolific wicket-taker in Langley Cricket's almost eighty-year history."

Jack looked at the group and smiled, "Thanks, Fred. In the last six months, I think you've shared that fact at least once every week!"

"Why are you looking so uncomfortable, Private Brampton?" mocked Adam Bostock, playfully. "Are you feeling a bit seasick?"

"Not at all," answered Robin. "I've just acquired a rather valuable artifact from the land of the Hun." He stood up and, in a dramatic gesture, produced a small sword from inside his thick coat. "This, my friends, is a genuine German foot soldier's bayonet, taken off one poor Fritz at Dunkirk – I'll be hanging that above my fireplace in years to come."

"I can beat that, my friend," said Andy. "And he put his hand inside his coat and pulled out – a live German grenade – with the pin firmly intact."

"For fuck's sake, Andy, throw that away. It could blow at any time," Jack shouted.

"But Jack, what a memento it would be! Please, can I keep it?" Andy pleaded.

"No!" came the collective response from the group.

Reluctantly, Andy let the grenade fall over the side of the vessel and sink into the depths, cursing the fact that he had nothing now to show for his time on the French beaches. "Poachers once, poachers always." Fred summed up Andy and Robin's ill-gotten bounty.

Everyone laughed, apart from Andy, who was fuming that his best mate, Robin, had got away with his bayonet mascot. Will and Charlie were on the other side of the vessel, looking back across the English Channel, amazed at the flotilla of small boats that they were part of. It gave them optimism that in times of trouble, everyone in Britain would unite to support the common good, and this would be sufficient to complete the mission that Winston Churchill was committed to – keeping Britain free and defeating Hitler's army.

"I can't wait to have a pint at the Dunstan again," Will gushed. "Old Percy Ricketts promised me that if I got back in one piece, he'd open up that lock-tight wallet of his and pay for my beer all night!"

"That'll be worth seeing," replied Charlie. "But all I want to do is get back to that sister of yours before I start kissing you!" Charlie cuffed Will on the forehead and they both laughed.

It was good to be back in England, and there was a slim hope that Jack's patrol would be able to make it back to

Cheshire on home leave before they were reassigned to further military duties. The fishing boat docked and they all disembarked, thanking the skipper and first mate with a rousing 'three cheers.' The Home Guard were on duty at Ramsgate and all returning troops were directed towards a large make-shift marquee where they would get billeted for the night and given instructions as to where they would go next.

The general atmosphere in Ramsgate was strange, the evacuation of Dunkirk was considered a success despite the huge loss of human life. It would allow a halt for the British Army to regain strength and stamina ahead of a secondary assault on the German occupation in Europe. There was tragic sadness at the realisation that sixty-two thousands of their comrades, or one in six, gave their lives on the beaches and dunes of Dunkirk. Any drinks that were had that night would be out of respect and in memory of those who had fallen.

Jack took the initiative and headed up the group as he had become accustomed in doing. He had never felt so closely bonded to this platoon of men. He had total confidence that they would follow him, and each of them would be willing to lay down their life for each other, and in turn, he would them. But not right now. They had survived Dunkirk; they needed to get their orders and enjoy the English air and a Kentish beer or more. Jack was also thinking that there might be a chance of him surprising Melissa with a visit, if only the army would allow two or three days of leave. He'd been married less than a year, and he was aching to get back to their little cottage in Langley and see his beautiful girl again.

The following morning, whilst most of his patrol were

sleeping off a well-deserved hangover, Jack stirred Charlie from the six-man patrol tent that they had been allocated, and they headed over to the command tent where senior officers would be able to pass on instruction as to whether they could head up to Euston station in London, and onwards to Macclesfield, before their next assignment. Alas, it became self-evident as they entered the command tent that the glum looks on fellow soldiers leaving, suggested that bad news was about to be broken, and most likely, this would be an immediate re-assignment of duties.

Jack turned to Charlie, "Come on mate, let's go and see what fate has got in store for us." He approached the desk and saluted, "Jack Moat, reporting for duty, Sir." Jack stood to attention in front of the desk sergeant.

"Stand at ease, soldier," answered the tired-looking officer. "What size of patrol is under your command, Corporal?"

"I have a patrol of twenty soldiers, sir," Jack stated.

"Any injuries incurred in Dunkirk?"

Jack considered Fred's minor shrapnel injury and thought about reporting it. However, he realised that Fred Needles would never want to be left behind without his Langley brothers around him, and in the same way, the platoon would be all the weaker without Fred as a component part. "Only one minor shrapnel wound, sir," Jack reported.

"Is he fit to travel, Corporal?"

"Yes, sir," Jack answered, feeling some guilt as this might have been an opportunity to save one of his men from whatever fate was that awaited them.

A senior officer with three diamonds on his shoulder, denoting a Captain, spoke, "Thank you, Jack. We have a special assignment for you and your group of brave fellows. You will report to Portsmouth for immediate deployment out to Cyprus for basic desert training. And from there you will be transferred to join the Cheshire 1st Battalion and head out to the mission in Tobruk, North Africa."

Jack saluted and stood to attention without saying a word. He found it odd that the captain did not look him in the eye and made his order without any real conviction or hope that this was going to be anything but a one-way journey.

"Bloody North Africa!" Charlie uttered with astonishment just as they exited the command tent. "And with immediate effect!"

"Bollocks!" Jack spat back. "It would have been ok if we'd had a few weeks or even a few days off."

Both men started trudging back to the tents where the rest of their patrol were still slumbering. "Hoy!" came a shout from behind them, and they saw the desk sergeant hailing them from the flap of the command tent. "I've got a telegram for Charles Aspinall. He's registered as being part of your platoon. Do you know him?"

"I'm Charles Aspinall, sir," said Charlie.

The telegram was passed across. "All the best then, boys, at least you'll bring back a suntan!"

Jack and Charlie looked at each other. It was unusual to get a telegram, and almost always was only used when important news needed to be communicated. Charlie opened it up. It had been sent from Langley Post Office. Charlie read it out aloud:

Charlie.

Hurry home to us. I'm pregnant and due to give birth in November. Congratulations Dad!

Forever,

Beth x

Charlie put down the note and looked at Jack. As he looked back at the telegram disbelievingly, Jack leapt on him. "Yes! What brilliant news. Congratulations Daddio!"

"Let me go, you idiot!" Charlie said, pushing Jack away so that he could reread the note – just to make sure the news was true. It was – the next generation of the Aspinall family was starting.

As soon as the platoon got to their barracks in Portsmouth next to the navy base, Charlie was granted permission to head off to the nearest post office to make a call to Langley. They only had one day in Portsmouth before being shipped off to Cyprus on HMS Suffolk, where they would be briefed and trained before moving across to North Africa to relieve the Desert Rats, who were besieged in various locations along the Southern Mediterranean between Egypt and Algeria.

That detail was a long way from Charlie's mind when he approached the Post Office that he had been directed towards by one of the local Military Police who were stationed at the gates of the barracks. Charlie's first instinct once he was back in the civilian world was to head towards the train station, catch the first train north, and go back to see Beth. But Charlie's values were such that his loyalty to the righteous cause of beating Hitler's Germany was steadfast, and he felt confident that he would return to Beth and his new baby only after he had helped to rid the world of fascist tyranny and injustice.

Charlie had been briefed by Will, who had furnished him with the Langley Post Office telephone number – still one of few telephones in the village. As soon as he had got through to Mr. Ricketts, he should tell Percy to tap on the wall to alert his neighbours, the Ledgers, that they were needed urgently.

The phone started to ring. "Brrrrr, brr… Brrrrr, brr… Hello, Langley Post Office. How can I help you?" Percy's unmistakable voice answered.

"Percy? Hi, it's Charlie Aspinall. Can you get Beth as quickly as possible, please?"

"Charlie – great to hear your voice again – hold on, I'll knock on the wall." In the background, Percy's ever-present walking stick was heard urgently tapping away on the wall. "How are all the boys? The village just wants to know that they're all safe and when are you coming home?"

"The good news is that we are all in fine health, but the bad news is, I'm afraid we're being sent over to North Africa for a while, so we won't be back for some time."

Charlie could hear a lot of shuffling in the background and some muffled voices. "Charlie! My beautiful boy!" Gwen's voice embraced him. "How are you? How is Will? How are all of my boys? I've sent Silas down the road to get Beth. She's over at Melissa's – she has some news for you. Oops, I should shut up."

Charlie jested, "Oh Gwen, you've not lost your ability to talk, I hear! No wonder Silas spends so much time up on Teggs Nose, but I suspect he can still hear you from up there."

"Charlie, you rascal! Tell me about Will."

"Your son is one of the best soldiers here, or so he thinks! He asked me to send his love and say that he'll write, or rather he'll tell me what to write soon. But he's in rude health, the rest of the boys are just rude!" he jested. "We all managed to survive the evacuation from Dunkirk, but we are heading out tomorrow to North Africa."

More shuffling was heard in the background, and Charlie imagined Silas, Beth and possibly Melissa entering the small Post Office. The phone receiver was handed over. "My darling Charlie," Beth started, "Did you get the telegram?"

Her voice alone choked Charlie up, "I did, my love. I just want to be with you." His voice broke.

"And I want to be with you too. Can you come home?" Charlie could not talk, but he could hear Gwen explain that they were heading out by ship to Africa.

With a trembling voice full of emotion, Beth started talking again, plucking up the courage to sound stronger than she truly felt. "Charlie, you will be the best dad, and we'll be waiting for you."

Charlie responded, "And Silas and Gwen will be the best grandparents too." He had known a father who was unloving and merciless in his selfish pursuit of money. His own child would be brought up with love all around. Henry Aspinall's parental poison would be banished from their child's life.

"Charlie, I love you so much, just get back to Langley as soon as you can. Melissa sends her love to Jack and you need to promise to look out for each other and Will. In fact, bloody hell, make sure all of you come back here or they'll be trouble."

"I promise we'll all stay together and come back together. Jack is our platoon leader and Corporal Moat is brilliant. All of us have a role to play. Fred is the comedian, Andy and Robin are our scavengers, Will is our muscle, 'Adam is our handyman, and I act as Jack's number two." He added, "When we are on board the ship tomorrow, I promise I will pen a letter from all of us to all of you."

"You better!" came Gwen's voice in a friendly threat from the background.

"I love you, Charlie Aspinall," Beth signed off.

"And I love you, Beth Aspinall," Charlie whispered in an attempt to have a final private moment in a crowded Langley Post Office.

Charlie returned to the army camp. The following day, having been re-provisioned, the platoon embarked on HMS Suffolk for three weeks of sailing, with stop-offs at Naval bases in Faro and Toulon. His life was worth fighting for even harder now.

CHAPTER 41 - *DARK SKIES*

It was 1941, the German hierarchy had committed to breaking the infrastructure and supply lines powering the British forces. U-boats were having a devastating impact in the North Sea and to shipping lanes across the North Atlantic. Yet it was decided a full-on air assault was also necessary on the manufacturing centres in the Midlands and the docks in Liverpool. Major Dietrich Von Zielberg was the pilot and Luftwaffe squadron leader of a planned raid on Liverpool dockyards on 8th May.

At 4 am, eleven Junkers JU88s took off from Hamburg, together with eight Messerschmitt BF109s, as escort cover. The forecast was perfect for an air raid with low cloud cover expected, sufficient for protection from any English ground-based anti-aircraft guns, whilst still being thin enough for air-to-ground radar to identify potential targets in and around the docks. It was even rumoured that HMS Hood was in Liverpool and had been given a mission to 'sink the Bismark' – the German flagship.

It was the thought of sinking the Hood that excited Von Zielberg. It would be a sure-fire way of him earning the Iron

Cross and hopefully a way of getting an audience with the Fuhrer himself.

As Von Zielberg throttled back on his Junkers and started rolling down the runway in Hamburg, he was thrilled by the power of the engines, magnified by the crisp early morning air. He had half a dozen thousand-pound bombs in his hold and ten similarly equipped planes in his squadron. The sheer firepower under his command got him excited. Alongside the squadron leader was a young wireless operator – Rudolf Schwalbe. He was a young student, fresh out of Luftwaffe training college in Bremen, immediately fast-tracked into active service. He had excelled in all of his classes and was considered so proficient and capable by his training officers that Von Zielberg demanded that the youngster take a role in his aircraft.

Very few people knew, but Rudolf Schwalbe was a pacifist who detested the notion of war. However, to openly object to war was the same as publicly sticking two fingers up at the Fuhrer and so tantamount to suicide. He felt that, at least as a wireless operator, he could provide a service that was not directly involved in the killing fields that he felt humanity was actively producing all over Europe. He had always graduated top of his class, and because of his skills – particularly in languages – his destiny was within communications. He had hoped that his vocation would be ground-based, but Hermann Goering, the Supreme Commander of the Luftwaffe, had seen some of his exam results and had personally demanded he join his air force for some practical experience. The mission to bomb Liverpool docks was to be

Schwalbe's first time on active service.

The German formation made its way across the North Sea and reached the east coast of England near Beverley, East Yorkshire. The lack of any anti-aircraft fire suggested that they had been high enough to avoid any detection, plus the early hour meant that perhaps the morning shift was yet to really wake up. This mission was highly unusual in terms of the size of the squadron, but surely, the British should have been more aware of how vulnerable they were to an air attack of this nature. Von Zielberg took a long drag from a cigarette, he mused that perhaps the British were too preoccupied with re-shaping their army following the evacuation of Allied forces from Dunkirk. Or perhaps they needed to be fully focused on protecting their navy from the constant howling of the 'wolf pack' – the nickname of the German submarine fleet.

At 5:56 am, Von Zielberg commanded the squadron to descend from 20,000 feet to 15 and then 10,000 feet in preparation for the attack on Liverpool. Things were going perfectly. Sheffield was below, and so far, there had been no indication that England was aware of what was about to hit them. Von Zielberg was picturing the sinking of HMS Hood and his name on the front pages of Das Reich – Joseph Goebbels weekly national propaganda newspaper. He was confident that his Iron Cross was only an hour away.

Suddenly, the sky was filled with brilliant flashes of light as they were strafed by anti-aircraft fire from sites around Sheffield. Some of the Messerschmitts were ordered to change course to try and draw the fire. In the back of the lead

Junker, Schwalbe was holding his head in his hands. This was the first bit of serious action the young man had experienced and he knew at that point that his constitution was not ready for this kind of brutal kicking. He tried to maintain focus on the radar and keep his headphones from being shaken off as the explosions happened around him. The headphones did nothing to dampen the external noise, in fact, it added to the static electrical scream coming through from his communications gear.

The acrid smell of phosphorous was permeating the fuselage, but the plane remained intact. This was sensory overload in every direction. Schwalbe looked up and saw the demonic eyes of Von Zielberg behind his goggles. A smile had spread across the major's face. This was his world. This was where his name was going to become as infamous as that of his boss – Hermann Goering. Von Zielberg would become 'the man who sunk the Hood and saved the Bismarck'. In fact, the act that he was about to commit might just become known as the one that turned the tide in favour of Nazi Germany as they became the single world power.

Rudolph, acted on instinct born out of logic. He knew that his squadron leader would rather die a hero by burying the Junker into the heart of HMS Hood, than try to preserve any life. This was the moment for Rudolph Schwalbe to have his say on history. Several re-calibrations of the navigation system, and Rudolph replotted the plane's course towards an outcrop of rocks. It would be better that the four crewmen died rather than hundreds of human lives were taken in Liverpool. This would be Rudolph's selfless act of humanity – unpublished and unheralded – yet unbeknown to them, many families would be in his debt.

As the plane was changing course, the left engine was hit by anti-aircraft fire and disintegrated within a second. A direct hit on the fuel line proved fatal. JU88-A5 dived and started to rotate. The Major needed to give the signal to eject, but his face was frozen in shock. Von Zielberg's dream was shattered and the only way honour could be preserved would be if he went down with his aircraft. Schwalbe braced for the impact.

Everything went black.

Silas was on Tegg's Nose earlier than usual. He was training a relatively new group of American, Canadian and Dutch soldiers who had been assigned to Thomas Whetton's Quarry Company as additional labour to cover British workers who had been assigned for war duties. The quarry business had gone into overdrive as more gritstone needed to be crushed and moved across to help extend runways to be able to handle larger delta-wing bomber aircraft that were still in their test phase. The group of soldiers had been involved in the simple moving of the stone during the month that they'd been in Cheshire, but they had not been used in the actual quarrying.

Silas had agreed to retrain the ten recruits, predominantly American, in the methods and techniques to extract gritstone slabs safely from the quarry face and then cut and crush the rock in readiness for transportation. Silas was impressed with the healthy look of these raw recruits, several of whom had been assigned from within the ranks of the US Marines – a much-heralded fighting force.

It was not until December 1941 that the US and its allies entered the war arena. Before then, they only provided non-fighting resources, and so it was in this capacity that Silas had his much-needed additional labour force.

"Morning boys – I'm Silas Ledger – people call me Sledge. I am your boss for the foreseeable future." Silas got the attention of the new recruits. "Listen carefully to what I tell you today, and you'll all learn to love the art of quarrying as I have for the last thirty years." A dull boom was heard over to the east, which distracted a few of the soldiers. "Don't worry, lads, that was likely to have been quarry explosives from works over in Staffordshire."

Battalion, the shire horse, whinnied gently in the background as if he were agreeing with Silas. The group of soldiers smirked, and Silas continued: "Let me introduce you to our mascot – Battalion. He used to pull carts with more gritstone rock in them than a group thrice your size could budge. So, we demand the utmost respect for this old boy. He brings us luck."

Battalion's nose nuzzled up to Silas' shoulder. The cloud was low over the Peak District that morning, and the sun was only just rising, and there was a light frost on the ground. Suddenly, the horse stood more alert and tensed, letting out a nervous neigh. "That's alright, boy," said Silas calmly, tightening his lead rope. A dull sound of a large aircraft engine was heard overhead, and then more. Through a small break in the cloud, the quarry workers looked up and saw a swarm of aircraft heading west. Although enemy aircraft had been seen before, they were usually in small units heading toward the manufacturing centres of Manchester and

Liverpool. This size of squadron was unusual.

The British Army Officer, who was overseeing the deployment of the allied soldiers, moved quickly towards the army lorry, where he had a radio that he could use to inform HQ. Within five minutes, air raid sirens would be wailing across Cheshire to the Wirral and up into Lancashire.

"Welcome to wartime Britain!" Silas finished addressing the troops. "Now let's get busy – there's work to be done. And if it's done well, the Setter Dog Inn is where we'll introduce you to the best of British – warm beer!" A cheer rang out from the newcomers. Silas then led them down to the quarry face, where he paired them all up with experienced quarry workers. The training began.

The Roaches was a gritstone escarpment in Staffordshire. It rose steeply to over 1800 feet and formed part of the edge of the south-east Peak District. In daylight, it was a useful navigational beacon for aircraft. At night or in low cloud, it was a geographical feature to avoid at all costs.

Major Von Zielberg had fought valiantly to halt the dive of the aircraft but struggled to get any kind of traction from the wing flaps to gain any real control. The Junkers hit Hen Cloud, an outcrop at one end of the Roaches and exploded on impact. The wreckage being strewn across a wide area of the hillside. Remarkably, Rudolph Schwalbe was thrown from the aircraft upon its initial contact with the earth, his body smashing into the branches of a large gorse bush and coming to rest in a nest of bracken and heather. He lost consciousness immediately and so was unaware of the enormous explosions hundreds of yards away where the rest of the fuselage containing the bomb undercarriage combusted in a gigantic fireball.

It must have been about thirty minutes that Rudolph was unconscious, he awoke to the sound of shouting. He just lay there and slowly mentally checked his body to see if he could move different parts. Only his left shoulder seemed to be giving him excruciating pain. His body was covered in cuts from the gorse bushes and branches he had hit when he had been thrown from the plane. It was remarkable that he had survived. He remained still and realised that the shouts were from English voices who must have been locals coming to check on the wreckage and see if there were any survivors. Thankfully, most of the voices were several hundred yards away, where the main fuselage was still burning. Rudolph felt safe just staying where he was. Even if he could have moved, a searing pain down his left side made it sensible to stay still for now. At least he knew that there was no major life-threatening injury.

The German airman fell in and out of consciousness for what must have been twelve hours, as it was dusk when he decided that he had to test out his injury and move or risk dying from a cold night on the hillside.

Rudolph had been an ace student at most subjects, and although excelling at linguistics, he was also a very competent navigator and had studied topography extensively at his college in Bremen. This allowed him to scan the Roaches escarpment and begin to plot in his mind a route that took him to the highest point from which he might be able to work out where he was compared to any urban settlements.

Thankfully, it was a clear sky and the stars could act as a compass bearing for him. His last memory from the flight was that they had crashed about ten miles to the southwest of Sheffield, as the damage to the aircraft had made them veer off their westerly path and descend into a shallow glide. Rudolph's first action was to manoeuvre his body to an upright position and assess how able he was to stand. After some disentanglement of bracken and painful gorse bushes, he discovered he was relatively ok. Deep bruising on his left hip and thigh, and possibly an injury to his left collar bone, which must have taken the initial impact with the boggy peat ground beneath the gorse bush. He gradually shifted around to observe more about the location and just to check whether there were still any locals or military personnel searching the site. In the distance, he could just see the movement of small figures surrounding what must have been the final embers and smoke of the main aircraft chassis. JU88-A5 had done a good job of spreading any evidence of its one-time existence across around half a mile of the hillside. Surely, he would have been the only lucky survivor, the rest of Von Zielberg's crew must have perished.

Rudolph turned around and noticed a long lake down below him with lights from a small village twinkling at one end. He'd later discover that this was Meerbrook, from where a British Army patrol had been on a training exercise when the Junkers had crashed. It was this patrol that was on the scene quickly and had missed checking the flight path for any jettison – human or not. Their eagerness to get to the main crash site had allowed him to maintain his liberty for now. Having fully checked the site, the Army had handed over the duty of securing the site overnight to the local Meerbrook

Scout group – who had diligently set up a security cordon close to the main fuselage – happy to serve their country and the war effort. Secretly, most of the boys were keener to pick up some souvenirs from the Junkers once their scout leader gave them the go-ahead.

Rudolph turned back to look at the escarpment of the Roaches. He froze, astonished he was six yards away from two adult wallabies munching on a bilberry bush. Was this a hallucination? It would only be later that he would find out that a colony of this particular marsupial had formed following an escape from a local private zoo in the 1930s. The wallabies were utterly disinterested in the sight of this strange human arising from the undergrowth and just nonchalantly carried on munching whilst Rudolph limped past them in the direction of the rock face.

He walked slowly as his stiff body gradually became accustomed to the challenge of movement, plus the fact that he needed to stoop in order to ensure he attracted no attention from any eager young Scout with binoculars. It was a miracle that he had survived the crash. His only recollection from the plane was that as it glided awkwardly towards its final resting place, the floor from beneath Rudolph had opened up and he had fallen through the gaping hole. His tough Luftwaffe flying suit had torn badly upon impact with the trees and bushes before he came to rest, but ultimately must have saved him from a more serious injury or even death. It was a thickly padded suit with many pockets. Rudolph was a meticulously well-prepared individual and had several items in his pockets that would prove invaluable. Bars of chocolate, a pencil and a map of North West England, including their planned flight path to and from Liverpool. He also had pictures of his family whilst holidaying in the Schwarzwald, Bavaria, a few years previous.

It took him over two hours, but eventually, Rudolph found a gulley and scrambled to the top of the escarpment. The sun had set an hour before, but there was still a glow coming from the west, confirming the direction in which he had decided to travel. For what reason, he was not sure, but his current idea was to remain undetected for as long as possible so that he could formulate a plan that might allow him to work out how he might survive in this foreign country.

CHAPTER 42 - *CULTURAL MIX*

Soon after the arrival of the foreign workers on Teggs Nose, they had ingratiated themselves to the Langley community in a most positive way. Initially resistant and suspicious of outsiders, their positive work ethic, amusing sayings and cheery attitude had meant that the group was always welcomed – and most regularly across the thresholds of the Setter Dog or Dunstan inns. The Americans were the loudest of the group, whilst the Canadians were more reserved. The two Dutchmen – Lucas and Jan – became the butt of many jokes due to the fact that they were identical twins that were never seen apart, and indeed no one could tell them apart. They also had a canny knack for finishing off each other's sentences. Gwen practically adopted the Dutch twins, and they were regularly invited to Sunday lunch, which they relished due to the size of the platters Gwen would furnish them with.

One night at the Setter Dog Inn, Dick Avery organised a music night, having been badgered by the Americans to allow them a chance to show off their talents with a new type of music called jazz. Posters were put up around Langley and Macclesfield and the word got out that an evening of American jazz would 'light up the night'. Dick Avery's pub – the Setter Dog – being a bastion for males, and dominated by farm and quarry workers, was missing a large number of regulars due to the war effort. He realised that he needed something to appeal to women, and what better than a new exotic style of dance music played by good-looking young men from foreign lands.

Beth was amused by the thinly disguised excitement that Moll Brampton exuded as she described this new music style, which was gradually getting played on more unlicensed radio stations. In truth, Moll was more interested in the infusion of new eligible males into the neighbourhood, as she had gotten through to her mid-twenties without finding a serious partner. One of the Canadian soldiers, Patrice, was the specific one on 'Moll's love radar' – as she regularly told Beth. Beth was now heavily pregnant and so was not willing to make her way up the cobbled Saddlers Way footpath to the pub, but Melissa agreed to chaperone Moll.

It was the first time that either woman had entered the Setter Dog Inn, despite Melissa's husband – Jack – being a regular there with his quarry worker friends, including Moll's brother – Robin. Both Jack and Robin were fighting the war in North Africa – but were remembered in the pub by their photos in pride of place, above the bar, together with the other five Langley boys who had enlisted. Above their photos – were the words 'God Bless Our Brave Boys.'

Dick was very happy that Silas had promoted his pub to the new international workers, and in turn, they had adopted the Setter Dog as a second home. This was conditional upon

Dick adding American bourbon and Canadian Molson beer to the bar. Given the quantity they drank, he felt that was a mutual win for both parties.

That evening, the atmosphere in the pub was building as more and more intrigued locals entered and crowded into the large single lounge area, stripped of seating for the occasion. Next to the bar was a small make-shift stage where the American soldiers had their instruments – the most unusual one being a bucket and a broom handle with a string attaching one to the other. Melissa and Moll looked at each other and pondered what sort of music could ever be produced by such an odd creation.

There was a swell of anticipation as the part-time musicians entered in their finest military uniforms. Unknown to the locals, they had managed to persuade two semi-professional jazz musicians from New Orleans to appear alongside them and add a level of quality to the evening. The two true musicians were soldiers from a USAF base near Warrington, and Thomas Whetton had given permission to Stan – one of the American quarry workers – to use the quarry wagon to go and fetch them earlier in the day, on the promise that he was allowed to attend that evening.

Thomas and Silas were supping their ales at the back of the lounge, bemused at the eclectic mix of people in the pub. They had grown closer ever since Whetton had helped Beth get her story of injustice against Silas published. Both had enormous respect for each other, and Whetton really enjoyed Silas' calm diplomacy in sorting out any matters arising from the Whetton Company quarry business.

The lights dimmed and the Dutch twins – Lucas and Jan –

hushed the crowd. They had taken on the responsibility of logistics as they had no musical bone in their combined bodies. A distant, smooth sound was heard as one of the real musicians started to work his saxophone. The sound got louder as it approached the main entrance of the pub. Suddenly, with a crash of sound and flash of lights, the three American soldiers and their make-shift instruments arrived on stage, accompanied by both of the New Orleans jazz musicians playing a trumpet and a saxophone. Stan jumped on stage and put one foot on the bucket, tightened the string on the broom handle, and started to strum out a steady rhythm. Another of the Americans had a crude washboard and was using a washing peg to make rapid clicking sounds as he drew the peg to and fro. The third American stood at the front and started to click his fingers to the beat and broke into a song that only he and the band seemed to recognise.

Owain Jones – who had been part of a Welsh male voice choir before his extended time in Strangeways – jumped up and started to vocalise, not knowing any words but feeling that his knowledge of melody and rhythm might add to the occasion. The Americans loved Owain's unorthodox sounds and invited him to join them on the stage for the rest of the performance.

It was such a colourful mixture of musical madness in front of the audience, with a style of music which was half decent considering the resources, that all they could do was join in. Patrice eyed up Moll and started to swirl her around the makeshift dancefloor that cleared to allow dancing to occur. And within minutes, fuelled by the liberal drinking, anyone who wanted to dance was trying their best to copy any of the jazz moves that Patrice seemed half competent to throw on Moll.

The evening carried on as it began, high octane, never heard before (or again) musical entertainment and greatly amusing for all present. Moll won her man over and managed to get him to walk her home afterwards. East Cheshire had experienced jazz – or at least its own unique form of jazz – for the first time.

The fun and excitement a few miles away was not being shared by Rudolph Schwalbe. His climb up the gulley had sapped all his remaining energy, and he found shelter behind a large gritstone boulder. He got out his map and oriented it so that he could identify any key landmarks. He looked down on Staffordshire to the southeast and saw Meerbrook's lights and the large stretch of water called Tittesworth, glimmering in the moonlight. The picture of his family on holiday was caught up in the folds of the map. His mind wondered, what coincidence that the family photo was of Titisee, a lake in the Schwarzwald region of Bavaria. England and Germany were really not that different, if only the politicians could find more similarities and finish this pointless war.

To the west, and the dying embers of the day, were the lights of Manchester and Liverpool. He wondered whether the rest of the Luftwaffe squadron had managed to blitz the docks successfully and scored a win for Germany or whether they had come up against a similar fate as JU88-A5. He really did not care either way – the meaninglessness of war was clear to him. His focus was now purely on survival.

It was mid-May, and the night temperatures were benign. After an hour's rest and in the light of a relatively full moon,

Rudolph moved along the ridge of the Roaches and dropped down into the heavily wooded valley of Gradbach. The scale of the map did not show detail, but it was clear to the German that other than the very occasional farmhouse, he was in an area where it was likely that wallabies far outnumbered humans. He found a deep chasm in the gritstone and used some heather and bracken to make a crude cradle in which he settled. The sound of the river Dane below and the occasional hoot of owls hunting for voles and field mice, coupled with the last of his chocolate ration, made a relaxing backdrop for a couple of hours of sleep, allowing his bruised body to recover further.

He awoke to the sound of a far-off bell ringing inconsistently. Rudolph had heard this kind of sound back in Germany and recognised it as likely being a cowbell. As dawn was breaking, he thought that this could be the stirring of the herd on their way to the dairy to be milked. He stretched out his stiffened body and headed towards the sound of the bell. He had a hope that if his intuition was correct, there might be fresh milk to quench his thirst, and maybe more. Following the tree line along for half a mile, he found a series of barns and heard the contented mooing of cattle being milked. The stockman was visible, leading the thirty or so cows gradually through an open barn door to the milking shed, where several milk stools were set up with two young female farmhands milking the cows. Once a milk pail was full, the girl emptied it into a large metal churn. There was much laughter and cursing going on in the milking parlour as the animals moved through their twice-daily routine, and the milking team tried their hardest to make a tricky job go as quickly as possible.

This scene of rural life enchanted Rudolph, who for much

of his life had chosen to spend any spare time in the library studying. If he managed to survive his time in England, he swore to himself that he would spend more time in God's great garden. For now, he needed to plot a way of extracting some of that milk without being noticed. The German edged along the side of the field until he was adjacent to the barn, about ten yards away from the back of the line of cows, waiting patiently to enter the milking parlour. From this location, he could see the urns, and fortuitously, there were several smaller bottles containing some fresh milk, probably for the purposes of refreshments for the busy milking crew. Rudolph quickly vaulted the wooden fence and snatched a bottle of fresh milk, and also a small package wrapped up in a white handkerchief. He turned and retraced his steps at speed, not resting until he was deep in the woodland again. There was no unusual commotion from behind, suggesting that he had got away with his petty crime. Rudolph got down to the river Dane and unwrapped the small package. Two boiled eggs, a thick slab of bread, some cheese and a small jar of sweet pickle – were all the contents inside – and the soldier hungrily devoured half of his bounty. Washed down with half of the milk. He felt that he should put some distance between him and the dairy, as the stolen lunch would surely be found soon and suspicions would arise.

If the British had assumed that there were no survivors in the air crash over on the Roaches, it would mean that nobody would be searching for him unless they had found the flight manifest – unlikely given the intensity of the explosion upon impact. More likely his discovery would be due to a mistake that he himself made. Rudolph was a meticulous planner and would only take risks as and when they were essential for survival. He took another look at the map and deduced that if he followed the river downstream for around three miles, he would get to Danebridge, a small hamlet. From there, he would recalculate his options and make the optimal decision.

The day after the jazz night at the Setter Dog was full of jokes and jesting. Owain had driven the semi-professional jazz players back to their barracks in Warrington, keen to have a final chat about music. The pail from the make-shift 'double bass' had been returned to the store room and the head of the mop had been reattached, having been used by Owain as a wig for half of the evening. Several quarrymen were whistling one of the catchier of the tunes from the previous night. Patrice was being very honourable and refusing to describe which 'base' he'd got to with Moll Brampton. He realised that Silas would allow a certain amount of coarse humour on site, but any disrespect to young Langley ladies would be punished by a scowl and additional labour assignments at the end of the day.

Both of the twins – Lucas and Jan – were suffering equally debilitating hangovers. Seemingly once they had managed the crowd in the lounge bar last night, they had then competed with Dick Avery in downing shots of bourbon. They had not learned that one should never play a drinking game with a publican. Dick had given them a dozen bourbon shots whilst surreptitiously substituting his own drink for tap water. The amusement was that everyone else at the bar was very aware of Dick's antics. Only the twins were oblivious to the game and found it hard to understand how, whilst they were sliding off their bar stools, Dick seemed able to hold his liquor without a problem.

Silas was keen to get the operation back into full production as there was an increasing need for rock to be excavated out of the quarry. Thomas Whetton had described the devastation that German bombers had caused at the docks in Liverpool the previous morning. Five merchant ships had been sunk – including two large barges – serving Liverpool from the North Welsh mines. HMS Hood had managed to remain afloat. The wreckage in the Mersey estuary would take some time to clear, and this put more pressure on home-sourcing crushed rock from Cheshire.

It was good that he had his work to focus on. Silas worried about the fact that no word had arrived from Charlie about Will and the boys. This was having a depressing effect on the household. Gwen was trying to keep Beth in a positive state of mind as she got closer to her due date. Melissa was also desperately worried that no news from Charlie meant no news about her own Jack.

During their time in Europe, Charlie had managed to get correspondence across to Langley every three to four weeks. He wrote on behalf of all of the Langley boys and had become so good at describing the mood and sentiment of the collective group and the individuals that all of their families had become accustomed to calling into the Post Office at 8 am every day to check with Percy Ricketts whether any mail had arrived from Charlie. Since being in North Africa, the mail had dried up, and only one letter had arrived which was an account of the voyage from Southampton to the port of Limassol in Cyprus.

The account of the journey was full of nervous energy as Charlie described his and his friends' fears as they traversed the Bay of Biscay, hoping for a major storm, as this would be one way that the U-boats from nearby La Rochelle – might not attack. It was from there that Hitler had based the wolf pack – the nickname used for his armada of submarines – aimed directly at Atlantic merchant shipping in an attempt to starve the UK of outside supplies. Charlie had described the relief after they rounded Cadiz in Portugal and entered the straits of Gibraltar. He had also described the game of canasta and had admitted that Will was the star player of the group and had won most of the chocolate rations of the entire unit thanks to his mean play. Charlie wrote in a way that allowed each of his friends to appear as a positive influence on the others, as he knew that his words would be poured over by all of the families. Beth paid particular attention to some of the letters and words as he had worked out a special code within his sentences that only she would understand and generally communicated his undying love for her and the soon to arrive baby.

However, two months passed without any further news from Charlie. The information appeared in public newspaper headlines announcing the tough battles that English forces were having with Erwin Rommel's German and Italian troops around Tobruk in eastern Libya. This was the main reason why HMS Suffolk had been quickly summoned to take reinforcements to the Mediterranean.

Silas was constantly worried about the war; he was finding it very hard to motivate his quarry workers. Thank God he had been allocated the international soldiers, who had become the life and soul, not only at the quarry but also in the village, and without them there, life would be much less colourful. Shortly after the jazz night, one of the American soldiers – a tall, gangly fellow called Arnold Cunningham – had asked if they could stage an exhibition game of basketball on the school playground down in Langley. Silas had immediately agreed, knowing that his sister – Martha – the headmistress – would be delighted to welcome Arnold and the other international soldiers to the school as it would help bring new meaning to geography lessons. Silas suggested that perhaps some of them could address the school assembly and describe what living in their home countries was like to the boys and girls. What this basketball was all about was another matter! The Americans readily agreed to help out at the school, and Silas promised that he'd get full permission and possible dates from his sister when he saw her next Sunday at the weekly roast dinner.

Silas had just introduced the idea to Martha when Beth's waters broke. Two weeks earlier than expected. Gwen, being Gwen, had everything prepared. Between her, Martha and Melissa, they coaxed Beth upstairs to her room whilst Nat ran next door to ask Percy Ricketts to phone Doctor Cartright – who lived in Sutton – and get the message across that he should please come to Langley as soon as possible. Silas was in charge of fresh towels, boiling water and cups of tea.

Twenty minutes later, Doctor Cartwright arrived breathless, having pedalled the three miles from Sutton in record time. His Ford Motor car had a garage service, so his push bike was his only mode of transport. As he entered the cottage, a high-pitched yell was heard, and then some small coughs, the baby had arrived – healthy and loud.

"Congratulations, Silas – it sounds like you're a Grandad to a beautiful little boy!" beamed Nat.

The doctor nodded. "It's no wonder that I was totally unnecessary – with Mother Gwen clucking around, and Martha – who must have delivered several thousand lambs in her lifetime, and the ever-efficient Melissa – Beth could not have been in better hands. I'll just check Beth and the baby over and then be on my way."

Beth was naturally tired and emotional. She and Melissa hugged. Beth whispered, "I'm so happy about the baby, but I just want Charlie here with me to see him and hold him. We haven't even discussed what name to call the wee fellow."

Melissa squeezed her and whispered back, "Don't worry, my darling friend. Jack has promised to bring Charlie home and then you will all be together. Until then – I'll be his surrogate daddy."

Four miles away across the hills, Rudolph Schwalbe had reached his initial objective, the bridge over the river Dane leading up to the village of Wincle. He drank from the stream beneath the bridge, well out of sight from the track that ran across the top. He caught a reflection of himself in the still pool at the side. His face was bloodied and his Luftwaffe flying suit was shredded from the gorse bush. This look, together with the limp and broken collar bone, would send any human screaming in the other direction. Thankfully, so far, it had only been the wildlife of Gradbach and the Dane Valley that had laid eyes on him, and he was hopeful that this would continue to be the case for a while yet. Even so, he resolved to try to do something about his appearance. He had a final gulp of stream water and then followed the track upwards, staying close to walls and coppices to the side and heading in the direction of a church spire that he had seen from one of his vantage points on the route.

St Michael's was an Anglican church with a bell tower and just the kind of location that Rudolph considered might be a useful resting point. The church served a very small and spread-out community of farmers, and it seemed likely that from Sunday to Sunday, it only served to welcome the very occasional visitor. Rudolph slipped inside the main door and found the church to be empty other than a cooing wood pigeon that seemed to be roosting in the rafters. A font dated 1861 was located in the nave – a perfect place for a recent survivor of a plane crash to wash his face and clean up. Following that, Rudolph tried the door to the vestry. It opened with a loud and prolonged squeak. Around the walls were several pegs with clothes on – presumably belonging to the vicar or verger. Possibly, they had been left behind by members of the choir. Whatever – they were a perfect opportunity for Rudolph to transform his outward appearance into something a little more acceptable to the human eye. The only item missing was new footwear, he would have to survive in his military boots for now. He returned to the nave and spied a platform in the tower with a long ladder leading up to it. At the top of it there was a large bell, but also just about enough room to one side for him to curl up. Using a prayer cushion for a pillow, he caught up on some sleep, confident that nothing would likely disturb him other than the fat wood pigeon whose home he'd rudely invaded.

CHAPTER 43 - *RATS OF TOBRUK*

It was a critical wartime effort to defend Tobruk for the Allied forces. Holding it would deprive the Germans of a supply port closer to the Egyptian–Libyan border. The only other option was Benghazi, 560 miles to the west. The siege of Tobruk, by a largely Australian force of Allied troops, had lasted for five months and had been a mammoth effort in the face of constant German and Italian bombardment by land, air and sea. Occasionally, a resupply convoy had got through, but often, these had been thwarted by large German artillery located to the east and west of the port. It was in one of these convoys that members of the Cheshire regiment on board HMS Suffolk had entered Tobruk without attracting the attention of any of the German guns, under the cover of darkness and in thick sea mist.

Jack Moat disembarked the vessel first and said a little prayer of gratitude under his breath. HMS Suffolk had been their home from Southampton to Cyprus, and even when in Cyprus, they had used the ship as their overnight quarters. They would now be saying farewell to her for quite probably the last time, as the captain had informed Jack that Suffolk would now replace another naval ship that had been sunk trying to deliver supplies into Libya, which was itself a replacement to another vessel now residing at the bottom of the Mediterranean.

Jack shouted behind him, "Will, can you make sure Charlie, Fred, Andy, Robin and Adam all make it off the boat? And if they grumble, bribe them with one of your bountiful supplies of chocolate bars!"

"Jawohl Herr Fuhrer!" shouted back Will irreverently and with a smile on his face. Will was delighted to be heading for dry land again. He was the one member of the unit who had suffered seasickness badly, and if truth be told, despite winning all of that chocolate at card games, he hadn't been able to stomach any of it due to his constant barfing over the side of the ship. However, chocolate was like money, and he was able to bribe the medical officer on board to supply him with Mothersills Seasickness Remedy, a new drug on the market that seemed to soothe his motion sickness better than any other.

Will gathered the unit together and met Jack on the dockside, who was discussing billeting arrangements with an Australian sergeant who used the word 'bloody' after every other word, yet Jack seemed to be making some headway.

"These bloody Italians are pains in the bloody ass," Will overheard the Sergeant report to Jack. "At least with the bloody Krauts, you know where they're likely to bloody well attack. The bloody Italians are all over the bloody place, even firing at them-bloody-selves sometimes!"

Jack looked at Will and signalled for him and the rest of the group to follow him. They walked up through bombed-out brick and stone warehouses, through some narrow alleys and found a bunkhouse which looked like one of very few that had not experienced any bomb damage.

"Okay, boys, find a place for your bedroll – and get some kip," Jack said. "We report for some serious duty in two hours' time."

The Cheshire Regiment quickly understood why the militia that they had joined was known as the Rats of Tobruk. The living conditions were horrendous, and although they had stayed in a relatively undamaged bunkhouse on the first night when they returned from duty after a sixteen-hour shift. They discovered that their bunkhouse had been shelled and they had to dig out their belongings before finding another location to try to seek some rest. Most of the British soldiers they'd met had been there for some time and seemed to have lost touch with reality and were walking dead. Jack resolved to ensure that his unit would not suffer likewise. The good grace was that the British reinforcements came with new ammunition and this would allow a more aggressive approach towards defending Tobruk.

"Sergeant Moat, please report to Lieutenant-General Leslie Morshead bloody immediately." Jack was awoken by the Australian Sergeant who he had first met at the port, giving orders for him to get up and follow him. In this state of war, soldiers slept with their boots on, and so Jack picked up his rifle, put on his hat and followed the Aussie out of the room. The rest of his unit did not stir, or more likely pretended not to hear, as they returned to their dreams of hunting deer in Macclesfield Forest or hitting a winning six, whatever delights their sub-conscience would concoct.

Jack entered the lieutenant-general's dusty, smoke-filled office. It contained a long table beneath two old chandeliers that were hanging precariously from rusty chains. The glass beads were constantly making sounds as the sirocco desert wind blew violently through the window frames, covered by tatty material. Two men were pouring over a map on the table. The senior of the two turned as the sergeant introduced Jack to the room.

"Ah, welcome, Sergeant Moat," Leslie Morshead growled in an Australian twang. "It's good to see some Limey soldiers join us in our own little piece of Hell. It's about time you lot bloody well turned up and did some work."

Jack got the impression that the Lieutenant-General was joking, but he wasn't too sure about the Australian humour just yet.

"Brandy?" Morshead enquired. Jack accepted the offer. "Come over here and have a look at this map, and tell us what you think?"

Jack walked over to the table and looked at a map of Tobruk and the surrounding area. The second officer at the table was adjusting the position of a number of black, red, and gold-coloured counters around the map.

The officer pointed at the map, "The Aussie gold counters represent our best intelligence on the latest positions we hold in defending the city and keeping the port open. The black counters are where we believe Italian troops are active, and the red counters are the bloody Hun."

Jack was now in no doubt why Morshead had used the term 'Hell.' The gold counters were few in number and they were surrounded from all sides by red and black counters.

"You asked my opinion, sir," Jack responded to the Lieutenant-General's original question. "I believe that just sitting here and defending our current position is doomed to eventual failure. We must secure the port and the supply line from the sea." Jack noted that he had got the attention of several other officers that were loitering in the room.

"Go on Sergeant, and how do you think we can succeed in that," said Morshead in a semi-mocking manner.

"We need to counterattack their own supply lines here and here." Jack pointed to the map, identifying one cluster of black Italian counters and one cluster of red German counters. "These two locations feed the rest of the enemy's supplies. If we can overcome these, we have a good chance of weakening their grip on the port, and this might allow further naval supplies to arrive. That's what I'd do."

Jack looked at the group of officers now studying the table surface more closely. These were hardened soldiers who had been defending this god-damned city for almost six months. Week after week, they had seen fewer gold counters appearing on the map and had lost the appetite to do anything but defend the few remaining. The thought of a counter-offensive to try to take back control grabbed their attention and they were busily digesting the possibility.

"Sergeant Moat, how would you propose we take out their strongholds?" asked one of the officers.

Jack offered up an idea. "Any kind of an attack from our side will prove a surprise to them, and if we manage to focus on both of these points in a synchronised manner, despite leaving our centre vulnerable, I believe that the surprise element will be sufficient to upset the balance. You have all built the reputation of being desert rats; we need to scrap like them now or risk being poisoned by inertia."

Jack recognised that this was a risky statement as it accused the Lieutenant-General and his team of being inactive, but he felt his naivety might be able to beg forgiveness later. As it was, there seemed to be general agreement around the table that this courageous move might be suicidal, or it might be just the kind of glorious counter punch that could break the siege and push Rommel back into the sand dunes of the Northern Sahara together with his Italian cousins.

"Sergeant Moat," Morshead announced with an authoritarian voice. "You and your platoon will be responsible for taking on the Italians and Captain Forsberg," Morshead turned to a large Australian officer. "You will gather a group of soldiers together and plan your assault on the German position. We have no time to lose, so let's target 23:00 this evening." He finally added, "We will call this Operation Crusader. Good luck, gentlemen, and make sure you both have sufficient Libyan soldiers with you, those that you can trust, to show you where us rats truly can do their utmost damage."

Jack saluted and wished Captain Forsberg luck with his mission, they agreed to share a brandy upon their successful return. Morshead interrupted, "Oh, Sergeant Moat, one more

thing, there's a telegram for you and your boys from England."
He handed an envelope across to Jack and wished him well,
"And let me introduce you to a fine man who will be of great
help to you. My interpreter – Farukh Khan."

Jack caught the eye of a man in Islamic clothing who had
been listening to the conversation around the table. Jack
beckoned for him to come over to him and introduce himself.
Farukh had been an interpreter at the Allies headquarters for
the last four months, ever since his home had been blown up
by the Italians and killed his entire family. He had
volunteered to become more involved in the war effort and
had been looking for a way to avenge his personal tragedy.
Jack Moat's fresh and bold plan was something that he had
wanted to be part of, and he knew the complex network of
streets and alleyways that might be an advantage to any
assault on the area that had become known as the Italian
Quarter of Tobruk.

Jack needed Farukh, and Farukh needed Jack. They both
headed back to the part of the building where the rest of the
Cheshire Regiment were resting.

"Boys, let me introduce Farukh Khan, he is a local man
born in Tobruk, and very knowledgeable about the layout of
this city and will give us the best possible chance of success."
Will and Charlie shook Farukh's hand warmly and the other
boys all waved a welcome from their sitting positions. Jack
continued, "We have our first mission. The Cheshire has been
asked to destroy the headquarters of the Italian operation in
Tobruk. It's the location from which all battle orders are
issued and all of their spare inventory sits. It all goes off at
23:00 tonight. At the same time, an Australian platoon will

attack the German central operation. Farukh, Will – come with me, we have some planning to do. The rest of you, check your equipment, including incendiaries, and get some rest, we'll need to be on top form tonight. These Italians will soon feel the full force of what a load of Cheshire quarrymen can do when we want something."

Full of thoughts as to how the Cheshires might fulfil their mission, Jack had stuffed the telegram from England into his jacket pocket and forgotten about it.

Rudolph must have slept for a full three hours. As he woke up, the bats had started to wake up too and start their early evening sorties out of the bell tower in order to catch insects. No human sighting had been made, and his wash in the font and new clothes made him feel more positive. He took one more look at his face in a mirror that was usefully hung in the vestry. Other than the facial scratches, he looked almost human himself. He gathered his Luftwaffe uniform together and stuffed it behind a drystone wall and an ash tree on the perimeter of St Michael's. He kept the map and the photo, but every other form of identity was abandoned alongside his uniform. He looked down at his shoes. These were standard issue Luftwaffe, and unmistakably so. At the earliest opportunity, he would need to sort these out, but for now, the flares on his trousers were able to cover most of the boot.

The dusk was sufficient for him to slink out of the church and over a field towards a hill that he had identified on the map as being Bosley Cloud, about five miles away. There were only isolated sources of light from the land, but the moon was again another strong source of light, meaning that he could move along in the shadows of the walls dividing fields without attracting attention other than the occasional grazing sheep or cow.

After three hours, Rudolph entered a farm building just below the summit of Bosley Cloud. A chicken coop to one side had provided him with three eggs that he gorged on, swilling it down with the last of the milk. At one end, the barn was stacked to the rafters with hay bales, whilst the other end had a number of pens with what must be some late Spring lambs. On approaching the barn, the majority of the fields had lambs resting, with watchful mothers stirring only if he got too close to them. He tried to avoid waking the barn up by stepping carefully around the pens and found a natural hole in the haystack, through which he forced himself and so he was out of view. Dust from the hay made him want to sneeze, and he swallowed two sneezes, but the third escaped and exploded out of his nostrils. A cacophony of baa's arose from the pens but calmed down soon enough. Rudolph hoped that this would not attract any attention from the farmhouse some four hundred yards away. Ten minutes later, he had noticed no activity through the peephole he had found in the side of the barn and at the back of the hay stack. He settled down for the night.

The planning for the Italian element of Operation Crusader had gone well. Jack and Will had briefed the platoon, whilst Farukh had drawn out in great detail the street plan and angles from which to approach the Italian stronghold. He had also confidently described the location of the arms depot, which would be a key target for incendiaries to be set and whose detonation would signal the frontal assault of the Italian compound by the British and, indeed, would also signal the Australian assault of the German headquarters on the other side of Tobruk.

There were two hours to go before the operation would begin, all weapons had been double-checked, and now was the time to get some final rest before action. Jack looked at his men, playing canasta and joking with their new Libyan friend Farukh, who had quickly picked up the idea of the game and, much to Adam Bostock's annoyance, had cleared him out of two bars of chocolate already. A closer, better group of comrades, he could not have chosen. They'd survived Dunkirk together and were now about to undertake their most daring mission. He knew that the chances of all of them returning were small, but that was war, and he knew that all of them would lay down their lives for each other. The greatest of sacrifices.

As Jack was having these personal thoughts, he suddenly remembered the telegram in his pocket. It was addressed to Charlie. How stupid he'd forgotten to pass it on immediately. Interrupting the canasta game, he shouted over, "Charlie, I have a telegram for you from England. I should have given it to you earlier." He handed it to Charlie, and as was a habit with the group, they stopped their game and all waited for Charlie to update them about what correspondence had come from home."

"Okay, boys, here goes," started Charlie. "It's from Beth..." They all sighed romantically, with Andy mock-kissing Robin. The jovial mocking manner was not lost on Farukh, who now understood that Beth was Charlie's wife or girlfriend from home.

Charlie smiled back at the group. "Shut up – let me continue... she says the following:

"Everyone here in Langley sends their love to all of our boys. We know that you've made landfall in Cyprus and/or North Africa. We have located you on a map at the Dunstan stan Inn! If you are in the desert, Adam, your mum reminds you to put sun cream on." They all laughed and pointed at Adam's fair complexion underneath his red hair.

"Melissa has been painting your house, Jack, and hopes that you like the colour when you get back. Oh, and she's also bought a sheepdog and called it Logan." Jack tutted but smiled at the thought of him and Melissa, hand in hand, walking up Teggs Nose with Logan.

Jack continued, "Fred, Andy and Robin – Silas says that you can stay in North Africa on holiday for as long as you want, as he has replaced you with some much better Dutch, Canadian and American quarrymen, who work twice as hard." Everyone laughed at Charlie's impression of his father-in-law.

"And Charlie... congratulations, you're a dad! And Will... congratulations, you're an uncle. I gave birth to our son on 21st April 1941. Hurry home!"

Charlie looked open-mouthed at his friends in front of him. There was silence for a few seconds and then mass hysteria. They all danced around crazily, congratulating Charlie and Will and hugging each other. Farukh didn't really understand very much about this reaction, but felt compelled to jump around too, with Adam eventually taking him to one side and explaining that Charlie had just become a father for the first time, and Will was a new uncle.

Jack was genuinely happy for his friend Charlie but also realised that the group needed to focus on the tough task ahead. He stood on a chair amidst the raucous behaviour and signalled for calm, "Okay, boys, the drinks will all be on me later. We will so wet young Aspinall's head when we get back from the operation. We now all have a new little mascot to fight for and even more reason to get ourselves all back home – which will only come after we've chased these Italians back to Roma."

Arnie Cunningham stood two clear feet above Martha Lovatt, but the diminutive school headmistress commanded great respect amongst her students as she addressed them in the school assembly. Arnie had been highly impressed with the polite manner in which he and his fellow Americans had been warmly welcomed at the school reception by a group of wide-eyed eleven-year-olds – the eldest that Langley's primary school accommodated. They were ushered through to the one large assembly hall that doubled as a classroom. The room fell silent.

"Girls and Boys," Martha started, "we have some very special guests today who have travelled all the way from America, and they will be telling us all about their homeland. Mr. Cunningham, over to you." Martha sat down and Arnie moved to centre stage.

"Howdy all you kids," he paused as he looked at puzzled faces, "or should I say, 'good morning, children.'" Arnie exaggerated his accent and made a funny face, which broke the silence as the children's faces started to smile at the American's amusing mannerisms.

"This morning, my friends and I will be telling you all about the great land across the sea called the United States of America and how we live our lives when we are not in the beautiful country of Teggs Nose, helping you English extract gritstone."

A hand shot up from the front row, it was Tommy Heghleigh, a nine-year-old, a nephew of Fred Needles, and a chatterbox. "Yes sir, how may I help you?" said Arnie.

"My uncle is in the war, you know, and he also plays cricket for Langley, he's a bowler, and I bet he can bowl faster than you."

Arnie smiled at Tommy and answered, "Well young man, how about me and my friends teach you a sport we play in America, and you can teach us how to play that funny old sport of cricket." Tommy nodded his head in happy agreement. Around him, his friends started to nudge each other with shared excitement about the challenge ahead.

Having divided the school into three groups by age, the teachers accompanied one of the American soldiers each and they showed the children all sorts of things American. From the design of the US flag to the singing of the national anthem to the names of famous Americans – like Abraham Lincoln, George Washington and Babe Ruth. The children loved the unusual sayings that the visitors had and their relaxed style. After break, the whole school emptied out onto the playground and surrounded a section that had chalk markings. At one end a scaffold had been erected and a hoop and board had been placed ten feet from the ground. The three Americans then proceeded to play 2 on 1 basketball with a score being given to the person who could shoot the ball through the basket. Arnie commentated throughout the demonstration, showing how the ball could be dribbled or passed to a colleague and how best to set it before taking a shot. The schoolchildren loved it and cheered each time a ball passed through the hoop. After five minutes of non-stop action, the three Americans breathing heavily. Stood together in front of the school and gave a dramatic bow. The children and staff cheered.

"And now," Arnie said panting, "it's your turn to play the greatest sport on earth – basketball."

The three groups were given a basketball each and went through drills to learn how to dribble, pass and shoot. At the end of the session, the Americans gave each child a cigarette card featuring a famous American basketball player in a mock graduation ceremony.

Just as the lunch bell rang, Martha collected everyone together again and thanked Arnie and his two colleagues for their time in sharing their culture and even more so for their effort in supporting Britain's war efforts.

Arnie took Martha to one side, "Thanks, Mrs. Lovatt, that made a lovely break for me and the boys and a chance to escape Sledge for a morning." He added with a wry smile, "your brother sure does drive his workforce hard!"

Chapter 44 - *Lambing*

The small hole in the barn wall was casting a beam of sunlight across the small hollow space that Rudolph had made for himself behind the haystack. As the warmth from the sun hit his bare face, his eyes opened. He was cocooned in hay, and relatively comfortable given that he was an air crash survivor from only two days previous. The greatest pain he was feeling right then was coming from the hunger pangs in his stomach. It was time to try and scavenge for more food. The lambs had decided it was also time to awaken, and the morning chorus of the lambing shed was in full cry within ten minutes. This also signalled some movement from the farmhouse that could be seen through the spy hole.

Thomas Whetton's land spread across the whole of Bosley Cloud, and most of it was farmed successfully for the last nine years by his tenant Nat Lovatt. Nat had made it his purpose to know every square inch of the farm, having been granted a very fair tenancy agreement by Whetton after Henry Aspinall had ejected him unceremoniously from Trentabank farm prior to the flooding of the valley and the formation of the Trentabank reservoir. Nat viewed Whetton as a saviour figure and felt he owed it to him to steward his land to the very best of his ability. And this he did with good grace and a huge amount of work. However, Nat was getting older, and Martha did more than her fair share as a working farmer's wife. Martha wanted to keep her teaching profession going down at Langley School, where she had been ever since graduating as a teacher. As a sheep farm, there were intensive labour periods over the lambing season, where Nat needed help, which he mainly found from itinerant farm workers. These were hard to come by, given the demands of wartime Britain.

The last of the lambs had been born and were due to be let out to pasture now that the late Spring days were warming up. It was a Saturday, and Nat was up at the break of dawn as usual. Today was the day that he would move the last lambs and ewes from the barn out to the pasture closest to the farmhouse, the safest from any local prey and farthest from any public footpaths where dogs could cause a nuisance. Martha was already in the kitchen putting bread in the oven and preparing a large chicken casserole for the weekend when they were due to head down to Gwen and Silas's house in Langley village to celebrate the naming of Beth and Charlie's son. It was agreed that the little boy would not be baptised until Charlie returned, but he deserved a name before then.

"Just off down to the lambing shed, love," Nat announced as he headed out of the door, two sheepdogs were in the outhouse, dutifully waiting for a day's work with the flock. "Should be back by lunchtime." Nat loaded a handcart up with a large pale of cow's milk for some of the orphan lambs who had lost their mothers in the process of birthing and a large sack of oats for some of the weaker ewes. The two collies were flanking the cart as he trundled along the rough track.

Rudolph was watching from the barn and noted the two eager dogs. It was too late to escape without being seen, so he decided to stay put and sit it out, hoping that the farmer's duties would be quick and the dogs would not be allowed in the barn for fear of spooking the lambs. He stayed in his curled-up position, hoping that the noise of the hungry flock demanding milk and oats would more than block out the angry growls that his ravenous stomach was making.

A cacophony of high-pitched bleats arose as the barn door creaked open. Daylight streamed in. Rudolph remained stock-still, confident that he was out of sight. Nat talked to his sheep. "Now, you lot, time for some fresh grass for you all after I give a bit of extra milk to the littl'uns."

He made his way towards the pen closest to the haystack where Rudolph lay. The pale of milk was placed down in the centre, and the orphans suckled on three rubber teats that Martha had expertly created from an old washing-up glove. Nat split the oat sack down the middle and filled up a shallow trough in another pen occupied by some of the smaller ewes. He checked all of the other pens and confirmed the numbers. "34 – all present and accounted for. Ruby, Jess – come by!" he shouted to the dogs as he put his fingers to his lips and whistled a high-pitched shrill. Jess reacted first and ran around to the left of the barn door, just out of sight of the sheep, Ruby was younger and still learning the art, she was excited by the chance for some action and ran into the main pen, causing the sheep to scatter. One lamb jumped through the fence and down a crevice between two hay bales adjacent to where Rudolph was hidden.

"Ruby, away!" Nat yelled and the collie reacted shell-shocked by the commotion she had caused. She reversed out of the shed and went and lay next to Jess. "You useless little bugger," shouted Nat, "I'll have to go and find that lamb now!".

The rest of the sheep and lambs were let out of the shed, and the two collies kept an eye on the flock whilst Nat moved towards the mountain of hay, armed with a large pitchfork.

"Perhaps you are looking for this?" Rudolph appeared through the bales carrying the startled lamb. Rudolph had thought it best to announce himself rather than risk being stabbed by the pitchfork.

"Who the hell are you?" Nat said, startled, still holding the pitchfork.

"I'm Rudi Ipsen, a mariner from Esbjerg, Denmark" he said, having pre-planned a story for when he would come into contact with any local.

Rudolph Schwalbe had been born in Kiel, Northern Germany, across the Baltic from Denmark – a neutral country – and one that he had learned the basic language from a teacher at his preparatory school. In addition, years before the war, he had been to Denmark twice on exchange trips, both times to Esbjerg, so he knew some of the basic facts about the town and Jutland, the Danish peninsular where Esbjerg was located. He felt confident that he could imitate a Danish-English accent sufficiently to remain unidentifiable as a German whilst he worked out his next move.

"So, what are you doing in my lambing shed, Rudi from Denmark," said Nat, perplexed at this sudden appearance from the haystack.

"I'm very sorry, sir." Rudi bowed his head and concentrated on his newfound Danish intonation. "I came off a merchant ship at Liverpool and am heading back across to Hull to catch a fishing trawler back home. I've got a little lost and decided to seek shelter for the night in your barn. I'm very sorry, but I've got no money to pay you. I'll happily do some labouring for you for the cost of the night's sleep. Perhaps you could throw in a bit of food, too, as I'm starving."

"Hold on!" Nat said, putting the pitchfork down, recognising that this person held no malice against him or his property. "Did you leave your ship willingly, or have you absconded?"

"Truthfully, I did jump ship at Liverpool. I'd had enough of these German U-boats taking potshots at us every time we rounded the southern Irish waters. We were attacked twice around Kinsale Head, and we only just managed to limp up to Liverpool on one engine." Rudolph almost convinced himself with the genuine tone of voice he was using. He decided to shut up and allow Nat to make the next move.

"Okay, Rudi, I believe you and I could do with a few days of manual labour for food and lodging, as long as Mrs. Lovatt agrees. It looks like you can handle sheep anyway." Nat pointed to the little lamb nestling in Rudi's armpit. They smiled at each other and shook hands. Nat continued, "First off, grab that pale and bring that stray lamb out and we'll find its mother."

CHAPTER 45 - *FIREWORKS*

"Shh!" Farukh signalled by raising his finger to his lips as he edged his way along a broken wall separating the market square from the myriad of alleyways making up the Italian Quarter. This area was relatively scarce of life as it had exchanged hands between the forces several times, and was consequently scarred by debris and buildings torn apart by explosions. Tonight, it was peaceful. Farukh and Jack had agreed on a two-pronged attack, with each of them leading their assigned men from the east and west of the Italian army's central headquarters. The timing was perfect as tonight was the Catholic festival of Saint Sebastian, a much-worshipped martyr in Sicily. There were many Sicilian conscripts fighting in the Italian army in Tobruk, so it would be likely that there would be plenty of grappa brandy being shared, and the lookout posts would be sparsely manned or manned by soldiers with more blurred vision and thinking than usual.

Jack's team consisted of himself, Robin and Andy. Their job was to draw fire from the Italians and distract them sufficiently to allow Farukh, Charlie, Adam, Will and Fred to get into the heart of the compound and, lay as much explosive as was possible, and then retreat fast before detonating. The plan was simple, but both teams were slowed by needing to navigate around the debris-strewn streets, trying to keep to shadows. Jack's team purely had light weaponry with them, as they needed to be able to flee at speed ahead of the expected Italian pack. An additional burden to Farukh's team was the bulky backpacks of explosives needed to cause ultimate damage to the Italian forces.

Lieutenant General Morshead and the remaining Australian soldiers were primed to go on the offensive over at the port as soon as the fireworks started in the city. If successful, decimating the Italian ranks and central supplies might be sufficient to secure Tobruk and its port long enough to allow a much larger regiment of reinforcements to land from the Allies base in Cyprus. Potentially – a successful outcome of this plan might end the siege and signal the start of the end of Erwin Rommel's time in North Africa.

Jack was uneasy. Whenever Charlie and Will were out of his sight, he felt a guilt complex. His promise to Silas, Gwen and Beth was that he would look after them both like his own sons. But there was a human resource reason for this, and it would give the mission a greater chance of success. Jack, Andy and Robin were the best marksmen out of the group, whilst the four soldiers with Farukh were all more capable of carrying heavy equipment and laying explosives. The decision was made and Jack would just have to trust the others and pray that all eight of the men would rendezvous at the agreed location by the lighthouse at the port - a location already secured by Australian forces.

Another five minutes and Jack's team were within earshot

of the Italian barracks. There was opera music coming from a scratchy gramophone and plenty of laughter and chinking of glasses. Jack smiled to himself when he thought of his own two companions – Andy and Robin – who had honed their rifle skills upon the wide expanse of Macclesfield Forest – illegally shooting Henry Aspinall's deer and selling the meat up at the Setter Dog pub. He turned to them both and smiled as he spoke softly, "Okay, boys, you remember all those fine stags you shot in the Forest when you were mere lads... Well, I want you to sharpen your aim once more, as we need to piss off these Italians so much that they start chasing us big time."

"Italian venison – not sure if the Setter Dog would want that on its menu!" Robin whispered back. "But let's see how we do."

The three of them climbed up the wall and onto different positions on the roof overlooking the courtyard. There were clouds obscuring the moon, so the only light was from paraffin lamps and candles lighting up around fifty soldiers on long trestle tables toasting their patron saint. Hell was about to be unleashed!

Jack gave the signal and received confirmation that the other two were in strong sniping positions. They had already planned their escape path and their secondary locations to target the first wave of the Italian pursuers. Jack identified the most senior-looking officer around the table. 'Crack' – the sound of the first shot echoed around the courtyard, followed by two more. Three Italian soldiers slumped to the ground, with one of them kicking over the trestle table as a final act of life. As further shots rang out, the Italian party was well and truly over. Soldiers scattered to find cover, trying to identify the angle from where the shots arrived from. Two more Italians fell in trying to escape and lay motionless on the ground. From a second-floor balcony across the courtyard, the sound and flash of small arms were seen, and this response signalled the start of the next phase of their plan - their retreat and the ensuing Italian pursuit.

The hope of Operation Crusader was that – hot-blooded, leaderless and confused - almost all of the Italians would seek weaponry and start to retaliate. Finding the attack no longer present on the upper levels, they would assume that the attack had retreated and so take up pursuit through the narrow alleyways and away from their headquarters and supply depot.

From the lookout point, Charlie had his binoculars focused on the carnage happening below, and after the initial shooting, he saw three shadows moving down from their sniper points and back into the network of alleyways. He refocused his search on the chaotic scene in the courtyard as the Italians tried to make sense of the murderous desecration of their patron saint's feast. It seemed as though the reaction was as the British had hoped – spontaneous and uncalculated – a large number of Italian soldiers left the courtyard in the direction of where the shooting had come from, leaving the barracks vulnerable from the side where Charlie, Farukh and the others were hiding with the explosives.

Jack, Andy and Robin had started the mortal combat and the Italians had taken the bait. Bloody retaliation was all they had on their mind, that and cursing that they had allowed their security to lapse under a false belief that the largely Australian forces were so shell-shocked and exhausted that any offensive was highly unlikely.

As the Italians streamed out of the western side of the compound, Farukh steered his team into place on the east and started to lay explosives around the edge of the main depot. Gunshots were now heard at a greater distance. The six soldiers preparing a new surprise for the enemy all hoped that Jack, Andy and Robin were fleet of foot enough to escape their pursuers or at least distract them sufficiently for the enemy compound to go up in fire and cause a more destructive blow to the Italian war effort.

Jack, Andy and Robin took up their secondary positions behind a ruined fountain in a square about two hundred yards from the barracks. Their intention was to fire on the first few Italians and then using grenades, cause a smoke screen to then escape individually and make their own way towards the lighthouse rendezvous point. Once the grenade explosions were heard by Farukh and the team, the detonations of the main explosives would begin.

Everything was working according to the plan; six large explosives were in place. The Italians had been drawn out of their compound and were moving through alleyways to the west. As soon as the Italians were spotted entering the square with the fountain at one end, the British started firing again, causing the Italians to seek cover. Jack pulled the pin on the first grenade and hurled it into the middle of the square, followed quickly by two more from Andy and Robin. As the grenades detonated, a large cloud of dust appeared signalling the retreat of the three soldiers.

They ran as fast as they could to a point where the square had several alleys. Jack signalled for the other two to stop.

"Okay – this is where we break up – see you at the lighthouse as soon as you can get there. Good luck, and tread carefully."

Andy and Robin disappeared into the dark. Jack started running towards his chosen alleyway, recognising that the dust cloud caused by the grenades was lifting and Italian voices were now readily audible, moving towards the fountain. He missed his footing and kicked a large piece of rubble. He fell. Everything went black.

During the first hour of working together, Rudi was proving to be a competent and friendly worker. Nat, who spent almost all of his working day alone, was finding him to be very pleasant company and certainly better than some of the other itinerant farm labourers he had employed in previous years. The two dogs – Ruby and Jess – seemed to have befriended him too. "Do you fancy some lunch back at the farmhouse?" Nat enquired.

"Thanks, Nat, yes please," replied Rudi, with a huge emphasis on the 'yes.' No need for a second invitation here. Rudi was starving and unseen by Nat, had even gorged down some of the sheep oats and drunk the last remains of the orphan lamb's milk out of the pale that he was still carrying.

As they approached the farmhouse, Nat shouted out, "Martha, one more for lunch today, please, my dear."

Martha opened the top half of the stable door. "And who do we have here?" she asked, looking Rudi up and down. Her eyes stopped at his boots, which looked out of kilter with the rest of his appearance.

"This, Martha, is Rudi Ipsen from Denmark," Nat said.

"And he's been helping me this morning."

Rudi held out his hand awkwardly as his collarbone was causing him severe pain. "Hello Martha, pleased to meet you. Your husband has been very kind. He found me in your haystack this morning, and I've been helping him with the sheep."

Martha had a good ear for accents, and she thought that Rudi had a very good, educated English accent for someone so young, although she also clearly recognised a Scandinavian twang. Martha opened the lower part of the stable door. "Very good then, come in and tell me all about yourself and life in Denmark. I hope you like a good Cheshire pie. How did you hurt yourself?" She added, having noticed Rudi rubbing his shoulder.

The cooking smells emanating from the kitchen had already got Rudi salivating. As soon as the slice of pie was placed in front of him, he launched into it, forgetting any pain from his collarbone. Between mouthfuls, Rudi mentioned – rather unconvincingly, Martha thought – that he had been knocked over by a dislodged container on board his last ship.

"Goodness gracious, Rudi, nobody is going to take your food, no need to rush so much!" Martha scolded jokingly.

Rudi slowed down, "I am sorry, Mrs. Lovatt, the last proper meal I had was at the docks in Liverpool, and that was five days ago. I've been wandering across the Cheshire Plain ever since."

"Just as well you weren't there two days ago then, the Germans bombed the hell out of the place. They sunk a number of boats in the Mersey." Nat said. "I heard it on the radio news yesterday morning. Good news though, they missed HMS Hood."

Rudi was careful that his face did not show any of the grim irony he felt, and he just added, "Well, I hope my old ship and shipmates are okay."

Nat added, "The other thing I heard on the radio news was that one of the German planes was shot at by anti-aircraft guns near Matlock and came down over the Roaches. Three bodies of the airmen have been recovered, and the fourth is missing but assumed dead and possibly bailed out over Tittersworth Reservoir."

"It's all horrible news, those young men all losing their lives. Have another slice of pie." Martha changed the subject, and Rudi eagerly accepted the food and wolfed it down. He was fast recognising that Martha and Nat's farmhouse might be a useful location to stay at for a few days whilst he worked out his next move.

The sound of the grenades going off in Fountain Square had triggered a sequence of events. The retreat of Jack, Andy and Robin towards the port and lighthouse, and also the detonation of the main haul of explosives. Farukh, Charlie and the team had put four hundred yards distance between themselves and the explosives. Only Adam had remained behind about one hundred yards away in order to hit the switch and, hopefully, light up Tobruk. Adam had volunteered as he was the most athletic of the group and thus argued that he would be able to catch the rest of the team up after the explosion.

On plan, Adam flicked the switch, but nothing. "Shit," he said to himself under his breath, something had gone wrong. He manually connected the two wires, but still nothing. He tried it several times, and still, there was none of the expected Armageddon. Adam started back towards the explosives and got to within 50 yards when he noticed that one of the main detonating cables had split apart. Adam, still feeling that it was safe to reconnect the cable, did just that.

The explosion that followed was fierce, followed up by two more that shattered windows around him, and several tiles flew from rooftops. He turned to start to run, and then an ear-splitting explosion happened. It must have been the Supply shed, and the Italians must have kept all of their ammunition pile inside. The earth shook and walls started to crumble around Adam. A piece of masonry hit him on the forehead and he fell. A massive fireball appeared in the sky.

Fred turned to Will and shouted, "Yes, we've done it! We've only gone and blown up Italy!" He turned to Farukh, "Well done, my little Libyan bugger – you are a hero now." Charlie calmed Fred down and reminded him that they needed to wait for Adam and then make their way to the lighthouse, they could celebrate more then.

There were stones and flaming material spewing out from a series of secondary explosions to the main ones, signalling more destruction. The fire was intense and it seemed to engulf not only the Italian compound but a large area surrounding it. The few Libyans still living in the city – most had deserted to live out in the desert – came out of their houses to witness the destructive event. A tear appeared in

Farukh's eye, realising that although this was revenge for his family, the inevitable result was the part destruction of his home city and one that he cherished dearly.

"Where's Adam?" he said, coming back to the present.

"He should be here by now," Fred replied, immediately replacing his premature frivolity with concern for his mate.

Charlie took command, "We need two people to retrace our steps to find Adam, and the others can stay here. I'll go. Who will come with me?" Will immediately stepped forward. "I'll come with you."

"We'll need five minutes. If we are not back by then, Farukh, you and Fred head out towards the lighthouse and we'll see you there." Farukh and Fred nodded in agreement, and watched as Will and Charlie made their way back through to where they'd left Adam.

Adam had been badly caught up in the blast due to how close he was to the unexpectedly violent explosion of the Italian explosives store. A burning timber from a scaffold had pinned him down and his left leg was taking all the weight. He was conscious but very aware that he was not going to be able to move without help. At least, he felt that the majority of Italians would be to the west of the compound now, chasing Jack's team, yet he did not feel strong enough to shout out for help. The pain in his leg became excruciating. He was semi-comforted by the fact – as planned – he could hear Australian artillery beginning their assault on the port, triggered by the detonation of his explosives.

Charlie and Will had got to the hundred-yard mark where

Adam was supposed to have detonated the explosives, but all they found was his rifle and ammunition belt. It dawned on them that something must have gone wrong and Adam must have had to get closer to the compound. They looked ahead of them and saw a partly collapsed building with fire shooting out of the lower ground windows.

Will and Charlie looked at each other. "Let's move to that building, it could be that Adam needed to get closer for some reason," Will said, and Charlie nodded in agreement. They edged forward. Just the other side of the broken lintel, there on the ground surrounded by broken masonry and smoking timber, was Adam's body.

They both rushed into the building, with the fire still raging in one section, spitting flames and burning ash their way. Charlie checked Adam's pulse, and it was faint but still there. Will used a length of timber as a lever to budge the weight slightly from Adam's leg, sufficient for Charlie to drag him out. They hooked their arms under his armpits and, lifted him out of the building and started dragging him towards the others. As soon as Fred and Farukh saw the silhouette of two men dragging a third, coming towards them through the smoke, they ran forward and the four soldiers carried Adam back to their original location, laying Adam on the floor in front of them.

Charlie, who was the designated medic of the group, checked the pulse again, Adam was grasping onto life, but barely. He opened his eyes a little and looked at Charlie and then closed them again.

Resurgent with hope, Charlie shouted, "Boys, he's alive! Make a stretcher. I'll stem the leg bleed now using a bandage and a belt, but we need to get him to the lighthouse quickly. Adam needs better medical attention."

Fred and Will made a framed stretcher and Farukh found a tarpaulin that he stretched over the frame, sufficient to hold 'Adam's weight. They carefully placed the body onto the stretcher and started to head out in the direction of the fort and lighthouse. It would be a good twenty-minute walk in normal daylight, but with the added challenge of darkness and the weight of the stretcher, they would be lucky to make it in ninety minutes. But they had to try. They vowed that this small unit of the Cheshire regiment would stay intact.

On the western side of Tobruk, Andy had escaped the built-up area of the city and was making his way along a coastal path. The lighthouse was about a mile away, and he was expecting to be challenged by Australian soldiers from their lookout points within the next few hundred yards. He wondered how Robin and Jack were doing. He didn't have to wait long to hear Robin's chirpy voice from up above on a sand dune.

"Hi buddy, that was easy enough. Jack can't be far behind." Andy turned and looked back towards the smoking city. "Bugger me, that blast was much bigger than just our explosives – we must have hit their armoury."

In tripping over the rubble, Jack had fallen and his head had smashed into a wall, knocking himself temporarily unconscious. The enormous explosion from the compound had rocked the ground around him and woken him up.

Burning debris was falling from the sky all around. Jack raised a hand to his forehead and felt a deep gash oozing blood. He had lost his helmet, and his gun was nowhere to be seen. He was unaware of how long he'd been lying there but was aware that the Italian soldiers that had been chasing them had turned and were looking back at the plume of fire above their former headquarters. One of them spotted Jack still on his haunches. Illuminated by the phosphorescence of the sky, Jack could see all of the features of the face of the Italian soldier. It was Gustav Coccini. Both men were motionless, staring at each other, trying to make sense of this bizarre reunion and trying to work out what their next move would be.

The senior ranking officer within the Italian ranks shouted, "Fanculo, andiamo." The soldiers started to retreat back towards their barracks, leaving the fountain square by the way they had come. Gustav remained rooted to the spot, standing between Jack and the Italian officer.

"Coccini, Andiamo," the officer stepped towards Gustav, curious as to why one of his soldiers was so statuesque. He saw Jack trying to get to his feet about five yards in front of Gustav. The officer raised his pistol and took aim at Jack. Gustav moved his body in order to block the shot.

"Jack – run!" shouted Gustav. Jack jumped to his feet just as a shot rang out. Jack staggered further along the alleyway into the shadows and then turned to see Gustav on his knees in front of the officer, his head was bowed, the second pistol shot was Gustav's execution. Jack momentarily froze, still groggy from the blow to his head, and now confused by the whole strange scenario. Was he dreaming about this whole situation?

Thankfully, the shadows were deep enough to mean that he was out of sight of the officer, who kicked the motionless body of Gustav, muttering "Bastardo," and then turned to follow the rest of his unit back to the roaring inferno that was formerly their compound.

Jack emerged from the shadows and stumbled back into the square and Gustav's body. He turned Gustav onto his back and looked at his former Teggs Nose quarry colleague, still finding it hard to believe that it was the very same person. Gustav was still alive, but his breath was very shallow. Gustav's lips moved as if he wanted to say something. Jack leaned down to listen.

His final words were, "Jack – tell Sledge I'm sorry."

CHAPTER 46 - *WIN & LOSE*

At the lighthouse, where the Australian command post was based, and the rendezvous point for Operation Crusader, Andy and Robin were anxious. It had been an hour, and there had been no sighting of Jack nor any of the explosives team. They decided to head back out to the outskirts of the safe zone, where the Aussie forces had security look-outs posted. They reached the bunker and went inside. The fire from the city was still blazing away but a little less intense than previously. The light from the flames helped them to identify all of the tracks from the city to the port and around the lighthouse.

A silhouette of a group of people was just visible through binoculars, and as the group got closer, it became clear that they were carrying something or somebody. The Australian guard, using a more powerful telescope, identified British uniforms. Immediately, Andy and Robin jumped down from the look-out post and started running towards the group.

Adam was dead. Despite stopping regularly to tighten the ligature around the wounded leg to stem the bleeding, he had lost too much blood. It was a sombre scene that met Andy and Robin. This was the first time that one of the Langley boys had been lost; they had lived a charmed life for the last two years, but one of their brothers was now no more.

Robin and Andy held the middle of the stretcher on either side, and silently, the procession continued. In respectful silence, Adam's body was carried past the security post and into the main lighthouse building. The pallbearers laid the stretcher in a side chamber and covered his body with a sheet.

Charlie broke the painful silence, "Where's Jack?" he said, looking around.

"He was behind us," replied Andy, looking over at Robin to try and find reassurance where none existed. "I'm sure he's ok, though; your explosion must have distracted the Italians; he'll be back soon." Charlie looked at the uncertainty in Andy's face and felt no comfort.

"I'm going back to the security point to wait for him," said Robin. "We'll come with you," said Will and Charlie in unison.

Thankfully, it was only five more minutes before they saw the lone figure of Jack moving across the sand dunes. He was staggering, but he was alive. The group made a collective sigh of relief.

"Andy, let's go and help him; he looks unsteady," Robin said, grabbing Andy by the shoulder.

Other than the deep cut to his forehead, Jack was ok. He was pleased to see the boys but decided that now was not the time to talk about how Gustav had become his guardian angel. None of the rest of the group could summon the courage to tell Jack about Adam until they got back to the lighthouse.

Fred was Adam's best friend; they had cricketed together since the age of six. Fred's wickets as a bowler complimented Adam's runs as a batsman. Fred was the right person to break the news to Jack.

Jack could tell from the group's sullen looks that there was something up, but he felt that the Cheshire regiment was invincible. As their leader, he should have done a head count and realised that – including Farukh – there was still a missing person. Fred broke down in tears whilst he told Jack about Adam volunteering to return to ignite the detonation and consequently becoming a casualty. He told Jack about their attempts at stemming the wound and carrying him back. After Fred finished telling him, Charlie led Jack through to Adam's body and drew back the white sheet. Jack's head throbbed with pain from the injury, but that was nothing compared to the pain his heart felt when he saw Adam's body – the reality and agony of war hit him hard.

Lieutenant General Moreshead entered the room, "Well done lads – a great success! We've put those Italians back months, if not for good. You bloody Pommies aren't as bad as I thought! Plus, us Aussies have smashed the Krauts down by the port. We own Tobruk now!"

Despite the well-intended humour, the Lieutenant General quickly realised that the mood was not one of celebration. He peered over and saw Jack kneeling next to Adam's body. Moreshead immediately realised his mistake. He removed his hat. "My condolences; I'm sure he was a brave lad." He backed off, signalling to the private - who had followed him in carrying three bottles of brandy - just to leave them on the side.

Whilst Jack was kneeling over the body, he pictured Adam's mother – Hilda – being told of her son's death and the emotional outpouring that would run through the whole village. He looked at the rest of his charges and vowed to himself that this feeling of desolation in losing a comrade would not be repeated whilst he was in charge.

Adam Bostock was buried in the military graveyard near the lighthouse, looking northwest towards England and home. There were no dry eyes. The six of his friends from Langley carried the coffin. Jack led the ceremony, with Fred summoning up enough courage through the tears to describe his best mate via a couple of cricketing tales of innings that defied the odds. Farukh blessed the occasion with an Arabic prayer to fallen comrades.

After the ceremony, Jack took Charlie to one side and reminded him that despite the sadness of losing Adam, he needed to focus on getting back to Cheshire and holding his new son.

CHAPTER 47 - *OLIVER*

"What can we call him?" Gwen asked Beth. Both women were looking into the cradle at the babbling shape of the baby.

"We can't call him anything until Charlie gets back." Beth said firmly.

Silas piped up from the back garden porch, having overheard the final part of the conversation, "We need to have a name, even if it is only temporary. How about just calling him Charlie junior?"

"Charlie junior, it is for now," said Beth, "and we'll sort out a proper name when we talk with his dad next."

There was a familiar knock on the wall. It was Mr. Ricketts with his walking stick, tapping on the intervening wall. Since Will had left for the war, Percy Ricketts had been using Beth as his runner. Beth was pleased to be bringing in a little bit of regular money for the household, as her political and social journalism was often in too radical a direction to be publishable. However, since the third trimester of her pregnancy, Percy had been told – in no uncertain terms – by Gwen that her daughter would no longer be running errands, and Percy would have to find someone else in the village. The sound of knocking on the wall had not been heard for a number of months. This was unusual.

"I'll head next door to find out what Percy wants," said Silas. As he closed the door to his own terraced cottage, he was only ten yards away from the Post Office. A Cheshire regiment army van was parked just to the other side. His heart missed a beat; this could mean only one thing. Percy was speaking to an army officer on the pavement and beckoned Silas over.

He turned to Silas. "Sledge, there's some terrible news; this officer has just informed me that Adam Bostock was killed in the line of duty over in North Africa."

The officer introduced himself and confirmed what Percy had said. Silas bowed his head, afraid of what came next. "Any news about the other boys?" he asked.

The officer replied, "I'm sorry, we are only told about those that have lost their lives. It is safe to assume that Adam was the only fatality, or we would have been informed."

"Thank you, sir. Can I show you where Hilda Bostock, Adam's mother, lives?" Silas said with a knitted brow and watery eyes.

The officer thanked Percy and accepted Silas' offer of help. The two men walked down the high street without any further words. Curtains twitched, and people were very aware that a visit from an army officer was only ever made during recruitment drives or to pass on bad news. There were no more recruits available, and so it was easy to deduce what this official call was for.

Silas and the officer stopped at the Bostock's small cottage, next door to Melissa and Jack's house. Melissa was outside in the small front garden, looking intensely into Silas' eyes, willing him to give her a comforting sign. Hilda Bostock opened the door and invited the officer in. Silas went across to Melissa and gave her a hug.

"Adam has lost his life. Our boys are ok," he whispered in Melissa's ear. She started sobbing, partly in relief and partly in grief for her neighbour and the loss of her only son.

A wail emanated from the Bostock's cottage – the news had hit home – and Hilda's emotional outpouring was heard along the street. More people came out onto the pavement and looked down towards where Silas and Melissa were standing. The officer left the Bostock household, and Melissa went inside to try to comfort Hilda. Other friends from the village started to walk towards the cottage. It was Hilda's son who had died, but it was a child of the village, and the grief was felt everywhere.

Silas walked solemnly back to his own home with the officer, having to move into the road due to the number of people making their way down the pavement to the Bostock's home. Enroute, he met his own family. He hugged Gwen and Beth, who was holding Charlie junior, reconfirming that Will and Charlie were ok, or at least no further bad news around fatalities had been received at the Cheshire regiment HQ in Chester. The officer's face looked encouraging. "Your boys will come home, I'm sure," he said, putting a hand on Beth's shoulders.

Silas walked the officer back to his vehicle and watched as it disappeared towards Macclesfield. He turned around and came face to face with Henry Aspinall.

Silas had rarely seen Henry Aspinall during the three years since he left the courthouse in Manchester, having been released from his prison sentence. He had known that the man largely behind his incarceration was now facing him. The man who had planted evidence sufficient almost to get him hung. The man who had consistently subverted the rule of law in order to wreak revenge on a family that had taken in Charlie and supposedly turned him away from his own father. It was just as well that Silas was not the type of person to hold grudges. He was not a practicing Christian but lived his life with certain values. Although wholly justified, Silas was not about to seek any retribution.

"Mr. Ledger, it's been a while," Henry said, removing his fedora hat.

"Hello, Mr. Aspinall, indeed it has," Silas replied, trying to hide any surprise in his voice. Neither man offered a hand.

"I saw the Army vehicle coming into the village and just wanted to know if there was any important news." Henry looked down at his feet.

"You mean you want to know about Charlie?" Silas challenged. Henry nodded, continuing to avoid any direct eye contact.

"Adam Bostock lost his life in North Africa. The lads are fighting against Rommel's army. They think that the other boys are all ok and should be coming back to Europe soon," Silas stated factually.

"Ok, thanks." Henry turned to walk back to his car.

"Mr. Aspinall, do you want to know about Charlie's son?" Silas shouted after him, not knowing whether Henry had any idea that he was a grandfather.

Henry stopped and stood still. Clearly, this was new information that had momentarily shocked him. He turned back to face Silas and looked confused. Usually, any news in the village was relayed to him by Arthur Brice, his estate manager, but with many of Arthur's contacts having left for the war, he'd lost some of his networks. Even if he did know, perhaps this news was too sensitive for Arthur to have communicated.

Silas broke the silence, "He was born three weeks ago, and we have named him Charlie junior for now. He will be named properly when his dad returns. Beth is learning motherhood, and my wife is proving to be a great teacher. He's in good hands." Silas thought he saw a tear in Henry's eye. Aspinall nodded his head but seemed unable to speak. He turned and walked away.

Up on Bosley Cloud, Rudi had been put to work by Nat fixing dry stone walls that had come down in the winter and were allowing the smaller lambs to escape. Rudi enjoyed the work, and the Lovatt's older sheepdog, Jess, had become a firm friend who followed Rudi everywhere. Weeks passed by, and there seemed no pressure or desire on Rudi to progress in his journey. His injuries from the air crash had disappeared, and his new identity was being perfected.

Martha returned from her job at the school one day and mentioned that there was a memorial service for a soldier down in Langley village, and Gwen had invited Martha, Nat, and Rudi to join them for a Sunday roast after the service.

"Young Rudi, we might need to get you a few new clothes if you're going to show respect in church. You've worn those clothes bare, building stone walls," Martha said. "There's a couple of community charity shops over in Macclesfield. Let's go tomorrow, and we can get you a few things."

Rudi nodded in agreement; he felt confident now that his false backstory was convincing enough to continue his current lifestyle. This trip would allow him to understand more about the local environment and where the nearest train station was, possibly with the thought of boarding a train to a destination he knew not where.

It was a sunny June morning, and Nat proudly drove an old Whetton quarry lorry – that Thomas had given to the farm the previous year – down to the outskirts of Macclesfield. Martha and Rudi got out. "See you in two hours," Nat said as he headed off towards Chelford's farmers market to pick up some fencing posts.

Martha knew the owner of the first charity shop they went to and proudly introduced Rudi as a distant relative from Denmark who was over helping them out on the farm for a few weeks. A pile of appropriate clothes, including a suit, was sorted, and Charlie tried on a couple of items to check for size. Martha had brought a sack with her, and the chosen clothes were put into the sack, knowing that she would be sure to wash them thoroughly before they were ready for Rudi to wear properly.

With her mind on showing Rudi off at the memorial service in Langley chapel at the weekend, Martha looked at his soiled boots. She scalded, "They will not do Rudi Ipsen; let's find some good shoes that you can wear on Sunday."

A decent pair of brown brogues were sourced from another charity shop, and after a pot of tea at Martha's favourite tea shop next to the Town Hall, they headed back towards the location where Nat had agreed to pick them up.

Mid-morning on the Sunday, Nat and Rudi returned from their morning errands around the farm. Martha had heated enough water for both of them to have a soak before readying themselves for the trip over to Langley. Nat was a traditional farmer who never felt comfortable dressing up for anything, so Martha laid his clothes out on their bed to make sure Nat got the message that she expected a certain appearance of respectability for Sunday, especially the memorial service element. The small attic room that Rudi occupied was up a ladder that was now too difficult for Martha to climb, so she had hung his charity shop suit on the ladder rungs with the brogues beneath and one of Nat's other shirts and a tie.

Whilst the men got ready, Martha busied herself in the kitchen, getting the flowers that she had bought for Hilda Bostock out of a vase of water and trimming them down. As she threw away the stems in the rubbish bin outside the back door, she noticed Rudi's dirty work boots. The ones that she thought looked odd the very first time she had been introduced to him a month ago. This was an opportunity for a closer look. She picked them up and took them over to the sink to brush and clean up. They were very well made of thick black leather. There was a small stamp on the sole of both boots; they were both obscured by mud. She scrubbed them – a spread eagle appeared; in its talons was a tiny swastika, the insignia of the German Luftwaffe squadron. The swastika had been partially scratched off; it looked like it had been done intentionally, but there was no mistaking the origin.

Martha quickly finished washing the mud off and put them back where she had found them. Did Rudi have an innocent reason for having these boots, or was there a more sinister explanation?

"Hello, Martha," Gwen greeted her sister-in-law in her usual bonny manner. "Come on in. Silas, offer our guests a drink."

"This is Rudi Ipsen, from Denmark," Martha announced as she introduced Rudi, watching his reaction closely as she emphasised his nationality. There was no sign of any discomfort on Rudi's face. He immediately made himself popular by approaching Beth, who was holding Charlie junior.

"We're calling him Oliver now," said Beth, pleased with how warm Rudi immediately was towards the baby. "One of the Dutch soldiers – Jan – suggested it, and it fits perfectly as Oliver Twist is a favourite Dickens novel that Charlie-his father- and I both love. It's early days, though, as I need to agree it with his dad, so we're testing it out for now." Beth looked towards the window, caught up with the thought that she had not heard from Charlie since the news of Adam's death had been received.

Gwen smiled and glanced at Martha, "Oliver is a good name for a baby. Now Martha, come through to the kitchen and help me with the gravy."

Beth snapped back into the moment, looked over at Nat's suit, and remarked, "My goodness, Uncle Nat, you do scrub up well; sheep farming must be a profitable business nowadays! Dad, you could take a style lesson from your brother-in-law."

Silas smiled and passed some sherry glasses around. "I'm quite happy with my quarryman's style, thank you very much. Now, has everyone got a glass?"

"Ladies, stop nattering, and come through. I'd like to say a few words before we eat." Gwen and Martha came through to the front room.

Silas started. "We know that we are lucky to still be living in a free world, thanks to the bravery of our boys. To Will and Charlie – may they both return to us soon, along with Jack and the others. Tragically, we know that they must be suffering, as we ourselves suffer, with the loss of Adam. Let's pray that no more will perish, and that this war will end soon. To safe returns."

They all raised their glasses and toasted, "Safe returns." Martha looked at Rudi and thought she detected a hesitancy. How would she be able to check the dark thoughts that had emerged following the discovery of the insignia on the sole of his boot?

The Ledger dinner was not as boisterous as usual, without Will and Charlie present, making fun of Gwen's mother's command of the regimented proceedings. The mood was low-key, given that much of the conversation were memories that they all had of Adam and his cricketing exploits. Plus, the fact that Oliver was in the front room trying to take a nap before the memorial service made voices lower out of respect for the baby's slumber.

Martha spotted a chance to test Rudi. "Rudi," she said

during a pause in the conversation, "why don't you tell us about life in Esbjerg, what your family is like, and how you managed to arrive on Bosley Cloud?"

Rudi finished his mouthful and replied, "I'm sure you all don't want to hear about my boring old life over there."

Martha responded with greater conviction, "yes, we do; it's always good for us to understand more about countries we are unlikely ever to visit."

"Ok," Rudi said, "but I'll stop if I see anyone yawn! I have two older sisters – Grethe and Karin, and my mother brought us up alone as my father had drowned in a fishing accident off the coast of Jutland in a freak storm. I was only six years old, and my sisters were nine and eleven. We were a poor family, and mother earned a bit of money mending fishing nets at the harbor. My sisters started working making lobster pots when they reached their teenage years. I had always loved boats and wanted to follow my father and go to sea."

So far, Rudi had produced a very convincing account of his life. Martha thought that perhaps there was a plausible explanation for the boots. Rudi continued. "At the age of thirteen, I first went out on a fishing boat and fished the waters between Denmark and Norway, but after a few years, I had earned enough money to contribute to the family home, but also attend maritime college to learn various trades around seafaring. When I graduated, I got a contract with a merchant shipping company called Maersk, which was exporting from Scandinavia around the world. Then, the war started, and I was assigned to a ship that was contracted to conduct regular voyages between Liverpool and New York. We were regularly targeted by German U-boats but survived.

Six weeks ago, we arrived in Liverpool after a particularly difficult voyage. We were in a convoy of thirteen ships, of which only three managed to make it through the U-boats. I decided that this was too much for me, and so I left the ship and started to make my way across England to hopefully catch a boat home from the east coast – possibly Hull or Felixstowe. On the route, I found a lambing shed for the night, which just happened to belong to the Lovatts. Nat and Martha have been so kind to me that I thought I'd stay for a little longer to try and earn some money for my onward journey. That's me done."

"That's quite a story," Silas said. "And what position is Denmark in the war?"

"Officially, they are a neutral country," Rudi started, "Sweden welcomed the Germans in, and quickly Copenhagen was occupied, and then they occupied Funen and Jutland, where my hometown of Esbjerg is located."

Martha was looking for any signal suggesting that Rudi might be falsifying his story, but there were none. She decided to let things lie for now, but she felt a strong desire to continue her fact-finding later. Rudi was inwardly celebrating the fact that his false back story had been communicated without hesitancy. It almost worried him that he could lie quite so easily and convincingly.

Following lunch, the group readied themselves to head across to the Chapel for Adam Bostock's memorial service. Unsurprisingly, it was an emotional affair, and many prayers were said for those family and friends who were still battling for Britain's freedom.

Although conscious of the irony of the situation, Rudi sat thoughtfully throughout the service, hymns, and readings, thinking about his own family back in Northern Germany. He wondered what messages may have got back to his parents about his whereabouts. Did they even know that he was still alive, or was a presumption made that a plane 'missing in action' meant that all of the airmen aboard would have perished. He could do nothing about communicating with Germany. He must bide his time and look for opportunities.

Seeing the sadness in the eyes of the congregation, witnessing the mourning mother, hearing the heartfelt stories of Adam's life from various friends – Rudi had realised that this was happening in multiple towns and villages across Europe – and what for? What was the meaning of this war? Would a world led by a dictator like Hitler be acceptable? Here was Rudi, having been taken into a loving family's home, surrounded by American, Dutch, and Canadian soldiers who had volunteered to support Britain in their war against his country. Although a proud German, Rudolph Schwalbe deplored this war and certainly questioned his role in it.

In the chapel, he found himself next to Beth and the little baby; he smiled as he looked at Oliver, gurning his face and dribbling – not a care in the world. He was suddenly aware of Martha looking directly at him, and as he caught her gaze and their eyes locked momentarily, he thought that she knew his secret.

Unseen by any of the Ledger family, Henry Aspinall had sat himself in the small balcony of the chapel. He was there to pay respects to Adam Bostock – as Adam had been the exceptional captain of the Cricket Club that he had heavily sponsored. But primarily, he was there to peer, for the first time, down on his grandson. Tears formed in his eyes when he saw the baby sitting in a wicker basket next to Beth. He knew that Charles was away at war, and in all likelihood, if he were not, then he would not allow Henry to have any influence over his grandson. Yet, Henry Aspinall was a very wealthy man with no prospects of any heir. He was likely to die a very rich man in terms of material wealth but destitute in terms of family. He sunk his head into his hands and prayed. Not something he was accustomed to.

CHAPTER 48 - *CALL HOME*

The destruction of the Italian camp in Tobruk was absolute. The Italians were forced to fall back into the desert to regroup, but this signalled the start of the end of the Italian involvement with Rommel's North African conquest. Operation Crusade had opened the Allies supply route through to Egypt, and from that point onwards, the Germans were on the back foot, losing ground to General Montgomery's forces. The Desert Rats had won this chapter.

The Cheshire regiment had joined a convoy of ships heading north to Cyprus and had enjoyed two weeks of leave on the beaches of this British outpost. As soon as they could source a bat and ball, beach cricket took place. They knew that their fallen comrade – Adam - would have loved to have taken up the bat and faced fiery Fred's bowling once again. As it was, the Australians made up one team, and Fred led the English team in a reenactment of the Ashes Series 1942. Jack took a role as an umpire as his head injury was still such that he was not yet able to participate fully. Charlie set up a scoreboard using an upturned blackboard and chalk, just behind the boundary, marked by a line scratched in the sand with an umbrella. After each six-ball over, he shouted the score onto the field. On regular occasions, both Jack and Charlie received light-hearted volleys of verbal abuse from the Australians.

"You Pommie wankers! You missed the no ball...." or "Pommie bastards, you can blow up the Roman Empire, but you can't play cricket!"

This was just the kind of break that the whole unit needed – although they would have all preferred to have been able to head home to see loved ones again. The war was far from over, and they realised that any home leave would be unlikely until the Germans had been truly defeated in Europe. They also realised that home for them was much nearer than for their Australian comrades.

One evening, whilst the group was chilling out with a few beers, the British Commander to Cyprus appeared, followed by a very smart-looking Lieutenant General Morshead, hardly recognisable from the disheveled Australian commander in charge of the rag-tag forces in Tobruk.

The British Commander asked for silence and addressed the fifty or so soldiers in front of him. "Men, I have just been given the go-ahead from London to recognise a few of you with honours medals for bravery in the face of enemy fire. Corporal Jack Moat and his men – Private Will Ledger, Private Charlie Aspinall, Private Fred Needles, Private Andy Soutter, and Private Robin Brampton – please all step forward." The Commander unfurled an official-looking document. General Lieutenant Morshead was beaming from ear to ear. The six men stepped forward, looking a little bewildered. The Commander started reading from the scroll-like document.

"On behalf of King George VI, I have the honour of presenting you all with the King's Gallantry Medal – 'exemplary acts of bravery in the face of the enemy during the siege of Tobruk.' And in the case of Corporal Jack Moat, his honour has been upgraded to a full Victoria Cross due to his additional bravery shown in remaining behind to ensure his unit were able to escape successfully."

Jack bowed his head; he would have given anything to have been able to share this moment with Adam.

The Commander saw this emotion and quickly continued. "Tragically, one very brave soldier – Adam Bostock – lost his life during the breaking of the siege. But without his bravery in returning to ensure detonation was initiated, there would have been no success. To Adam Bostock, he is presented with the Victoria Cross posthumously."

The Commander put down the scroll and saluted the six members of the Cheshire regiment, who all responded with their own salute. General Lieutenant Morshead – who had nominated all of the recipients – called for three cheers from the crowd of soldiers that had gathered around. Plenty of backs were slapped and beers drunk that evening – but in the sober light of day – the war was still raging, and the Cheshire regiment was awaiting its next orders.

Reveille sounded at 6 am, just as the sun was rising over the Mediterranean. Strong black coffee was served at the mess tent before Charlie, Will, and Jack made their way to join the queue. The queue was for the telephone that – if lucky – would connect them to their loved ones at home. It worked sporadically, and over a hundred troops were wanting to use it at any one time. Each soldier was allowed one minute, and if nobody answered in the UK – they had to queue up again. The three men recognised that with three of them there, that would allow three minutes – sufficient time for old Percy Ricketts in the Langley Post Office to bang his stick on the wall and hopefully alert Beth, Gwen, or Silas to run around and take the call. Charlie's last letter to Beth indicated that this might be happening, and so they all hoped that the Langley side would be prepared for some fast movements.

Will had come along to help with the allocated time, Jack too, although he would have loved to have spoken directly to Melissa. It was Charlie who was rehearsing in his head everything he needed to communicate for all six friends. Will – having been a runner for Percy's Post Office in his youth, knew all about the likely process that would happen. Percy always allowed three rings to occur before picking up; he then confirmed with the operator that an incoming call would be accepted. He then picked up his walking stick and knocked on the wall, alerting the Ledgers that he needed help to get a villager to the phone, pronto.

Jack, Will, and Charlie got to the head of the queue and explained to the sergeant in charge what they needed. One three-minute call to this specific number. He accepted the unusual request, having been present the night before when the gallantry awards had been announced.

Charlie took the receiver; Jack carefully checked the number before handing it to the sergeant to dial. "Brrrr, brrrr. Brrrr, brrrr. Brrrr, brrrr."

The ringing stopped, and some crackling on the line was

heard, possibly being the Operator validating the number. Hopefully, Percy had already alerted the Ledgers, and somebody was moving fast. "Hello, Langley Post Office, Ricketts speaking." Came Percy's familiar voice.

"Hi Percy, it's Charlie – are any of the family there? I only have a couple of minutes."

"I've summoned next door, Charlie; they'll be here soon. Great to hear your voice. We were all devastated to hear about Adam. We'll be having a drink for him and all of you at the Dunstan tonight. We've also decided to hold a Memorial cricket match for Adam later in the summer. Here's Beth...."

Beth raced into the Post Office, knocking a sweet stand over in the process, and grabbed the phone receiver. "Charlie, my darling, how are you? I miss you. Little Charlie junior is wonderful, and we've started to call him Oliver as I know that Oliver Twist was your favourite book, and it was the first film we saw together at the cinema in Macclesfield. Is that okay?"

Hearing her voice again and the lyrical rhythm of her words momentarily choked Charlie up; his mouth went dry, yet he knew that every second on this call counted for his friends, not just himself.

"Beth, I love you so much, and I can't wait to hold my little boy. I love the name Oliver – it's perfect. Listen, I only have a very short time, and I need to tell you that we are about to get new orders for our next assignment. And I don't know how easy it will be to contact you from there."

Charlie looked at a scrap of paper that he had tried to memorise. "Can you pass the news on that we are all doing well and are pleased to be away from North Africa and back in Europe – one step closer to you all. Jack is a fantastic leader of our little gang and has just been awarded the Victoria Cross for his bravery in Tobruk. Adam has been too, which we were all pleased about. The rest of us all got gallantry awards."

Beaming with pride, Beth gasped, "That is amazing; we are all so pleased for you – but make sure you stay safe – the village cannot do with any more memorial services. We need you all home in one piece. Tell Jack that Melissa loves him dearly and can't wait to see him again."

Charlie jumped back in. "My darling, I promise that we cannot be in better hands. The six of us are brothers now. You may well have a brother called Will, but he's ours too – and nothing will hurt him or any of us, with each other alongside." Charlie was free-wheeling now, having forgotten his script completely. Being able to hear Beth's voice was so special. The line went dead. The Sergeant nodded, confirming that time was up.

Even though Charlie was speaking, both Jack and Will were listening intently, knowing that Beth's voice generally carried a fair distance, even over a shaky telephone line. The three of them started walking back towards the tented camp.

Will was the first to speak. "Just think of that, eh? The Dunstan will be full tonight, with everyone drinking in memory of Adam. And they'll also be holding a memorial cricket match in his honour. I wonder who'll captain the sides. If it becomes an annual event, perhaps I can play in it."

"I'll be in the scorer's hut for sure," said Charlie, "that's the only fit place for me on a cricket pitch."

Jack added, "I do feel so sorry for Hilda Bostock; she's now left all on her own; her only son is dead. But maybe making a bumper cricket tea for that event will be a fitting memory for her and act as therapy of sorts. I'm sure Andy and Robin will somehow manage to procure the finest meats possible for an 'Adam Bostock Memorial Game Pie' – Adam would be laughing out loud up there with St. Peter."

CHAPTER 49 - *A FUGITIVE*

Two weeks after Adam's memorial service, Martha found herself in Macclesfield catching up with friends who had come in from Chelford. The talk was about all sorts of things, including the challenges farming families were having with the lack of available labour and the likelihood of not being able to harvest the summer crops properly. Martha mentioned the good fortune that they had had in finding help in the form of a young stray Danish mariner called Rudi. The other ladies congratulated her, and the conversation rolled on to the war effort. One of the ladies commented on the current slowdown in bombing raids on Manchester and Liverpool and the fact that air raid sirens were heard much less in recent times.

She offered up a thought. "It seems like the Germans have slowed down their raids ever since they lost so many planes in May trying to attack Liverpool docks. Our anti-aircraft guns have been a good deterrent."

Martha stopped halfway through sipping her tea. A thought sprung to her mind. That was around the time that Rudi had entered their lives – could it be linked in some way?

She excused herself from the other ladies and made her way to Macclesfield town library. She started thumbing through back copies of newspapers to see the date of the air raid and any other information she could glean about the aircraft that had been shot down. She discovered that the main attack on Liverpool docks was early on 8th May 1941. Martha looked at newspapers on proceeding days. None of the national nor Cheshire copies she found had any great detail about the air raid other than the weather was cloudy, which inhibited the ability of the anti-aircraft guns to target the bombers. Still, there were sketchy reports of around twenty planes being involved, mainly Junker bombers and Messerschmidt escorts. One report stated that at least one of the Junkers was shot down over Staffordshire, near Meerbrook.

Martha asked an elderly librarian where Meerbrook was compared to Macclesfield and was informed that it was around 15 miles away, in the direction of Stoke. Perhaps it was feasible that Rudi could have survived an air crash and found his way across the country to Bosley Cloud. It was a long shot, but in her inquisitive and suspicious mind, Rudi's alibi seemed too well rehearsed, and the concrete evidence of his work boots branding made up to a story that needed to be further checked out. She headed back to the farmhouse with a plan to ask him directly that evening whilst Nat was out at a Farmer's Club meeting at the local pub.

Nat was very happy to have such a hard-working labourer as Rudi working with him over the summer months; the lambs were growing older and more adventurous, which meant that they were finding ways and means to escape the farm fields into adjoining properties. Each lost lamb was a hit to the profit of the farm, and although Thomas Whetton was very fair to Nat and Martha. Nat was committed to always making a profit on the farm. He had proudly maintained that promise in the decade that they had been on Bosley Cloud. Rudi, aided by the sheepdogs, had proven very successful at retrieving the escapee sheep and blocking up any holes in the fencing that they had likely escaped through.

So far, Rudi had not suggested that he wanted to leave the farm before the winter months, and Nat had no intention of encouraging him, although he did find it strange that Rudi was content to stay in Cheshire whilst his family were waiting for him in Denmark. "Do you want to come down to the Harrington Arms tonight, Rudi? There's a Farmer's Club meeting, but they do serve a lovely pint of Robinson's beer, much better than your Danish ale!" Nat asked.

"No thanks, Nat, I'll stay home tonight; I really must write a letter home to my family explaining where I am and what I'm doing," Rudi replied.

"Fair enough. I'm sure Martha will be happy that someone is home as the nights are getting shorter. If I'm singing when I get home, you'll know that I've won the monthly raffle, and the boys have forced me to drink more than my fair share of the yard of ale prize!"

Rudi laughed at the prospect of a drunk Nat yodelling his way home after midnight. "Perhaps you should take Jess and Ruby with you to shepherd you home!"

The ears of both dogs pricked up as their names were mentioned, but their places by the warm hearth looked too good to move from. Martha smiled from her seat at the kitchen table. She had to catch up on her knitting, having fallen behind the task that Gwen had set her for the Langley knitting club – who were knitting rugs for the wounded soldier's welfare trust. "Just you be careful, Nat, that's a good thirty-minute walk across the fields; I'll not go to sleep until I hear the front door open." She warned.

Nat had been gone an hour when Martha noticed Rudi had stopped scratching behind Jess's ear and was staring into the embers of the fire.

"Rudi, you ok?" she asked. "Fancy a cup of tea?"

"Thanks," Rudi replied, "I would, but I've also got something to tell you."

Martha got up and poured tea out of a freshly made pot and gave a cup to Rudi. She sat back on a chair by the fire, nervous about what Rudi wanted to talk about. "Martha, you and Nat have been so good to me in the last few months; I need to be honest with you now. I have sensed that in the last few weeks, you have become uncomfortable with me, and I owe you an explanation as to why that might be so."

Martha looked directly at him and braced herself to hear whether her suspicions were about to be justified. "I am not Rudi Ipsen from Denmark. I am Rudolph Schwalbe, and I am a German Navigator who was shot down in early May near the Roaches. I survived the air crash and managed to make my way here."

Rudi looked at Martha and recognised that she had guessed his back story already, as the level of shock was not as great as would have been the case if she had no idea at all. "I am very sorry for deceiving both of you and your family and friends. I have never supported the war between our countries. I was conscripted into the Luftwaffe at the age of 18, and this was my first ever flight in battle." He paused for a moment. "You and your family have been so kind to me, and all I have done is deceive you. I'm sorry."

Martha saw that the young German held no malice, and his eventual honesty showed that he respected his hosts; she spoke without any ill-feeling in return. "Thanks, Rudi – for I shall not call you Rudolph! I appreciate your honesty, and I will not tell anyone else – even Nat. But you need to decide what you do now. You are a German living in a country that is at war with Germany. If you give yourself up to the Authorities, you will be interned as a prisoner of war."

Rudi looked up, "I understand that, and I am opposed to this war. My country would expect me to continue to fight, but in my heart, I know that this is an unjust war. Perhaps I can continue to live here for as long as you will have me, but I fully understand if you need me to go, as I do not want you to be blamed for hiding a fugitive." Rudi looked down at the sheepdogs slumbering.

Martha started, "Here's the deal, Rudi, I will say nothing. You will continue to be Rudi from Denmark, and you'll work here for as long as Nat needs you. Once the war has ended, you can disappear back to wherever it is you call home – with no ill feelings. How does that sound? But you need to make sure the marks on your work boots are more fully removed, as that was what raised my suspicions in the first place."

"Thank you, Martha, I will," Rudi said, relieved that his honesty policy had produced the right outcome – for now.

CHAPTER 50 - *D-DAY*

The remainder of the Cheshire regiment in Cyprus was sent across to Sicily as an invasion force, which proved to be quick and decisive as the Italians were disillusioned with the war and felt let down by their German overlords. Jack was particularly interested in walking through the deserted streets of Palermo and just thinking about Gustav and his tough upbringing, as well as what led him to Cheshire in the thirties. He walked past a shelled-out tobacconist with a shop sign, 'Coccini's cigarette.' No doubt the surname was a traditional Sicilian name. Perhaps Gustav's relatives were once honest shopkeepers. Jack suspected that Gustav's life would always be more colourful. The fact that despite his darker side, Gustav had saved Jack's life and sacrificed himself - perhaps as a way of making up for the hell that he'd put Silas through. It was his way of trying to correct the wrongs in his life in one final act of ultimate sacrifice.

It took another two years, but eventually Mussolini was overthrown, and Italy surrendered to the Allies. The war was heading towards its final year, with Germany weakening by the day due to the Soviets launching successful offensives to regain territorial losses and pushing toward Berlin.

It was now the final months of 1943. Jack's unit was transferred back to the Cheshire 2nd Battalion and asked to push towards the German coastal defence line in northern France, Belgium, and Holland, in preparation for Operation Overlord, D-Day, and the Normandy landings. Charlie had been writing letters more regularly as there was more guarantee of them reaching their destination now that they had access to better-structured military postal services. This meant that their families in Langley had more of an idea of where their loved ones were and how they were faring.

Silas was down to a bare minimum of workers at the quarry as all of the foreign military personnel had been moved down to southern England for training in preparation for the crossing of the English Channel – planned for early Summer 1944. Silas and Owain had laid on a farewell evening in the Setter Dog Inn for their American, Canadian, and Dutch quarry workers, whom they had grown very fond of. In his brief speech, before Owain could break into Welsh song, Silas thanked Arnie and the others for all of their blood and sweat on the rock face and wished them well in their next challenge. He thanked them for introducing jazz music and basketball to Cheshire. Silas finished by saying how confident these boys made them all feel as they headed towards the liberation of Europe from the north, whilst his son – Will, and his friends were liberating Europe from the south. "With this kind of force against them, the Germans will be running for Berlin in no time!"

The big American – Arnie – made a speech in return,

thanking Sledge and Owain for their superb hospitality and made a special point of thanking Dick Avery for his endless beer supply, despite it being on the warm side. Owain then started to sing 'Sosban Fach,' a traditional Welsh folk song, with everyone else encouraged to sing along with the chorus, having no clue of the meaning but enjoying the tune.

Teggs Nose would be quiet without the regular quarry work happening as Whetton Quarries consolidated the workforce into a new quarry over in Kerridge. Thomas Whetton had divested away from canal haulage due to the fact that more and more freight was being moved via rail or road. He had invested in road transport and had based a fleet of heavy goods vehicles in Sandbach right next to one of the core north-south roads from the Midlands up to the industrial heartland of the North West. This road would eventually be upgraded to become Britain's first motorway – the M6.

Thomas himself was spending more time in London with his friend Elliot Chapman, and they had purchased a London apartment together just off Pall Mall. With trusted people looking after his businesses in the North West, his accountant, who was based in an office within the Sperry & Burroughs Law building, sent him weekly accounts from all of his businesses, and he had part-employed Melissa to manage any local administrative matters.

Beth and Thomas had developed a very close relationship during the period in which they were fighting for her father's innocence. And Beth continued to stay in regular contact, using Thomas and Elliot as mentors for her writing, which they both enjoyed as it was always raw with passion and sky-high in energy, if not always directed at the right cause. Several times, Elliot had commissioned Beth to write speeches for him on safe subjects, that he delivered from the back benches of the House of Commons, receiving praise from fellow MPs for their passion and originality.

Both Elliot and Thomas were overjoyed to hear about the birth of Oliver, and Beth started to refer to them both as 'Uncles.' Beth also asked Charlie, via a letter, whether he felt it appropriate to ask Thomas to be a Godfather alongside Jack. Charlie readily agreed. Thomas was overjoyed as he realised that he was never going to father his own child. He did rather wonder how Henry Aspinall might react to knowing that his estranged grandson had Thomas Whetton as a new Godfather, but that wasn't his problem. Thomas recognised that Oliver was not to be formally christened until after his father returned from war. He swore to himself that despite Aspinall's blood, this child would be much loved by him and Elliot, as would their parents.

Whenever there was a dearth of news from the war in Europe, Beth often contacted Elliot directly just to enquire whether he had any news via his parliamentary contacts within the War Cabinet. Elliot was always able to get reassurances across to Beth that confirmed that Charlie and his friends were alive and located in such-and-such a foreign field. They had been based in Toulon on the Mediterranean for almost a year. Later, Beth discovered that this was the location of the surrendering French navy. The boys were being used to help police the naval barracks as there were many French sailors unable to get home, and their boredom was generally getting them into trouble in the bars and brothels of the city.

Through Elliot, Beth knew that from Toulon – Charlie, Will, Jack, and the others – would be moved north to help liberate Paris. Then, they would then await instruction as to how they could start to weaken the retreating German army to allow Operation Overlord its greatest chance of success. She also learned from Elliot that there would need to be a period of postal silence due to the confidentiality of troop movements. Charlie would be unable to make contact for the foreseeable future.

Elliot was also keen to support another intelligent young person who came to him via Thomas. He and Rudi corresponded regularly by mail about what life in neutral Denmark under Nazi occupation was like. Elliot found it useful to further his political career by having contacts outside of the UK who could better illustrate the pressures of war. He wondered whether Rudi would ever consider visiting him in London.

The month of May rolled past with Allied troops led by Eisenhower and Montgomery amassing in southern England and the Germans – under Rommel – fortifying their defenses in France and the Low Countries, building what was dubbed by the Reich as the Atlantic Wall in anticipation of landings in France.

Due to canny military deception, the Allies managed to convince the Germans of different dates and locations for the invasion. 160,000 Allied forces landed in Normandy on 6th June 1944 and quickly captured the port city of Cherbourg, thus setting up a foothold for the arrival of the main strike force. By the end of August, the Allied forces numbered over two million, and the overwhelmed German army retreated towards the German border, hotly pursued by the Allies.

In mid-August, under General Patton, the US Third Army, assisted by a now very active French liberation force under General de Gaulle, moved into the outskirts of Paris. The now much depleted German militia's leader – Dietrich Von Choltitz –surrendered meekly at the Hotel de Meurice, the newly established French Army Headquarters.

The Cheshire 2nd Battalion was able to link up with other forces in Normandy and join other Cheshire and Staffordshire units, moving eastwards, and driving back the Germans towards the Belgium/Dutch border. Field Marshall Montgomery termed the offensive – Operation Market Garden – and was intended to drive the Germans all the way back and beyond the Rhine. A number of German Panzer tank divisions were successfully holding back the Allied army's progress, as they were agile enough to avoid detection by the Allie's aerial bombers, hiding in woodland at the merest sound of plane engines. Holding key bridges and road junctions meant that heavier tank-busting artillery could not get into position to do any damage.

Jack Moat and the Langley members of the Cheshire Regiment were facing just this scenario. Frustrated by the lack of progress, they were camped down in a bombed-out farm, about two miles from a small intact road bridge – one of few – over the Meuse River in Holland. This was only twenty miles from the German border.

The majority of the hundred and fifty-strong Allied Forces in this part of Holland were made up of Canadians, with around twenty British and a similar number of local Dutch Resistance soldiers. Without larger artillery, any attempt to take the bridge over the Meuse would have been futile against a stubborn Panzer division, likely commanded by a Nazi captain who realised that this was their last stand.

"Why do they not just head home to their young Frauleins and allow us to do the same?" pondered Robin out aloud, thinking about these Germans having already reversed hundreds of miles, almost back to their own country. Why stop here?

Generally, there was a positive feeling amongst the Allied troops. There was a growing sense of victory following the success of D-day and the Normandy landings. Behind them, this advanced force knew that there were over a million strong making up the Allied army and ahead of them was a demoralised, almost defeated, under-supplied, battle-weary German army. Jack had taken a leadership position with all of the British troops present at the farmstead. His cool, calm approach varied hugely with many of the hot-headed leaders present, keen to massage their own vanities by exaggerating past battle victories won. Few of them knew that Jack had already been awarded the Victoria Cross. His close friends also had their own bravery commendations from their time in Tobruk. One such egotistical leader was the Colonel in charge of the Canadian force, and because of his higher military ranking, Jack's senior officer.

"Corporal Moat," barked Colonel Fletcher of the 2nd Canadian Infantry Division, "What state are your men in right now?"

"Colonel, I have twenty lads, of which all but one is fighting fit and raring to go." Replied Jack, keen to keep Fred away from any action as he was struggling with a bout of dysentery, having drunk from a stagnant well a week previous. Many of the men had not drunk or eaten well in recent weeks, as out of malice, the Germans had made it their business to steal or destroy any food sources they had come across. This was causing the local Dutch population to starve and increase their hatred for them even more.

The Colonel looked at Jack. "That size of team is about right. Ok then, I have an operation for you and your men to take on tonight under the cover of darkness. I need you to perform a reconnaissance exercise on the bridge to ascertain where the Germans have established their tank units and whether there are any weaknesses. What troubles me is that they are waiting for us to start to cross the bridge before blowing it up. I need you to look to see if they have mined the area around the bridge on our side of the river."

Jack peered over at the rough map that had been drawn up by one of the Dutch Resistance personnel who used to live five miles from here and so had a good understanding of the topography of the land and had crossed that bridge on many occasions in peacetime. The map had been written on an old piece of cardboard from a box once containing tins of coffee.

A vague smell of coffee rose from the map as Jack studied it closer. He pointed to the woodland about two hundred yards from the bridge, perfect if they were to remain unseen by any German sentries. "What's your name, soldier?" Jack asked the creator of the map.

"Private Gerd Kroll – Dutch Army, Sir," came the sharp response.

Jack looked at the Dutchman, suddenly impressed that he heard such enthusiasm in the voice of a soldier. After four years of soldiering, any conversation Jack had been part of tended to be fatalistic and weary. This Dutchman had real vigour about him, reminding him of his dear friend in Libya – Farukh Khan. "Well, Gerd Kroll, is this area likely to be mined too?" he asked, pointing to the map, "and could we use this woodland as cover?"

"Sergeant Moat, Sir, in my opinion, the woodland may be mined, but it does have a number of defensive trenches which could be used to move safely. I would recommend using the wood," Gerd said this with such conviction Jack started to pay more attention to this bright young soldier.

"How do you know about these trenches, Gerd?" Jack queried.

"Because I dug them for the Germans about four months ago." Gerd looked down shame-faced to the floor. "My mother and sister were raped by a German Panza unit and then shot dead. My father and I were then made to dig these ditches; I know every inch." Gerd looked up, and Jack recognised pure hatred in the tearful eyes of the young man. "My father was shot after we had completed the last trench, and I was made to bury him in that woodland. I think that they would have killed me too, but there was an Allied bombing raid that happened, and I managed to escape amidst the chaos of German soldiers and tanks trying to take cover."

Jack recognised a burning desire in young Gerd and felt like it was worth harnessing. Farukh had lost his whole family and had fought valiantly in support of the Cheshire regiment; this Dutchman had a similar motive and could perform just the same. "Private Gerd Kroll, will you do me the honour of helping my team and me check out this bridgehead and secure it for the Allied forces and in honour of your family?"

The Dutch soldier tried hard to check his emotion and nodded his head. "Corporal Moat, it would be my biggest honour." Jack saluted Colonel Fletcher, picked up the cardboard map, and returned to his unit, accompanied by Gerd, to plot the evening's reconnaissance mission and to tell Fred that a good-looking young Dutch lad had replaced him.

Fred was in the latrines, where he had seemingly taken up permanent residence. Through the toilet door, Jack broke the news that the rest of the unit would be on an exercise that night, and they had to leave him behind due to his overactive bowel. He then gathered the rest of the unit in the mess tent and introduced Gerd as a new recruit and a scout who knew the area around the bridge. He decided not to tell Gerd's harrowing story and left that for the Dutchman to tell if he needed to; he just said, "Gerd has some unfinished business over near the bridge."

Andy shouted up from the back of the tent, "Fred's also got lots of unfinished business!" to which he got a raucous round of laughter from those who knew of Fred's gut problem.

This was the first planned exercise that Jack had been asked to lead specifically since the attack on the Italians in Tobruk, which led to the death of Adam Bostock and a near-death experience of his own. His angel, in that instant, took the shape of Gustav Coccini. He hoped that there would be no need to call on more angels tonight. He was not going to lose any other soldier, and he would willingly lay down his own life to save that of the friends he had joined the army with. In the same way that Gustav had sacrificed himself to keep him alive.

It was just before midnight when the twenty-strong unit from the Cheshire Regiment moved out from their temporary base in the farm buildings. As the crow flies, they had two miles to cover before they would be at the bridgehead. It was a clear, crisp spring night, and the moon was nearing a full orb. It was too bright, and Jack was very aware that a cloudy darkened night would have been much more suited for the task they had ahead of them.

He was very aware of the shadows they cast as they moved along a muddy dyke to the southern perimeter of the woodland that marked the final resting place of Gerd Kroll's father. Gerd was leading the snake of soldiers with Jack following close behind. Gerd's job was purely to navigate the landscape, he was not qualified nor equipped for combat, and Gerd was proving to be an invaluable source of knowledge about the local terrain. Jack signalled to him about the shadows that were being cast. Gerd understood instantly and moved the line of men closer to the dyke wall so that their shadows merged with the dark earth of the bank. Occasionally, a foot dislodged mud or rock that slid into the murky black water in the ditch running along the foot of the embankment.

After about fifteen minutes of traversing across this terrain, Gerd signalled to Jack that it was time to head up over the dyke and into the woodland. He would go first and ensure that the coast was clear for the rest of the unit to advance. Jack was the only person who knew the significance of this woodland for the Dutchman and admired his ability to show no external emotion as he gave a thumbs-up sign, and nodded his affirmation of Gerd's plan. Jack watched Gerd nimbly moving up and over the dyke and across a marshy strip of land before entering the woodland. A minute later, two flashes from Gerd's torch indicated that it was safe for the others to advance.

Working in pairs ensured that each person provided possible weapons cover for the other as they moved across the marsh and into the woods. Jack watched Will and Charlie working together expertly, with one moving quickly whilst the other shouldered his rifle, looking for any potential enemy intervention. Jack was last across the marsh and found the group in a natural hollow caused by the uprooting of a large elm tree. He looked at Gerd and mouthed, "Thanks, good job."

Gerd was supposed to wait there in order to assist with the retreat following the completion of the reconnaissance. However, Jack knew that Gerd wanted to stay with the group, and his knowledge of the environment in which they were working was proving invaluable.

Jack whispered: "Gerd, you stay with me up front, I want your local knowledge to help inform where we might come across any defensive trenches. Will and Charlie, you two next, and so on. Andy and Robin – you two at the rear."

"Oh, we'll miss all the excitement," moaned Andy, with a smile on his face.

Jack turned his head, "we want no excitement tonight. We just need to get to a place where we can see the bridgehead and identify where the German tanks have sights on the bridge, and whether any areas are likely to be mined. If this bridge is not captured, our supply chain will be pushed back two weeks or until we can build a pontoon bridge. So, this is an important piece of work."

Gerd and Jack moved forward into a shallow trench and made their way through it until it became much deeper. The floor of the trench was a foot deep in water. At an intersection, Gerd rested a hand on Jack's shoulder. "There's a deserted store and mess room on the left." Sure enough, there it was. "My dad was very proud about how he had created that room using the trunk and roots of another fallen tree to help create the covered space," Jack noted that Gerd's naturally gentle voice had softened further, and he was briefly lost in a much darker thought.

The unit got to the outer edge of the woodland and started their detailed surveillance of the bridgehead, usefully bathed in the moonlight that had caused the Cheshires a problem earlier. They could quite clearly see four Panzer tanks, two on either side of the bridge on the far side of the Meuse River. Coordinates were written down in order to communicate later to the RAF Bomber Command. Failing the availability of an air strike, these coordinates would be used as targets for any of the expected heavy tank-busting artillery that had been due to arrive in the farmstead the previous week. There were no obvious signs of the area around the bridge being mined, but – Jack wrote on his notepad – 'any troop movement would need to proceed with extreme caution and likely need to be preceded by a tank with a mine plough attached.' Gerd attracted his attention to a small jetty sticking out into the Meuse, a single mooring attached to two rowing boats. As the river was fast flowing and wide, these may come in useful for any advanced unit to cross the river following the removal of the tank threat. This information was also quickly scribbled into the notebook.

Jack signalled to left and right, directing his men back into the deeper shade, the trenches, and the route home. After about ten minutes of wading, Gerd whispered to Jack. "Sergeant, can I just pay my respects to my father? His grave is just over there, I think."

"Of course, I will come too." Jack signalled for the unit to continue onwards whilst he and Gerd scrambled out of the trench and into a small clearing in the woods.

In the clearing was a patch of newly dug earth – Gerd's father's grave. Both men bowed their heads. Gerd's shoulders started to shudder with emotion, and Jack placed his hand on one of them.

"Your father is in a better place now, and he'd be very proud of you. Just remember that." Jack picked up two sticks and tied them in a cross using a spare piece of tape from his pack. "Here you are soldier, mark your father's grave for now with this. When we've liberated this area, you can decide how you mark your father's passing with the dignity he no doubt deserved." Gerd took the cross and planted it at one end of the newly dug earth.

An ear-splitting explosion seared the air behind them. It came from the direction of a trench that they had not previously used. It was throwing earth, flame, and smoke high up in the air and lighting up the trees around them. Jack looked at Gerd and signalled for him to follow him along the surface on one side of the trench. He could see members of his unit scrambling up out of the ground and onto the woodland surface, away from the explosion.

"Fuck – what's happened?" he demanded from the nearest soldier.

"Sir, I think it was a land mine; somebody stepped on it."

Jack shouted an order, "Troop - buddy up and check on your partner." All the soldiers looked around and checked the person they had been originally partnered with.

"Who is not accounted for?" Jack shouted.

A soldier called Lewis was the first to respond. His voice was shaky, "Sir, I was behind the explosion. I think it was Sam Forsyth who stepped on the mine."

Robin Soutter stepped forward, wiping blood and dirt from his face, "Sergeant – it was Forsyth – he was blown sky high. There's nothing left of him."

"Where's Will and Charlie?" Jack gasped, unable to hide the fear that gripped him.

"They were out ahead of the rest of us; they must be beyond where the explosion happened," Andy Soutter muttered.

Jack took control again, "Let's all proceed above the trench and look for them, tread carefully; there may be more explosives."

They moved along the top of the trench, peering down at the smoking ground where the mine had exploded; the sickly sight of Forsyth's dismembered body parts were all too recognisable. Ahead of Jack, down in the trench, were two figures standing motionless. It was Will and Charlie. Will was behind Charlie, holding on to his waist.

"Will, Charlie – are you alright?" shouted Jack.

Will turned his head upwards and shook his head very slowly. "Charlie believes he has just stepped on a mine and cannot shift his weight for fear of triggering it."

"Shit. Shit." For a split second, Jack was lost in the thought that he was going to break his promise to the Ledgers and witness the death of their beloved boys.

He came back round to full consciousness by the sound of a large lorry coming from the direction of the bridge; at least, that had answered one question about explosives on the bridge. It must be German troops coming over to investigate the explosion. They needed to move quickly.

Jack ordered his unit with authority and without his usual calm. He was scared, not for himself, but for the position that Will and Charlie were in. "Okay – all of you, get into defensive positions between here and the road. We need to expect enemy troops to come towards us and we must keep them at a sufficient distance for long enough to try and get the boys away from the mine."

The patrol spread out in a semi-circle about ten yards away from the lip of the trench. Jack handed Gerd his rifle and directed him to a tree stump next to Robin Soutter. "Corporal Soutter – make use of that boy – he has a strong motive to protect this woodland."

Having checked the position of all of his men and found it to be as strong as one minute's worth of preparation could make it, Jack then slipped his body down the side of the trench and approached the motionless bodies of Will and Charlie. He approached them as gently as possible, "Okay, boys, let's sort out this problem. Will, are you able to step back towards me without causing Charlie to move?"

Rifle shots started to be heard above them. The Germans must have believed that it wasn't woodland wildlife that had set off the explosion that killed Sam Forsyth. They seemed to have a heavy machine gun with them, and when it fired, it was like a psychotic lumberjack, whole tree trunks shattered under its fire.

Jack was fully back in control and shouted the instruction, "Will, I need you to go and strengthen the defence – keep those Germans away from us; I'll sort out Charlie," Will whispered reassurances in Charlie's ear, then nodded to Jack and slowly started to back away from Charlie.

"Stay completely still, Charlie," Will said as he moved back up around ten yards to where Jack was standing. Both of them looked at the statuesque Charlie, knowing that if anyone could stay calm during this chilling predicament, it would be Charlie Aspinall.

Will cupped his hand and whispered in Jack's ear, well beyond the earshot of Charlie. "I have confirmed that there is a device beneath Charlie's left foot; I checked it with my knife. It may not be active, but the suggestion is that it is given the other explosion that killed Sam."

Jack whispered back, "Okay, I'll take it from here. Thanks, Will. Just make sure those Germans don't get any closer until we can get Charlie out."

Will hugged Jack hard and pleaded softly, "Please, Jack, we have to get Charlie home to Beth and his son."

No more words were needed. Will scrambled up the trench side and joined the fracas up above. It seemed like the German guns were getting closer; Jack had no time to lose. He strode the ten yards towards Charlie, talking calmly as he moved. "Charlie, here's what I have to do. I will use a large piece of wood, which I am going to get into position to replace the weight of your foot so that you can move away from the device."

Charlie had said nothing, but the words he now used had been thought about carefully and were words that Jack would always remember. "Jack, I know that the chances of this working are low, but if I am to die, I do not want you to die too. I need you to step away. I need you to be around to lead the fight that's going on up there. I may need you to act as a guardian to my son and bring him up as I would have. I need you and Melissa to love and support Beth, Will, and my parents. I'm sorry, Jack, but I need to do this."

Charlie moved his foot.

Jack was thrown back by the power of the explosion, he opened his eyes and saw the moon and stars through the trees. Momentarily, there was peace and silence. And then chaos returned.

"Charlie! No!" he yelled. He looked back down the trench, and there lay Charlie, his body horribly mangled and torn. Jack realised that Charlie had sacrificed himself rather than risk taking anyone with him. Jack picked up Charlie's rifle and, baying like a banshee, clambered up the side of the trench. He quickly oriented himself to where the semi-circle of British troops were, and pulling two grenades from his belt, with tears running down his face and adrenalin pumping, he started running towards the German machine gun.

Will had heard the explosion in the trench and had guessed what had happened. He couldn't lose Jack as well as his brother-in-law, so he shouted at the rest of the unit to follow Jack towards the German line.

Good fortune had blessed the timing of Jack's assault as the machine gunners were re-loading, just at the time that one of the grenades landed by their feet. "Fuck you!" Jack screamed as it exploded, killing both gunners instantly. He then hurled the other grenade towards the truck that had brought the Germans across the bridge. It landed by the petrol tank, and a huge fireball rose as the initial explosion caused the rupture of the fuel tank.

That was the last thing Jack was aware of; he was shot in the stomach, shoulder, and leg. He fell and lost consciousness.

CHAPTER 51 - *CITY LIFE*

Life up on Bosley Cloud at the Lovatt's farm was carrying on positively. Rudi's support work was allowing Nat to complete a number of projects to improve the overall quality of the sheep flock. Thomas Whetton was seeing the figures coming from the farm and complemented Nat on the positive profits from both meat and wool sales.

Nat was quick to remind Thomas of Rudi's presence and the help he was being. Thomas had met Rudi briefly at Adam Bostock's memorial service. He had been impressed with how well-spoken the Dane was, especially as English was a third language behind his native Danish and German. Thomas mentioned this to Elliot one day, and correspondence between the pair had commenced – with Elliot keen to understand 'occupied Denmark and the Nazi regime'.

Martha was keeping her and Rudi's secret intact, and Rudi was making sure that he was helping Martha in every possible way when Nat wasn't asking him to rebuild walls or move sheep from one pasture to another – always with the aid of Jess – the ever-faithful sheepdog. The only item that Rudi was keeping secret from Martha was his regular correspondence with Elliot. It was an uncomfortable secret, as in his writing, he was further developing the character of Rudi Ipsen, the Dane. Yet this alter ego was intriguing and he felt that Elliot Chapman MP, based down in London, was a contact that could provide him with a new avenue to explore. When Elliot's last letter suggested that Rudi could come to London and potentially take up a research assistant role, Rudi had not felt such a surge of excitement before. Perhaps this opening provided him with an opportunity to step back into helping his fatherland in their ailing war efforts, not through espionage but via actively looking for a peaceful solution.

At dinner that evening, Rudi dropped a hint to the Lovatts that he was thinking about moving to see city life before heading back to Denmark. This was met with wide-eyed surprise by both Nat and Martha – for very different reasons. "What will we do without you, Rudi, my boy? Jess will be heartbroken!" Nat said with a smirk. "No, seriously, we would miss you enormously, but the spring will follow winter, and we'll all just have to cope, won't we, Martha?"

Martha nodded, but chose not to say anything until Nat had got up to get more firewood from an outhouse that doubled as a wood store.

Checking to see if Nat was out of earshot, Martha turned to Rudi. "What do you think you're doing? London is full of people who will be more suspicious of what a Danish sailor is doing in London working with a politician. You have many more chances of being caught and imprisoned."

"Martha, that's true, but I have to make an effort to get back to mainland Europe somehow. I'm a German soldier who objects to this meaningless war. I cannot reveal this openly to anyone for fear of the German state taking retribution on my family back in Germany if I can get some forged identification papers; in that case, I may be able to reach the Danish Consular and plead my case that I was a German who had emigrated to Denmark just before the war, and then joined the Danish merchant navy, before my journey from Liverpool to your home."

Martha looked questioningly at Rudi, "Your story seems to be evolving fast. Are you sure you can keep this going? London will ask many more questions of you than hiding up here on Bosley Cloud."

Rudi looked at her, "You and Nat have been so kind, but I feel that I really must make this move now." Jess was by his feet and whimpered, sensing the impending departure.

Nat and Martha wanted to take Rudi to Macclesfield train station in order to catch the train down to London. Nat quickly engaged in conversation with the station master – Jon Shankins – who he had been at school with. Martha linked Rudi's arm, and they walked along the platform. There were ten minutes until the express from Manchester to London stopped to pick up Macclesfield passengers. "Are you sure you want to go to London, Rudi? This is your last chance," Martha nudged him warmly.

"Martha, I promise you that this is what I need to do. Mr Whetton has introduced me to his friend Elliot Chapman, and he asked me to call on him whenever I'm in London, so that's what I'll do. Don't worry, I promise I'll write regularly and tell you what your German friend is up to!" Rudi teased.

"But I'm worried that your nationality will be discovered, and the British Authorities will think that you've been spying, and what's more, they may think that Nat and I have been colluding with the enemy." She looked at him seriously.

"Martha, please don't worry; the way I read the newspapers, it seems like the Germans are retreating following D-day, and it is only a matter of time before they must surrender."

"I wouldn't be too sure about what you read in these newspapers," Martha said. "War propaganda would have had it that we'd won the war in 1940 if you believed every word you read. It's the letters that we get back from Charlie that gives us a real glimpse of what's happening on the front line."

Rudi replied, "Facts are that there are now no air raids happening both in the north or south of England because the Luftwaffe have lost so many planes. The Allies have won in the air and at sea, and now they just need to finish off on the ground. I promise that if I am discovered as a German, there is no evidence in existence to suggest that I have harmed British interests; in fact, there's plenty of evidence to show how I have helped the Great British economy by supporting the sheep rearing industry!" He winked at Martha.

Nat joined them both, and helped Rudi put his small suitcase into the overhead rack of the train. "Thanks, Rudi, for everything. You're always welcome back on the Cloud. We'll miss you, and Jess is distraught." They both laughed. Nat shook his hand and descended back onto the platform. He joined Martha and Jon, who blew his whistle to signal the departure of the train to London. Rudi was on the next leg of his journey home.

Chapter 52 - *The Convent*

"Corporal Jack Moat," Jack had just regained consciousness briefly. He heard his name announced by a military doctor to the army chaplain, "He has lost so much blood that you need to read him his last rites." Jack blacked out again. Perhaps he'll be with Charlie again soon.

The medical tent was positioned right next to the farmhouse where Colonel Fletcher had set up his own field HQ. A debrief was taking place with the Cheshire Regiment, who had undertaken the reconnaissance exercise on the bridgehead the previous night. The Colonel was aware that things had not gone to plan. As soon as he had heard reports of explosions coming from the direction of the bridge two miles away, he had ordered a unit of Canadian soldiers to advance in support of the British. They had arrived to see the final shots in the skirmish. The Cheshire Regiment had fought off a German unit successfully but had suffered casualties.

"Private Ledger, I believe you took charge of the unit following the incapacitation of Corporal Moat," the Colonel barked out. "Can you provide a full account of what happened?"

Will described the woodland and the successful reconnaissance. Gerd had taken Jack's notebook and passed it to Will to help provide the required information to the Colonel. He placed the notebook on the table in front of him as he spoke, "Unfortunately, sir, as we retreated, two of our soldiers suffered catastrophic injuries caused by landmines in a trench in the woods that we had not used on the earlier approach. Private Sam Forsyth and Private Charlie Aspinall." He paused for a moment, and the Colonel noted the emotion.

"Was he a friend of yours, Ledger?"

"Yes, sir, he was my brother-in-law and the finest friend a man could have." Will bowed his head, knowing that tears were not an accepted reaction in front of a senior officer.

"That's okay, son," said the Colonel quietly. "I'm sure Charlie was a fine man, and we have been honoured to serve with him."

Will raised his head and nodded. "Sir, can I ask permission to recover their bodies from the woodland? I have volunteers who would like to help me. It would mean a lot to their families."

"Yes, son, as soon as we get anti-tank backup and air support, it's due to arrive tomorrow. I don't want to lose any more men at this bridgehead." The Colonel added, "Before I dismiss you, Private, can you tell me what happened to Corporal Moat?"

Will described the blind courage that Jack showed in charging the German machine gun post, taking it out with grenades, and destroying the German truck, allowing the rest of the unit to strengthen their positions and kill the remaining Germans, just as the Canadian backup arrived. Jack's body had been then put on a stretcher and brought back to the farmstead. "Can I ask how he's doing?" Will asked, fearful of the reply.

"Your brave officer is still holding on, Corporal. We pray that he will recover, but the odds are not good. The chaplain is in with him right now."

"May I go and see him, sir?"

"You may. And Private, thank you," the Colonel added holding up Jack's detailed notes on the Panzer unit's locations, "This notebook has all the detail we need to take that bridge. I've ordered the air support and given coordinates." The colonel stood and saluted him.

Will headed straight to the medical tent, and passed the chaplain leaving. "How's Jack doing?" he asked. The chaplain laid his hand on Will's shoulder and said, "Just pray hard for your friend; he's in God's hands now."

Will pulled back the crudely hung sheet that was providing Jack's bed with some privacy. Jack was covered with bandages from his abdomen to his right shoulder, and a sheet covered his legs. One of his arms was out in the open by his side, with several drips connected to medication hanging from a stand. He looked pale but peaceful. At least all the blood loss had been stemmed, as there was no more plasma available that matched Jack's blood type.

Will sat down by Jack's uncovered arm and gripped his hand. Jack's hand was warm, and despite the paleness of his face, he seemed to be gently breathing very shallow breaths. "Jack Moat – you are going to get through this. You owe it to Melissa to get home. You owe it to Charlie. We cannot lose you, too. Please, Jack – fight for your life – like you've never fought before." Will lowered his head and said his own prayer. Just as he let Jack's hand go, he thought he felt a little squeeze. Perhaps there was some hope.

Three Hawker Hurricane bombers arrived as per the Colonel's orders and hit the far side of the Meuse Bridge where the Panzer tanks had dug in. In the aftermath, binocular surveillance revealed that the German defenses had been obliterated, and the Allied units were given the approval to advance to capture the bridge and set up a new base to await reinforcements. It was with great relief that the Cheshire Regiment was asked to remain alongside their injured Corporal at the farmstead. Jack remained critical, yet he was still holding in there, and the reinforcements would bring better medical resources to support the injuries.

Fred Needles was now over his bout of dysentery and keen to contribute to the tragic loss of both Charlie and Sam. He volunteered to complete the gruesome job of collecting both bodies with as much dignity as possible, given the circumstances. Will had gained permission, despite the ongoing risk of further incendiary devices, for five soldiers to take on this task and bring back the body bags. Andy and Robin were quick to volunteer to join Fred and Will. Gerd also wanted to return to the wood to honour his father's grave by placing a new cross on it – one that he had been whittling during downtime in the preceding days.

Jack's blood readings had been improving for five consecutive days when he regained consciousness fully. Will and Fred were with him and made sure he was aware of the plan to move him back to a real field hospital twenty miles behind the frontline. A decision had been made to withdraw the remaining Cheshire Regiment soldiers back for a prolonged rest, so Jack would have his comrades escort the military ambulance.

Jack's first conscious thought was of Charlie and the horrific scene he had witnessed a week earlier. It would be seared on his memory forever, haunting him. He would need to come to terms with the fact that Charlie's final act had saved him, although Jack had almost killed himself with his foolhardy – albeit successful – destruction of the German's machine gun placement. "Does Beth know yet?" Jack whispered to Will.

Will shook his head and replied, "We wanted to know if you were going to make it or not before we made contact with Langley."

Jack thought for a moment, tears welling in his eyes at the thought. He mustered enough strength to move his hand and hold Will's firmly. "I am going to make it, be assured. You must forewarn your dad before telling your sister. Sledge will need to be strong for her, and I know he will."

"What about Melissa?" Will asked. "Shall we tell her about your injuries?"

"They're not important, and I'll be fine," Jack responded stubbornly. Will knew the truth that some of Jack's physical injuries were so serious that he would need to return to England to convalesce. He resolved to be honest with his father and allow him to manage the Langley end.

It took almost a full day to move the twenty miles back to Liege across the Dutch border into newly liberated Belgium. The roads were in appalling condition, following tank movements and regular bombing. The ambulance needed to divert slowly around large craters. Every movement of the vehicle caused greater agony to Jack despite the high dosage of ether that he had been given. The field hospital in Liege had been set up in an Old Catholic convent and was well-resourced with Belgian and Canadian doctors supported by the resident nuns. Will had travelled in the ambulance with Jack whilst the rest of the troop had cadged a lift in an empty food truck, returning to Liege to restock.

Jack was taken into the convent's intensive care unit, as the wound in his abdomen had become infected, and there was also concern over the quality of some of the transfused blood that had been given. The rest of the unit set up home in patrol tents in the apple orchard – and were immediately given several flagons of local cider as a welcome gift. Fred and Will had been dropped off in the middle of Liege in order to find the senior officer and report their presence. Although not ranked as senior, Fred had taken the lead role within the unit. His relatively senior age and physical stature made it easy for the others to look up to him, and Will was too caught up in the emotions revolving around Charlie's – death. They found the Allied army HQ quickly enough as it was in the town hall, and had British and Belgian flags flying on a makeshift flagpole.

"Private Fred Needles, sir," Fred announced himself to the desk sergeant, who looked somewhat bemused at the formality of this almost seven-foot soldier trying to stand to attention and salute him in a small, low-ceilinged office.

"At ease, soldier," the officer said in a Mancunian accent. "Which company are you with?"

"2nd Cheshires, sir," Fred replied. "There are seventeen of us, and we have been withdrawn from the frontline, having suffered several fatalities and a number of injuries."

"Thanks for your bravery, son," the officer said, not needing to know the details further. "Whereabouts in Cheshire?"

"Langley, near Macclesfield," Fred responded in a more relaxed way. "God's own country!"

"It sure is, mate; I'm from Stretford," said the sergeant.

"United or City?" Will asked with a grin.

"There is only one team in Manchester – the red one!" replied the officer, smiling back.

"We'd both agree with that!" said Fred, "can't wait to see them again too."

The sergeant nodded his approval. "Now, you'll be fine at the convent; we'll let you know what your next instructions are in the next fortnight; in the meantime – enjoy the cider!"

The two soldiers left the HQ and headed towards the post office that had a queue of soldiers outside. They joined the queue having ascertained that there was an operational telephone inside. "Percy, it's Will Ledger. Can you get my dad, please?" said Will, as the Langley Store keeper picked up the phone after the usual three rings.

Very used to receiving calls from active servicemen now, Percy knew the importance of speed, "Hi Will, hold on, I'll get Sledge to the phone". Will could hear the familiar tap, tap, tap of the walking stick on the wall. Within thirty seconds, Sledge had arrived and had grabbed the phone receiver from Percy. It had been several weeks since any communication had taken place between the boys from Langley, and everyone had known that they were back on the frontline, pushing the Germans back towards Germany. Nerves had been increasing with every day that passed without news.

"Will, my boy, I'm so pleased to hear your voice," Sledge said, trying to maintain a steady voice. "How is everyone else?"

There was a pause; Will was struggling to find the right words to use. Sledge could hear his son's breathing, but the silence was ominous. Suddenly, a new voice appeared, "Sledge, it's Fred here. Charlie died in action last week."

Fred's stark factual statement numbed Silas' senses and emotions. He dropped the receiver and staggered back to lean against the wall. He clutched his heart. The news that any relative dreaded had hit his own family, and he would have to manage the fallout. He passed the receiver back to Percy. "It's Percy here; Sledge can't speak right now. Is there anything I need to know?"

Fred spoke slowly, "Hi Percy, I have just told Sledge that Charlie has died, the cause of death being an enemy landmine. He died immediately, and his act saved the lives of others. You should also know that Jack has been badly wounded, and we'll know more about his condition in the coming days. We are all praying for a positive outcome. Our unit has been moved back to Belgium, and we are far from the frontline for now. The Germans are on the run."

"Thanks, Fred; send the boys our love, and I'll make sure Sledge's family and Melissa have our full support." The line went dead.

Will looked at Fred and mouthed the words "Thanks." Fred and Will left the post office; they needed something to dull the pain that they knew would be hitting Langley by the news they had just shared.

"Let's have a drink to the memory of Charlie and the recovery of Jack. I'm buying." Fred pushed Will through the entrance of the first bar they passed - 'Le Trappiste.' It was early evening, but the bar was already heaving with soldiers heading towards the frontline or returning. The fresh faces of the soldiers who had not witnessed action yet were easy to pick out. Will and Fred had seen enough of war for their lifetime. They sat outside the bar in silence, just looking at the stars and trying to understand their own forms of grief.

Percy had poured out a strong brandy for Silas and was thinking ahead as to how they could let the community know once the important people had been told. Thankfully Gwen was yet to return from her mill work in Macclesfield, and Beth had taken Oliver into town to meet up with Melissa. At least they had avoided the heartbreak and agony of the news being delivered by an officer of the Cheshire regiment appearing unannounced in a van in the way that Adam Bostock's death had been revealed.

Silas slugged the brandy down in one and pulled himself together. Percy updated on the other information that Fred had passed on. "Thank you, Percy, I needed that. Now, we must coordinate this carefully to manage the pain. Gwen and I will need to focus entirely on Beth and the baby. I'll ask Nat and Martha to come over and help support Melissa. Once I tell you, can you inform Reverend Pottinger and Ned at the Dunstan. The Reverend will arrange prayers in the chapel, and that will bring comfort to many." He paused to review the actions. "I need to go and meet Gwen coming home, so that we can prepare for Beth's return. Thanks again, Percy."

Heading out of the door, Silas turned and added, "I also need to let Henry Aspinall know about his son."

CHAPTER 53 - *GRIEF*

It was now early Autumn 1944, and the late evening air was starting to develop a chill. A primeval scream erupted from the Ledger's house. The village recognised the utmost in human pain. Gwen held Oliver's hand whilst Beth was held tightly by her father. She pounded his chest with her fists until she went limp. Silas just held his daughter, knowing that she would have swapped anything to be in Charlie's arms – indeed, he wished he could have replaced Charlie right now. The extreme sense of loss was palpable within the household.

Charlie had been a soulmate to Beth and as close as a son to Gwen and Silas since his teenage years. Oliver had never met his dad, but his four-year-old senses recognised his mother's emotions, and he hugged Gwen's leg tightly, before running to Beth and cuddling her.

Percy met Martha and Nat at the edge of the village and explained the urgent message that had come from Silas and his request that they go with Percy to inform Melissa of the situation with Jack. As they were heading down the street, they saw the worried face of Melissa hurrying towards them. Beth's scream had either been heard or reported down the village high street, and neighbours were appearing in doorways. "Melissa!" Percy shouted. "Can we have a quiet word with you over here."

"Is it Jack? What's happened, Percy? Tell me now!" Melissa demanded.

"Jack has been seriously injured and is fighting for his life in Belgium. But he's safe with Fred and Will and the others. We need you to be brave for now. Charlie has lost his life."

This news was too much for her to take on. She looked at Percy and the others. "Jack will be fine, I know it. He's not allowed to leave me now." She refused to recognise anything but a positive outcome. "Poor Beth, can I see her?"

Martha put an arm around her shoulder and said, "Let's get you home, where we can have a nice cup of tea. Gwen and Silas are looking after Beth and the baby. Nat, you come with me and Melissa, please."

Martha's intuition was right, as soon as they had arrived back at Melissa's cottage, she went hysterical. "Jack Moat – you dare leave me now! That would not be fair. You promised me you'd come home to me. Don't you dare..." Melissa sunk onto a chair and started to sob uncontrollably.

In the Ledger's terraced cottage, Beth was now holding little Charlie and soulfully singing him a lullaby. Gwen was also resorting to tea as the best tonic for this solemn occasion. Silas had decided that things were sufficiently calm for him to leave the house and head up to Ridge Hill in order to inform Henry Aspinall of his son's death. He called in to see Percy first and asked him to inform the local village pub, a sure way of communicating news to the village – good or bad.

Silas wrapped a scarf around his neck and pulled his coat collar up. It was the same coat that had been used as evidence by Henry Aspinall all those years ago to frame Silas as a criminal. He reflected on the irony of his clothing choice as he walked up the road. Adding to this, two rabbits ran across the road ahead of him, fleetingly looking at him, before heading off into the hedgerow. It was Will's borrowing of his coat on that fateful night and his forgetfulness in remembering to remove the snared rabbit that had meant that Silas had spent almost a year locked up in Strangeways.

As he mused over the turns his life had taken, he returned to the pains of the present. How was Henry Aspinall, an estranged father, going to react to the death of his estranged son? More significantly, how was Beth going to live her life and bring up a little boy without a husband and father?

Silas rang the bell on the gate of Aspinall's manor house. A smartly dressed man appeared from the gatehouse. "Hi, Sledge – how are you?" the suited gentleman asked enthusiastically.

"Young Jimmy!" Sledge exclaimed. "I didn't recognise you in all that finery."

"It's 'James' now, Sledge; Mr. Aspinall insists that I'm James now. I picked up this job after the quarry closed, and it's a cushy number and paid a bit more too."

"Good for you, Jimmy – James!" Sledge said. "Is your boss at home? I've got some important news to pass on."

"You may want to see him, Sledge, but are you sure he wants to see you?" Jimmy replied, recalling the past animosity between the two men.

"This is serious news that Mr. Aspinall will want to hear. It's about Charlie – Charles – his son," Sledge responded.

Jimmy opened the gate and beckoned Silas through. "I'll ring the house; you head up there now, and the butler will let you into the drawing room."

As he walked up the meandering driveway, Sledge looked at the imposing manor house growing in size as he approached. He thought that every one of the Langley population could quite possibly live in this enormous structure – yet one man was living here now, together with a staff of who knows how many.

As he walked up the stairs, the front doors opened, held by not one but two doormen. The butler bowed and ushered Sledge through to the drawing room, offering to take his coat; Sledge politely declined, not wanting to risk any further miscarriages of justice.

The ornately decorated hearth had a roaring blaze heating the room. The flames danced their shadows all around the oak-panelling. The imposing chandelier dominated the high ceiling. Sledge wondered who on Aspinall's staff had the job of individually lighting and extinguishing each of those many candles.

The butler re-entered the room, announcing the appearance of the master of the house. Henry Aspinall was dressed in his business suit and had just returned from an evening at the Macclesfield Chamber of Commerce. The war had been good to Henry Aspinall's fortunes, and his wealth was growing exponentially. "Good evening, Mr. Ledger. What an unexpected pleasure it is for you to visit at this late hour."

Henry noticed the overcoat that Silas was holding. "Have you come to return any more of my poached game?" he said with a heavy tone of sarcasm.

"Good evening, Mr. Aspinall. I am here to inform you of a matter that I felt was unfair coming from anyone else." Silas paused; he felt Henry shifting his gaze. A realisation had struck him that there was one matter that Silas might know before he would.

"What's happened?" Henry demanded. "Is it Charles?"

"Yes, I'm sorry." Silas recognised the pain etched on Henry's face. "Charles was killed in Holland by an enemy landmine, I was informed earlier this afternoon. I'm very sorry."

Henry remained open-mouthed and still. Then he collapsed onto the nearest chair and stared into the flickering flames. "My Charles is dead," he wailed. He looked up at Silas and said with spite in his voice, "He would never have gone to war if he'd stayed with me. He was never built for war."

Silas remained silent. He felt Henry's loss just as much, given that he had acted as a surrogate father to Charlie for all those years in which he and his natural father had been estranged. Yet Silas could feel that he and Charlie had parted this world as more than just friends – he was part of the Ledger family. Henry would be tormented by his decision to push Charlie away by forcing him to follow a lifestyle that was against his values and preferences. Ultimately, Charlie's love for Beth had won over any love that he had for materialism and his father's greed.

Henry maintained his stare into the burning embers of the

fire. The butler had backed out of the door minutes before and gently closed it behind in order to ensure the conversation was private. Having heard his master's reaction to the news that had been imparted, the butler reopened it again and approached the motionless Henry. "Sir, would you like to be left alone? Shall I escort Mr. Ledger to the door?"

Silas walked towards the door without any further need of affirmation. Henry raised his head and, looked directly at Silas and asked an unexpected question, "Mr. Ledger, can I meet Charles's son?"

Silas turned, surprised by the question. "I will need to check with his mother first, but I think you should meet the child; he's already got so many features of Charlie. I'll make contact once I've spoken with Beth. Please understand, though, that Beth has lost the most precious man in the world, and she herself will need time to grieve."

Henry nodded and returned to his gaze into the fire, lost in thought. Silas left the drawing room, exited the house, and walked back to Langley. The cold, fresh air gave him an opportunity to clear his head. How was Jack? How was Will coping with all of this? And how could he support Beth as she came to terms with her own grief?

CHAPTER 54 - *EARL GREY TEA*

Rudi got off the train at London Euston and walked to Elliot's Kensington address. He recognised a very smart apartment block with a shared foyer managed by a doorman. He knocked on the door and asked if Elliott Chapman MP was at home. "No sir, Mr. Chapman is not at home, but his friend Mr. Whetton is here. Can I tell him who called?" said the friendly doorman in a very strong London accent, very different from the rural Cheshire accents that Rudi had become accustomed to.

Now, having only briefly been introduced to Thomas Whetton at Adam Bostock's memorial service, Rudi thought it would be an imposition to ask Thomas if he might stay and await Elliot's arrival. "That's kind of you sir, but if you could just tell Mr. Whetton that it is Rudi Ipsen from Denmark, calling to see Mr. Chapman, and I will call back later. Good day." Rudi touched his flat cap, a going-away gift from Martha, and reversed back down the steps.

He turned to walk away, but a shout came from a first-floor balcony – it was Thomas Whetton. "Rudi. Rudi Ipsen from Denmark. Come on up; I want to hear all the fine things you've been doing with my sheep up on Bosley Cloud." Thomas beckoned him up.

Thomas had already prepared a pot of tea by the time Rudi had ascended the grand staircase up to the level one apartment. "Come on in, Rudi, my boy. Elliot will be delighted that you've come to visit, although why swap the wonderful Cheshire air for the smog of London is a bigger question to ask?" Rudi was impressed that Thomas remembered him from the one brief introduction in Langley, and equally that he was warm and welcoming.

"Mr. Whetton, thank you so much..."

"Now, less of the formality – it's Thomas, no more Mr. Whetton, please!" Thomas said, pouring a cup of tea without even asking whether Rudi wanted one.

By now, and living in the Lovatt household for so long, Rudi realised that a cup of tea for English folk was the equivalent of breathing air. Life was unsustainable without it! "Thank you... Thomas," he said as he was handed a fine Wedgewood cup and saucer. "Martha and Nat gave me many lessons in the art of tea and its importance to English society."

Thomas responded, "Not least, the tea will cleanse the London smog from your palate. Now let's sit down, and you can update me on my sheep flock."

The two men sat for an hour exchanging news of the farm and life in Macclesfield. Thomas was impressed with how this young, sea-faring Dane was so easily able to communicate in English. He had clearly been educated to a high standard to be able to speak as he did, especially if he had been on Danish boats for so long a time where the likely conversation would have no doubt been befitting of the tough life of the merchant navy.

Intrigued, Thomas delved deeper – "Tell me, Rudi, how come you are so fluent in English? Nat's hardly the most eloquent of English speakers given that he is alone with his sheep most of the day," he smirked.

"No, you're right there, Thomas," Rudi started. "Nat is no talker, but like his brother-in-law – Silas Ledger, when he does speak, you listen." Thomas nodded in agreement.

"Martha's schoolteacher habits continued around the kitchen table, and she was exceptional at picking up on any small language error I made and correcting it. In eight months of Martha's constant corrections – I've improved my English language immensely."

"Bravo to that," Thomas said.

"Bravo to what?" Elliot announced his entrance, dressed in his Parliamentarian finest.

Thomas got up and gave Elliot a warm embrace; Rudi recognised it as unusually warm for just friends. "Hello, Ell; I was just saying to our young friend Master Ipsen how good he was at the English language, considering his Danish background."

Elliot held out his hand to Rudi, "Rudi Ipsen, at last we meet face-to-face. The pleasure is all mine."

Until then, Rudi had only corresponded with Elliot over a couple of letters. In Beth, Elliot had found one source of youthful inspiration to aid a perspective on Britain's domestic policies, and he was hoping to gain further insights into

Britain's foreign policies from another Cheshire resident – albeit a foreign worker – who had fortuitously come to him via Thomas. "Give me five minutes to get out of this stiff suit into something more casual, and we can chat over tea. Thomas, pour me a cup of Earl Grey; I'll be back in a tick."

Rudi relaxed; what a stroke of luck that he had found these two individuals in London and they were so welcoming to him. This position of comfort gave him a different perspective on life. Perhaps now was the time for him to reveal his true identity and allow fate to dictate the next phase of his journey.

The phone went off in the hallway, and Elliot answered it. Only a hushed voice could be heard from where Thomas and Elliot sat, but it sounded like a serious conversation. Elliot appeared at the doorway. "I've just had some terrible news from the War office. Earlier today, I read in dispatches that a British soldier with the surname of Aspinall had been killed in action near the Dutch-German border. I have just had it confirmed to me that the soldier was Charlie Aspinall of the Cheshire regiment." Elliot moved to sit next to Thomas and put an arm around his shoulder. "I'm so sorry."

Thomas' mouth opened as he stared back at Elliot. Thomas had accepted the honour of being Oliver's godfather years previous and was committed to that role. He had great regard for Beth and recognised her soulmate in Charlie. He was looking forward to when Charlie could return from war and meet his son for the first time. Beth had ensured that Charlie had been sent photos of Oliver, but no official christening would occur until the whole family could be together. Given the way that the war was progressing, Thomas felt certain that this would be soon.

Thomas turned to Rudi and explained who Charlie was related to in Langley and how he had a four-year-old child who he had never met. Also, he was an aspiring lawyer before signing up for the war. "I'm so sorry, Thomas," said Rudi. "He sounds like he was an outstanding man." Rudi decided that perhaps now was not the time to reveal his German ancestry.

Thomas asked Elliot if he could use his phone and called the Langley post office number. He quickly learned from Percy Ricketts that the tragic news about Charlie had already been shared with the village. Thomas asked for his thoughts and prayers to be passed on to Beth and the Ledgers. Percy also shared the news back that Jack Moat was hanging on to life by a thread, and they were waiting for more information from Will in Belgium.

"There's only one thing for it," said Elliot. "Let's go to the RAC club and drink some of its finest wines to honour those young men and their sacrifices. To coin a phrase from Winston Churchill – 'if you're going through hell, keep going.'"

Thomas turned to Elliot, "I know you're right, my friend; we cannot let these tragedies drag us down; we must fight back. Let's go to the Club, and you can hear all about Rudi's colourful life before he turned up in Cheshire. Tomorrow I will make contact with Sledge and Beth and see what more we can do to help."

"Agreed," said Elliot, "and I can try to find out more information from the War Ministry. They may have an understanding of Jack's situation."

CHAPTER 55 - *NEWSPAPER HEROES*

In Liege, the constant movement of troop reinforcements and additional hardware for the frontline gave a heightened confidence that the Allies were on a one-way path to victory; it was only a matter of time. The 2nd Cheshires were directed to move up towards the frontline and ready themselves for the final push across the Rhein, which would eventually happen in March 1945. Fred Needles, together with Andy Soutter and Robin Brampton, were asked to rejoin the main unit. There was no hesitation; they all felt it was critical to see this war to its final outcome – for themselves – but more importantly – for the memory of Charlie, Adam, and other valiantly fallen comrades.

It was an emotional farewell. The senior officer had permitted Will Ledger to escort Jack Moat – when sufficiently recovered – and the body of his brother-in-law – Charlie, back to Britain. Jack had stabilised, and the medical staff at the convent were confident that he would be able to survive the journey back across the Channel and would be better off convalescing at home. This plan was relayed back to Langley, and more exact dates would be communicated as soon as they knew the details of the route that they would be heading home.

Jack was in a wheelchair now, and although still in regular pain, it had been a month since the fateful day of Charlie's death and Jack's feat of insane bravado in attacking the machine gun fortification. Given his heroics in Tobruk, which had already gained him a top commendation award two years previous, this latest act of bravery had further raised Jack's soldiering profile, and a war correspondent from London had been asked to interview Jack and send a report and photo back to London.

The journalist found Jack at the convent and was given permission by the doctors to conduct an interview. "I'll only speak to you if I can have all of my unit around me," Jack said. "Anything I have done was only possible because of the team."

The journalist – whose name was Mike Hodgkinson – conceded. This meant that Will, Fred, Andy, and Robin piled into the small recovery room that Jack was occupying. Gerd had also joined them, following insistence from the others. Despite the shadow that was cast by the loss of Charlie, the boys were in a positive mood because of the daily improvement in Jack's health and the fact that tonight they would be having a send-off at Le Trappiste – the bar in Liege that had become a favourite for British and Canadian soldiers.

Slightly discomforted by the five soldiers crowding around the bed, the journalist started by asking Jack to describe the events leading up to his attack on the German machine gun post.

Jack was very factual about the events, yet underplayed all of his own involvements, building Gerd up as the brave young Dutchman who was fighting for the Allies in memory of his father. Jack also paid special attention to Charlie and described his selfless sacrifice as the bravest act of any soldier he had seen in the almost five years he had been at war. He described his charge on the German guns as a split-second decision as he'd seen a chance appear as they reloaded.

"Now, now, Corp!" Andy called out. "That needs explaining further. Mr. Hodgkinson, do you mind if I call you Mike?" Mike nodded, thinking that being as outnumbered by battle-hardened soldiers he should generally be submissive. Andy continued. "Mike – what actually happened was that this German machine gun was shredding all of the trees that we were hiding behind. A further minute and none of us would be here for you to talk to. We were all shitting ourselves – mind my Flemish! None of us could get an angle to shoot at the dominant position where the Germans were located. A landmine had just killed our friend, Private Charlie Aspinall, and we all thought that we would die in this forest." Andy turned to Jack, "Jack, are you good with me continuing?" Jack nodded his approval. "Suddenly, Corporal Moat appeared from the trench, screaming like a madman, charging towards the German gun positions. He got to within ten yards before being cut down, but not before he could throw two grenades, both of which hit their targets. The machine gun position exploded, followed by the troop carrier behind it. We were then all able to advance and finish the job whilst also recovering the Corp." Andy paused for a moment. "That was the bravest act any of us had ever seen. And most certainly the final act that most of those Germans ever saw.

He put his life before us all, and I am proud to call him my Corporal and my friend – Jack Moat."

The rest of the group cheered Andy's words, and Jack blushed. The journalist thanked the group for their vivid description of the events and got them all together behind Jack's wheelchair for a group photo. "Now Mike, before you file that story, come to Le Trappiste with us – we have a big send-off planned – and I hear that press men generally have large expense allowances!" Fred added, winking to the group.

Gerd and Robin helped to lift Jack and his wheelchair into the back of a delivery lorry that was heading back two miles to Liege. The journalist was helped in by Andy and Will – there was no escape – even if Mike had wanted to. The lorry driver was surprised to see that Jack needed so many carers, but he was about to go off duty, so he was willing to help for a few francs.

The next day, the whole group was nursing hangovers. Fred felt very stiff and was covered in straw, and it was decided that he must have spent half the night in a haystack on the walk home to the Convent. Andy had not appeared at all until halfway through breakfast. His recollection was that he had gotten lucky with the barmaid, although he also vaguely remembered being chased across a field by her irate father and a beagle hound. Mike, the journalist, had been keeping up with the rounds, consuming large quantities of cider that would have made Fleet Street proud. His antics would further guarantee that any article published would surely paint Jack and his friends in a good light. Will had been in charge of getting Jack home in one piece, although the angry looks of the convent's head sister as the wheelchair was slalomed into the grounds just before midnight – suggested that this was not a suitable programme of convalescence for a wounded war hero!

All agreed that 'Le Trappiste' bar had provided a most colourful environment in which to have a final farewell. For the first time in almost five years this small group of soldiers were heading separate ways – but all for the right reasons. Jack and Will would return to England, whilst Fred, Andy, and Robin would rejoin the ranks of the 2nd Cheshires as they pushed the Allies onwards towards Berlin and expected victory.

During the six-week period since Jack's injury, Will had been making phone calls to Langley to update Melissa on his steadily improving health. Each time she had received the news, she immediately informed Percy Ricketts, as this was a sure-fire way of communicating the news with the entire village, especially those who frequented the Dunstan Inn.

Having taken two weeks' leave to support Beth during the depths of her grief, Melissa had returned to work at Sperry & Burroughs Law firm in Macclesfield, positive that she too would not become a widow based on the upwards trajectory of health that was being reported about Jack's condition.

It was extremely hard for her not to feel guilty about Jack's likely survival whilst her friend's husband Charlie had died. The fact that a child was now orphaned, having never even met his father – only worsened the situation.

It was now early December, and Will phoned once more,

but this time, he called the office where Melissa was working. "Melissa, it's Will," he said following the Operator in the Macclesfield exchange having rerouted the call from British Army H.Q Liege to Sperry & Burroughs. Melissa's heart missed a beat. "What's wrong, Will?" replied Melissa. "Is it, Jack? Is he okay?"

"I'm fine, my darling," Jack's unmistakable voice could be heard. "I can't wait to hold you again."

Melissa went weak at the knees and collapsed onto a chair. Her love, her husband – who she thought was so badly injured that he would never make it home to her – was on the end of the phone! "Oh, Jack, how wonderful to hear your voice again," she said, holding back tears. "When may you be coming home?"

"Soon, my darling. Will is just sorting some of the paperwork out with the local army administrators here, and we will be assigned a crossing back to England. It might be in the next two weeks. I'll be home by Christmas."

Will took the receiver back from Jack. "Melissa, I'll confirm the details with Silas, and we will also be arranging for Charlie's coffin to travel with us. We want to make sure he comes home to his family for his final resting place."

"Of course, Will," Melissa said. "Beth will be so pleased, she is struggling right now, but bringing Charlie home will help in her grief."

The Exchange Operator cut back in and confirmed that the call was now over, as any conversations with mainland Europe were limited to two minutes only due to the volume of calls from military personnel.

Melissa called Thomas down in London and gave him the good news. They agreed that he would share the news with Elliot, and Elliot could then find out the exact transport details that they would be booked on via the War Office. "And Thomas, will you come down to the South Coast with me to meet them as they get off the ship? I'm sure the Ledgers will want that." She asked.

"Of course, I shall – it will be a poignant moment – rejoicing in the living, yet mourning for the dead." In saying this, it hit Thomas just how difficult this would be emotionally for everyone involved. He was honoured to be asked and vowed to be strong for them all.

As it was, Silas received the message first. Will and Jack – together with Charlie's coffin – would likely be on a cargo ship out of Zeebrugge on 10th December – a week away – landing at lunchtime in Portsmouth Harbour. Two days later, these details were confirmed in a telegram that Thomas had sent to Langley following information received in the War Office by Elliot.

Silas first spoke with Gwen about his intentions to travel to Portsmouth to welcome the ship in. He had been told of Melissa's plans and felt he should be there too. His son – Will – would need support, as would his good friend – Jack. And he felt compelled to help ensure the transport of Charlie's coffin was carried out with the dignity and respect that the young man deserved. He had heard that Thomas Whetton would also be there, which was befitting given that he was very much a part of the extended family now and was Godfather to Beth and Charlie's son – Oliver.

It was the day before the ship would sail when Percy Ricketts not only tapped his stick on the adjoining door between his Post Office and the Ledger's cottage but also let out several yells that brought out several neighbours from further away. "Look at this!" he said, holding up a copy of The Times. "It's our boys – and they're all heroes!"

Percy had been astonished not only at the front-page feature and the strong dominant picture of Jack in his wheelchair surrounded by his comrades, but he had also poured over the words that Mike Hodgkinson had written. It highlighted the bravery of each of the men and emphasised the selflessness that had led to Charlie Aspinall's death, and the immense bravery shown by Jack to storm the machine gun placement. Already a Victoria Cross holder from the Siege of Tobruk, in his article, the journalist had also suggested that Jack should be further honoured, and posthumously, Charlie should be considered for a formal honour, a Victoria Cross – the highest and most prestigious in the British honours system.

Curious neighbours, unused to hearing such a kerfuffle in the early hours of a weekday morning, grouped around Percy and stared at the image. The handful of Times newspapers delivered each day were all quickly bought up, although Percy held two back to make sure that he could pass one to Melissa and one to Beth.

Ned Croucher – the landlord at the Dunstan Inn – was already considering how he could frame the front page and hang it in pride of place above the hearth, where folk could admire the fact that Langley had been a highly decorated part of the war effort.

Silas and Gwen were already at their respective workplaces, so Percy knocked on his neighbour's door. He could hear movement from inside, and Beth's voice, "Oliver, there's someone at the door; who do you think it could be?"

Since Charlie's death, Percy had rarely seen Beth leave the house, other than when she was playing with her son in the back garden. Gwen and Silas had done a good job at providing a safe haven for her to grieve in peace. Neighbours and friends had kept a respectful distance, although all had shared their condolences in their own ways.

Beth opened the door, and looked tired. Still in his bedclothes, Oliver was holding a teddy in one hand and his mum in the other, keen to see who was calling at this early hour.

"Hello Percy," Beth said, stifling a yawn. "To what do we owe the pleasure of your early morning wake-up call?"

Percy smiled, "I am sorry, my dear, and sorry to you too, young Oliver." Percy bent down and playfully tugged at Oliver's teddy. "What's his name?"

Oliver looked up at Beth, who gave him an encouraging smile. "His name is Charlie, and he's a very brave soldier bear," Oliver announced proudly.

Percy took a step back, saluted, and stood to attention. "Young Oliver, I see I am in the presence of greatness." Percy put on a mock official army tone, "May I present this to your mother on behalf of the village of Langley." He winked at Beth as he passed across a copy of the Times newspaper. He added in a whisper to Beth. "You may want to take a look at the front page – you'll both be very proud."

CHAPTER 56 - *IDENTITY REVEALED*

Elliot Chapman, M.P. followed similar political leanings to that of the then P.M. - Winston Churchill. A follower of liberalism in early life, he had moved towards conservatism later in life and had gained a seat as the M.P. for Winchester at the relatively young age of 38, a decade before Churchill became Prime-minister in 1940.

Winston Churchill liked Elliot and considered him to be a young Conservative who could see beyond today's Britain and help shape tomorrow's. Elliot had done some early work with Churchill on domestic policies whilst in the opposition, and the two had become friends. Now that the war was nearing a likely end, Churchill was exhausted and that was showing in his mannerisms. The British people wanted to know what post-war Britain would look like on a world stage. The P.M. had asked Elliot to lead some independent work on Britain's foreign policy.

Elliot Chapman was an anglophile – through and through. Summer days at Lords in the pavilion or at Henly on the river bank, were his idea of heaven. Never once had he dreamed of traveling the world, and indeed until he had become an M.P., he had not even owned a passport, despite having the financial means – inherited from his family – of travelling the world many times over. This lack of foreign experience smacked of deep irony in a parliamentarian who was supposed to work on an international scope for Britain. However, Churchill had faith in him, and so he owed it to his country to invest his best thoughts.

Rudi's arrival into Elliot's life was perfectly timed for him to absorb thoughts from an international perspective. Rudi had told him about Danish life, how his family had suffered under German occupation, and how he had travelled across the Atlantic to America, many times with consignments of produce, working for Maersk.

In these travels he had seen first-hand the opportunities that existed in America – in terms of entrepreneurialism on both sides of the law. He was able to eloquently describe his own feelings in being a citizen of one country working in another country. A refugee – yes, but also a man who could add value by doing a job that others might not want to. His plight away from his homeland was a better option than what he would experience if he were to stay. The fact that Rudi's whole life was built on a false foundation would only surface later.

For now, Elliot believed that Rudi Ipsen could provide him with all of the ammunition needed to build a foreign policy that could embrace internationalism and allow Britain to rebuild its shattered economy, post-war.

"Rudi, tomorrow you will come to Parliament with me; I

would like you to work with me on something that the PM has insisted I lead," Elliot announced over a morning tea soon after Rudi had arrived in London.

Rudi nodded and breathed in the fragrances of his Earl Grey tea. How could a German, and a recent Luftwaffe airman, who had been on a bombing mission to destroy HMS Hood in Liverpool docks, suddenly be invited to enter the epicentre of British power – the Houses of Parliament? Pressure was building up inside him – his lie was getting out of hand.

As he mused over his thoughts on foreign policy, Elliot was already instructing Thomas to pick out a selection of his suits that might fit Rudi so that he could appear suitably dressed for a day in Westminster. Rudi could take it no longer. He saw the kindness of these two relative strangers, willing not only to take him in as an orphan but also to believe his story so fully that they were willing to employ him in supporting British Government policy based on a complete lie. He had never meant any harm to befall anybody when he first concocted his Danish persona, but his values determined that his integrity could not take this falsehood any further.

He stood up and addressed both Elliot and Thomas together. "Gentlemen, I have a confession to make. I am very sorry, but I need to be honest. I am here under false pretenses, and you have both been so good to me that I cannot continue to deceive you both. I am not Rudi Ipsen from Esbjerg, Denmark." Thomas stopped laying out suits, Elliot put down his recently delivered mail, and both looked astonished at their guest. "Please, both, if you sit down and let me tell you the real truth."

With stunned and perplexed looks, both men sat down on a chaise longue. Rudi stood in front of them. "I am really Rudolph Schwalbe, and until recently, I was a communications officer and junior navigator in the German Luftwaffe. We were flying a Junkers bomber over the Peak District en route to bomb the Port of Liverpool – and specifically, I knew that my squadron leader and pilot – Major Dietrich Von Zielberg – wanted to destroy HMS Hood."

Thomas and Elliot sat staring at Rudi, not really knowing how to react to now knowing who they were now facing. "I am a pacifist, a taboo subject in Hitler's Germany, and I was forced into joining the Luftwaffe due to my strong exam results and excellent language skills. Hermann Goering himself demanded that I join up to gain experience.

"I am German and have only been to Denmark on occasional vacations during my earlier life. I have never been to America nor worked for a shipping company. I made that whole story up. I'm sorry." He paused for a moment.

"One final fact – before we were hit by anti-aircraft fire and crashed, I had altered the navigation systems on board the plane. I felt it was right to do my bit to save potentially hundreds of human lives in Liverpool by at least diverting Von Zielberg away from his intended target. I recognise that this does not sound credible, but it is true."

Elliot looked at Thomas and raised an eyebrow questioningly. Rudi continued – "I survived the crash into the Roaches on the Staffordshire border, spent two days walking across the moors into Cheshire, and ended up on Nat and Martha Lovatt's farm on Bosley Cloud."

Thomas remarked to Elliot, "That's my tenant farmer." And turning back to Rudi, he added, "Do they know who you really are?"

Rudi looked down, knowing that this might cause problems for the Lovatts. "Yes, Martha guessed that I was not Rudi Ipsen from Denmark, but she trusted me that I was not a person to cause any intentional harm to anyone. And she decided that revealing my background might lead to my own imprisonment or worse. I understand if you want to call the Authorities, I am resigned to that."

"Thank you, this is all a bit of a shock," Thomas said whilst Elliot was standing there wide-eyed and open-mouthed. "Can you step out of the room now, please Rudi – if that's what we should call you now? Elliot and I need to talk."

Rudi, stepped out of the room, with his head bowed. What would his confession mean to him?

In the Macclesfield Old Boy's Club, many members had also been reading The Times' front-page story. Upon understanding the details surrounding Charlie's sacrificial death, many of them had grouped around Henry Aspinall. They clapped him on the back, commiserating and congratulating him for his son's bravery in battle. Even Joshua Padgett, who was now a retired honorary member of the Old Boy's Club, called over from his fireside seat.

"Aspinall, that's the best epitaph any person could hope for. Shame neither of us will be written about like that."

Henry himself just stared at the photo. As he looked at Will Ledger, he could clearly see Silas' features. A nemesis in life, Silas had taken his son from him and had supported Charles going to war – leading to his tragic death. And there was Will – Silas' own son - smiling for the camera. He could not bear this sense of injustice. Henry neglected to remember that it was injustice that he had employed – in collusion with Joshua Padgett – to frame Silas Ledger a decade ago.

Henry left the Club, brooding, wondering if he had the energy and commitment to try one final act of revenge. Now that Charles was dead, could he employ the law to claim greater access to his grandson Oliver? Perhaps he could use his financial clout to influence Oliver and somehow at least recover family credibility and legacy. Right now, he recognised he was growing old alone, in a large manor house with a set of staff who disliked him, and few friends. He headed towards his offices, resolved to change his fortunes.

CHAPTER 57 - *HOME AT LAST*

The train journey down to Portsmouth was uneventful. Melissa was excited but recognised that she needed to keep her emotions in check, given that she was meeting her husband again after almost five years.

One of the Cheshire Regiment trauma officers had visited her and discussed that any soldier who had been through the horrors of war in the way that Jack and his men had would find it hard to move back into civilian life without a few permanent scars. And in Jack's case, there would be scars on the outside and on the inside. The latest prognosis from the medics who had been in charge of Jack had suggested that he would need a wheelchair for at least the next six months, but there would be every chance of him relearning to walk. The bullet to his leg had caused some nerve damage, and this would need time to heal.

The biggest unknown were the mental scars. Jack had promised Beth that he was going to look after Charlie and bring him home. He was bringing him home but in a coffin.

The whole grieving process would be hardest on Beth, of course, but also Jack and his friends, who had fought together, would have a different way of dealing with loss, and that would need respect.

At Euston, they met up with Thomas, who had arranged a taxi down to Waterloo, from where they picked up a connection to Portsmouth Harbour. On the train, Thomas was tempted to share the news that Rudi had just imparted about his secret life, but he had agreed with Elliot to keep it hush until they had fully figured out how the situation could best be managed. Elliot was developing a plan that just might help him and Rudi too; it might also be a final script to the ending of the war setting a firm direction towards peace in Europe and the start of rebuilding foreign relationships.

They arrived at Portsmouth Harbour just before 2 pm, having set off from Macclesfield at 4 am. Silas and Thomas had spent the final two hours of the journey discussing how they should reopen the quarrying business on Teggs Nose and what they could do to make it more productive whilst not compromising workers' health. Owain Jones figured high up on their agenda, as his personality and work ethic had impressed both of them. Silas felt that his active days in the quarry were coming to an end, and as a new grandfather, he'd like the chance to spend more time with Oliver, given that Charlie would not be around to act as a father figure, and Beth would need plenty of help.

The three of them walked across the platform to the docks and could see a large cargo ship just dropping anchor in the middle of the river Hamble estuary. Ten minutes later, a small boat left the cargo ship and docked about two hundred yards away from where Thomas, Silas, and Melissa stood.

"Is it them?" Silas asked.

"I think so? I think I can see Will, and there is a man in a wheelchair – that must be Jack," Melissa added, finding it hard not to shout out.

A sailor helped Will lift Jack and his chair onto the walkway. There were several other army kit bags to retrieve before the two of them could make their way towards the dockside building. A naval officer walked with them, checking various documents as they got closer.

Melissa couldn't contain herself any further and started running towards them, throwing herself at Jack. Silas could see Will laughing and trying to cope with holding the weight of several kitbags as well as keeping control of the wheelchair. Jack was laughing but with tears streaming down his cheeks. The naval officer backed away, stood to attention, and saluted – the paperwork was complete.

Silas hugged Will, and further tears were shed. Silas whispered in his son's ear how proud he was of him and how much his mother was going to dote over him when he got back to Langley.

"Sledge – great to see you again!" said Jack, still with Melissa hanging around his neck. "I've got a special message for you from Gustav Coccini. But that can wait until the train."

Thomas welcomed the two boys with a warm but more formal handshake. "Great to see my workers back from their holidays," he joked.

The initial embraces over; it was the moment that Silas,

Thomas, and Melissa had been most concerned about – understanding how Jack and Will would talk about Charlie's coffin. As it was, it happened very naturally.

Will looked back and pointed at another boat leaving the starboard side of the cargo ship. "Charlie's on his way across on another boat it should take about ten minutes. The naval officer has arranged for his coffin to travel in the army rail freight carriage. He'll be with us all the way."

Before Thomas left to meet up with Silas and Melissa at Euston station, he and Elliot had discussed a radical thought about how they might use Rudi's revelations to progress several subjects of importance. Firstly, Rudi needed support in his position as a German army pacifist who had decided that the war that he was forced to be a part of was no longer something that he should actively support - or secretively deny whilst in the guise of an absconder from the Danish merchant navy.

Rudi, or rather Rudolph, had an opportunity to be a public voice that was likely echoed many multiple times across Germany, and the European mainland. Could he become an advocate for peace? Could he turn his knowledge of Germany's declining military might into a forceful argument for the end of the war? Might he be convinced to use the miracle of him walking away from an otherwise fatal air crash of a German bomber – destined to wreak havoc on Liverpool docks – as a sign that there was a greater calling for him in the desire to stop this needless destruction? Could the generous hospitality that he was shown by Martha and Nat, even after Martha discovered that he was a German airman, act as a message that it was possible for humanity to forgive and live together?

Lots of questions and ideas formed in Elliot's mind as he and Thomas parted on that frosty winter morning in Kensington. Thomas left his partner, wondering what he would return to, as he knew Elliot had a way of acting on impulse. It seemed that all of these ideas were theoretically sound, yet he had not thought about how he might convince Rudi to come along for the unknown journey into infamy or righteousness and what risks were involved on both sides.

The following day, Rudi appeared downstairs for breakfast. Elliot had been up for several hours, measured by the fact that he was on his third teapot of the day. "Earl Grey?" Elliot said, offering Rudi a seat at the breakfast table and putting down his copy of the Times. "Toast? Orange juice? How did you sleep?" Elliot was excited at the prospect of accelerating past the pleasantries of the morning. He wanted to get down to a serious conversation as quickly as possible.

Rudi sat down, "Thank you, Elliot, I slept well, although the London night-time noise is very different to the peace of the Cheshire countryside. I've forgotten that city life rarely stops."

Elliot poured the tea, having formulated his plan of attack in his mind. "Rudi, I have been speaking with Thomas, and we think there's an opportunity to achieve a number of shared objectives. Do you mind listening to this proposal?" Rudi was simply pleased that he wasn't being led out of the house in handcuffs. Elliot continued, "You are a unique individual who has an enormous opportunity to make a statement towards a goal that many of us desire – an end to war and the start of peace." Elliot paused to check on Rudi's reaction. By the manner in which the German was looking at him, it certainly seemed to suggest that he had grasped his full attention.

"Please carry on, Elliot. I am intrigued," Rudi said, grabbing another large sip of his tea.

Elliot was given the green light and went into full dramatic flow. "Rudolph Schwalbe – a Luftwaffe officer – who, unwillingly, had been forced by a desperate dictatorship – to attack the industrial heartland of Britain. Survived an air crash in Staffordshire and was taken in by a kindly local English farmer. Learned to see the heartless insanity of war through the lives of English country folk, and felt that it was now right to share with the world his feelings. Peace needs to be grasped with both hands, German and English. We must collectively finish this war as quickly as possible and turn all our attention to creating a world in which war is not the answer." Elliot briefly stopped for breath and to build to his conclusion.

"Now, what do you think of coming to Westminster with me today and telling some of my more cynical Parliamentarian colleagues that sentiment and using your unique position to hold the torch that could eventually bring light to the darkness and despair of so many lives today."

Rudi put down his teacup. "My goodness, Elliot, you have been plotting. Give me a moment, please."

He stood up, walked over to the window, and gazed across the mews to a small enclosed park. On one side of the grass, three children were playing with a ball, not helped by the intervention of a dog, all too keen to be involved. He thought about Jess, the border collie dog from Bosley Cloud, who had become a devoted friend. Life through the eyes of dogs was so much simpler. Rudi's eyes moved to the other end of the park, and there were some soldiers gathered around smoking, watching two workmen digging away, filling a hole that a bomb could have well caused during the blitz years. A generation was growing up in a wartime scene of carnage and depression – this had become normal life. What was being seen in London was replicated in Munich, Berlin, Hamburg, Cologne, and Frankfurt many times. Could he really do as Elliot had asked and become a voice for change and good in this world of uncertainty?

He turned to Elliot. "Okay, let's do it! I'm ready to speak out. I know that this might be hard for my family back home, but I owe it to Martha and Nat. I owe it to everyone who has lost their lives – in Britain, Germany, and elsewhere. Let's do it!"

Elliot jumped up and clapped him on the back. "You know that it might mean that you will need to face some sort of justice here in the UK as a German prisoner of war. Although, I do feel that as soon as you register your public views, then that will be taken into consideration? And, of course, I will do everything in my power to ensure that you remain a free man."

"I understand," replied Rudi. "It will be a small price to pay if it can help ease the pain of others." Boyed with this shared enthusiasm and his own emotions, Elliot gave Rudi a hug. "Together, we can do something great. Let's get to it."

CHAPTER 58 - *HIDE-AND-SEEK*

Beth had been just about hanging on to existence. Almost two months after Charlie's death, she needed to have Oliver with her day and night. His fidgeting four-year-old body asleep in her bed at nights, was the only source of comfort she had, knowing that she would never see her Charlie again, and Oliver would have never ever seen his father. Perhaps this would be easier for him to cope with. Gwen was doing all she could to ease the pain, but it was simply a matter of time to allow grief to flow unabated until something allowed life to move on. They all hoped that now a date was known for Charlie's body to return for burial locally, then this would be the opportunity. Silas had been the rock that all leaned on, and he had been present at all of her low points. He said nothing, but in those moments, no words were necessary – just the warm, strong bodily presence of her father was all that was needed.

The one difficult conversation that Silas did have with her was about Henry Aspinall. A man who had tried to have her father executed – wrongfully – for the Kidsgrove canal explosion and death of the lock-keeper. A man who had done this to avenge his inability to love his son by forcing him to decide between family money and power or true love and friendship. Henry Aspinall had lost in every way and had now lost any hope of reconciliation with his son. Beth had known that Silas felt it his duty to inform Henry of Charlie's passing, but she had not known that Silas had offered to ask her if Henry could meet Oliver. She had been aware that over the last four years, Henry had appeared at a distance at various public village events where Oliver was present but had never had the tenacity to approach, not knowing how Beth would react, but doubtless fearful of the reputation Beth had of being a firebrand of a human who would likely become an aggressor given the figure of hate that he had held in her life.

Gwen had been much more tolerant of Henry's role in village life. As the wealthy local landowner, he was a benefactor and supporter of many clubs and events that happened – much of it anonymously. Henry had been the one who had paid for Adam Bostock's memorial service and wake at the village cricket club, where he was also the main patron. Ironically, and unbeknown to Henry, if he had not sponsored the fine cricket scorebox that was located on the boundary rope at Langley Cricket Club, then perhaps there would not have been the opportunity for early romance that his son and Beth had had during their latter teenage years. Gwen had regularly made it her godly duty to remain courteous and considerate to Henry, updating him on his grandson's wellbeing whenever there was an opportunity. He seemed very grateful for that, although he did not once ask about news from Charlie in the war overseas.

Beth's view of Henry had mellowed over the years, but she

was of a view that she could never forgive him for what he had done. In her eyes, Henry Aspinall was a sad, ageing man who had made the wrong choices in life and deserved his current unhappiness. Silas knew Beth's view very well and realised that this topic would always be sensitive for her, especially given Charlie's death and pending funeral. However, he decided that it was appropriate to raise the prospect of Henry meeting Oliver now rather than let it rest any further.

The week before, Silas and Melissa travelled south, but just after the publication of the Times article on Langley's 'brave brothers,' there was a knock at the door from a journalist from the local Macclesfield newspaper. Gwen had answered the door and turned to Silas before allowing the journalist to enter the cottage.

"Silas," she said in a hushed voice. "Do you think it would be good if Beth talks to this man from the local paper?"

Silas approached the hallway. The journalist immediately cowered from the imposing size of the giant in front of him. "Don't worry mate, I don't bite!" Silas said smiling, used to this kind of reaction from people he met for the first time. "Tell me what you would like to discuss with my daughter, and I'll ask if she's willing to talk. But be warned, she knows the journalism trade very well, so you'll not get any cheap story here."

The journalist was still only in training and so nervously described to Silas the kind of article he wanted to write as a follow-up to the nationally published story of heroism and tragedy. Silas felt it was credible and so disappeared inside again in order to discuss it with Beth. After five minutes, he reappeared at the door.

"If you head over to the bench in front of the chapel, Beth will meet you in a little while, and I hope you don't mind, but I'll be there with Oliver, her son, as he needs some fresh air today."

The young journalist happily consented to this idea and headed over towards the chapel. Five minutes later, Beth appeared and strode over towards the journalist. Trailing behind was the enormous frame of Silas holding the tiny hand of a little boy crossing the road, following his mum.

"I hear you want to know about my Charlie?" Beth said. "And what kind of a man he was?" The journalist nodded his head in acknowledgement of the brief that he had described and added that he had also read several of Beth's published articles and would also love to know more about her life and how she had met Charlie and also found journalism as an interest.

Silas had been playing hide and seek with Oliver inside the chapel for thirty minutes; in fact, at one stage, he had recruited the help of Reverend Pottinger, who had been preparing a sermon in the vestry. Pleased for a break, the Reverend and Silas took turns to hide from Oliver amongst the pews and acted surprised when the youngster eventually found them. Oliver's giggles filled the church and regularly produced equally loud yet much deeper laughter from the two adults, who were enjoying the game immensely.

Beth appeared at the vestry door, having finished her interview with the journalist, which had become much more of a career development session than any hard-hitting interview. However, she felt refreshed that she could talk so openly about her very happy life with Charlie and that she now had the privilege of raising a young son in Charlie's honour. The sight of her giant father squeezed into the pulpit, with a finger on his lip – demanding her to look away – caused her to add to the comic sounds of the chapel. Oliver was searching every pew and had already found the Reverend, and so together they were trying to find 'Grandad Sledge' as Silas was known by his grandson.

Having tried for a few minutes, Oliver got impatient and demanded that his grandad show himself. Silas then made some amusing mouse-like squeaks, and the giggling little boy ran up towards the pulpit and pointed with glee at the amusing sight of his grandad crammed into the small space. Having extricated himself, Silas let out a great big sigh and suggested an end to the game. He was pleased to see both mother and son laughing together. A sight he had not seen for a long time. They thanked the Reverend for the use of his chapel as a playground and exited. Whilst Oliver ran amongst the gravestones for a few minutes, Silas and Beth sat down on the bench again.

"So, how was the journalist?" Silas asked.

"He was fine. He's agreed to send me any article he writes and genuinely wanted advice about how he moves further in freelance journalism. I enjoyed discussing the business of writing with him," Beth said.

"And what about Charlie? Were you able to speak about him?" Silas added.

"Yes, that was fine, and I even stopped short of calling his father an ogre and a shit!" she looked at Silas, and they both laughed again.

This was the moment Silas had been looking for. "What do you think about allowing Henry to meet Oliver as a one-off and see where it goes? It would be nice for Oliver to know that he has another relative out there, and in the long run, it might help him understand his father's side of the family." Silas was uncertain about how his daughter might react and whether it was the right thing to do. In life, Silas had always believed it was right to give someone a second chance, and although Henry Aspinall had been given countless chances previously. This one was different, as it involved the only 'flesh and blood' that Henry had left on earth.

Beth turned towards her father. "I'm okay with that. Given what that man put you through, if you are willing to forgive him, then deep down inside me, I feel Charlie would also want to forgive him. However, I do not want anything to do with him. Dad, you can arrange to take Oliver to see Aspinall, but only just to meet him, and that's that for now."

CHAPTER 59 - WESTMINSTER

Elliot was excited and on edge. He hadn't felt this adrenalin rush since some of the early days in Westminster when Beth had prepared some of his most powerful arguments around land reform and public access. He felt that he was becoming stale at the slow progress the Government made in some of his more liberal stances on life. However, now, he had received a new injection of life from Cheshire in the form of Rudi. This new individual could help him shake the foundations. A German military man allowed to address a Parliamentary sub-committee during wartime – yet speaking about the need for a concerted push for peace.

Rudi was less excited; he was sitting alongside Elliot in the black Hackney cab that was turning into Whitehall. He suddenly felt very alone and foreign as he saw the famous public buildings of London's Parliament Square. The German wartime doctrine he had been taught was all about the destruction of these edifices of British power, and now he was about to enter them. He looked into the faces of British people on the pavements going about their daily business. A postman was emptying one of the famous red letterboxes. Bowler-hatted civil servants were walking along, thrusting their umbrellas out, making them look like they were almost in a military marching band. Shopkeepers were finessing their shop window message boards, trying to make some meagre profit from the scarce ration stamps that were out there. A baker's boy cycled unsteadily along the road overburdened with bread. A group of women in army uniforms were being briefed on something by a senior officer.

Rudi's mind drifted to his memories of Hamburg and Bremen and other Northern German cities; all of them would have similar scenes being played out, although he feared that German cities would all be in a much more desolate state. And the rations available to families would be scarcer than here in London. He knew that there would be a risk to his family at home once it was known that he had started to speak out in public, but like the decision he had made to redirect the Junkers plane away from Liverpool docks and the likely death and destruction of hundreds. He felt that his words and actions just might help avoid the further pain, death, and destruction of many more.

Elliot had secured an initial private appointment with none other than Prime Minister Winston Churchill at Number 10. Downing Street. Knowing that he would not have been able to get security clearance as Rudolph Schwalbe – the name was simply too Germanic – Elliot had used the name Rudi Ipsen to secure passage into Downing Street. The plan was once they had a private audience with the P.M., Elliot would reveal Rudolph's true identity to Churchill and explain the potential of using him as a willing political pawn. This was a high-risk strategy given that Elliot was smuggling an 'active'

German military serviceman into the home of Britain's highest statesman – on a whim that he could leverage his friendship with Churchill to convince the P.M. that this could become a landmark publicity opportunity to convince the British public that the war was almost over and that peace with Germany was close at hand.

The inside of Number 10. Downing Street was a hive of bustling activity. Rudi was astonished as to how a normal-looking terrace house could be entered from the pavement and reveal an interior of staircases, corridors and multiple meeting rooms. Civil servants rushed around, with the constant 'excuse me or sorry' remark echoing as they brushed closely passed each other – reminding him of the British and their inherited politeness. The political architecture of Germany in the form of Berlin's Reichstag could not have been a greater contrast to No10. Downing Street.

A stooped, balding figure with a cane approached them, puffing on a large cigar. Winston Churchill carried an aura about him, along with clouds of Cuban cigar smoke. The sea of civil servants parted and bowed their heads in reverence as he passed by. "So young Chapman," Churchill addressed Elliot. "What's all this about? Come into my private office, and let's hear what your latest wild idea is."

Elliot smiled to himself; few relatively junior politicians got so much as an acknowledgement from the P.M., but he had somehow sparked interest thanks to his liberal views and writings, particularly around the need for a tolerant social view of homosexuality. Despite pressure from more right-leaning Conservative party members, Churchill had never denounced the practice. He likely employed a number of gays amongst his staff, although as it was considered illegal at the time, they could never have admitted it and remained in employment. "Sir, thank you for agreeing to meet us," Elliot said as the door was closed by a staff member. "May I introduce a very special person to you? Rudolph Schwalbe, a Luftwaffe officer."

Churchill, who was now sitting in a large brown Georgian leather armchair with a portrait of George IV above him, exhaled a large cloud of cigar smoke and said, "How very interesting – Herr Schwalbe – how may we help each other?"

Elliot and Rudi left Downing Street and headed towards Westminster to find a public house to sit in and just reflect on the surreal conversation that had just happened with the Prime Minister. "Did he really suggest what I think he suggested?" Rudi said as Elliot returned with two pints of frothy Whitbread beer from the bar.

"I think dear Winston suggested that you tell your story to one of our most respected journalists. Become a media sensation and pronounce that Nazi Germany is a spent force and that peace is now the answer. Simple, eh?!" Elliot looked at Rudi with a grin. "What do you think of that?"

"I've seen enough propaganda in Germany to know the power of the media. I'm not sure if being used as a British spokesman is any different?" Rudi answered, blowing some of the froth off the top of his pint.

Oozing with enthusiasm, Elliot started his pitch, "I can see I may have some convincing to do here, Rudi, but just open your eyes to the prospect of what the P.M. has suggested. If

Winston Churchill has endorsed this, then the whole of Britain, the whole of Europe, and the world will see this story as emblematic of what's to come. A German officer of the Luftwaffe renouncing the philosophy of Nazism and fascism and being allowed to freely state a true belief in humanity and peace."

Rudi looked uncertain; Elliot continued, "This would be a chance for you to say what you really believe rather than do what your masters have commanded you to do. This would be free will – witnessed on a central stage. I've also thought about a photo opportunity back in Cheshire, in the barn where you were taken in and adopted by that lovely farming couple on Thomas's farm. Cloudy Hill or something."

"Bosley Cloud," Rudi corrected him.

"Yes, Bosley Cloud," Elliot repeated. "It makes the story so much more personal and also illustrates the kindness shown by the Bosley Cloud couple – normal English folk."

"Nat and Martha" Rudi was getting used to filling in the detail, whilst Elliot allowed his imagination to run free.

"Of course, the lovely Martha and Nat," Elliot said, "Well, this could be positioned as the 'come to Damascus' moment where you realised that good honest humanity would always conquer the darker forces of dictatorships." Elliot paused for a moment. "What do you think of that?"

Rudi still looked uncertain. "Elliot, you and Thomas have been true friends, as have many other people here in Britain. The fact that within the last hour, I have had an audience with Hitler's sworn enemy just blows me away. I'm not sure what to think right now."

Elliot recognised that his friend needed more time to consider the case presented. "Okay, Rudi, have a few more sips on that fine ale, and I'm sure it will help lubricate your thinking. I am certain we are on to a winner."

Two miles away, Mike Hodgkinson was being celebrated in the Times' Fleet Street offices. His front-page story of Jack and his band of brothers from the Cheshire Regiment in Liege had captured more readers for that edition than any in the previous three years. The Editors realised that what the nation needed were more 'hero' stories featuring normal people. The fact that Jack Moat – a quarryman and pipe-layer from Langley, East Cheshire – had, in the space of just over four years of active service, become a holder of the Victoria Cross, not once, but twice. The photo that Mike had taken in the convent in Liege, had been reproduced many times over, bringing more revenues in for the paper. For this reason, it was Mike who they had summoned up to their offices, having received a phone call from the Downing Street Press Secretary.

The highly confidential brief was interesting: to interview a German Luftwaffe officer who had 'seen the light' and decided that war was not the answer. The fact that this would be the first time that a British paper interviewed a German and that the subject was the peaceful conclusion of this painful war excited Mike's journalistic blood. He was chomping at the bit to be introduced to this airman – Rudolph Schwalbe. A nice bit of added irony was that the interview was due to take place at the RAC Club in Pall Mall, a bastion of Britishness. A private room had been arranged, and an M.P. was to be present – one Elliot Chapman, M.P. for Winchester. Mike had little more to go on than the brief that had come from Downing Street and that it was important enough for the then owners of the newspaper – the Astor family – to send a telegram to him with a good luck message. An unheard-of act previously, which made him rather on edge as he entered the small private meeting room on the third floor of the RAC Club.

"Mike Hodgkinson – The Times," he announced himself.

"Great article, Mr. Hodgkinson. I'm Elliot Chapman MP." Elliot started, "You captured the mood of the nation brilliantly; we all needed a little 'pick-me-up' with your story from Liege a few weeks back. I think we have another one here, and there may well be an intriguing connection."

"May I introduce Mr. Rudolph Schwalbe to you? This is the man with a story that I feel needs telling." Elliot backed away and made room for Rudi and Mike to shake hands.

"Very pleased to meet you, Mr. Hodgkinson; you may call me Rudi."

"And please call me Mike; no need for formalities here. I find that the reader wants to know the honest truth in an article, and formalities tend to hide facts, I find."

Rudolph visibly relaxed. "Thank you, Mike. I will be fully open with you, but I need you to know that what I tell you could impact my family back in Germany, so I just need you to understand this and treat it sensitively."

"You have my word, Rudi. I promise," Mike said as he took out his notepad and pencil.

CHAPTER 60 - *CATCHING UP*

Thomas had arranged for a private carriage on the train north for the returning heroes. Melissa cuddled up next to Jack, who had managed to manoeuvre himself from the platform side in Portsmouth onto the train and into the carriage, with just a little bit of help from others. Thomas, Silas, and Will sat facing the couple, relieved that the travel logistics had gone so smoothly. They now had a seven-hour journey to Macclesfield, hopefully arriving in just before midnight. The Station Master at Macclesfield – had been forewarned that he needed to ensure he was able to unload the special cargo arriving in the freight carriage and the need for sensitive handling. He had arranged for the coffin to be handled by a local funeral parlour, and Reverend Pottinger was already very aware of the scheduling of a Langley funeral in ten days-time.

Almost five years ago, Silas had bid farewell to his boy – Will – excited as he and his young mates headed off to do their service for King and country. Today, he was looking at a man who had grown up so much and seen too much. Will looked tired, but he had survived the war, unlike many of his comrades, particularly his brother-in-law. There was plenty of discussion about Charlie and how proud Oliver would be when he understood how his father had lived and died – to save his friends whilst serving his country. The posthumous gallantry medal, confirmed in dispatches, would be a permanent memory for the child to hold. His Uncle Will would always remind him all about the true courage that his father had shown, the same kind of courage in which he should be living his own life and taking on his own challenges.

In the train carriage, the whole tale about the Siege of Tobruk had been retold again, and the tragic death of Adam Bostock. Jack described the scene in the marketplace by the fountain when he was about to be shot by the Italian lieutenant. This was the first time he had revealed all of the details and the incredible coincidence of the identity of his guardian angel that day.

When Gustav Coccini's name was mentioned, Will gasped. "But that was the little bastard who was responsible for dad's imprisonment."

Jack replied, "I know, and this was perhaps his way of making it up to all of us and finding inner peace. Without Gustav throwing his body in front of the gunfire – I would be dead."

"Well, bugger me!" Silas muttered, as astonished as the others. "Thank God that he did what he did."

"Indeed," Jack added, "and his last words to me before he died were that of a confessional. He said, 'Tell Sledge – I'm sorry.'

Silas could not find further words to convey the thoughts that flooded his mind. What a strange twist of fate that, having had Silas almost killed for a crime that Gustav had committed, he was then in a situation in which he could seek penitence by committing the ultimate sacrifice in dying to save Jack. Perhaps equilibrium had returned.

Silas' puzzled face said it all to Jack, but he felt he needed to say the words that Silas portrayed. "Gustav had respect for you, Silas, and I think that the brotherhood developed in the quarry at Teggs meant that deep down inside, despite his criminal sidelines, he suffered painful guilt from which he needed to find peace."

Silas looked out of the window, and if Jack's shared thought was correct, he felt grateful that Gustav had been able to clear his conscience before finding eternal peace. Silas had never felt any direct grudge towards Gustav, as he had known that the Sicilian had never intended that the blame for his crime had fallen on his quarry boss. It was Henry Aspinall who had manufactured the story such that evidence was stacked against him.

Breaking the silence in the train compartment, Jack asked about Oliver and Beth and how they were coping with the news of Charlie. Melissa shared that they were managing the grieving process as best they could and were being well cared for by Gwen, Sledge, and the Langley community. "You know how determined Beth can be." Melissa started, "Well, she's outwardly showing stacks of strength and courage in trying to continue normally, but those closest to her can feel the utter desolation she feels at home in her room. All we can do is be on call for when she wants us and allow her the space to come to terms with the loss of Charlie." She continued, "Oliver has only ever known his dad through photos and the letters that Beth has read out to him. He is not yet old enough to fully understand the loss of his father, but when he looks and speaks to you, you'll see an uncanny resemblance in his mannerisms – it brings a tear to my eye every time I recognise it."

Jack and Will asked about every person in the Langley community. They heard about the memorial service to Adam and how Hilda Bostock had managed the most magnificent memorial tea at the cricket club. In turn, Silas asked about his quarrying friends – Fred, Andy, and Robin. They all laughed when they heard that the army had commended Andy and Robin for their riflery skills – having honed them in Henry's Aspinall's estate – poaching for wildfowl, deer, and boar. "The least Charlie's dad should give them for their heroism is a couple of free shooting permits for his land!" Will suggested.

Thomas responded with a wry smile, "That's a very fine idea, Will; I'll suggest it anonymously to the Macclesfield Chamber of Commerce clerk. If it gets raised in a committee meeting, it has to be answered, and as Henry sits on the Board of Trustees, I think it will be hard for him to reject." He added, "I know that the Chambers want to show their appreciation for their returning heroes – especially now, given the national news coverage."

Will smirked, "That would be epic.... Poachers turned Gamekeepers, in a whacky sort of way." The carriage erupted in laughter.

Jack was enjoying having Melissa snuggling up to him, and despite his physical injuries, life felt good for the first time in a long time.

The train to Macclesfield was on time, and Jon Shankins, the Station Master, had been true to his word. He had managed to get the Funeral Director and his team direct access to the platform, and they were easily able to identify and offload Charlie's coffin and transport it smoothly to the mortuary to await the funeral. As the train had pulled in, Jon Shankins and about twenty other people were lining the platform with their hats respectfully lowered from their heads.

Melissa recognised the two partners from the law firm she worked at – Harold Sperry and Jonathan Burroughs. Silas caught sight of a few older quarry workers and their wives who would have wanted to show their appreciation to Jack and Will – both having worked the quarry in more recent times. He guessed that Owain Jones must have let them know about the train timings. Two other men, one quite old, turned out to be Alistair Grainger and Wyatt Montgomery – old friends of Charlie's from Hoarwithy School – who had made the trip across from Bakewell to be there. Two female uniformed officers from the Cheshire regiment stood respectfully on the platform. They stood to attention and saluted as the train slowed to a stop.

Gwen, Beth and Oliver were not present, as Silas had said that they could say their welcomes back in the cottage at Langley – if they were able to stay awake that long. Gwen protested about not being present but backed down for the sake of Beth and Oliver. However, their presence was felt as a 'Welcome Home Our Heroes' banner was hanging on a wall at the back of the platform, created by the boys and girls from Langley Sunday School. Reverend Hamish Pottinger and Old Percy Ricketts stood on either side of the artwork, as they had been under strict instructions from Gwen as to where to hang it up and to make sure it was then returned to Langley, where she had planned to hang it over the Dunstan Inn sign, for a proper reception that was planned for the following evening.

Silas was touched by the human compassion on the platform. He noticed one more figure in the far shadows, away from the light. The person was holding a cane with a silver top that reflected as it caught the platform light. The Bentley in the small car park revealed that Charlie's father had decided that his presence was also needed at this poignant moment to see his son's coffin returning for burial.

Having watched Charlie's coffin taken off to the mortuary in silent, solemn respect. The welcome party then broke out into three cheers, led by Percy Ricketts. Melissa quickly got frustrated that Jack – now back in his wheelchair – was receiving too many hearty slaps on the back.

"Did these people not realise that his body was still recovering from multiple injuries?" she thought to herself. Thomas read her unease and intervened, ushering Jack and Melissa towards his chauffeured car. Silas thanked Jon Shankins for managing the train disembarkation so well, and then he and Will got a lift with Percy and the Reverend – together with the precious 'Welcome Home' banner.

The twenty-minute journey by road to Langley was uneventful, but the sight of Teggs Nose with the moon behind it caused Will to sigh and pronounce. "Home at last. There were many times in the last four-plus years when I never thought I'd see that sight again."

Silas replied, "You just wait for the hug your mum is about to give you; you may wish you'd have stayed away a bit longer."

The Reverend parked the car at the vicarage, and Percy, Will, and Silas walked the hundred yards back to the Post Office and the Ledger's cottage. A candle was burning in the window, creating a glow behind the curtains. Gwen and Beth were both downstairs waiting for them. Oliver was asleep upstairs; he would see his uncle – for the first time – in the morning. As the door opened, no words were exchanged. Mother and sister hugged Will; of course, they all desperately wished that Charlie was there too, but they understood that life had changed and needed to accept that this was the new reality.

Mike Hodgkinson was spellbound by the eloquent German in front of him in the RAC Club. He occasionally had to look across at Elliot to check that he was hearing what he was hearing. Elliot just sat there, seemingly as enthralled by the detailed description of Rudi's life in Germany and forced recruitment into the Luftwaffe by Hermann Goring. The manner in which the Nazi party doctrine had been forced upon Rudi and all teenagers and the fact that free speech became tantamount to a crime – were insights into why the disciplines of Germany's army were so successful in the early days. Also, when things started to unwind, how a hit on their Nation's confidence could spell disaster for the regime, recovery could never have been fully achieved if confidence was undermined from within. Rudolph Schwalbe was the personification of Germany's challenge – a man who was not afraid to ask questions. Successful dictatorships relied upon a society that followed the leader's philosophy without challenge.

A RAC housemaid knocked at the door and appeared with a fresh pot of tea and a plate of delicately cut sandwiches. Elliot thanked the lady and excused himself for a moment, suggesting that Mike and Rudi continue their conversation without him present.

Rudi recalled perfectly the details of the air crash, and the relatively spontaneous creation of his Danish alter-ego. The kind compassion he was shown by Martha and Nat, even after Martha had discovered his true background and identity. He described his emotions after having attended a memorial service of an English soldier – Adam Bostock – killed by Italians in Tobruk. Finally, he spoke about the chance meeting of Thomas Whetton, the landlord of the farm where he was staying, and then Elliot Chapman and how he had felt a compunction to reveal his true identity and tell his story.

Elliot had carefully briefed Rudolph not to speak about the involvement of the P.M. at this stage, as there was still political risk being taken. The warmongers amongst the Conservatives wanted to crush Germany into oblivion, whilst the P.M. and the moderates within the party – including Elliot – had always sought to find a solution that involved lasting peace and the ability to help rebuild Britain and Europe as a whole – including a democratic and peaceful Germany.

Elliot had returned to the room, carrying a broad smile on his face. Sensing that Rudi's story was at an end, he plunged in. "Gentlemen, apologies for leaving the room, but I had an idea and felt that I had to make contact with my good friend Thomas Whetton to see if he felt it was plausible." Elliot remained standing, as his highly energetic demeanour often meant that if he sat, he fidgeted, especially if he had an idea he needed to express. "Thomas has a very good relationship with Martha and Nat Lovatt; they would do anything for him. How about a photo of Rudi and the Lovatts at their farm?" Elliot looked directly at Mike, "And this – Mr. Hodgkinson – is where we could link in the soldiers you met in Liege. Will Ledger is the nephew of the Lovatts and lives in the same village as Jack Moat – Langley. They are both now home and will be at the funeral of Charlie Aspinall. As you know, Charlie was their close friend who tragically died in Holland in the fight for the bridge over the river Meuse. They returned only a few days ago and brought the body of their friend with them for burial in Langley."

"It might be a good way of wrapping up Jack Moat's story," Mike said. "Given that he was still in a hospital bed when you last saw him, and his longer-term prognosis was not great. If he is willing, then that would be a positive piece to the story. It would really herald this little part of England as a place where people are at peace."

Elliot was fidgeting again and exploded with his latest idea. "We might even get Jack – England's hero and double VC medal holder, sharing a pint with Rudi or shaking his hand. What a story of reunification that would be!"

Rudi was open-mouthed at the flow of ideas appearing before him – he jumped in. "Hold on, Elliot, last time I was there, in all but Martha's eyes, I was Rudi Ipsen from Denmark. The reaction of knowing a German was living a double life may not create the harmony that you describe."

Elliot thought further about this. "That's a good point. We will have a good amount of groundwork to do first, and we must ensure that whatever else we pay Charlie Aspinall's death, the full respect it deserves."

Mike nodded in agreement, "If, and it's a big if, we can get the Langley community onside, then I think this has got the potential to be a massive story – front, middle, and back pages."

"Elliot, the key to this is Martha," Rudi suggested. "Her brother is Silas Ledger, who also lives in the village and is a highly respected barometer of sentiment in Langley. Because Martha knows my secret, we should seek her views first."

"I agree," said Elliot. "Mike – you develop the editorial piece, and we will work on the photo opportunity to help you complete the story. We'll be in touch in the next two or three days."

CHAPTER 61 - *DRINKS ALL ROUND*

The 'Welcome Home' banner had been hung above the sign for the Dunstan Inn. Villagers crowded into the main bar room to await the arrival of Jack and Will. There was a strange atmosphere in the air. Everyone was conscious of the need to pay respect, considering that the funeral was due to take place the following weekend, but there was also much pent-up excitement about the first return of some of the village heroes after four-plus years of absence. Will was born and bred in the village of Langley, and his family was much loved. The loss of his brother-in-law, Charlie, was devastating, and everyone recognised the tragic juxtaposition that this presented. The picture in the Times newspaper had been framed and hung on the wall by the publican – Ned Croucher. A small gaggle of villagers were crowded around it, with one of them again reading out aloud the words that Mike Hodgkinson had penned about the heroic story of victory and tragedy.

The sentiment that the journalist had used in the article, summed up the moment well. 'With great joy, one often has to suffer intense pain,' and this was being recognised within the village that evening.

Beth's appearance in the street caused a temporary hush. Beth had not really been seen out of her cottage for a number of weeks, and the villagers had maintained a respectful distance despite wanting to show her that they cared deeply for the loss of her husband. Will and Silas quickly followed, with a laughing Oliver swinging joyously, hand-in-hand, between the two men It presented a show of family unity that broke the uneasy tension. Gwen was following the four of them, carrying a large teddy bear that Thomas Whetton had bought in London for Oliver. Thomas himself was due to arrive later in the evening.

Dick Avery, who had come down from the Setter Dog Inn to help serve drinks at the Dunstan, started to clap his hands, and a ripple of applause broke out down the street, quickly becoming a roar. The applause was an emotional gesture of support for Beth and a welcome home for Will. The village cared deeply about their kin. Simultaneously, more applause was heard from the other end of the street as Melissa wheeled Jack out of their cottage and down the main road towards the Inn. It felt like it had been synchronised, but pure coincidence was appropriate.

Nat and Martha Lovatt were the first to properly greet their nephew. "Welcome back, Will," said Nat.

"We so missed you," added Martha. Unable to hold back, she grabbed him and gave him a big hug.

"Steady on Auntie Martha! You'll crush me." Will laughed as he hugged his diminutive Aunt back. Nat looked at Beth and hugged her without a need for any words.

Gwen saw Jack from a distance and squealed with delight as she passed the teddy bear to Silas and ran towards him and Melissa. "Jack Moat, you are my hero!" she announced. "Thank you for keeping my boy safe."

Jack accepted the thanks, although Melissa noticed the slight anguish on his face. Jack would have to live his life knowing that he was unable to keep his promise about bringing Charlie back alive. He had worried about the moment that he would have to face up to Beth and Oliver, knowing that he was unable to bring home Charlie. His worry was quickly doused – Beth followed her mother over to Jack's wheelchair and presented Oliver to him.

"Oliver – this is your Uncle Jack – he was best friends with your father, and now he'll be your best friend." She leant down and gave Jack a hug, and whispered in his ear. "I know you did all you could, thank you."

"Why has his seat got wheels?" exclaimed Oliver. "I want a go!"

Jack smiled at Oliver but was too choked up to speak. Melissa helped to ease the tension, "Oliver, it's to help him race along the street. I'm sure Jack will give you a go in it later."

Beth winked at Melissa, "Oliver, it's to help Uncle Jack move as he has a poor leg at the moment, but I'm sure he'll play with you when he's able."

Still choked with emotion, Jack looked at the boy and smiled, recognising many of Charlie's own boyish looks. "That's right, Oliver, you and your Uncle Jack are going to have plenty of adventures. I promise."

"Don't leave me out of any adventures!" added Will, smiling and recognising that Jack must have been intensely affected by seeing a much younger version of Charlie.

Reverend Pottinger appeared from the Dunstan's porch – "Come on in everyone, the Cheshire Regiment have very kindly put money behind the bar for a number of drinks – so first come, first served!"

This was the signal for the start of an evening that felt like the start of a new chapter for the village. Of course, there were still many more sons and some daughters to return from wartime duties, but at least this day had arrived.

Thomas appeared an hour later and met Jack just as Melissa had decided that it was time for him to head home for some rest. Jack had spent much of the time in the pub, sitting beneath the newspaper cutting, with Oliver and his teddy sitting on the arm of the wheelchair, meeting and greeting well-wishers. Beth stayed close to her brother, who was being bought and immediately downing, pint after pint. She had several herself. Gwen stood with Silas, Martha, and Nat – surveying the scene and preparing herself to take charge of Oliver and the homeward trip. She knew that Beth needed to release some of the stresses of her life, and doing it amongst her family and friends was the best place.

Thomas caught Jack and Melissa at the doorway. "Can I have a quiet word outside, Jack?".

Thomas had spent a lengthy period of the afternoon on the phone with Elliot and Rudi down in London. They had described their meeting with the journalist – the very same one that had interviewed Jack and the boys in Liege. Elliot also indicated that the request had come from the highest of political offices. Thomas had questioned Elliot to confirm that the PM's office was involved, but Elliot played the classic politician by neither denying nor acknowledging this fact. However – the message had been clear that the British public could benefit from a reconciliation message, and Rudi and Langley had a part to play in this.

Thomas walked with Jack and Melissa towards their cottage, explaining the proposed article, positioned as a follow up to the very article hanging on the wall of the Dunstan. Jack was not opposed to it but was very clear that nothing should detract from Charlie's funeral in ten days' time. He was intrigued to know that this German officer he was to meet together with Mike Hodgkinson – the Times journalist – had knowledge of the Langley community.

Thomas headed back towards the Dunstan; he wanted to speak to Martha alone first, as Rudi had made it explicit that she should give permission for his story to be told and her part in it before any further discussions took place. Thomas also knew that he wanted to gain Will's support alongside Silas, and of course, Martha would need to gain Nat's agreement, given he might feel that he'd been hoodwinked by a German soldier benefitting from their goodwill.

As he returned down the road, fortuitously, Gwen, Martha, and Oliver, accompanied by the teddy that Thomas had bought as a present, were heading home. Grandma Gwen had decided that the pub had become a little too raucous for a youngster, plus the fact that Oliver was protesting that his new friend – Uncle Jack – had to leave, but that was no reason why he should also leave! As Grandma tended to do, she got her way.

Thomas called over to the group. "Evening everyone, I'd like a word with that teddy, please."

Oliver turned around and announced that the teddy was in need of hot cocoa and was too tired to talk to anyone. Gwen took Oliver inside the cottage and got busy at preparing the bedtime drinks.

"It's actually you; I need to speak with," Thomas whispered to Martha. "Can we just have five minutes alone?"

Whilst Gwen was busy heating up the milk in the kitchen, supervised by Oliver and his teddy, Martha and Thomas sat in the lounge.

Thomas started, "What I am about to say to you may sound far-fetched, but you are in a unique position to support a story that could hasten the end of the war." Thomas was surprised by his own dramatic effect; perhaps Elliot's colourful prose was rubbing off on him! Whatever, it had certainly captured Martha's attention.

"Really, Mr. Whetton, you're sounding like a politician. But go on, I'm intrigued."

"It's about your friend Rudi Ipsen, or should I say Rudolph Schwalbe!" Thomas paused, noting Martha's look of astonishment.

He continued to detail how Rudi had revealed his true self to Elliot and he in London, including the fact that only Martha had guessed his true identity, yet maintained confidentiality on a whim of trust in his values and approach to humanity.

Thomas then described what Elliot had shared with him over the phone and the idea about Rudi returning with a journalist to meet up with Jack and write a story about how Germany and Britain need to finish this war and focus on how peacetime should be shaped.

As Thomas described the idea, a thousand thoughts went through her mind. Primarily, though, it was about how Nat would react to her keeping all this secret from him and then how the rest of the community would react to knowing that a German had, unwittingly, walked amongst them despite Martha knowing the truth.

"I realise that there's no way that I could remain anonymous here. Too many people knew that Rudi lived with us for six months, but could we suggest that I never knew about his true background? Could we keep that secret?"

Thomas looked at Martha. He knew that she was such an honest, god-fearing lady and that the deception she had been harbouring thus far had been hard on her. To prolong the deception further would likely simply add to the torment. "It's up to you, Martha, but I feel that both Nat and the community know what an upstanding citizen you are, and you have been proven correct in your assessment of Rudi and his values." Thomas continued. "Not revealing his identity at the time has worked out in the long term, as your trust in him has led to him trusting the British system and agreeing to reveal himself and support the reconciliation message."

Noise from the kitchen suggested that Gwen would shortly be reappearing with a hot cocoa. "Okay, give me this evening to talk to Nat," Martha said, "I'll let you know tomorrow morning."

Chapter 62 - *A Story Told*

Rudi and Elliot were due to arrive in Macclesfield at 6 pm. Mike Hodgkinson was heading onwards to Manchester as he was meeting up with a professional photographer before returning to Macclesfield for the meeting with Jack, Will, and Rudi.

Martha had discussed the situation with Nat, who had himself admitted to some concerns about Rudi's story, but had given him the benefit of the doubt as he was such a willing worker and he had desperately needed help with dry stone-walling. In addition, the fact that Jess the collie dog had been so faithful to him – Nat had always thought that animals had better intuition than most humans – except for sheep!

Nat was also enthusiastic about supporting the Times article – as he saw none of the potential pitfalls that Martha had in terms of a possible adverse community reaction. He also felt an obligation to support anything that Thomas Whetton supported, given that it was Thomas who had saved them following the loss of Trentabank Farm fourteen years ago. Martha contacted Thomas immediately to give him a positive reply but added that she would not want any photography to include any images of herself. Fame was not something Martha Lovatt sought.

Thomas had also taken it upon himself to wait until the morning to talk to Silas and Will. He felt it unfair to talk to either of them that night due to the excess of free drinks being bought, but he felt positive that they would be fine if Jack and Martha were okay. He felt that Silas would be able to gauge the mood of the village and also be able to speak about it with Beth to ensure that any sensitivities around Charlie would be recognised and respected. Will would also provide continuity with the Liege story and provide support for Jack.

In the morning, both Silas and Will were positive about the story and felt that the community would be further impressed with any publicity generated for Langley. They acknowledged and underlined the need for Charlie to be recognised respectfully. Mike Hodgkinson provided a commitment that publication of the story would happen after the funeral; he also confirmed that he was happy for them to review the feature ahead of going to print.

Everything was now set for a private meeting between Will, Jack, and Rudi, followed by a facilitated conversation with the journalist and then a photo shoot. The photographer would have a chance to look at Langley's scenery and consider the best options to illustrate Rudi's story and the message of reconciliation. Rudi had asked if it might be possible to revisit the site of the Junkers crash at Roaches End. There was still a chance that once the story was made public, the authorities might want to sanction charges on Rudi for being part of a plan to cause atrocities on British soil. However, Elliot had already gained legal backing that this would be unlikely given the fact that Rudi's story was all about a realisation that no gains were being made from continuing to fight. In fact, the story could become a beacon for peace, and so any chance of an arrest being made, would seem contradictory. If anything, Elliot knew that having the confidential backing of Winston Churchill himself would be a considerable weight in favour of Rudi's protection.

The morning shone brightly across the Peak District. December's frosts had provided a sugary sprinkling of snow on the upper fells. Elliot's energetic mind was working ahead of others and had already pictured an amazing photo of England's natural landscape alongside an incredible story of positive hope, described by Rudi and written by Mike Hodgkinson. He was also thinking about the great old man – Winston Churchill – in his Chesterfield leather armchair, smoking a Havana and smiling whilst reading the Times newspaper. Comfortable in the knowledge that his young friend, Elliot Chapman, had delivered on his promise.

The group had agreed to meet at Langley Chapel, and as the weather was so good, they would then head out towards Sadlers Way and up Teggs Nose. The path was good enough to manoeuvre Jack's wheelchair up the path – especially given the fact that Silas and Will would be with them – both knew every inch of that track – and certainly had the muscle power to push their friend up the hill. Jack also knew the route intimately and was desperate to get back up to the quarry, having not been up there for almost five years. Silas had asked Dick at the Setter Dog Inn to have a kettle on the boil and a plate of sandwiches prepared to cater for the group as they could well be in need of a snack after the uphill climb. There was a seat near the summit where the group could sit and talk, and the photographer might want to take some pictures with Langley, Bosley Cloud, and the Peak District's moors in the background.

Before they started their walk, Jack and Will were introduced to Rudi, and the three of them sat on a bench in the graveyard next to a memorial stone remembering Adam Bostock. Thomas thought that it was a very poignant moment seeing the three soldiers, two British and one German, paying respects to a fallen soldier. The photographer, having opportunism as a requisite of the job, had already perched himself on a peripheral wall to get a photo of Will and Rudi, standing on either side of Jack, reading the inscription on the memorial stone.

Rudi was slightly younger than Will, who was ten years younger than Jack, but the German spoke with such honesty and composure about the remarkable events and reasons that had led him to the Lovatt's farm and a six-month stay, living as a supposed stranded Danish mariner. Both Will and Jack were immensely impressed and felt that the sincerity with which he spoke about wanting to help send a message of hope for Europe's future through advancing the publication of this story was one that they could fully endorse.

They started to walk towards Saddlers Way and the hills. Mike joined the three soldiers, listening in on their conversation. Rudi enjoyed hearing the amusing anecdotes that Will shared about his Uncle Nat and his passion for his sheepdogs. Jess was mentioned as a collie who also favoured Will whenever he used to visit Bosley Cloud before the war. Both of them agreed that Jess' was most skilled at running along any dry-stone wall and barking as soon as she reached a weakness in it that sheep might exploit as an escape hatch. Rudi also learned much about Langley's village life, the closeness of the community, and how that sense of affection was a driving force that helped soldiers survive in the most bitter of times. Those who lived amongst the village communities and who had been drafted and fought together – became true brothers-in-arms.

Jack found himself recalling how he had led that final reconnaissance mission on the bridge in Holland in a way that he had not previously remembered. He found a clearer memory of the fateful trench and how he had found Charlie standing still, looking at him. That final moment in which he knew that Charlie was willing to sacrifice his own life to give others a chance. Jack then described how, with tears flowing down his face, he mounted the trench and charged towards the German machine gun, intent on stopping this madness that had just taken his friend's life. He recalled throwing both his grenades and then silence as he lost consciousness.

There was silence amongst the group, with only the sound of squeaks from Jack's wheelchair mounting the cobbles of the drover's path.

"I'm very sorry," said Rudi, breaking the silence. "I'm very sorry that my fellow countrymen – and I – were forced into a position to play a part in an unjust war." He continued, "Nazi Germany, led by a fascist dictator, needs to be stopped. And thank God that it looks like he will be, sooner rather than later." He paused for a moment. "Beneath the surface, Germany is just like Britain; we have villages with communities that live in peace. We have farmers like Nat, who dote over their sheep flocks. Germany has hills and lakes and forests, just like these here", pointing towards the reservoirs and the pine trees of Macclesfield Forest.

"Humanity needs to heal political divides – and create peaceful ideologies that all of us can accept and live by."

Will clapped Rudi on the back. "Well said, mate! Just round that corner, we'll find the Setter Dog Inn, and I want to buy you a Cheshire ale so that we can toast to a new age in Europe."

The second group, walking fifty yards behind, consisted of Thomas, Elliot, and Silas. The photographer was moving between the two groups like a mountain goat, snapping as many angles as he could get, blessed by being out in a wonderful wintry landscape, so refreshingly different from the many cityscapes that he was more used to.

The lower group was conscious that the soldiers ahead were involved in some heavy discussions, but Thomas and, particularly Elliot, were confident that Rudi would win over the other two with his logic-led passion, intelligence, and his crystal-clear anti-war sentiment.

Elliot started to complain about the pace that the other two walked at, "Come on boys," he gasped. "There are no hills like this in London or Winchester," Elliot said inhaling deeply. "Have pity on my short legs and small lungs!"

Silas laughed at Elliot's heavy breathing. "Thomas – just

remind your friend here that I did this walk-up Teggs twice every day of my life, as did Jack and Will before the war. Perhaps Mr. Chapman might like to join me for a day at the Teggs quarry next month for a bit more hearty exercise?"

Thomas smiled – "Sledge, Elliot here could not even move the hammer you use, let alone swing it and break the stone. I'm afraid he'll do a better job arguing with other politicians at Westminster and probably expend just as much energy!" He looked ahead into the distance, "Elliot, this might motivate you. See that white house, just below the skyline – that is our destination – the Setter Dog Inn. The landlord there – Dick Avery – serves some of the best game pie, with most of the game coming from the nearby estates, although he'd never admit to that." Thomas looked at Silas and winked.

The whole day was a real success; true to his word, Will bought Rudi a pint at the Inn, and Dick had made sure a large game pie was warmed in the oven to reward the walkers for their climb. Elliot sat down in a window seat next to the journalist and the photographer and went over the options for the most impactful of story angles and the most appropriate photos. He wanted to make sure that the P.M. benefitted from the final published article, and so he was looking for some suitable reference without politics hijacking the purity of the story. Mike and Elliot reached an agreement on the overall sentiment of the article and also the timing – that being – publication following Charlie's funeral. The group said their farewells and parted company. Thomas had arranged for his car to pick up Elliot, Mike, and the photographer directly from the Setter Dog to take them back to the train station. Rudi had agreed to walk back to Langley and wait for Martha's school day to finish before being picked up by Nat and taken back to the farm on Bosley Cloud to a – no doubt – panting Jess, delighted to meet up with her old buddy.

That left Silas, Jack, and Will alone in the pub, with the landlord willingly topping up their pints from a frothy, bottomless jug of beer on the bar. Dick was keen to hear about his two young mates – Andy and Robin – who, together with Fred, were still with the Cheshire Regiment marching towards the river Rhein and the inevitable surrender of the German army. Silas had not really had any alone time with Jack and Will and was keen to double-check their feelings towards Charlie's death and his pending funeral. Jack revealed that he did not think he was strong enough to talk about Charlie at the funeral; the emotions were still very raw. However, he would write something for another person to deliver. Silas, but mainly Gwen, was arranging the funeral, with input from Beth whenever she felt strong enough to contribute. Amazingly, Beth wanted to say some words about Charlie. Will, who was never good at public speaking, felt that his involvement should purely be as one of the pallbearers together with any number of villagers who would be honoured to shoulder Charlie's coffin to and from the Chapel. Silas wanted an opinion on how involved they would allow Henry Aspinall to be.

Silas spoke, "Charlie's father is a different man from the one you knew many years ago. He paid for Adam Bostock's memorial service and plaque, and since I informed him of Charlie's death, he has been very respectful of Beth and her wishes, amongst all others. In fact, Beth has agreed for me to introduce him to Oliver soon after the funeral."

Both Jack and Will looked sceptical. "Dad, how can you so easily forgive a man that could have got you hung?" Will said, looking very uneasy.

"Sledge, I agree with Will. Henry Aspinall was evil and there's no way he has suddenly redeemed himself in my eyes thanks to a few small gestures," Jack added.

"I agree. It was tough to consider at first, but I thought about what Charlie would have wanted for Beth and Oliver." Silas paused for a moment and then continued, "I concluded that he would want any hostility to be put to one side. Charlie had seen what his father had done to his mother and how easily a loveless family could fall apart. I think that's why he was attracted to our home, in the heart of a community that cared for each other."

Will smiled at his father, "Dad – please – it was Beth that Charlie was attracted to; it just so happens that she has the best of brothers and not bad parents, too."

Silas smiled at his son, "Okay, I agree it was Beth, but it was also the way that village life provided a practical and safe environment for him. Unlike the 'win at all costs' commercial lifestyle of his father. The flooding of Trentabank and the way he treated Martha and Nat – were an example of his lack of human compassion. Thank God – Thomas Whetton was around to balance out the justice."

Will added: "And what about Sid Bayley at Nesset Farm? Henry Aspinall was responsible for Sid's suicide, no doubt whatsoever."

"Will, I agree Henry's actions back then were deplorable,

but that was over fifteen years ago. We have to consider Henry will have learned from his mistakes, and in my view, if Beth can support a reconciliation on behalf of Charlie and Oliver, I would hope the rest of us can."

There was a nod of agreement from Jack and Will, and although the subject of Henry Aspinall was a difficult one for them to accept, they all felt that they needed to respect Beth's decision.

CHAPTER 63 - *THE FUNERAL*

The day of Charlie's funeral was overcast, and the clouds lay low over the moors. Beth woke early and looked out of the window, above Macclesfield Forest and beyond. She recalled the time, up there, when she persuaded Charlie to commit his first crime when he helped to cut the barbed-wire fence that acted as a barrier to free-roaming, how they loved being able to run and leap from peat bog to heather clump – at one with nature. She remembered their first kiss at the signpost at the bottom of Saddlers Way. And then there were all those times in the score-hut at Langley Cricket Club, where Charlie had patiently tried to explain the rules of cricket to her, whilst all she was interested in was playfully mocking all of the different coloured pencils with which he used to annotate the scorebook so neatly. She would take Oliver up to the cricket club this summer and hopefully find a friendly scorer who could start to teach him the art and science of the score hut. Perhaps her brother and Fred Needles would be on the field and could start to give young Oliver a few bowling and batting lessons as well. Beth rather hoped that Oliver would reject the battle on the field in favour of the art and science of the score-hut.

"Tea's up", came the shout from downstairs; Gwen had been busying herself for several hours already, and this was her morning call to make sure she gathered a few helpers to manage the jobs to be done before the funeral started at 10 am.

Silas was stoking the fire in the hearth, with Nat providing helpful hints on the best way to get more ventilation beneath the coal. Martha was in charge of a large frying pan that spat with the sound of sizzling bacon. Nat and Martha had said goodbye to Rudi, who was traveling back down to London. Elliot had already headed south, but Thomas, as a Godfather to Oliver, wanted to be at the funeral to support Beth and his godson.

Gwen headed over to the chapel to ensure that the flowers were appropriately placed around the altar and that Reverend Pottinger was primed with any last-minute changes to the order of service. The local printer had kindly provided his service free of charge as Beth had been a regular Saturday worker there during her teenage years.

A familiar knock was heard at the wall; Percy Ricketts at the Post Office needed some attention.

"Will," Beth shouted up the stairs. "Will" she increased the volume of her voice. "Percy needs you!"

A yawning Will appeared at the foot of the narrow stairwell. His body completely filled the space. "Why me? Isn't Oliver old enough now to take on this job?"

"No, Will," Beth scalded, "Oliver is not even five yet, although I think Percy would love it if his little face appeared at the door."

"Please, mummy, can I go..." said Oliver, appearing from beneath Silas's bent frame. He'd been helping his grandad throw smaller sticks onto the fire.

Will scooped him up and ruffled his hair, "Come on then, soldier, time for your first adventure next door to see old Percy, and maybe he'll have a couple of gob-stoppers for you." Oliver's face sparkled with excitement as the two of them headed next door.

Percy was standing next to an uniformed officer. By the stripes on his lapels, Will quickly recognised a Major General, the highest-ranking officer he had ever seen, let alone met. Will immediately put Oliver down, stood to attention, and saluted. Oliver impressed by his uncle's actions, copied him perfectly. The Major General, who had come across from his headquarters in Chester, saluted back and asked the soldiers to stand at ease.

In a playful yet serious tone of voice, he asked for Will's name and rank. "Ledger, sir. Private William Ledger of the 2nd Cheshire Regiment." Will stood to attention and saluted for a second time.

"And you, young sir?" The senior officer looked down at Oliver, who grinned and tried to copy his uncle again.

"My name is Oliver Aspinall, sir, and Charlie Aspinall was my dad." Oliver said proudly, getting a little muddled over his salute as he smacked himself in the face." Percy let out a roar of laughter, quickly joined by the Major General and Will.

The senior officer spoke again, "Young Oliver, and his Uncle Will, I am deeply honoured to be here today. I am Major General Godfrey Budgeon," he quickly looked at Oliver specifically. "But you can call me Budgie"; he smiled and winked, and looked back at Will. "I am a representative of the army and of the Commander in Chief – King George VI. I believe Corporal Moat has asked if I might be able to say a few words at the funeral on his behalf. Again, I would be honoured."

Will gathered himself, "Sir, thank you. I know that Oliver and Beth – Oliver's mum and Charlie's widow – and all of the village would be very grateful. Jack has prepared some words, I think, that he would like you to read out."

Percy sniffed the air. "First things first Will Ledger, I do believe I can smell fresh bacon in the air. Perhaps the Major General might like a cup of tea and a bacon butty before anything."

"What a good idea." said the Major. "But first, I'd like to award a shiny penny to the person in the shop who can salute first." They all looked at Oliver to prompt him into action. And this time, Oliver managed to salute correctly – and the Major passed a penny to him to buy any sweets he wanted, but not to be eaten until his mum allowed him.

The Ledger cottage was now overflowing with humanity, with Oliver now firmly perched on the Major General's knee, joking with him about being called Budgie, just like the little caged birds Oliver had seen in Reverend Pottinger's vicarage. The bell on the chapel started to peal, indicating that there was only half an hour until the funeral cortege was due to turn up. The plan was that the horse-drawn hearse would stop at the outskirts of the village and then slowly make its way to the chapel, allowing mourners to walk behind, gathering numbers as they went.

Henry Aspinall was waiting for the hearse down at Gurnett aqueduct; he felt that he could walk alongside it for a mile until it reached the edge of the village. He wanted that time to be more alone with his son, to share some of his thoughts and feelings. To ask for forgiveness and apologise for the wrongs he had dished out on many people. The fact that his son had chosen to be a lawyer and to fight for people's rights, was an ironic underlining of their differences. He had hoped that Charles would follow in his footsteps and become an entrepreneur and industrialist, making a fortune and building the Aspinall empire. But right now, as he saw the black shire horses approaching the aqueduct, he knew that money and fortune meant nothing compared to a man's happiness, beliefs, and values. His son had been a much richer man than he could ever be. He watched as the funeral director walked ahead of the carriage, dictating the pace at which the horses moved. Already a small group of people had joined the procession but walked at a respectful distance. Henry recognised a few of them as workers from the law firm that Charlie had been employed at before the war.

He also noted that the coffin had 'Charlie' in white lilies on one side and 'Dad' in flowers on the other side. His mind wandered again – what would his own funeral look like? Who would be there? What had he done for others to make them feel as if they should show him any respect in his death? These were difficult thoughts, and he demanded that he put selfish thinking out of his mind. This was his son's day, and the attention should only be on him and the courage and bravery he showed to shape a life that he had himself determined. Henry very much hoped that in the coming weeks, he would be allowed to meet his grandson – Oliver – and he swore that all the pain and suffering he caused his own son would be replaced with love and affection for the next generation – if he were to be granted this favour. He had Silas and Beth Ledger to thank for this act of compassion, again one that he did not deserve in any form.

The funeral procession halted at the boundary line between Sutton and Langley, and Langley villagers filed in behind the carriage. Henry saw Silas and Will leading Beth and Oliver to the very front of the procession, followed closely behind by Martha, Nat Lovatt, and Gwen Ledger. Then came Jack Moat, walking unsteadily with a cane but nonetheless walking, helped by Melissa. Jack had promised himself that even if he was not able to help carry Charlie's coffin, he would walk alongside him. Thomas Whetton walked a few steps behind the Moats. After that, there were a number of villagers mixed in with uniformed army personnel and any number of other mourners. The procession must have contained over three hundred people tailing back down the road towards Sutton.

Will and the other pallbearers lifted the coffin from the hearse and began the short walk from the road into the chapel. The chapel bell had stopped its solemn peal, and silence prevailed. Jack took the place of the funeral director and led the coffin down the aisle, with the congregation standing in respect. Silas had offered Henry a seat with the family, but Henry had politely declined. He was not yet ready to forgive himself for the wrongs of the past, nor perhaps, would he ever be able to.

Oliver was aware that his father was there in the chapel, but only in a spiritual form. The wood container seemed unnecessary, but as everyone else was focussed on it, he kept quiet. Beth had convinced him that Dad would be playing hide and seek in that chapel for ever more. Oliver had taken that quite literally and had been busily scanning around the rows of male mourners to see if there was someone who he could recognise as his dad. To a person, they all looked back at him and gave him a smile or a wink. He felt reassured that all of them represented his dad in some way. He wasn't so sure about his mum's tears, gently rolling down her cheeks. He held her hand tightly, and that seemed to help her.

Reverend Hamish Pottinger welcomed everyone and introduced the first hymn, 'Abide with Me', followed by an opening prayer. The Reverend then spoke about his own memories of Charles Aspinall, quickly correcting himself to use the name Charlie. "Charlie was schooled away in Staffordshire near Bakewell, so we only saw him during holidays, but what a delightful young man he was; never happier than when he was in the cricket scorebox, ensuring the match was being correctly administered. In fact, an old friend of his, and I believe the man responsible for teaching him the fine art of scoring – Alastair Grainger OBE – has been asked by Beth to say a few words."

An old man started to walk down the aisle towards the front of the chapel, where the coffin lay on its stand. He was helped by Charlie's old school friend – Wyatt Montgomery,

'Monty', whom Beth had stayed in contact with during the war, and had now become a teacher himself back at Hoarwithy School. Alastair Grainger spoke so eloquently and lovingly of Charlie during his school days as a prodigious scholar and someone that he felt so deserved the bursary that the Old Boys Alumni had presented him, having fallen out of favour with his father. Henry Aspinall looked down to the prayer mat, shamed by the reference, but also felt that any public humiliation coming his way today was deserved and would be small compared to the immense guilt and pain he was feeling inside. Alastair finished his speech. Both he and Monty touched the coffin, bowed their heads, and then returned to their seats.

Major General Godfrey Budgeon then stood up and walked up to the coffin, taking his hat off in respect and bowing his head. He then turned to the congregation and invited Jack to join him. As Jack unsteadily got to his feet and walked towards the front, he stumbled. Will was positioned on the end of an aisle, and shot out a steadying arm.

"Private Will Ledger, will you also join Corporal Moat?" In the past, Budgie had attended so many funerals; he had gauged the mood of the village quickly enough and knew that it was important to have people they knew representing their fallen comrade, not some highly decorated, senior nobody. "It is fitting that Jack and Will are here today to mourn the passing of their dearest friend and brother – Charlie. I know how proud they were to walk alongside him in battle, and they should be proud now to be beside him as he rests in peace." The Major General paused and took a deep breath;

he'd caught a glimpse of Oliver cuddling Beth and giving her strength to go on. The emotions even got to a hardened, experienced soldier who had fought in World War One. "Beth and Oliver need to be the proudest of all here today as they bid farewell to their husband and father. I have been asked to read some words that Jack Moat has written, and I am so honoured to do just that."

"Charlie was more than a friend. He was calm and rational, whilst all else around was wild and lawless. Charlie was never a fighter. Firing a gun was always his final option. His judge and jury were, above all else, fairness and love for humankind. Pulling the trigger was a last resort. I should have known this due to his choice of law as a profession and his choice of Beth as a partner. They were made for each other – both with a passion for the rights of people, regardless of background or status. They found each other as two halves of a whole, and that whole was a beautiful world that created young Oliver. Oliver, I am very proud to call you, my Godson."

Jack looked down towards Oliver – smiled, and nodded. Budgie continued Jack's eulogy, "Charlie was welcomed into Sledge and Gwen's family and lived his teenage years there during holidays away from Hoarwithy School. It was during this period that I got to know Will and Charlie. I know Will won't mind me saying that he was the brawn to Charlie's brains." Will smiled at Jack and the congregation, acknowledging the truth. Budgie continued, "Often, Sledge or I would be faced with problems laying pipes or up at the quarry, and our answer would be manpower – put more muscle into the problem. Charlie taught us to take a step back and think rationally about the challenge. It was he who saved the Hollins pipeline by suggesting that lengths of pipe be brought by canal to Gurnett and then offloaded and dragged up the hill by a shire horse – old Battalion. None of us would have thought of that, but Charlie did." Jack nodded his head in agreement.

"In summary, and on behalf of Will and the other boys from Langley who are still actively serving in Germany right now – Fred Needles, Andy Souter, and Robin Brampton – we'll miss you, mate. We think of you and Adam Bostock now up in heaven. Adam will be racking up the runs whilst you'll be happily scoring for him." A ripple of amusement appeared from the congregation, and the Major General paused. "I know that Beth wants to say some final words now, so that I will leave it at that. Thank you for listening." Budgie nodded to Jack. He and Will then made their way back to their respective pews. "Thank you, Jack and Will, for your bravery and comradeship. You two and Charlie have all been honoured with rewards for the service you have been to the country. We are all in your debt."

Budgie then turned to the coffin, stood to attention, saluted, and returned to his own seat. Reverend Pottinger then made eye contact with Beth, quite prepared for her to shake her head, given the emotion that must have been swirling in her body. However, he was met with a look of steely determination. Beth walked up to Charlie's coffin, Oliver still holding her hand.

She spoke clearly, "Oliver never knew his dad, but through his friendship with his Uncle Will, his Godfathers – Thomas and Jack – and his Grandad Sledge, and the whole community of the village. He'll learn the values and attributes that Charlie had as a man. And I fell in love with a decade ago." Beth looked up at the congregation and located where Henry Aspinall was sitting. She continued, "I also hope that Charlie has shown all of us that the way to live life is through honesty, hard work and fighting for justice. Wealth comes from the values in which you live your life. I hope that Oliver will also be able to forge a strong and positive relationship, going forward, with his Grandad – Henry."

A small murmur arose from the chapel; it was well-known what animosity had been in the Ledger-Aspinall relationship for years, and here, very publicly, an olive branch was being extended. Henry Aspinall bowed his head, hiding his face from any member of the congregation who sought to see a reaction. Henry was struggling to accept what had just been said. It was hard enough facing Silas and his show of support a few weeks previous in the immediate aftermath of finding out about Charlie's death, but to hear those very public words from Beth was something he had never imagined. Indeed, it had been Beth and Charlie's love that had triggered the initial hatred that he felt towards the Ledgers. Ultimately, it was this that led him to plot against Silas and try to get him killed.

By the time Henry had raised his head again, Beth and Oliver had sat down, and the pallbearers were gathering to carry the coffin out of the church and into the graveyard for burial. Only family and close friends were invited to the internment. As Beth walked down the aisle following the coffin, she beckoned to Henry to join her and Oliver.

CHAPTER 64 - *WAR IS OVER*

Three days after the funeral, there was the familiar knock on the wall of the cottage quite early in the morning. None of the Ledger households had yet gone to work, and so Percy knew that he could possibly muster some help in the post office from his neighbours.

"How about us sending Oliver around this time?" Will suggested. "Percy will find it quite amusing that he's demanding child labour, although I'm sure it will be paid for handsomely in sweets!"

"Please, mum", Oliver wailed. "Let me go; Uncle Will can watch from the door if you're unsure."

"Okay, Oliver – you can go. Make sure you stay on the pavement and come straight home with the message from Percy." Oliver jumped up excitedly and ran to the door, getting his Wellington boots on in a hurry.

Percy was leaning on his counter studying something that Oliver wasn't able to see as he was too small. "Hello, young Oliver," said the old man. "Do you want to become my runner now?" he laughed, remembering the years that Will used to do exactly that. More people in the village had phones now, so he was not as reliant as previously on needing someone to run down the road with messages. He lifted Oliver up onto the counter. "Now see this picture – who is it of?" He pointed to the front page of the Times newspaper.

"Wow - that's Uncle Will and Uncle Jack, and who is that man there?" He pointed at Rudi's image.

"That is the name of a very brave German soldier who lived in this area for some time but has now decided to speak out against the German State and that nasty little man – Adolf Hitler." He lifted Oliver back down to the floor of the shop. "Now here's an aniseed ball, pop that in your mouth, and don't tell your mum. Run along and take this paper to your family; they'll be keen to see the picture, and perhaps you can get them to read the words out to you." Oliver ran out of the shop, happy with his first paid errand and happier to be sucking on a delicious sweet.

Ten minutes after Oliver had delivered the newspaper back home, Melissa was in the shop getting her own copy to take back to Jack. "Does it reflect well on the village and our boys?" she asked Percy.

"Does it just!" he exclaimed. "We'll be lucky if we don't have bus-loads of tourists pulling up shortly. A couple of the pictures that the photograper got of the local snow-capped hills look like they're out of a Swiss travel brochure. The Alpine pastures of Langley!" Percy joked. Melissa took a copy and headed home to share the newspaper with Jack.

The main photo on the front cover was the picture of Jack,

Will, and Rudi paying their respects at Adam Bostock's memorial stone. Jack was pleased that Adam had featured in the story given that he had been dead now for almost three years. "Gone, but not forgotten," he muttered. Charlie also got a very positive write-up. Jack was pleased there was no mention of his foolhardy charge on the German machine gun, as although incredibly brave, it was also incredibly stupid and would have been sufficiently fatal, but for the machine gun needing to be reloaded for him to be able to throw the two grenades that he carried.

The article highlighted the need to focus on sustainable peace and how the shape of Europe would look. The realisation of the threat from Russia was gaining traction, as it looked like they would be rewarded and compensated with sovereignty over other Eastern European countries in gratitude for their weakening of German resolve to the East, allowing Allied forces to strengthen in the West.

Rudi gave a very good account of how Nazism had ruined Germany, with fascist leadership breeding fear amongst the people. Mike wrote that Rudi had experienced unity and an upbeat resolve amongst the British people that he acknowledged was missing in Germany. He also found that there was war fatigue and a genuine desire to find peace. This he thought Germany shared whole-heartedly but was not allowed to admit it out of fear of Hitler and his SS guard.

Down in London, Elliot had received an early edition of the newspaper. He was delighted at how insightful Mike Hodgkinson had been in writing the article with just the right amount of emphasis on the human story, as well as the political message. He was certain that Winston Churchill would be pleased.

The phone rang. "Chapman, is that you?" the gruff old voice of a man who had sucked on too many cigars was unmistakenly heard at the other end of the telephone. "Do you have that young German staying at your's still? I'd like a word."

Elliot was gobsmacked; he'd never received a telephone call from the PM before. He immediately passed the phone across to Rudi, mouthing that it was the British Prime Minister on the phone. "Herr Schwalbe," Winston started, "Vielen dank for your part in progressing the idea of peace between Britain and Germany. History will mark your contribution to be..." He paused for dramatic effect. "Significant. Please accept my government's thanks, and I hope that Mr. Chapman is making your stay in London most enjoyable."

Rudi was astonished by the call, "Thank you, Mr. Churchill. I to hope that Germany moves quickly to accepting a peace treaty, and together, we can rebuild in a more mutually beneficial way. The phone went silent.

Following the publication of the Times article, despite a highly positive public reaction, there were still people in London and in more extreme right-wing political circles who were unhappy that a German who had participated in a bombing raid on the UK was walking free, seemingly immune to any form of prosecution. Letters received by the Times newspaper in preceding days suggested that it would be safer for Rudi to be placed under voluntary house arrest in Kensington at Elliot's apartment until any anti-sentiment disappeared.

"I'd feel much safer up in Cheshire," said Rudi. "Nobody would find me on Bosley Cloud. In fact, nobody did find me, he said with a smile."

"Stay here for now," Elliot replied. "Thomas gets back in a few days; we can review the situation then."

In Berlin, Hitler's intelligence services were still monitoring foreign press closely. Although operationally, they had been severely impaired by reduced resources; they still had sleeper cells active in a number of foreign cities. Rudolph Schwalbe's act of gross disloyalty to his country and challenge to the Third Reich demanded a response.

The police weren't able to determine how the intruder had gotten into Elliot's apartment, but one week after the article was published, Rudolph Schwalbe was dead.

The police report and post-mortem indicated that toxic substances were found in the medical analysis of Rudi's blood, pointing towards a planned and professionally targeted assassination. The likely perpetrators were foreign (German) agents still active in Britain. At the time of the murder, Elliot had been in Westminster in the Commons, and Rudi had been alone in the apartment, writing a half-finished letter to his parents. Thomas was due back later that afternoon and had been the person who found Rudi's lifeless body slumped over the writing table.

Elliot looked at the letter. Rudi had been explaining his actions to his parents back in Bremen. Elliot could tell that the words he had used had been carefully crafted to explain how, in his heart, he knew that this war was unjust, and he felt that his actions might be able to help accelerate the end. Elliot put the letter to one side, committing to passing it on to the Schwalbe family, adding his own eulogy to the bravery of the man who had put humanity above politics and his own life.

It was devastating news and made further headlines in all of the newspapers. The fact that Germany still had connections to active assassins in London made anyone of political notoriety double their security. In Hitler's deranged thinking, disloyalty to German nationalism was the ultimate of crimes, and death was the sole option. The media covered the murder widely, yet there was a definite swing in sentiment from the right-leaning papers. In their eyes, patriotism – above all else – demanded total loyalty. In Rudi, they saw an individual who stood for European unity but someone who had blatantly betrayed his mother country, regardless of whether it was Germany. These were the voices of nationalists who wanted to exact full retribution upon the German state and all their allies. 'Germany in chains' was the hope and expectation of these people.

Rudi was cremated after a secret ceremony in Highgate Cemetery, North London. Mike Hodgkinson attended, as did Nat and Martha Lovatt. Martha left a wreath at the crematorium 'from the villagers of Langley – much love to Rudi Ipsen – our Danish friend.'

Elliot was devastated that it was his apartment that had

been the location where Rudi had been killed. He and Thomas moved to the RAC Club and his house near Winchester. The Kensington apartment was put up for sale immediately. Elliot was also deeply disappointed that Winston Churchill distanced himself from any involvement in the incident. Unbeknownst to Elliot, Winston was already planning to step down as the PM, with his wartime deputy Clement Attlee replacing him. It was felt that a high-profile diplomatic incident involving the PM was not needed, especially as peace treaty papers were already being drafted in Berlin.

In Langley, the news of Rudi's death was felt deeply, particularly by those few who had met him and realised that they were in the presence of a man genuinely committed to peace. He was to be the last casualty of the war that Jack and Will knew, and it felt chilling that even back on English soil, evil was present. Many messages of condolence were passed to Martha and Nat before they embarked on the train to attend the cremation. Percy refused to sell some of those national papers that were carrying 'served him right' messages. Prayers were said in the Langley chapel on the night of the cremation – praising the humanity and good nature of Rudi Schwalbe, the friendly German officer.

Otherwise, life was getting back to normal on the edge of the Peak District. The quarry on Teggs Nose was back in full production, as gritstone was needed to help rebuild some of the infrastructure lost in the war. Silas and Owain had done a good job in reworking manpower plans and machinery around the five quarries in the area that were now managed collectively under the Whetton company name. Despite the mechanisation of quarrying, they still needed plenty of men, and more were becoming available as soldiers signing off from active service were now looking for work again.

The Potsdam Agreement was signed in August 1945, ending the war. In May 1945, Germany unconditionally surrendered, and those British troops still active in the field were sent home in a phased way. The 2nd Cheshires came home in June, and it was on 14th of June that Langley's main street was filled with villagers, bunting was tied along the trees, and Union Jacks were everywhere. The Dunstan Inn was the focal point and had celebratory music pouring out of the window on a gramophone that Ned Croucher had been able to acquire – with the help of Arthur Brice – from the Aspinall Manor House on Ridge Hill. In fact, it was Henry himself who had helped Arthur carry the gramophone into the pub from the car outside and set it up. Dick Avery had insisted that he should be in charge of the records, and Henry had accepted that for the price of a free beer.

Since Charlie's funeral and being granted permission to spend time with his grandson Oliver, Henry had become a different man. He was a much more benevolent individual in every way. He now always attended Sunday Services at the Langley chapel and had even joined the choir. Gwen was aghast the first time she saw him lining up to attend rehearsals for the Easter service, but his voice was very strong, and the female-dominated choir needed some baritones. Henry had stayed clear of the Chambers of Commerce in Macclesfield and his other Committee duties, recognising that the politics of business were often shady and where he had played in the past, he was unwilling to play ever again.

The East Cheshire Cricket League benefitted from a sponsored trophy called the 'Adam Bostock Memorial Trophy', which was to be played across the county, but the final of which had to be played at Langley. Henry Aspinall asked Hilda Bostock to become an Honorary President, although her sole responsibility was the teas on finals day. The whole village benefitted in different ways from a landowner who had seen the light and now understood where he could best honour his son. Foremost in Henry's mind was how he could perform as Oliver's grandfather now that Beth had given him full license to become part of his life.

'Roll out the barrel' – a cockney drinking song was blaring out of the Dunstan, with plenty of vocal accompaniment of questionable quality coming from the pavement outside as the chapel bell started to ring. The pealing of the bell had been choreographed between Percy and the Reverend, and some youngsters who were stationed at the edge of the village had been included. As soon as they saw an army truck approaching, they were to run up the road and signal to Percy at the Post Office; Percy was then set to signal to the Reverend to start pulling the bell rope.

Fred Needles was the first to get out of the back of the army truck. Silas thought that he'd got thinner since he'd been away – no doubt army rations helped to keep the weight down. Then came Andy Soutter and, finally, Robin Brampton. Silas thought that the fact that these two troublemakers had made it through five years of war without any visible sign of injury was amazing.

Jack was now walking unaided, and he and Will flung themselves at the three men. To see all five soldiers back together again was so touching – made more so by those who should have been there with them – Adam and Charlie. The whole village crowded around them, and a spontaneous 'three cheers' was shouted. Moll Brampton flung herself at her brother and then quickly turned to Fred and gave him the longest lingering kiss that Langley Main Street had ever seen! The flickering romance that had been present when Fred went to war was being well and truly set on fire again!

Fred, with Moll by his side, looked over at the Dunstan Inn, pointed and shouted, "I believe the Cheshires have purchased several of Ned's finest barrels – the beer is on the regiment!"

Cheers arose from the throng of people as they pushed their way into the pub. Silas decided to stay at a distance and just observe; it was proper that Will and Jack had space to be with their friends again. The atrocities that they all must have witnessed together could only ever really be understood by those who stood alongside them. He was aware that Will was suffering nightmares on regular occasions and was waking up screaming with terror. He had been referred to a military psychiatrist to start to work through the traumas. The outpouring of joy that was happening in the Dunstan right then could still not compensate for the pain and suffering each of these soldiers had endured.

Gwen noticed her husband sitting on a bench, observing the jollity. She sat down next to him and held his arm tight. Without words passing, she understood that her caring, loving husband would have preferred to take all of Will's and the other's pain and tackle it in his own way. He was always willing to sacrifice himself for others. "They'll all be okay," she whispered to him. "We'll be there to pick them up when they fall. That's all we can do."

Inside the pub, dancing had started, with the gramophone taking centre stage. Jack and Melissa were sitting in a small alcove to one side of the bar. Will approached and asked Melissa for a dance. Unusually, she declined such an offer. Will looked quizzically at Jack. Jack smiled and looked at Melissa, who nodded her head. "Yes, Will, we're expecting a child; Melissa is twelve weeks pregnant."

"Wow!" exclaimed Will. "Who knows?"

"Only Beth to date," said Melissa, "but I think more are going to know very soon." She smiled at Jack, who was standing up, tapping his empty tankard on the table to gather everyone's attention.

"Everybody... it's great news that Fred, Andy and Robin are home again." Cheers rose from the revellers. Jack raised the volume of his voice. "Hush for a moment as there's more good news of a personal kind." He looked over at the beaming Melissa, "Melissa and I are expecting a child." The bar room exploded with more cheers and applause. Silas and Gwen came to the door, intrigued to understand what all the commotion was about. As they got close to the porch, Moll came out of the pub and gleefully announced, "Jack and Melissa are expecting a baby!"

Later that night, Henry Aspinall and Dick Avery spent several hours together in the Dunstan Inn, discussing the merits of various records in Henry's music collection. Dick was trying his persuasive powers to play more jazz-style music – having got the bug for it from the American soldiers who worked in the quarry a few years previous. Two more contrasting individuals, one would be hard pushed to find. But it seemed as though Henry and Dick were hitting it off fine, no doubt helped by the plentiful supply of special thirty-year-old port that Ned had promised to open on the night that the final few soldiers arrived home.

"How about announcing it now?" Dick said to Henry, "You'll have a very supportive audience." He turned the gramophone down, causing a tirade of friendly heckling from the dancefloor.

"Hush, everyone!" said Dick. "Our local landowner has something to announce." Turning to Henry, he handed over the floor.

"Ladies and Gentlemen." Henry started with a slight slur in his words, "I know that my friend Dick here has fallen on hard times recently, as his magical supply of prized game has dried up somewhat. Possibly because the source of that game was away fighting for our country."

Robin and Andy looked aghast for a moment, suddenly understanding that their former years as Dick's poaching duo had been rumbled by the very landowner from whom they had been stealing. Dick's smiling face reassured them, and they soon realised that arrest warrants were not about to be issued.

Henry continued, with a broad grin on his face, "So in light of the downturn in trade, I am delighted to announce that

Andy Soutter and Robin Brampton will, from now on, be offered annual 'legal' shooting and fishing licenses, honoured across the whole of my estate." Cheers broke out in the room. "And what's more, The Setter Dog Meat & Fish Trading Company, managed by Dick Avery, will now become a licensed Aspinall partner and trade officially, with heavily discounted prices to all Langley residents."

More cheers erupted from every one, with Robin and Andy forced through the throng to accept Henry's congratulatory outstretched hand. "And I expect both of you to poach responsibly now that it's legal, you little buggers!" he added in a lowered voice.

Dick had managed to manoeuvre a jazz record onto the turntable and turned the music up. Moll grabbed Fred and started whirling him around the room, to everyone else's general amusement, as Fred had no idea about what dancing to jazz looked like. His helicoptering arms better resembled his cricket bowling technique than any sort of dance move.

CHAPTER 65 - *FISHING*

Melissa and Jack had a daughter named Sara. She was born on the same day as Oliver but five years later. Destined to be linked by their family's friendship anyway, the two of them now also had birthday celebrations they could share.

Henry Aspinall became a devoted grandfather to Oliver, taking him on adventures around his estate every weekend. Sometimes, the two of them would ride a horse up on the moors and look over towards Kinder Scout. Beth would remind Oliver of the story of his father, Charlie, getting wrongfully arrested for trespass in 1932 – a useful lesson in sticking up for what you believe in. Henry had asked Arthur Brice to remove all 'Trespassers will be prosecuted' signs from the estate. An action massively appreciated by Beth, although she still secretly harboured an idea that he could put up signs welcoming ramblers instead. Perhaps in time!

On other trips, Henry and Oliver would climb Teggs Nose, meet his other Grandad and watch the quarry workers splitting rock with the mechanised saw. On occasions, Oliver was allowed to sit in the workshop, sharing sandwiches with Owain Jones, who had tremendous stories about the Welsh hills and mystical dragons that lived in Snowdonia. Even though Oliver had lost his father before they'd even met, Charlie seemed to come alive through all of the characters that filled his life with rich images of the kind of man he was.

The following spring, Henry asked Beth for permission to take Oliver up to Trentabank reservoir in order to fish. Beth was trying to finish a research paper for Elliot's latest work on prison reform, so she was delighted that Oliver would be out in the fresh air all day. A young forest now surrounded the Trentabank reservoir at the far end of the dam wall.

A heronry had just started to get established on one side, and on the other side, Henry had been informed by Robin and Andy that the best trout could be found, feeding off the mayflies that were abundant at that time of year. Henry set up both rods close to each other but far enough away to cover a broad sweep of water. Oliver was so excited to be able to watch the float bobbing around, imagining what was happening beneath the surface of the water. Henry was also watching his float, but his mind wandered to the middle of the lake, and what he knew was under the water there. Two eery ruined farmhouses, no doubt now inhabited by all sorts of water life. He remembered his role in the flooding of the valley and his despicable behaviour in evicting his tenant farmers, one of which took his life as a consequence. He swallowed hard; how could anyone have been so callous? Perhaps, as a consequence, he had been punished himself by losing his own son, spiritually and physically. Now, it was time to make up through his grandson. A heron swooped low on the lake, looking for any small ripples in the water,

575

indicating a surfacing fish.

"Oliver, are you getting any bites?" Henry asked in a hushed voice.

"No, Grandad, but I think I'm about to get a whopper," the young boy said, stretching his arms wide across his chest to exaggerate the size of the imaginary monster trout.

The bank of the reservoir was quite steep at the area where they were fishing and was sodden through thanks to a very wet April. Oliver was on his little camp chair, sitting well back from the edge to ensure there were no accidents. A picnic basket, provided by Gwen, had been dropped off by Arthur Brice, Henry's land manager, and was located between the two fishermen.

"I'm hungry," said Oliver, looking eagerly at the wicker picnic basket.

"That's okay; how about getting one of Grandma's sandwiches now? I'll keep an eye on your float," Henry said.

Oliver jumped up and raced towards the basket, undoing the leather strap. Just as he was lifting the lid, he was suddenly aware of ripples appearing in the water. He turned to see his float disappear.

"Oliver – I think you've hooked a whale!" shouted Henry.

In his excitement, Oliver turned and ran back towards his fishing station. He tripped on a silver birch tree root and lost his footing, falling down the bank and into the water.

He was too shaken to make any audible noise, and as he was now out of sight of his grandad. Henry could only hear the splash to understand the exact location where he entered the reservoir. Henry sprang up from his seat and ran towards where Oliver had gone over the bank. He had grabbed a landing net that had been placed between them as it had a long pole, which might prove useful.

Henry looked over the bank and saw Oliver floundering around half in and half out of the water. He was so shocked that he wasn't really making any sounds other than a quiet whimper. "Oliver, I'm coming!" Henry shouted as he slid down the bank himself. The water was icy cold on his legs as he struggled to find a position in which he could hold Oliver up out of the water. There was a small ledge on which he was able to sit the small boy, but it meant that he had to stay almost fully submerged in the water.

He spoke to Oliver, reassuring the young boy that it'll all be ok. Oliver was wet and cold sitting on the ledge, although at least the upper part of his body was still mainly dry, and his mother had put on extra layers that morning. Henry was in a more threatening position. His whole body was wet, and he had to stay almost wholly immersed in water in order to keep one arm outstretched, keeping Oliver balanced on the ledge. Without assistance, Henry could not see a way out of their predicament. Perhaps there was a chance to swim with the child to a shallower place, but Henry himself was not a strong swimmer, and by the minute, he felt himself getting colder and weaker.

The only option was to keep Oliver's spirits up and shout for help, hoping that someone was within earshot of the reservoir. "Oliver," said his grandad, breathing heavily. "I need you to be very brave and think about your dad and how brave he was during the war." Henry stopped for a moment to summon up more strength, "I need you to shout as loudly as you can." He stopped again, realising that he was only going to be able to keep the boy on the ledge for a few minutes at most.

Oliver started yelling whilst his grandad concentrated on keeping his grandson on the ledge. Suddenly, a voice responded to the child's high-pitched yelling. It was Arthur Brice; he had come to check that everything was okay with the fishing rods and tackle that he had brought that morning from the gamekeeper's cottage.

Arthur was older than Henry but had always been a practical outdoorsman. Assessing the situation, Arthur used the landing net and got Oliver to hold it tightly. This then freed Henry up to reposition himself and try to find a part of the bank in which he could stand. Arthur hauled Oliver up, and once at the top of the bank, he quickly swaddled him in the picnic blanket to give him some heat. He then went back to the bank and peered over to find Henry.

Holding Oliver up out of the water for that long must have used up all of Henry's strength and energy; his body was limp in the water, and hypothermia must have set in. Henry was unresponsive to Arthur's shouts. Again, using the landing net, Arthur was able to bring Henry's body to a shallower area and then pulled the body out of the water. His face was blue, but his mouth moved, trying to say some hardly audible words. Arthur leaned closer to try to make sense.

"Oliver – look after Oliver. I'm so sorry." His breathing then faded.

Arthur laid Henry on his back and started to massage his

heart. After several minutes of trying and simultaneously shouting in vain to attract attention, he had to rest himself. There was no pulse. Henry Aspinall was dead.

Assessing the situation and having Oliver out of sight, decided Arthur on the only course of action he could take. He had to leave the older man and make sure the young boy was ok. Oliver was shivering but wrapped up in the blanket; he was comfortable, oblivious to his grandfather's condition.

"Come on, Oliver, we need to get you to a place where you can change your clothes and get warm. I'll come back and look after Grandad Henry later," Arthur said, believing that others would be better placed to break the news of his grandad's death to him.

Arthur carried Oliver to the nearby estate truck and put him in the front seat, strapping him in tightly. Arthur drove immediately to Langley and the Ledger cottage, where he knew Beth would likely be. Beth and Gwen were at the door. "What's happened?" Gwen exclaimed. Oliver was being comforted by his mum.

"Mum, I'll just take Oliver through to the kitchen and make him some hot cocoa." Beth said. "Will, can you come out? I think we might need you."

On the doorstep, Arthur described the scene that he had come across on the side of the reservoir to Gwen and Will. Then, he quickly excused himself as he needed to use the phone at the post office to call P.C. Keith Aikin, the local policeman and a friend of Arthur. They needed to get an ambulance up to the reservoir. Will joined Arthur at the post office and waited for the police vehicle to arrive before leading them back up to Trentabank and the scene awaiting them.

It was the same as Arthur had left an hour previous. Henry's cold, still body lying to one side. PC Aikin lay a blanket over the body and did a cursory search of the area, peering over the bank to see the small ledge that Oliver had perched on and the still disturbed muddy water below, where Henry had fought to maintain footing whilst holding Oliver above the water.

"How very sad!" the police officer remarked.

"Indeed, it is," Will answered. "But in some ways, this is a fitting end. It allows Henry some level of redemption from all of the wrong-doing he did with his own son. His final act being to save his grandson."

Despite Silas having forgiven Henry, Will could never find it in his own heart to forgive. However, in this one single act of self-sacrifice, Henry had earned the kind of respect that had forsaken him in life.

CHAPTER 66 - *THE WILL*

Following the required formal procedures from the Authorities, Henry Aspinall's body was released for burial. His solicitor – Mr. Linus Farbrother – had details of Henry's wish to be buried in his estate next to his wife, Florence. The funeral was intended to be a small affair, although many Langley villagers attended as a show of gratitude and respect for Henry's more recent benevolence. The Ledgers were there in full attendance.

The six-year-old Oliver could have been traumatised by the whole incident but was shielded from the full truth by some carefully woven words from Beth. According to her, Grandad Henry had died from a heart attack unrelated to the incident at the reservoir. A good outcome for Oliver had been finding a new 'old' friend in Arthur Brice. Being the Aspinall Estate Manager, he had access to all of the gamekeeper's equipment – and all of the hunting and fishing trophies collected over the years on the Estate. There were many majestic-looking mounted stag heads and ferocious wild boar and cunning foxes in the collection. There were even stuffed buffalo and antelope heads from hunting safaris in Africa. All of these were made more vivid and enchanting by Arthur's grossly exaggerated and amusing stories of the hunts that took place. However, the collection that impressed Oliver the most was the fish. Massive pike, sleek salmon and multi-coloured trout caught on the Estate, were all mounted in glass exhibition cases. Oliver's first fateful fishing expedition had not put him off the thought of many more, and Arthur Brice definitely seemed to be the right person to lead in future, and he knew that his mother would insist on a second adult being present at all times.

Four weeks after the funeral, Linus Farbrother requested a meeting at the Ridge Hill manor house. Invitations had appeared for those people who would be beneficiaries of Henry's will. A number of people were surprised to be asked to attend. This included all of those soldiers who had fought with Charlie; it also included a number of Langley villagers – Percy Ricketts, Ned Croucher from the Dunstan Inn, Dick Avery from the Setter Dog, and Reverend Hamish Pottinger. Also invited were Nat and Martha Lovatt. Silas and Will attended on behalf of Oliver and Beth, who felt it was best that they didn't attend such a serious event. The whole of the Estate staff was also invited to attend, unsurprisingly, given that their future jobs were linked to whatever the will commanded. More surprisingly, Thomas Whetton was invited to attend the reading. Given their sparring in life, Thomas felt that Henry's death would certainly not provide for anything.

However, as Oliver's godfather, then perhaps it was relevant for him to be there. Oliver, being the single-blood relative, was likely to be the main beneficiary, but given the falling-out of Henry and Charlie, nobody really knew how the next generation might be impacted.

The solicitor addressed the room. "Ladies & Gentlemen, I have been asked to read the will of Henry Franklin Aspinall of this address on Ridge Hill." He paused for a moment and then started again. "Oliver Aspinall will inherit the Aspinall Estate, House and most business interests. Before Oliver reaches the age of eighteen, I kindly request that Mr. Thomas Whetton take on full guardianship of all commercial interests of the Aspinall Estate on Oliver's behalf and receive commensurate compensation. I believe that all areas of the commercial estate have been audited such that all meet the regulatory requirements of their respective industry sectors. I have found Thomas Whetton to be a formidable industrialist, but one who leads his business interests fairly. I could have learned from him earlier in life." Silas looked at Thomas and acknowledged the sound judgement that Henry had only belatedly recognised.

Mr. Farbrother took a drink from a glass of water and continued, "All of my staff here at the manor house will be retained and will all receive enhanced retirement payments. In recognition of poor decisions on being a landowner in earlier life, I would like to provide all of my tenants in the area of the estate with a free year's tenancy starting immediately and then a lower fixed tenancy for the next decade." A cheer stirred amongst the audience, many of whom were tenants. "I thought you might like that!" the solicitor said with a smile before continuing on. "I treated several tenants very poorly, costing one of them his life. I hope to seek forgiveness from Sid Bayley in the next life. For Nat and Martha Lovatt, I am genuinely sorry for the pain and suffering I put you through at Trentabank. It is to your credit that you have now rebuilt your lives and are thriving in Bosley.

"I would like to offer my life president status and guardianship of Langley cricket club to Fred Needles, together with monies to develop the pavilion and grounds further. I want to pay for a phone box for the villagers of Langley to take some strain off Percy at the Post Office, and I bequeath sufficient monies for this," Percy cheered, bringing laughter to the room. "Hush, please. We've got a fair way to go yet," requested the lawyer.

"On top of the fishing and hunting licenses presented to Andy Soutter and Robin Brampton in recent years, I would like to offer them both full-time employment in the vacant position of Aspinall Estate Gamekeepers – reporting to Arthur Brice. In addition to providing Dick Avery full ownership of the Setter Dog Trading Company, inheriting my half, and wishing him good luck with the business. Any Langley villager will continue to receive large discounts, decided by Dick, and depending upon market prices."

A cheer went up from Dick, Robin and Andy. They shook hands vigorously. Arthur Brice smiled at the thought of looking after these two reformed poachers for the latter years of his working life.

"To Jack Moat and Will Ledger, I would like to leave the Aspinall pipeline business and make them co-owners. Supported and guided for as long as needed by Thomas Whetton. I do this in appreciation of their friendship and loyalty to Charles – my son."

Again, Silas looked across at Thomas Whetton. He wondered whether Thomas was aware of his heavy involvement in the administration of Henry's will. Thomas acknowledged Silas' look and nodded his head, affirming his prior knowledge.

The solicitor continued, "I will leave a significant sum of money to Langley Parish council for use in the community, supporting all village events and clubs in some way each year. I would ask Reverend Pottinger to oversee this." The Reverend nodded acceptance to the solicitor.

"I would like to thank Beth for loving my son Charles when his own father struggled to do so. Your love of my son made him the man he was, sadly, a man I neglected and only got to know through his own son – Oliver. Your mother – Gwen, gave you your energy and dynamism. But it is your father – Silas – that I must now publicly address."

The solicitor paused and looked at Silas, as did the rest of the people present. Silas shifted uncomfortably in his seat, not being a person who overly enjoyed attention. Mr. Farbrother then continued, "Silas Ledger – you are a man beyond reproach. We clashed several times over matters at Teggs Nose quarry – all of which I now acknowledge you were doing on behalf of the men and their conditions of employment. Back then, I was unwilling to back down and accept anything but a drive towards greater profits."

Silas looked across at Jack, and both men recalled those early days of quarrying gritstone in the harshest of conditions. Silas' mind drifted. The dangers inherent in that industry were omnipresent, and the fact that Silas had survived three decades of working with that unforgiving material – mostly using hands as tools – made him feel very fortunate. He looked back at the solicitor.

"I would like to apologise to Silas now and offer all quarry workers who have worked on Teggs Nose in the past – when it was owned by Aspinall's – a month's salary as a bonus for every full year of employment. I would also like to add a sizeable amount of money to the Quarry Worker's Trust Fund, started two years ago by Thomas Whetton, to support any injuries sustained in the line of duty. Silas Ledger, you, more than any other individual who I came across in my lifetime, opened my eyes to the fact that materialism is unimportant compared with the impact you can have on human relationships through the values in which you live your life. I wanted to punish you for being the man you were; I tried to finish you."

At this, the solicitor looked up, surprised by this revelation despite having read the will earlier in the day. The stark admittance caused the rest of the room to inhale a breath. Only Silas looked unmoved, having already had this conversation with Henry face-to-face.

The solicitor broke the silence and continued, "But you were too strong, and your resolve and the power of the love that surrounds you meant that you survived to return to Langley and help Beth and Charlie to adopt similar life values to your own. Others before self. God bless you, Silas Ledger; we all live in your protective shadow. Thank you."

The solicitor looked up and closed the leather binder containing the will. "Thank you, everybody, that concludes the reading of Henry Aspinall's final will and testament."

Chapter 67 - *Passing Years*

Elliot Chapman MP continued to fight for justice from the back benches of the House of Commons. There were certain causes that he felt very strongly about, having been closely involved in his lifetime.

Thomas Whetton, his life-long companion, provided a comfortable home life in Winchester, allowing Elliot to pursue his passion for societal advancement in Westminster. Sharing Elliot's passion was his faithful Parliamentary researcher, Beth Aspinall. She decided to recognise Charlie fully and make it easier for Oliver by fully adopting her married surname.

Elliot and Beth worked on several key Government papers that led to positive change. In 1965, capital punishment was finally abolished, with Silas' miscarriage of justice in 1930 still being quoted as a clear example as to why death was not a suitable punishment for a modern society.

In 1967, an Act was passed that made headway on decriminalising homosexuality. Although Elliot and Thomas would never in their lifetimes be able to publicly profess their love for each other, they were able to do so in the privacy of their own home – small steps.

In 1971, an Immigration Act was passed, a commitment that Elliot had made to himself following the tragic murder of their German friend Rudolph Schwalbe. All in all, Elliot and Beth could both look at their public work and feel very proud that their input had led to a major step forward for British society.

Beth was earning a substantial retainer salary for the research work and speech writing that she was producing for Elliot. In truth, she would have willingly done much of this for free, as the fires inside her for just causes burnt as fiercely as they did in earlier days. She still lived in Langley.

Oliver had followed his father's profession and became a lawyer working out of Manchester's court system. Ironically, he had found himself defending several 'Sons of Strangeways', now a gang with more of a mythical status than actual. The old leadership of people like Edgar Fitch had met various grisly ends befitting of the way they lived their lives.

Will Ledger and Jack Moat, together, built a strong business following the inheritance of Henry Aspinall's pipeline company. They moved their office into the old Aspinall Company building. Each year, they would invite Silas to sit around the old boardroom table, where he had once been threatened by Henry while trying to negotiate better terms for the quarry workers. The dark wall panelling had been lightened, and new oil paintings of scenes from the Peak District added a much more friendly and uplifting atmosphere, as befitting the new management team.

Percy Ricketts had nobody to leave the Post Office, too. Still, knowing that it was a vital community hub, he asked if the Village fund that Henry Aspinall had provided could be used to buy the shop and employ an individual to run it. Moll Brampton was successfully interviewed and became the new Post Office manager.

Martha and Nat continued to manage Thomas Whetton's sheep farm on Bosley Cloud until both were too old to cope with the physical nature of farming. As part of a retirement gift, Thomas purchased a small cottage on the outskirts of Langley on the condition that he and Elliot could stay in their spare room whenever they were visiting the village.

The Macclesfield Water Authority owned Macclesfield Forest and the Langley reservoirs, but the hunting and fishing rights were closely monitored by Andy Soutter and Robin Brampton, maintaining a healthy discount to any resident of the Langley valley.

Silas Ledger, now over seventy years old, was still walking up Teggs Nose on a daily basis – rain, wind, or snow. If the weather was fair, he always sat on the same seat overlooking the Langley valley and recalled old times, often with his former quarrying friends – Fred Needles and Owain Jones. If the weather turned, then the small hut – formerly used as a store room – was still standing and provided them with cover from the elements. The quarry had been closed for a decade now, and all of the heavy equipment decommissioned, but the gritstone seams were still visible and provided endless reminders of decades past. The good and the bad. Gwen would religiously pack Silas a slice of cake and a thermos of tea to take with him.

Oliver Aspinall and Sara Moat, now thirty and twenty-five years old, respectively, were engaged to be married. They had been friends forever but only recently taken the next step. When Oliver wasn't wearing his lawyer's wig in Manchester's Crown Court, he supported the Cricket Club in Langley, but not on the field of play – in the scorer's hut.

On the sunnier afternoons, Sara would collect a packed lunch and seek shade alongside him. In the wood on the back of the door was an engraving that defined their very existence and told its own story of love and loss – 'Beth & Charlie 1927.'

Oliver and Sara were just setting out on their own journey of destiny, but they knew in their hearts that home would always be where their roots were deepest, surrounded by gritstone crags and the freedom of the moors.

THE END.

ABOUT THE AUTHOR

A novice writer who has returned to his roots and fallen in love again with the foothills, moors and villages of England's Peak District. The rugged gritstone cliffs and farm walls of Cheshire define the region, and all have tales of industry to tell. Surrounded by this scenery and learning new historical facts about the area inspired the writer to pick up a pen and create his first novel.

With a lifetime in the corporate business behind him, this story has allowed the writer to unapologetically show that fundamental human values are always worth fighting for, and he hopes you enjoy the journey.

And incidentally, he also loves village cricket!

Printed in Great Britain
by Amazon